WARPSWORD

HAVING BEEN POSSESSED by the ancient daemon Tz'arkan, dark elf Malus Darkblade is faced with a stark choice – recover five items of unimaginable power within one year or forfeit his soul forever! Darkblade's quest leads him to the dreaded city of Har Ganeth and the legendary Warpsword of Khaine. Time is running out and as Darkblade becomes embroiled in religion and assassination, the daemon within is becoming stronger...

DAN ABNETT AND Mike Lee team up to bring a cruel tale of deception and power in the dark and gothic Warhammer world.

A WARHAMMER NOVEL

WARPSWORD
A Tale of Malus Darkblade

DAN ABNETT & MIKE LEE

A Black Library Publication

First published in Great Britain in 2007 by
BL Publishing,
Games Workshop Ltd.,
Willow Road, Nottingham,
NG7 2WS, UK

10 9 8 7 6 5 4 3 2 1

Cover illustration by Clint Langley.
Map by Nuala Kinrade.

A CIP record for this book is available from the British Library.

ISBN 13: 978 1 84416 194 2
ISBN 10: 1 84416 194 3

Distributed in the US by Simon & Schuster
1230 Avenue of the Americas, New York, NY 10020.

See the Black Library on the Internet at
www.blacklibrary.com

Find out more about Games Workshop
and the world of Warhammer at
www.games-workshop.com

THIS IS A DARK age, a bloody age, an age of daemons and of sorcery. It is an age of battle and death, and of the world's ending. Amidst all of the fire, flame and fury it is a time, too, of mighty heroes, of bold deeds and great courage.

AT THE HEART of the Old World sprawls the Empire, the largest and most powerful of the human realms. Known for its engineers, sorcerers, traders and soldiers, it is a land of great mountains, mighty rivers, dark forests and vast cities. And from his throne in Altdorf reigns the Emperor Karl Franz, sacred descendant of the founder of these lands, Sigmar, and wielder of his magical warhammer.

BUT THESE ARE far from civilised times. Across the length and breadth of the Old World, from the knightly palaces of Bretonnia to ice-bound Kislev in the far north, come rumblings of war. In the towering Worlds Edge Mountains, the orc tribes are gathering for another assault. Bandits and renegades harry the wild southern lands of the Border Princes. There are rumours of rat-things, the skaven, emerging from the sewers and swamps across the land. And from the northern wildernesses there is the ever-present threat of Chaos, of daemons and beastmen corrupted by the foul powers of the Dark Gods. As the time of battle draws ever nearer, the Empire needs heroes like never before.

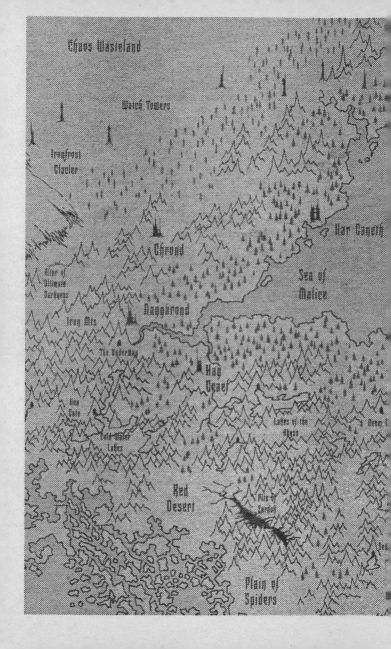

Chapter One
BAG OF BONES

Two FULL MOONS hung low in the evening sky, gleaming like burnished pearls in a band of indigo just above the sharp mountain crags to the west. Their light cast a shimmer of faded gold across the restless surface of the Sea of Malice, and the wind blowing in from the water was cold and damp. Tendrils of mist coiled along the rocky shore, reaching tentatively northward through the rustling fields of yellow grass and touching lightly on the dark stones of the Slavers' Road. As the night wore on the mist would thicken, swallowing the road entirely and pressing hungrily into the dense forest of dark pine beyond.

The small group of druchii walking along the winding road eyed the swelling fog with a kind of weary dread. After many days of travel along the seacoast, they knew that the wind and the mist would sink through their light summer cloaks like an assassin's knife and settle deep in their bones. They were all young and strong – and had demonstrated so on more than one occasion since leaving their homes – but their muscles ached and their joints were stiff after weeks of sleeping on damp, cold earth. So when one of their number spied a small, cleared area with a fire pit at the edge of the tree line the band stopped in their tracks and spoke amongst themselves in low, hushed tones.

Their leader, a tall woman with finger bones plaited in her black hair, turned and looked along the road to the north, searching for a sign that their destination might only be a short way away. She wanted to press ahead a bit further, but when the man who'd first spied the clearing walked to the fire pit and pointed out a stack of ready firewood tucked beneath a nearby pine, that settled the debate. With a last, searching glance to the north the woman joined her compatriots by the fire pit, throwing back the folds of her cloak and shrugging her travel bags from her shoulders. Lengths of wood clunked and rattled as they were tossed into the pit and the druchii murmured easily amongst themselves, pleased at the thought of a warm fire to keep the fog at bay.

Preoccupied as they were with flint and tinder and unwrapping what remained of their meagre rations, none of them noticed the lean, haggard figure step quietly from the concealing mist close to the shore. Droplets of water glittered like shards of broken glass on the dark surface of Malus Darkblade's heavy, fur-mantled cloak and ran in thin streams across his worn and split-seamed boots. His long black hair hung loose in a thick, matted tangle, almost indistinguishable from the wolf-fur that weighed upon his narrow shoulders. Moonlight limned the hard lines of his weathered face, sharpening the bony angles of his cheekbones and the dagger-point of his pale chin.

Shadows pooled in the hollows of his cheeks and the sunken orbits of his eyes as he studied the four men and two women forming a circle around the fire pit just a few yards away. As he watched, one of the druchii stuffed a wad of tinder beneath the piled logs and took up his flint, scattering a stream of thin red sparks with a few deft strokes before bending low to blow gently on the smouldering wood shavings. Within moments a tongue of fire rose from the tinder and licked along the cured wood, and the druchii all leaned forwards expectantly, reaching out with slim, pale hands for the warmth that was soon to follow. Malus smiled coldly, scarcely noticing the offshore breeze caress his face with cold, damp fingers. A few moments more, he thought, nodding to himself. They'd taken the bait, but now he had to set the hook.

Within a few minutes the druchii had a roaring fire going, filling the clearing and painting the sides of the dark pines with flickering orange light. The druchii ate cold meals of hard biscuit, dried fish and cheese, and stretched their feet wearily towards the blaze. After a long, hard day of travel the men and women seemed to come unclenched at the heady sensation of warmth and food in their bellies. None of them noticed Malus's approach until he limped like one of the walking dead into the circle of the firelight.

Conversation stopped. Several of the druchii straightened, hands reaching for their swords. Their faces were carefully neutral, but Malus could see the calculating gleam in their eyes. They were sizing him up, deciding whether to treat him as predator or prey. Malus reached both hands from beneath the folds of his faded cloak and showed his empty palms. 'Well met, brothers and sisters,' Malus said carefully. The words came out in a low, hoarse voice – after two and a half months of living like an animal in the woods along the Slavers' Road he'd had little use for conversation. 'Might a fellow traveller share your fire for a while?'

Without waiting for a reply, he unclasped his cloak and pulled it from his shoulders. Beneath, Malus wore a ragged shirt of blackened mail and a battered kheitan of human hide, cut in a rustic style common to the north country. A broad, straight northern sword and a set of knives hung from his belt above a set of faded and torn woollen robes. His black boots were ragged as well, the soles pulling away from their pointed tips. But for a large ruby ring glinting brightly on his right hand and a plain silver band glinting on his left, he looked like a half-starved autarii or a crazed mountain hermit.

Malus spread the cloak carefully on the ground and shrugged a plain cloth bag from his shoulder. Sharp, measuring stares flicked from Malus's face to the stained brown canvas bag and back again. All of the travellers carried similar bags, kept close by their sides. Like Malus, the other druchii were dressed simply: plain robes and kheitans, light armour or none at all, and a single sword or broad knife to deal with encounters on the road. Had they horses and clinking bundles of slave irons they could have been traders on the way to Karond Kar in anticipation of the autumn flesh harvest.

After a moment the leader of the small band leaned forwards with a soft rustle of layered wool and studied Malus thoughtfully. Her hair was drawn back in a series of tight braids, accentuating her long face and severe features. The woman's brass-coloured eyes shone like polished coins in the firelight. 'Have you travelled far, brother?' she asked.

The highborn met the woman's gaze and struggled to conceal his surprise. The woman's eyes marked her as a high priestess of Khaine, the Bloody-Handed God. They set her apart even among other members of Khaine's temple as especially favoured by the Lord of Murder.

Malus nodded slowly. 'From Naggor,' he replied, thinking to describe his route down the Spear Road past Naggarond but holding back at the last moment. Say no more than you must, he cautioned himself. 'And you?'

'From the temple at Clar Karond,' the woman replied, and then nodded to two men to her right. 'And they from Hag Graef.'

Malus continued to nod, keeping his face carefully neutral and giving the two men only the briefest of glances. His mind raced and a fist tightened around his heart. A voice hissed inside his head, like a blade drawn across naked bone.

'I warned you of this, little druchii,' the daemon said, its voice dripping with contempt. 'They will recognise you any moment and your pathetic scheme will come undone.'

'AFTER TONIGHT YOU will not be able to return to Hag Graef,' his mother had told him, her voice cutting through the howling wind as the city burned around them. 'You must seek the Warpsword of Khaine in the city of Har Ganeth. Your brother Urial awaits you there, seeking to make the sword his own.'

And so he had travelled north and east, slipping from the corpse-choked Vale of Shadow with food taken from the ruins of the Naggorite camp. He moved at night and stayed off the roads whenever he could, knowing that his kin would be sniffing for his trail as soon as they were able. Once the fires had been put out and order restored in the city, his half-brother Isilvar would send his troops into the Vale to check every bloated and torn body to see if he lay among the fallen. When they realised he'd escaped, word would spread, and every druchii in the Land of Chill would be watching for him. For the man or woman who delivered Malus Darkblade – living or dead – into the clutches of the Witch King would reap a drachau's ransom in wealth and favour. Not because Malus had led an army against his former home, but for the crime of taking the life of his father Lurhan, the Vaulkhar of Hag Graef, and by extension a sworn vassal of Malekith himself. No one slew the Witch King's property without his leave, and for that Malus had lost everything – rank, property, wealth and ambition, all stricken from him with a single stroke of a sword.

He had thought himself clever, but in the end he'd played right into his enemies' hands. Now Isilvar was Hag Graef's vaulkhar and possessor of not only Lurhan's wealth, but Malus's as well. His half-sister Nagaira had conspired with Isilvar; together they'd known more about Malus and his secret quest on behalf of the daemon Tz'arkan than he'd realised. They knew of the five relics he needed to find in order to free the daemon from its prison and reclaim his stolen soul. They knew he would seek the Dagger of Torxus in the tomb of Eleuril the Damned, and so they'd arranged for Lurhan to get it first. And he, blind to everything except recovering the relics and ridding himself of the daemon, had done their bidding like a trained dog.

It had taken a week to reach the Slavers' Road, and two weeks more to reach Har Ganeth, City of Executioners. Malus had stopped there, hesitating warily before the city's open gates and sombre streets.

The gates of Har Ganeth never shut because the City of Executioners hungered for flesh and blood. It was Khaine's city, seat of the temple's worldly power, and no one came or went from it without the approval of the priests who ruled there.

Malus knew they would be watching for him. His half-brother Urial would have seen to that, if nothing else. Urial had every reason to hate and fear Malus, and desired the warpsword for reasons of his own. It figured into an ancient prophecy, one that the crippled highborn believed to be his birthright.

Malus had reason to believe otherwise. Prophecies were often slippery things, and had a tendency to turn in the hand of those who thought to wield them.

Nevertheless, he knew nothing of the city and hadn't a coin to his name to bribe anyone with, so he had no confidence that he could slip quietly into the city and remain hidden beneath Urial's very nose, much less go poking through the temple fortress in search of a sacred relic. More than once he found it bitterly amusing that before, when he had everything to lose he would have just charged headlong into the city, convinced he could think his way out of any mess he found himself in. Now, however, since he'd lost everything, he found himself much more circumspect.

He needed more information about the city and its inhabitants, he'd decided. So he retreated into the wooded foothills north of the city and waited for someone to leave.

The first thing he'd learned was that, unlike every other city in Naggaroth, few people came and went from Har Ganeth. It was almost a week before a lone traveller emerged from the city gates and headed west on horseback. Malus shadowed the solitary figure until nightfall, when the man left the road and built a fire at a campsite along the edge of the tree line. After watching the man for half an hour, Malus walked into the camp and offered to share some of his wine in exchange for a spot close to the fire. After sampling Malus's wine, the man grudgingly agreed.

He was a stranger to the city, as it happened – visiting a cousin in Har Ganeth who kept a chandler's shop close by the temple fortress. As Malus had feared, every stranger entering the city had to report to the temple straightaway and receive the blessing of the priestesses, or else he took his life in his hands. There were only three sorts of people in the City of Executioners: servants of the temple, guests of the temple and sacrifices to Khaine. A druchii caught on the street – by day or night – without the temple's blessing could be slain out of hand as an offering to the Lord of Murder, and the people of the city were zealous in their devotion to the Bloody-Handed God.

The man knew nothing about the temple fortress. Only members of the cult were permitted to enter, leaving the devout to worship at any one of a dozen smaller shrines located across the city. He had heard a recent bit of gossip, though. There were rumours throughout the city that a holy man had appeared before the temple elders bearing signs and portents that the culmination of a great prophecy was at hand. What that meant the man could not say, but there were acolytes in the streets exhorting the faithful to prepare themselves for a time of blood and fire, and bloodied skulls began to appear in piles on every street corner. Fearing that soon his head would be added to one of the piles, the man fled for his life.

The news filled Malus with dismay. They finished the wine in dreary silence, and then he stabbed the man in the heart and went through his belongings for anything useful. Spite feasted on man and horse that night, and Malus had bread and sausage for a week after.

As the days passed Malus settled into a grim routine, stalking travellers leaving the city and learning what he could from them. Sometimes the conversation ended at the point of a knife; other times he chose discretion and slipped away into the darkness once the

wine was done. Once he nearly had the tables turned
on him, and it was only the Dark Mother's own luck
and his familiarity with the forest that allowed him to
escape with a whole skin. Little by little, his knowledge of the city grew, but nothing he learned helped
solve the most crucial riddles of all: how to avoid the
notice of the temple without winding up an unwilling
sacrifice, and how to find the Warpsword of Khaine.

It never once occurred to Malus to ask either
Tz'arkan or his mother Eldire for help. The silver ring
he wore had been a gift from his mother, one of the
most potent sorceresses and seers in the Land of Chill.
He could use it to speak with her on nights when the
moon was bright. As for the daemon, it had never
passed up a chance to tempt him with tastes of its
supernatural powers – but after the night in the burning city, its behaviour had changed. It was warier now,
questioning Malus's every move and offering nothing
unless asked. The daemon feared Eldire's power for
some reason, and that both pleased and troubled
Malus.

As the summer wore on the pattern of travel changed.
Druchii began heading for Har Ganeth – singly at first,
and then in small groups of up to half-a-dozen, arriving
at all hours of the day and night. They came down the
Slavers' Road from the west or crossed the Sea of Malice
in boats, and they all travelled surreptitiously, without
fanfare or finery. They came from all walks of life, as
near as Malus could tell: highborn and lowborn,
princes, bakers and thieves and everything in between,
and once they entered Har Ganeth, they didn't emerge
again. Malus found himself thinking about Urial and

his prophecy once more, and wondered whether there might be something to it after all.

Seeking answers, Malus headed down the road and looked for a solitary traveller to share a bottle of wine with.

The first man he found welcomed him like a long-lost brother and barely took a sip of wine before trying to cut Malus's throat. He'd laughed like a lunatic as they'd rolled across the damp ground, wrestling over the man's serrated knife. When Malus had finally gained the upper hand and searched the body afterwards he found a brown canvas bag filled with body parts: hands, ears, noses and genitals, many still sticky with gore.

Malus approached a second man a day later, and received another warm welcome. This time he was ready when the druchii leapt at him with a knife. He, too, had a bag full of freshly severed bits of flesh. In a fit of pique Malus tossed the druchii's head into the bag and took it with him.

After that he watched the people on the road much more closely. Man or woman, young or old, they all carried a sword or a broad-bladed knife and a stained bag hung from shoulder or belt.

Was there some holy ceremony in the offing, calling the faithful to the city to present their offerings to Khaine? He'd never heard of such a thing before. One thing was clear, however: the travellers seemed happy to kill any stranger they met except those carrying bags of their own. Malus had no idea why that mattered, but finally a glimmer of a plan began to take shape in his mind.

* * *

'WINE, BROTHERS AND sisters?' Malus pulled a clay bottle from a second carry-bag and offered it to the group. One of the men from Hag Graef leaned forwards and took the bottle eagerly. Malus caught the man's eye as he surrendered the wine, but saw no glint of recognition there.

'I hadn't realised there were any followers of the true faith living at the Black Ark,' the temple maiden said.

The true faith? What did that mean, Malus thought? 'I hadn't known of any in Karond Kar either,' he answered. 'I suppose that makes us even.' Eager to change the subject, he nodded his head eastward. 'We'll be in Har Ganeth by midday tomorrow.'

The other travellers from the Karond Kar murmured in approval. 'We should have listened to you after all, holy one,' the second woman said to the temple maiden. 'If we'd continued on we would have reached the holy city by midnight.'

'Let's go then,' one of the men declared. 'We have a sacred duty, do we not? The heretic and his minions could be battling with the faithful even now–'

The temple maiden cut the man off with a curt wave of her hand. Her gaze never left Malus. 'You look as if you've been wandering in the mountains for weeks,' she said to the highborn

Malus affected a shrug, his mind churning. The heretic? That had to mean Urial. Who else had recently come to Har Ganeth shouting about the end of the world?

'I... well,' Malus stammered, looking away. 'I confess that I've tarried a while on the road, holy one.' He reached over and hefted the bloodstained sack. 'There are meagre pickings on the Spear Road this time of year, and I didn't want to reach Har Ganeth with a poor offering for the god.'

Several of the faithful nodded their heads approvingly. He'd taken a wild guess about the contents of the bag, and the gamble had paid off. The temple maiden considered him for a moment more, and then leaned back against a fallen log and resumed her meal.

The man from Clar Karond eyed Malus. 'Have you seen many other faithful on the road, brother?'

'Oh, yes,' Malus nodded. 'They've come from all over. I'd wager there are thousands in the holy city, ready to fight the heretic.'

At the news, the man's eyes glinted with a savage light. 'At last! The day of reckoning is at hand. We've suffered the heretic's lies long enough!'

'I couldn't agree more, brother,' Malus said with feeling. The man from Hag Graef passed the bottle back to him and he took a hearty swallow. This was going to work. If he kept his wits about him he could slip into the city with the rest of the faithful and no one – least of all Urial – would be the wiser.

Grinning broadly, the man from Clar Karond reached for the wine. 'With so many of the true faith returning to the city the streets must be busy indeed,' he said. 'We have a place prepared for us at the home of Sethra Veyl. Where will you be staying?'

'With my cousin,' Malus replied. 'He is a chandler, with a shop close to the temple fortress.'

The man from Clar Karond froze, his hand still reaching for the bottle. His grin faded. Suddenly Malus noticed that everyone else had fallen silent.

The temple maiden rose to her feet, a curved dagger in her hand.

'Seize the heretic,' she hissed.

Chapter Two
EYES OF BRASS

MALUS BIT BACK a curse. So much for blending in with the herd, he thought bitterly. Thinking quickly, he grabbed his bag of offerings and rose slowly to his feet.

'Where I choose to stay inside the city is my business,' he said sharply, fixing the temple maiden with a steely glare. 'Just because I'm careful doesn't make me one of the enemy. Obviously you're as concerned about infiltrators in our ranks as I am, or you wouldn't be asking all these questions.'

Malus saw the two men from Hag Graef hesitate, their weapons half-drawn. They looked to the temple maiden for guidance.

She paused, the muscles in her jaw clenching as she wrestled with her bloodlust. The maiden opened her mouth to speak, but whatever she meant to say was lost as her female companion shrieked like a scalded slave and threw herself at Malus.

The woman's serrated dagger whistled through the air as she slashed at Malus's throat. He blocked the stroke with the stained bag of offerings, and the razor-edged blade split the damp cloth like wet paper. Withered, rotting body parts flew across the campsite, some landing in the fire with a sizzle and a flare of sparks. Malus planted his back foot and snapped the empty bag at the woman's eyes, checking her advance. Then he reversed his grip on the wine bottle and smashed it against the side of her head. She fell with a howl of rage and her companions took up the cry, rushing across the damp earth towards Malus with weapons held before them.

Malus back-pedalled, cursing fiercely as he dragged his broad sword from its scabbard. The zealots rushed at him from both sides, swinging wildly with swords and knives. The highborn blocked a knife stroke with his half drawn sword and then twisted wildly to the left to dodge a downward slash of a sword that struck sparks from his shirt of blackened mail. With a roar he freed his blade and drove the zealots back a step with a fierce swipe at their eyes, but less than a second later they were back on the attack, hemming Malus in with a net of glinting steel.

What the zealots lacked in martial skill they made up for in utter fearlessness, apparently unafraid of losing their lives in the process of bringing Malus down. They kept up their relentless advance, forcing Malus to remain on the defensive against the flashing points of sword and knife. He could tell that the zealots were gauging his reflexes, and the attacks were falling into a deadly rhythm. The two men from Hag Graef pressed him from the right, while the temple maiden and the man from Clar Karond circled to his left. One of the men from Hag Graef reached in with a long thrust to Malus's neck. As he swept the blade aside with a quick shift of his sword, the temple maiden's dagger flickered in at the same moment and dug into his side. Mail rings popped and the dagger point carved a furrow through his leather kheitan, but the armour stopped the worst of the blow. Snarling, Malus aimed a savage blow at the maiden's neck, but she nimbly leapt back out of the highborn's long reach. As she did, the second man from Hag Graef stepped in and sank his dagger into Malus's right thigh.

The blow was overextended and weak and the point of the blade sank only a few inches into the muscle of Malus's leg, but the fiery explosion of pain made the highborn stumble. The man from Hag Graef showed his red-tinged blade to his fellows and cackled with glee, showing crudely filed teeth.

Malus met the man's frenzied stare and let out a furious bellow, swinging at the hand holding the bloodstained blade. The man leapt back, just as the temple maiden had done, but the move was wasted, because the highborn's attack was only a feint. Checking his blow at the last moment, Malus reversed his swing, just as the man from Clar Karond rushed in on his left. The man was at full extension, slashing low with his knife, and Malus's heavy sword buried itself in the side of his head. The druchii staggered beneath the blow, a choking, bloody rasp hissing past his shattered jaw. Then he let go of his knife and gripped Malus's sword in his bare hands, trapping it in a death grip.

The zealot fell, blood pouring from his ravaged face and hands, and pulled Malus along with him. Without thinking, Malus put his boot in the man's face and took hold of his sword hilt with both hands, but he was not fast enough to pull his weapon free. The dagger-man from Hag Graef tackled him around the waist, knocking the highborn off his feet.

Malus hit the ground with a roar, feeling the sword wrenched from his grip. The zealot's dagger was trapped beneath the highborn for the moment. Malus pounded and clawed at the druchii's head, but the zealot tucked in his chin and closed his eyes tight against the highborn's stabbing fingers.

The highborn changed tack, fumbling for his dagger, but the temple maiden and the remaining zealots swept down on him, weapons ready. 'Hold his arms,' she ordered. The maiden ran a pink tongue over gleaming white teeth. 'I want him to watch while I sip from his living heart.'

Malus thrashed and kicked, but the men from Hag Graef seized his wrists and pulled his arms back over his head. The maiden knelt and with one hand hiked up Malus's mail shirt until the leather kheitan was exposed. Her saw-edged blade would make quick work of the tough leather. She set the point of the knife just beneath Malus's ribs and flashed the highborn a lustful smile. 'Servant of the false Swordbearer,' she hissed, 'you were a fool to think you could face us alone. You placed your faith in a false prophet and now you will pay the price.'

The highborn tried to wrench free one last time, drawing muffled curses from the zealots, but their grip was like iron. Finally he subsided, shaking his head. 'Alone? I think not,' Malus said coldly. 'Let me show you where I place my faith, temple whore.' The highborn drew a lungful of air and bellowed. 'Spite!'

There was a shrieking hiss, like water poured on a hot forge, and a huge, dark shape burst from the deep shadows beneath the trees. The nauglir was small for its breed, no more than twenty-four feet long from blunt snout to tapered tail, but its gaping jaws held fangs as long as daggers and its taloned forepaws were as broad as a man's chest. It propelled itself forwards on two powerful hind legs, shaking the earth with its tread. Lean, cable-like muscle rolled fluidly beneath its armoured green hide as it charged like a lion at the stunned zealots. The woman from Clar Karond was rising to her feet, blood streaming from the side of her face as the cold one reached her. Her scream was cut off with a thick, wet crunch as Spite's jaws closed on her torso and bit her in half. The war beast never broke stride, throwing the lower half of the druchii's body high in the air with a sharp toss of his head and a thunderous roar.

The temple maiden met Spite's hunting bellow with a shriek of her own, but it was like a war scream in the face of a howling storm. She leapt to her feet, dagger ready, but the dagger-man from Hag Graef let out a terrified scream and ran for his life.

Spite was on them in moments, clawed feet crashing down to either side of Malus and the zealots holding him. Gobbets of flesh and poisonous slime dripped from the cold one's jaws as it snapped at the man still holding Malus's arm. The highborn cursed and screamed along with his foes, rolling on his side and pulling at his trapped arm for all he was worth. The cold one would just as easily bite off Malus's arm in the heat of the moment and never know the difference.

The man from Hag Graef refused to let go of Malus, yelling his own curses at the scaly war beast and the temple maiden alike. Spite lunged at the man, snapping his drooling jaws, but the zealot ducked at the last moment and narrowly avoided losing his head.

Still screaming in fury, the temple maiden tried to drive her knife into the cold one's neck, but she didn't reckon on the thickness of the nauglir's leathery hide. The serrated blade sank barely a couple of inches into the dark green scales and was caught fast. Spite snarled and rounded on the maiden, but the woman anticipated the move and leapt backwards, out of reach of the war beast's jaws. Or so she'd hoped.

Just as she made her move Malus caught her ankle with his free hand and checked her flight. The maiden stumbled, but Spite caught her before she hit the ground. Her scream of rage turned into a rising shriek of pain as the nauglir shook her like a rat in a terrier's jaws and then flung her at the man still holding Malus's arm. Both zealots went tumbling across the ground, the impact nearly wrenching the highborn's arm out of its socket before the druchii's grip was broken.

Spite leapt after his stunned prey, bloodstained jaws gaping, and Malus fumbled his dagger free as the man pinning his legs saw his chance to escape and tried to get clear. The zealot rolled to his feet, eyes bright with hate, and Malus threw his dagger left-handed, burying it in the man's throat.

By the time Malus staggered to his feet the only sound in the clearing was the crackle of the fire and the brittle crunch of bones. Spite stood over the remains of the temple maiden and the man from Hag Graef, devouring clothes, flesh and bone in quick, snapping bites. The highborn gave the cold one a wide berth while it fed, looking for the man who'd fled towards the Slavers' Road. After a moment he caught a glimpse of a pale face, several hundred yards along the road to the north-east. He could not see any details, but Malus could imagine the man running as hard as his legs would take him, casting terrified glances over his shoulder every few yards for fear that the terrible nauglir had given chase.

'Spite!' Malus called. The cold one looked up from its meal, steam rising from the hot blood coating its snout. It snapped its jaws once, scattering streams of gory slime, and then loped heavily towards the highborn like a faithful hound.

Malus pointed down the road. 'There, beast of the deep earth,' he said coldly. 'Smell his fear? Hunt, Spite. Hunt!'

The nauglir raised its snout, nostrils flaring, let out a rumbling growl and started off at a ground-eating trot. It wouldn't be long before the zealot cast a glance over his shoulder and saw nothing but red eyes and dagger-like teeth.

Malus turned back to the corpses of the faithful and bit back a snarl of dismay. 'Damnation,' he said wearily, reclaiming first his dagger and then his heavy sword. 'One day I'll have a plan that works to perfection. The shock of it will likely kill me.'

'You were a fool to think they would be deceived, little druchii,' Tz'arkan sneered. 'All cults are born of secrets and deception, the better to identify outsiders. One wrong word, one wrong look, and your skull will be sitting atop a pile on a Har Ganeth street corner.'

'And what would you have me do?' Malus shot back. 'March into Har Ganeth and ask them politely for the sword?'

The daemon's presence slithered against his ribs like silk. Malus had come to think of the sensation as Tz'arkan's version of a smile. 'Why not? It was meant for you, after all.'

Malus let out an involuntary snarl and began searching through the zealots' bags. One of them was bound to have a bottle of wine. 'I'm not interested in your riddles,' he growled. 'I am not bound by fate or prophecy – least of all yours.'

Back in ancient times, when the druchii still ruled lost Nagarythe, the cult of Khaine was outlawed for its violent excesses and refusal to acknowledge the authority of cursed Aenarion, king of the elves. In those days, the faithful who worshipped the Bloody-Handed God clung to a prophecy that one day the Lord of Murder would send his chosen servant to lead the druchii to eternal glory in a time of blood and fire.

Urial thought he was that man, chosen by Khaine for his purity and devotion in spite of his physical deformities. He certainly fit the criteria set forth in the prophecy. But then, so did Malus.

The Scourge was destined to take up the Warpsword of Khaine. If Urial was indeed the figure of prophecy, he was going to be very surprised indeed when Malus pried the blade out of his half-brother's cold, dead hands. He had to have that blade, and to the Outer Darkness with the rest.

'Your mother has filled your head with lies,' Tz'arkan hissed.

'You sound jealous,' Malus replied absently, tossing aside the last of the bags. No wonder the zealots were such miserable wretches. Not a drop of wine among them. It was unnatural.

'I have never lied to you,' the daemon said querulously. 'I have shared my power with you when you needed it, even when it caused me great pain to do so.'

'And you've destroyed me into the bargain,' Malus snapped. 'No wealth, no rank, no prospects – I've lost it all thanks to you.'

'Trinkets,' the daemon sneered. 'Cheap gewgaws unfit for one such as you.' Tz'arkan slithered gently beneath Malus's skin, setting the highborn's teeth on edge. 'Have you ever considered that perhaps this quest is but a test?'

'A test?' Malus spat. 'Of what?'

Again, came the silky, scaly rustle of the daemon's smile. 'Malus, dear Malus. Think for a moment. I am not born of flesh. I am Tz'arkan, Drinker of Worlds. I am eternal. Do you honestly think I suffer in my crystal prison to the north?'

The answer seemed evident. 'Of course.'

'Foolish druchii. To you, a millennium of entrapment is a horror beyond imagining, but to me? It is an eye blink. If I remain bound to that crystal until the sun goes dark in the heavens it would be about as onerous as wiling away a long afternoon.'

The highborn paused. 'So you do not truly care if you are freed?'

Tz'arkan laughed. 'I will be free, Malus. That is beyond doubt. The question is whether you will be able to free me.'

Malus frowned. 'Now you're speaking in riddles.'

'No, you're being obtuse. Must I spell it out for you? I care nothing for pitiful little worlds, or the nations of pale grubs that writhe upon them. I am like unto a god, Malus. You could be, too. If you are worthy.'

The highborn laughed, shaking his head in amazement. 'And you expect me to believe that? You'd make me a god, just like that?'

He expected the daemon to sneer at him. Instead, Tz'arkan's reply was strangely sombre. 'How else do you think gods are born?'

The thought brought Malus up short.

He's lying, the highborn thought. He must be. He's trying to get the upper hand again now that Eldire has allied herself with me. And yet... it all made a terrible kind of sense.

Malus thought it over. 'All right,' he said slowly. 'Give me my soul back.'

'What?'

'You heard me,' the highborn said. 'If this isn't about your freedom, there's no need to hold my soul to compel my cooperation. Give it back, and I'll get your relics for you.'

The daemon writhed within Malus's chest. 'Impertinent druchii! I offer you power undreamt of, and you insult me!'

'I'll take that as a no,' Malus said, pleased at the thought of discomfiting the daemon. Slowly but surely, he was learning how the game was played.

Tz'arkan roiled like a storm inside his chest, but Malus gritted his teeth and tried to focus on the matter at hand. He had thought that with a bag of bones and a quick wit he could pretend to be a pilgrim and bluff his way into the city, but he'd underestimated the tensions running within the cult. It sounded as if the temple was on the verge of civil war.

Still, now he knew more about the situation than he did previously. He knew that the faithful were flocking to Har Ganeth to stop the false Swordbearer, which was encouraging. He also knew that the zealots were gathering at the house of Sethra Veyl.

Deep in thought, Malus walked over to the remains of the temple maiden. Spite hadn't left much. Her head and part of one shoulder lay amid the pieces of the man she'd landed on. The maiden's face was frozen in a rictus of hate, defiant until the end.

The highborn knelt, studying the face. What he needed was an extra layer to his disguise, something that would make the zealots think twice about suspecting him.

'All right, daemon,' he said thoughtfully. 'Forget giving me the power of a god. Right now I'll settle for a pair of brass-coloured eyes.'

* * *

Tz'ARKAN HAD OBLIGED without hesitation. That was a bad sign.

The pain had been immense, and it seemed to last for hours. There was a point when Malus thought that the daemon had decided to take him literally and turn his eyes to molten metal. After a while longer he wasn't thinking much of anything, hugging his arms tightly around his chest to keep from clawing his own eyes out.

The fog had reached the wood line and the fire had burned down to embers by the time the pain subsided. His face was flushed and each eye blink sent shivers of agony through his body.

Malus could hear Spite moving around the clearing, nibbling idly at the remains of the zealots. After some thought, the highborn rolled painfully onto his hands and knees and crawled towards the embers of the fire. Even the dull red light of the coals sent needles of pain into his eyes, but after some searching, he managed to find the maiden's offering bag. Malus called the cold one over and fumbled his way into the saddle. Then he pointed Spite up the road towards Har Ganeth and gave the nauglir its head.

They rode through the night. Malus swayed in the saddle, holding his eyes tightly shut. Well past midnight, his parched throat felt so tight he could barely breathe, and he groped behind his saddle for a water skin. The highborn drank deep of the brackish liquid, and then on impulse he poured a little into each eye. The pain was so sudden and sharp he cried out, but afterwards his eyes felt much better.

False dawn was colouring the mountains to the east when they reached the City of Executioners. The sea breeze shifted, carrying with it the burnt copper tang of blood, and Malus slowly opened his eyes.

The city shimmered like a ghost in the pearlescent light.

Har Ganeth, the Fortress of Ice. Before the druchii built Karond Kar at the mouth of the Slavers' Straits, Har Ganeth had been the northernmost city in the Land of Chill. Its walls and towers had been built from the purest white marble, quarried from the mountains near the Houses of the Dead. The Fortress of Ice was cold and cruel and everlasting, a symbol of the merciless druchii heart.

That had been before Malekith had given control of the city to the temple of Khaine, before the night of slaughter centuries past when the streets had turned to rivers of blood.

Walls of stone towered thirty feet above Malus, their sheer faces painted in layers of crimson from foot to crown. The bloodstained walls could be seen for miles, but up close, with the dawn light wakening the white marble beneath, Malus stared in wonder at hundreds upon hundreds of bloody hand prints, layered one on top of another to create subtle shades and murderous hues. The red sheen looked fresh. Malus was tempted despite himself to touch it, to add to it, deepening the mosaic of slaughter one thin layer more.

The city gate was unusually broad and low, wide enough for six mounted knights to ride comfortably abreast but not with their lances held high. An

enormous gatehouse loomed overhead, its wide face
pierced by arrow slits and murder holes. Oil gutters
hung like arched tongues from the carved mouths of
dragons and basilisks, ready to pour searing death on
any invader. The gates of Har Ganeth were long gone,
however, and its portcullis dismantled. The gateway
yawned like the wide mouth of a leviathan, ever
hungry for more prey.

There were no guards upon the battlements, no
green light of witchfires burning behind the arrow
slits. Beyond the gate Malus saw streets cloaked in
eddies of pale fog.

Somewhere in the distance, a voice cried out in
anger and pain. Malus put his heels to Spite's flanks
and entered the City of Executioners, seeking the
house of Sethra Veyl.

Chapter Three
CITY OF RAVENS

MALUS SOON LOST count of the dead.

They lay everywhere in Har Ganeth's streets and gutters, contorted by pain and violence and left to cool in drying pools of gore. Some were piled in narrow alleys like old rubbish; others lay slumped against the red-tinged marble walls, having painted the stone with bright swathes of their own blood. Most were druchii like him, although more than once Malus caught sight of the corpse of a slave, stripped naked but for his collar of service. Every victim had been hacked to death. Many bore the gruesome wounds of axe or draich, the great two-handed swords favoured by the temple Executioners. There were men and women, young druchii and old. Some died fighting, with swords and daggers in hand and mortal wounds to head and neck. Others simply ran and took their wounds in the back. The end result was the same.

Many of the victims had been beheaded. Their skulls had been added to pyramids of similar trophies, some stacked as high as a mounted man along the sides of the roadway or next to the door of a business or home. Nearly all of the piles of skulls rested in thick layers of dirty grey dust. The sight puzzled Malus at first, until he noticed that there was a gruesome stratum to the pyramids. The heads nearest the top were the freshest, of course, still cased in tattered flesh and skin. Closer to the bottom vermin and the elements had stripped them clean, leaving a layer of bleached bone at the very base. In time, even those sturdy bones crumbled, pressed down by the weight of the bones above and ground into pale dust.

The city stank like a battlefield. In the open squares it was bad enough, but climbing the narrow, winding streets towards the upper districts was like walking through a dimly lit abattoir. Spite grumbled and sniffed at the heavy odour of rotting blood and spilled organs, and Malus fought the urge to cover his face with a fold of his cloak. Even in the brutal battles on the road to Hag Graef he'd never seen the like.

The City of Executioners had been built on commanding ground on the shore of the Sea of Chill. At first just a collection of forbidding spires rising into the sky from atop a broad, granite hill, over the centuries the city had spread like a mantle of white stone down the hill slopes and along the flat ground around the hill's base. When Har Ganeth was given over to the temple by edict of the Witch King the temple in the lower city had been abandoned and the elders seized the districts surrounding the crown of the high hill. Many of the city's richest citizens had been turned out of their homes, and the buildings demolished to create the massive temple fortress that surrounded the drachau's stained white towers in a fist of dark stone. No matter where one stood in the lower city one felt the ominous shadow of the temple of Khaine.

Like all druchii cities, Har Ganeth was a warren of narrow, twisting streets and alleys, purposely designed to confound intruders. Tall, narrow buildings channelled would-be invaders into dead ends and cul-de-sacs where they would find themselves at the mercy of citizens waiting on wrought-iron balconies high overhead. But for a few main thoroughfares meant for commerce or war, no road was wide enough to admit more than two riders abreast, and in many cases the streets were narrower still. Sunlight rarely found its way into these claustrophobic lanes, and even in daylight every other house was lit by an intricately wrought, iron lamp hung outside the heavy oak door.

Upon entering Har Ganeth, Malus had found himself in the city's merchant district. Eddies of pale fog swirled around Spite's flanks as Malus led his mount past shuttered warehouses and through market commons littered with trash. Next came the slave quarter, with its broad squares and ironbound cages. The first of the city's many shrines lay just off the quarter, and it was here that the highborn saw the first signs of slaughter. Malus couldn't help but wonder how much flesh was bought at the markets and marched across the square just to bleed on the altar of the Lord of Murder.

The narrow streets of the artisans' quarters lay past Khaine's shrine, and further still were the flesh houses and blood pits of the entertainment district. Every lodging-house and tavern was tightly shut; their stoops empty of the indigent or the drunk. There were no signs of exhausted revelry, only piles of leering, tattered heads. For weeks he'd fantasised about a bath, bottles of wine and a soft bed in such a lodging-house, but the eerie stillness of the district drove all temptations from his mind.

Beyond the neighbourhood of lodging-houses and taverns the road began to climb the wide hill. The tall, shabby houses of the lowborn rose around him, and the way ahead became difficult. Malus's hair stood on end as he led Spite into the close-set streets. The narrow windows were shuttered and the overhanging balconies were empty, but he could not shake the sensation that he was being watched. The highborn drew his heavy sword and rested it in his lap, suddenly wishing he'd thought to put on the plate armour bound up in rolls of cloth and hung from the back of Spite's saddle.

The more scenes of carnage he passed, the more his wariness grew. Some of the bodies still steamed in the chilly morning air, suggesting that the killers were close by. The thought of a running battle with a mob of fanatics – on their home ground – set the highborn's teeth on edge.

He knew, from his conversations with travellers, that the highborn districts lay around the top of the hill, but he wasn't certain how to get there. How long could he wander down the maze-like streets before he stumbled across an armed band looking for more trophies to stack outside their door? Would his appearance give the attackers pause? Malus had no way of knowing. Nothing he'd seen so far made any sense to him. For the first time since the long, harrowing trip back from the Chaos Wastes, Malus felt vulnerable and exposed.

It wasn't as if he could go door-to-door and ask the way to the house of Sethra Veyl. Briefly he contemplated heading straight for the temple and simply presenting himself there – surely with a heresy simmering in the city the priestesses wouldn't scrutinise any offer of help too closely. The solution was simple and direct, but it gave Malus pause. There had to be a reason why the faithful were being lodged in houses in the city proper. Perhaps the temple ranks had been infiltrated? If so, how could he be certain that the priestess he spoke with wasn't a secret ally of Urial? With no other recourse open to him he nudged Spite onward, ears straining for the sounds of movement from the alleys or the balconies overhead.

As the dawn broke to the east Malus heard the first stirrings of life, high up in the shadows of the eaves along the street. Feathers rustled and bits of loose stone rattled down the stained facades of the houses. To Malus, far below, the shadowed ledges up near the slate roofs seemed to bob and writhe with invisible life. Then, with a querulous squawk and the beat of heavy wings, an enormous raven launched itself from the shadows and swooped low over Malus's head before alighting at the peak of a pyramid of fresh trophies. The carrion bird glared impetuously at the passing highborn before cocking its sleek head and contemplating its resplendent red feast.

Within minutes the air was black with gore-crows, flapping and calling to one another as they soared down the city streets. They passed so close to Malus that he felt the wind of their wings against his face, and they showed no fear at all of Spite. Once the cold one stepped right over a sprawled body covered in hungry ravens, and the birds paid no attention whatever to the lumbering nauglir.

The constant chatter of the birds made Malus uneasy. Some of the ravens even croaked at Malus in passable druhir. 'Sword and axe!' one bird called. 'Skulls! Skulls!' cried another. 'Blood and souls! Blood and souls!' croaked a third. Their eyes glittered cruelly as they jabbed at torn flesh with their dagger-like beaks.

He kicked Spite into a trot and rode on. Every house looked just like the next: stained walls and iron-banded doors of dark oak, without sign or symbol to identify who lived inside. At every turn Malus chose the uphill path, scattering ragged clouds of squawking birds before the nauglir's one-ton tread.

When Malus heard the ringing clash of steel and the screams of wounded men he turned Spite in the direction of the sounds without hesitation, his previous fears eclipsed by the morbid celebration of the birds.

He headed up a long, straight lane, certain the fight was dead ahead. Moments later Malus reached a dog-leg and found himself abruptly heading downhill.

Snarling, he pulled on the reins and turned Spite around in the cramped space to retrace his steps, and headed down another road that appeared to circle the hillside in the general direction of the battle.

That ended at a cul-de-sac piled with old bones and bare, white skulls. A lone, elderly druchii stood at the rail of an overhanging balcony, glaring down at Malus as he brought Spite about. The cold one knocked over piles of bones and crunched them underfoot, snapping irritably at the pall of fine dust kicked into the air. Snarling, the highborn kicked the nauglir into a canter, eager to be out from under the old man's silent stare.

He nearly missed the knife-slit of an alley as they careened back along the street. Malus caught the path out of the corner of his eye and reined Spite in roughly, causing the war beast to growl angrily and back-pedal along the cobblestones. The alley seemed to point in the direction of the fight, and was barely wide enough for the cold one to wriggle through. The fit was so tight that Malus had to draw up his feet and rest them on the saddle's cantle as the nauglir stalked down the narrow passage.

The alley intersected another street that seemed to climb the side of the hill at an angle. Malus reined in, cursing the damn labyrinth under his breath. Then he heard the unmistakeable ring of steel slicing flesh and a man's agonised shout just ahead. 'Slowly now, Spite,' Malus said quietly, prodding the cold one's flanks with his spurs.

They turned up the cross street and followed only a few dozen yards to the first bend. Predictably, the road came to a dead end just ten yards farther on. It was there that the killers had cornered their prey.

Five men had been backed up against the sheer wall at the end of the lane; only one of them was still standing, and he bled from a score of deep wounds. There were six druchii arrayed against him, locals, Malus guessed, by the similarity of the dark robes they wore. Their pale faces were streaked with patterns of dried blood – the five-fingered sigil of the Bloody-Handed God – and they wielded a mix of axes, clubs and knives. Their intended victim wore a highborn's kheitan and a breastplate of steel, and he fought with a knife in one hand and a long-hafted axe in the other. Despite his wounds, the man roared like a nauglir at his attackers, whirling his axe in a lethal pattern that drove the locals back. They had good reason to be wary of him; four others were already splayed out on the cobblestones, hacked open by the man's ferocious axe work.

As Malus watched, the locals gave ground before the man, staying just far enough back to avoid the reach of the axe, but close enough to threaten him if they got a chance. All they had to do was wait, the highborn thought. The axe wielder was already white as Har Ganeth marble, his robes dark and heavy with his own blood. Soon enough he would slow, and falter, and then the knives would strike home.

The highborn was just about to turn away when he saw the pile of cloth bags set neatly side by side along the sheer wall behind the beleaguered axe man. He was one of the faithful.

Malus slid quietly from the saddle and stepped close to Spite's head. He pointed to one of the locals. 'That one,' he told the cold one. 'Hunt!'

The cold one's jaws gaped wide as the war beast crept with surprising stealth towards the unsuspecting man. The highborn picked out a victim of his own and stole quietly up behind him, his broad sword raised.

At the last moment Spite's prey stiffened. Perhaps Khaine had sent him a premonition, or perhaps he'd simply caught a whiff of the nauglir's carrion breath. He whirled, weapon ready, and barely had time to scream before the cold one's jaws bit the man in half. Blood and entrails splattered across the cobblestones as the nauglir latched onto the druchii's lower torso and began to feed.

Malus struck at the same moment, striking the man's head from his shoulders with a single, sweeping blow. The headless body collapsed, bright arterial blood pumping from the severed neck, and the highborn leapt at the next man in line with a savage scream.

The surviving attackers recovered with surprising speed and two men turned on Malus, deeming him the greater threat. One of the locals, teeth bared in a bloodthirsty snarl, rushed at the highborn with a sweeping diagonal cut aimed at the point of his right shoulder. At the same moment the second attacker swept in wide from the left and swung his blood-stained club at Malus's knee. Laughing hatefully, Malus gauged the speed of the axe and dodged backwards at the last second. Then he slapped the weapon aside with a hard stroke from his blade. It sent the man's axe into the path of his companion, snapping his shin with a brittle crack. The club wielder fell face first with an anguished shriek, and Malus finished off the axe wielder with a backhanded stroke that opened his throat to the spine. The highborn turned back to the fallen man and took a moment to kick him in the side of the head. Then he turned back to the wounded zealot, but his foe was already down, blood pumping from a half dozen brutal wounds.

Smiling in satisfaction, Malus went back and finished off the druchii with the broken leg. He gave the axe man a comradely grin. 'It's well for you that I came along when I did, brother.'

The zealot was still standing over the body of his fallen foe. His head hung low and his shoulders trembled. Rivulets of bright blood shone against the pallid skin of his face and hands. He took a single, racking breath. 'You... you saved me, holy one,' the man breathed.

Malus bent to wipe his sword clean on the dead druchii's hair. 'Well, I confess I had a question to ask you—'

Had the zealot not been half-dead from blood loss his first stroke would have split Malus from crown to navel. As it was, the highborn heard the faint scrape of the man's boot and battlefield instincts threw him to the side. The axe came whistling down and split the dead druchii in two, but the zealot scarcely skipped a beat. He pulled his weapon free and leapt after Malus, his expression a rictus of madness and hate.

There was no time for confusion or shouted commands; the axe was a crimson blur, reaching for Malus's head, neck and chest. The zealot's skill was incredible, and it was all Malus could do to parry the rain of razor-edged blows. The street rang from the clash of axe and sword, like the tolling of a madman's bell.

Malus gave ground, his anger rising with every step. The axe blade sang past the highborn's sword and sliced through the sleeve of his upper left arm. He felt warm blood soaking into the fabric of his robes. 'What kind of gratitude is this?' he snarled.

But the man only redoubled his attacks, howling in fury. The zealot leapt forwards, feinting at Malus's neck and then sweeping upwards to smash his skull. It was all the highborn could do to throw himself back out of the weapon's reach. He felt the edge of the blade nick his chin in passing.

'He can still answer questions without his arms,' the daemon suggested in its silky voice.

'True enough,' Malus gasped. Just then the man aimed a vicious backhanded cut at the highborn's head. Malus dropped to his knees and the swing of the heavy axe pulled the man off balance. Before he could recover the highborn hacked off the man's foot just above the ankle.

The zealot screamed and fell, still swinging at Malus. The axe scored a glancing blow to his right arm, popping mail rings in a long, ragged cut. Furious, the highborn rounded on the bleeding man and chopped off his right hand. Steel rang on the cobblestones as the axe cartwheeled across the street.

'Kill me!' the zealot moaned, trembling with shock and despair. 'Give me back my honour, holy one! I've done nothing to offend you.'

No, you just tried to turn me into sausage, Malus thought furiously. He leaned over the man. 'I care nothing for your honour, you fool,' he hissed. 'I just wanted to ask you a question. You brought this on yourself.'

'I did this? How? If you hadn't come along those men would have killed me. We'd been fighting for nearly an hour!'

The man was obviously delirious. Malus was frankly surprised the zealot had any blood left to lose. 'Just tell me: where is the house of Sethra Veyl? That's all I want to know. Tell me…' Malus paused, trying to think of a suitable threat. 'Tell me… or I'll let you live.'

'No!' the man wailed, his eyes widening in horror.

'I can tie off your stumps; find a torch and cauterize the wounds. I could see to it you lived a long time.' He couldn't believe what he was saying.

The man looked at Malus as if he was a monster. 'All right, all right! His house is in the highborn quarter, near the city armoury. A house with a white door.'

'A white door, you say?' Malus snapped. 'That should be easy to spot in this blood-soaked place.' He rested the point of his sword against the man's neck. 'If you're lying…' The highborn paused. 'I'll… Oh, never mind.' He finished the man off. The zealot died with a grateful look in his eyes.

Shaking his head in wonder, Malus turned and called for Spite. 'In Har Ganeth you spare your foes and kill your friends,' he muttered. 'What do I do when I meet Sethra Veyl? Offer to burn his house down?'

BY SHEER LUCK – good or bad, Malus could no longer say – the next uphill street he found took him straight to the highborn quarter. The streets were starting to come to life; servants were emerging from the forbidding homes on errands for their masters, heading to the market or perhaps to restock the house's supply of slave flesh after a night's revelry. The servants moved with purpose, shoulders hunched and eyes downcast, never meeting another's eye or tarrying on the street for more than a moment. They wove gracefully among the piled skulls and the fresh bodies, and gave the fat, presumptuous ravens a respectful berth.

It took another hour of searching to find the city armoury, where the spears and armour of the city's militia were stored in anticipation of war. Using that as a point of reference Malus began exploring each nearby street, until at last he found a house with a spotless white door.

Malus dismounted, going over his story one last time in his head as he pounded his fist on the oak door.

Several minutes passed. Finally Malus heard the sound of a bolt being drawn back, and the door's spy-hole opened. A dark eye regarded him dispassionately.

'Greetings brother,' Malus said. 'I've come a long way to answer the call of the faithful. I was told there would be a place for me here.'

The eye regarded him a moment more, and then the spy-hole snapped shut. Larger bolts rattled in their housings and the door swung open. A young woman in startlingly white robes stood in the doorway. A long, fresh cut traced a red line down the side of her pale face, still seeping a thin line of blood. Her expression was eerily serene. 'Welcome, holy one,' she said in a measured voice.

Malus paused. Do I step inside or draw my sword, he thought?

He decided on the former. Stepping just inside the doorway, he found himself in a small, walled court-yard full of armed druchii. They all wore white robes, like the woman's, and little or no armour, but every one of the zealots had a bared blade in hand. They studied Malus with barely concealed belligerence.

Malus studiously avoided the stares of the assembled druchii, focusing on the wounded woman instead. 'I will need a place for my nauglir,' he said. It occurred to him that nearly every zealot he'd seen on the road had been travelling on foot.

'It will be seen to,' the woman said. 'There are nauglir pits in the quarter, with people we can trust.' She motioned to one of the armed men, who bowed and ran across the courtyard to a flight of steps that led into the house proper. 'Your arrival is propitious,' she told him. 'The heretics have learned how many of the faith-ful have slipped into the city over the last few weeks and they have decided to move against us.'

Malus nodded. 'I saw a bloody battle on the way here. The heretic's servants cornered five of our men and slew them not far from here. Where is Sethra Veyl?'

The woman's serene expression darkened. 'Dead, holy one. The heretics sent assassins in the night and slew Veyl while he slept. Tyran the Unscarred is the new elder, and he vows that the atrocity will not go unavenged.' A thought struck her. 'I should take you to him, holy one. You may be of great use to his plans.'

'Of course,' Malus said smoothly, considering the possibilities. Anything he could do to gain the zealots' confidence would make his position that much more secure. 'We will have to act quickly,' he said. 'Take me to the elder. If the heretics are on the move, then Urial must be close to claiming the sword.'

'Indeed,' the woman said with a fierce smile. 'The elders cannot deny him much longer. Soon he will take up the holy blade and we will sweep the heretics away on a tide of blood. If Tyran's plan succeeds, you will open the way for the Rite of the Sword to begin. Think of the rewards you will reap when the true faith is reborn and the Swordbearer takes his place at the head of the temple!'

Chapter Four
KEEPERS OF THE DEAD

THE WOMAN USHERED him into a large, empty chamber on the top floor of the house, and left him to wait as she announced his arrival to Tyran the Unscarred. A variety of swords, axes and knives hung from three of the room's walls, and the floor had been dusted with talc. The room was clearly meant for practice and perhaps meditation, although it was strange to find it at the top floor with the master's quarters. There was no fireplace to warm the open space, and the woman had made no attempt to offer Malus food or drink. Cold, hungry and deeply confused, he walked to the tall windows that dominated the north wall of the room and glared down at the city streets below. Suddenly he was envious of all the damned ravens and their sleek, black wings. At that moment he wanted to fly from Har Ganeth as fast as he could.

'This place is a madhouse,' he muttered darkly. 'Urial is the hero of the faithful and the temple elders are the heretics? Is everything turned backwards in this cursed city?'

'Heresy is mostly a matter of perspective,' Tz'arkan replied, clearly amused. 'The true faith is the one ruthless enough to wipe out all its rivals.'

'Or the one that has the support of the State,' Malus said. 'The heretics in the temple fortress have the support of Malekith, and Urial has sided with the opposition. How interesting.' The highborn tapped his lower lip thoughtfully. 'I wonder how long this has been going on for.'

'How long has he believed himself to be the Sword-bearer?'

Malus nodded. 'A good point. Urial survived Khaine's cauldron and was marked by the Lord of Murder, but perhaps the temple elders balked at the idea of a cripple emerging as the heir to their precious prophecy.'

'As well they might, for we know who the true Sword-bearer is.'

The highborn grimaced. 'I'll take up that cursed sword because I must, and the prophecy be damned.'

Tz'arkan chuckled. 'A prophecy cares not what you think of it, Malus. It is like a map, showing the road ahead. You can curse it all you want, but the road remains unchanged.'

'Indeed?' Malus replied. 'Eldire thinks differently.'

'The witch knows nothing,' the daemon spat. 'She intends to shape you to her will, little druchii. You are her pawn, and she will cast you aside the moment you are no longer useful.'

Malus laughed scornfully. 'Next you will tell me that the sun is warm and the night is dark. You will have to do better than that, daemon,' the highborn sneered. 'At the moment she makes a far better ally than you. For one thing, she doesn't hold my soul in her clutches.'

'No,' Tz'arkan replied, 'but she sent you to me. Think on that.'

The highborn's smug grin faded. Before he could reply, the door to the practice room swung open. The druchii woman beckoned to him from the doorway. 'Tyran wishes to speak with you.'

Malus nodded curtly and joined her. She eyed him curiously. 'Are you troubled, holy one?' she asked.

'No more than usual,' he muttered. 'Life is never at a loss for ways to vex me, it seems.'

She led him to a tapestry a short way down the corridor and without preamble pulled it aside, revealing a narrow opening and another stairway climbing into darkness. The zealot bowed slightly, gesturing for him to precede her. Frowning warily, he stepped across the threshold and peered upwards. Pale light shone steadily from under another door at the top of a short flight of stairs.

Malus climbed the wooden steps carefully, feeling them creak beneath his boots. A breath of sorcerous power brushed across his face, setting his black hair on end and causing his cheeks to tingle. Tz'arkan tightened painfully around his heart, and cold threads of daemonic energy withdrew from Malus's extremities, receding like a tide back into his chest. The sudden absence made his entire body ache. When had he gotten to the point that he only felt Tz'arkan's power by virtue of its absence? *What will be left once I drive the daemon out*, he mused?

He paused at the top of the stair, his throbbing fingers brushing the door's cold, iron latch. Another wave of power brushed against him, invisible as the wind. He was reminded of his mother's sorcery at the top of the witch's convent at Hag Graef. *Tz'arkan isn't the only power in the world*, he reminded himself, *and where the soul is lacking there is always hate to sustain me. With hate, all things are possible.*

Malus thumbed the latch and pushed open the door, letting in a blaze of cold, biting sunlight.

The door opened onto the tower's flat roof, providing a panoramic view of the eastern highborn quarter and the white-capped sea off to the south. The dark bulwark of the temple fortress rose to the west, a permanent stain against the summer sky. A sea breeze whistled fretfully over the battlements and across the flat expanse of the roof, carrying to Malus hints of pungent incense and snatches of whispered chants from the ceremony unfolding only a few score paces away.

A block of polished black basalt sat at the exact centre of the roof, its head and foot oriented to face east and west respectively. The body of a man lay on the block, his pale face stained with dark blood and his hands wrapped around the hilt of a gleaming draich. His body was attired in the clothes in which he had died: simple white robes, similar to the other zealots, but his were soaked in red from a gaping wound that ran from his shoulder to his hip.

Three women danced slowly around the corpse, their thick, white hair billowing like banners in the wind. Each wore a witch's black headdress, and their naked bodies were sleek and voluptuous. Sweat glistened on their powerful arms and gleamed coldly from white throats and heavy breasts as the witches swayed to a rhythm only they could hear. Their eyes were like shadowed pools, depthless and dark, and their full lips moved, whispering words of power that he could feel pulsing against his skin. With a start, he saw that their slender fingers were tipped with long black talons, and their white teeth were sharp and fanged like a lion's. All at once Malus was reminded of the dreadful statues lining the road to the Houses of the Dead.

'Are they not magnificent? They are true blood-witches,' his guide whispered in his ear. Malus hadn't even heard her approach. 'Heshyr na Tuan, the Keepers of the Dead. No one, not even Sethra Veyl, knew any still existed.' The zealot's voice was tinged with awe. 'This rite hasn't been performed in thousands of years. It is a great honour just to witness it.'

And in full view of the temple fortress, Malus thought, looking up at the watchtowers looming at regular intervals from the black walls. Honour or not, he suspected that Tyran wanted to send the temple elders a message. More than a half-dozen zealots stood in a tight bunch just to the left of the doorway, dividing their attention between the fortress walls and the hypnotic movements of the ritual. They were taut and alert, as if expecting a flight of arrows to rise from the fortress battlements at any moment.

One man stood apart from the rest, about halfway between the ongoing rite and the doorway where Malus stood. His back was to Malus and he was bare to the waist, revealing broad, powerful shoulders and strong arms that could have been sculpted from pale marble. The man's black hair had been pulled back from his face and bound with a rough leather cord. A long, curved draich rested in one hand, its polished edge gleaming like ice in the sunlight. For all that he stood with the ready poise of a skilled and experienced swordsman, his bare skin bore not a single scar.

'That would be Tyran, I presume,' Malus said softly.

'Yes,' the guide replied. 'We will wait here for a few moments. The rite is almost complete.'

Malus wasn't certain how the woman could tell. The blood-witches continued their slow dance around the corpse of Sethra Veyl, staring at the body with their hooded eyes and whispering supplications to the Lord of Murder. As he watched, however, the trio suddenly stopped. One stood to either side of Veyl's body and the third stood just behind the man's head. The blood-witches reached towards the corpse, stretching their long, taloned fingers, and the woman at Veyl's head bent with a bestial grin and pressed her lips to his.

The corpse convulsed, arms and legs spasming as if in the throes of death. The blood-witches withdrew, throwing back their heads and letting out an ululating howl that set Malus's teeth on edge. Then with a furious roar Sethra Veyl sat bolt upright, his bloody face twisted in an expression of hatred.

Several of the druchii witnesses drew back with startled shouts. Tyran, however, spread his strong arms as if welcoming a lost brother, and let out a joyful laugh.

'Arise Sethra Veyl!' Tyran shouted. 'Shake off the black veil of death and heed your vow to Khaine!'

The risen corpse glared at Tyran. Veyl's face worked spasmodically, as if wishing to hurl curses at the laughing druchii but unable to make its mouth form the words. Nothing but a choked rattle escaped Veyl's bloodstained lips as he slid from the stone and raised his two-handed blade.

After a moment the corpse gave up trying to speak. Veyl's dark eyes glittered with bitter humour. Malus suddenly wondered if the dead elder wasn't trying to curse Tyran, but to impart some dark wisdom from Khaine's blood-soaked realm. The realisation barely had time to sink in before Veyl rushed soundlessly at Tyran, his sword flashing in a complex pattern of deadly blows.

The speed of the attack shocked Malus. Whatever else could be said of the zealots, their dedication to the arts of war was astonishing. Tyran was motionless, and the highborn wondered if he too was stunned by the ferocity of the corpse's assault. If so, there would soon be another corpse for the blood-witches to dance for.

But just as the corpse's long blade sliced for Tyran's throat the bare-chested zealot exploded into action. One moment his sword was hanging calmly from his hand, and the next he was past Veyl's onrushing form, his draich held high. Malus barely registered the ringing sound of steel against flesh.

Veyl staggered to a stop, still frozen in mid-swing as if confused. Then Malus heard a wet, slithering sound, and the upper quarter of the corpse's torso slid off at an angle and fell to the floor with a spray of clotted blood. Incredibly, the rest of Veyl's body remained upright for a moment more before toppling forwards and spilling steaming organs across the slate tiles.

With an ecstatic shriek the witches fell upon Veyl's bisected form, pulling away robes and tearing into the shorn flesh with fang and claw. Tyran turned gracefully on his heel, lowering his sword slowly to his side, and Malus was struck by the eerie, serene look on his handsome face.

Tyran approached the crouching witches, moving as if in a trance. The blood-witches eyed him over their carrion feast, their chins dark with blood. They studied Tyran with large, leonine eyes.

Tyran held out his left hand. 'Give me my due,' he said, 'in Khaine's holy name.'

One of the blood-witches smiled, showing blood-stained fangs. She reached into Veyl's ruptured chest and pulled forth his heart. Tyran took the organ respectfully, threw back his head and squeezed the heart's contents into his open mouth.

There was a subtle change in the air. Malus felt the sudden absence of an electric tension that he hadn't realised was there. A sigh went through the assembled zealots.

'Now Tyran possesses a part of Veyl's strength,' Malus's guide whispered, more for her own benefit than his. 'It was ever thus, when an elder died in ancient days. Truly our time of reckoning is nigh!'

When the last drop of blood was gone, Tyran turned to the looming walls of the distant fortress. Slowly and deliberately, he raised his blade and his grisly trophy high over his head. 'The call of blood is answered in sundered flesh!' he cried.

'Blood and souls for the Lord of Murder!' the faithful answered.

Tyran lowered his sword and returned the heart to the waiting blood-witches. His face, neck and upper chest were streaked with dark blood. At that moment he noticed Malus. Tyran favoured the highborn with a calculating smile. 'Ah, here is our new pilgrim,' the zealot said. 'How was your journey, holy one?'

Malus paused but a moment, uncertain how to respond. Tyran's eyes were dark, not brass-coloured like Urial's or like those belonging to the other favoured servants of the temple. How did one address such a man? Malus knew with icy certainty that if Tyran wished, the zealot could split him like a gourd before he even realised he was in danger. 'My travels were profitable,' he said carefully, 'although pickings between here and the Black Ark were poor.'

Tyran studied Malus thoughtfully. 'It looks as if you travelled through the mountains to get here,' he said. 'Did you take to hunting autarii for your offerings?'

The highborn shook his head. 'I have no skill at catching ghosts, elder.' He offered his stained bag to Tyran. 'I gathered what offerings I could along the road, but I confess that I spent more time out of doors than I'd intended.'

Tyran took the bag and emptied its contents onto the roof beside the hungry blood-witches. They eyed the collection of body parts with feline disdain. Tyran did not seem much impressed either. 'You say you came from the Black Ark of Naggor?'

The highborn took a slow breath. 'I did. The temple there is small, but there are still a few of us who honour the old ways.'

'I didn't know there were any.'

'Didn't Veyl tell you, elder?' Malus asked. 'He was expecting me.'

Tyran considered this. 'What of the rest? Surely you are not the only true believer at the ark?'

'The others are dead, elder,' Malus replied. 'Perhaps you have heard the news of the feud between the ark and Hag Graef? The Witch Lord lost his entire army against the forces of the Hag. It was a tragedy for the ark, but a glorious day for Khaine.'

Tyran's smile turned cold. 'It's a convenient story, holy one, but your manner is strange, and you could easily be a heretic spy.'

Malus forced himself to remain calm. 'You would not be the first man to mock my rustic manners,' he said, 'but why would the heretics bother with spying on you when you hold your rites in plain view of the fortress?'

The zealot's smile faltered, and Malus felt his guts clench. Then Tyran threw back his head and laughed.

'Well said, holy one,' he replied. 'Forgive my impertinence, a man's heart blood is heady stuff, and it's left me addled. Welcome to the house of Sethra Veyl. What is your name?'

'My name is–' he caught himself saying 'Malus' and paused. 'I am Hauclir. Tell me,' he said quickly, eager to change the subject, 'is it wise to provoke the temple with such displays?'

Tyran's expression darkened. 'Do you fear the heretics and their slaves?'

'Of course not,' Malus replied, 'but neither are we in a position to challenge them openly. Otherwise we would have destroyed the heretics long ago.' The highborn was making it all up as he went along, his pulse pounding in his chest.

The zealot shrugged. 'They already know we're here. The fact that they sent a handful of assassins last night instead of turning out the temple guard tells me that they don't wish to provoke a confrontation. If they did, they couldn't be certain of killing us all, and then they would have to explain to their worshippers why they tried to wipe out the Swordbearer's disciples.'

'And what news of Urial?'

Tyran chuckled. 'They remain cloistered in the Sanctum of the Holy Blade. When he and his sister came through the Vermillion Gate there were far too many witnesses for the temple elders to hush it up. Urial presented his sister as the Bride and declared himself Swordbearer in front of almost a hundred witnesses. So they've made a big show of honouring his claim and have spent the last three months using the scriptures to discredit him.'

'And?'

A gleam of triumph shone in the zealot's dark eyes. 'They have failed. Our sources in the temple say that the elders have already been forced to admit that Yasmir is indeed a living saint of the Bloody-Handed God. So now I expect they are panicking.'

Malus very much wanted to know why the temple elders would be panicked over such a thing, but he feared that the question might give him away. 'Which is why they killed Sethra Veyl.'

Tyran nodded. 'It was a clumsy, crude gesture, which speaks to me of the elders' desperation. They seek to thwart Khaine's will by silencing his true believers, as if that would spare them from his wrath.' The zealot stepped forwards and put his bloodstained hand on Malus's shoulder. 'That is why I wanted to speak with you.'

'Is there some rite you need me to perform?' Malus asked, praying fervently that there wasn't.

The zealot laughed. 'I like you, Hauclir. For a priest you've a fine sense of humour.' He took another step closer and lowered his voice. 'No, I need you to lead a band of true believers into the temple fortress and kill the bastards who were responsible for last night's attack.'

Chapter Five
THE ASSASSIN'S DOOR

THE DOOR LAY at the end of a narrow street that only knew the touch of sunlight for about an hour each day. Tall houses, the homes of highborn lords, rose to either side of the close-set lane. Malus noted that the windows facing the street were tightly shuttered. Clearly the local nobles wanted little part in the temple's clandestine affairs.

He cursed himself for not anticipating Tyran's plan. In retrospect, the druchii's interest had been obvious. Veyl's death had to be avenged and the zealot leader needed expendable men for the job. Malus was new to the city, of uncertain provenance, and had no patrons to argue on his behalf. If he died in the depths of the temple fortress the zealots would scarcely feel the loss.

The highborn turned away from the mouth of the narrow alley and looked over at his two companions.

The zealots were nearly invisible in the deep shadows of the rubbish-strewn passage, their faces concealed in dark woollen wrappings and shrouded by close-fitting hoods. They seemed utterly relaxed, poised and ready for action at a moment's notice. The prospect of certain death seemed to affect them not at all. For the first time, Malus found himself wondering what rewards the cult promised in return for their devotion. He'd never shown any interest in the temple as a child; many highborn families cultivated strong ties to the cult for political reasons, but the children of Lurhan the Vaulkhar had little need for such affiliations. What do you think awaits you beyond the veil of death, Malus thought? Splendid towers and vassals? A thousand virgins? Feasting halls and an eternity of battle? He could still vividly remember the night he walked in Urial's sanctum and trod on the threshold of Khaine's realm. The highborn wondered if the true believers would be quite so sanguine if they knew what awaited them.

Like the zealots, Malus had been forced to don the robes of a dead temple assassin. The black woollen robes had been carefully cleaned and patched during the day to conceal the fate of their previous owner, and Malus had been forced to scrub the dirt of the road from his face and clean his tangled nest of hair, which caused him no small amount of apprehension. The grime had served to conceal the grey cast of his skin and the thick, blue-black veins that climbed all the way up his right arm, across his shoulder and up the side of his neck. He'd been able to conceal the corrupting touch of the daemon's curse for a time by a simple act of will, but the more he'd opened himself to Tz'arkan's gifts, the more the taint had spread. Now gauntlets covered his hands and he kept his own scarves bunched tightly around his throat. Over his robes he wore the assassins' lightweight kheitan of human hide and a shirt of fine black mail. Two short, broad-bladed swords were buckled to a wide belt at his waist. Malus nodded to the pair and pulled his hood up over his head. 'The sun is setting,' he said quietly. 'It's time.'

Without waiting for a reply he turned and slipped out of the alley, the sound of his movements lost amid the noise of the bustling avenue at the other end of the shuttered street. Horses trod across the cobblestones, men shouted to one another or cursed their slaves, and servants chattered together as they hurried to complete their masters' business before the sun went down. By day, Malus found Har Ganeth was much like any other city in Naggaroth. It was during the hours of the night that it became a very different place indeed.

The Assassin's door was made of bolted iron, with a small spy-hole covered by a cage of steel bars. There was no latch or knob; the flat, tarnished surfaces of the metal plates were inscribed with ancient, rust-stained carvings of leering skulls and piled bones.

Malus raised his fist and pounded on the rusty iron, calling to mind the strange words Tyran had told him to say. Somehow the witches had got the password from the temple assassins. He wondered if they'd made the men talk before or after they'd died.

There was a sound of scraping metal immediately and the spy-hole cover opened. A pair of dark eyes studied Malus and his companions warily.

The words tumbled from his lips, spilling out in a rush. The phrase was in an archaic form of druhir, the language of scholars and theologians. Perhaps it was a proverb of the temple, or an exhortation of the god – he simply concentrated on repeating the words as they'd been given to him. 'Khaine's will is done,' the highborn finished. He had no idea if it was the right thing to say, but it seemed appropriate. 'We have returned from the house of Sethra Veyl and must make our report.'

The spy-hole shut so quickly that Malus feared he'd made a mistake. Then there was a rattle of heavy locks and the highborn relaxed slightly as the assassin's door creaked open. Without hesitation Malus stepped through the widening gap into the chill darkness beyond.

He found himself in a narrow tunnel lit by a pair of flickering tallow lamps. Long shadows flitted and danced along the curved, soot stained walls. A small, pale face peered around the edge of the iron door as Malus and the zealots stepped hurriedly inside. The druchii who pushed the door shut was no more than a boy, clad in stained white robes and wearing a brass hadrilkar fashioned in the shape of a ring of linked skulls. The young novice shot home the door's heavy locks and then sat back down on a wooden stool beneath one of the guttering lamps. The highborn noticed a second, empty stool and reasoned that someone had run ahead to warn the elders that their assassins had returned. With a nod to his companions, Malus set off down the tunnel at a swift pace.

The plan that Tyran and the other elders had devised was a sketchy one, but the zealot leader was very specific in his orders: only the temple's master of assassins and the elder or elders who ordered the death of Veyl were to be slain. Of course, no one knew which of the elders had sent the temple assassins to Veyl's house, nor did anyone know what the master of assassins looked like, or where he could be found. Finally, after lengthy debate, Tyran concluded that once Malus and his companions reached the temple their targets would invariably come to them. The elders and the master of assassins would want to hear their report of the attack, delivering them into the zealots' hands. There was a straightforward, audacious simplicity to the plan that Malus couldn't help but admire, although bitter experience left him appalled at the number of ways that the whole thing could go disastrously wrong.

Within a few dozen steps the zealots were swallowed in reeking darkness. Malus was forced to slow his pace and move more carefully, his senses straining to penetrate the cavernous blackness that surrounded him. His hands clutched the twin hilts of his stabbing swords, and not for the first time he wrestled with the notion of turning on the two men with him and cutting their throats. After more than two months he was finally within the walls of the sprawling temple fortress. He could leave the zealots' corpses rotting in the darkness and lose himself in the temple's maze of tunnels. Tyran and the true believers would simply

think him dead, and if he went back and killed the
boy at the assassin's door then there would be no one
to describe him to the temple guards.

It was a tempting notion, but again, experience told
him that things wouldn't be quite so simple. He had
reason to believe that the blade he sought was kept
within the Sanctum of the Sword, but he had no idea
where that would be or how to get inside. Finding out
would take time, which he suspected was in short supply. Urial was eager to claim the warpsword for
himself, and it would be reasonable to assume that he
and Tyran were plotting to force the temple's hand.
Why the temple would be reluctant to accept Urial as
Khaine's chosen one still intrigued Malus. What sort
of agenda did the temple elders have, and how could
it be turned to his advantage?

The highborn walked straight through the trailing
edges of a dusty cobweb, the invisible tendrils clinging
to his face and the rim of his hood. He snatched at the
strands in irritation, slowing his steps even further.
I'm out of my element, he thought angrily. The
intrigues of the temple were similar enough to politics
in the Hag that he had a sense of what was happening,
but the rules of the game were altogether stranger and
more confusing than he was accustomed to. He
needed more information before he could make his
own play for the sword.

As preoccupied as he was, it was some moments
before he was aware of a shifting orange glow outlining the far end of the passage up ahead. Malus
resumed his brisk pace, quickly composing himself
before stepping through the arch and finding himself

in a vaulted, fire-lit gallery that stretched to either side of the highborn for as far as his eye could see. Pillars of white marble, stained and streaked with centuries of soot, rose more than thirty feet into the air, supporting thick stone arches worked in the shapes of fearsome, imperious blood-witches.

Don't gawk, he reminded himself fiercely, forcing himself to lower his eyes and study the gallery with feigned indifference. Red coals glowed and popped in the base of iron braziers set every dozen feet or so along the gallery, outlining narrow archways that opened off the gallery on either side. Many of these archways were dark, but in a few Malus saw rearing shadows and flickering candlelight glowing against the walls of narrow cells.

Acolytes of the temple shuffled quietly through the shadows, their heads bent in contemplation. They were pale-skinned, young and fit, and the highborn noticed that many of them moved with exceptional grace and speed. All at once Malus was reminded of his former retainer Arleth Vann, himself a former temple assassin who'd forsaken his oath and found his way into the highborn's service. The last he'd seen of Arleth Vann he was being dragged away into the darkness with two crossbow bolts in his back.

Such a waste, Malus thought bitterly. Like the rest of his retainers, Vann's honour had been ruined when Malus had slain his father at Vaelgor Keep. When the highborn had returned to the Hag at the head of the Naggorite army, the former assassin had done the only thing he could do to escape the stain of Malus's crime: he'd slipped into the Naggorite camp and tried to kill his former master. But for the timely arrival of a band of autarii scouts, Vann would have succeeded. Malus vividly remembered the touch of Vann's razor-edged sword at his throat. The man had most likely died in the forest outside Hag Graef, coughing up his life's blood and cursing Malus's name.

A figure in dark robes entered the gallery from a shadowy archway opposite Malus. For a moment the highborn was speechless, thinking he was looking at a ghost. The druchii's alabaster skin, pale hair and brass-coloured eyes resembled Arleth Vann's in eerie detail, as well as the paired swords that hung at the man's hip. Another young novice accompanied the assassin. He pointed at Malus and his companions and then backed away into the shadows, his head bowed.

The temple assassin stepped forwards, holding out his hands at waist height, palms up. 'The blessings of Khaine be upon you, brothers,' he said. 'This is a glorious day indeed. When you didn't return this morning we believed you had fallen to the blades of the heathens.'

Malus mirrored the assassin's gesture. 'Far from it,' he replied, speaking softly and counting on the hood to muffle his voice. 'The fools never saw us. We merely had to be patient in order to slip away while their leaders bemoaned Veyl's fate. In the process we heard much of the heathens' plans, and need to make our report.'

The assassin nodded. 'Master Suril has been summoned, as have the elders. Follow me.'

Malus relaxed slightly as he fell into step behind the temple assassin. As far as he was concerned, the hard part of the plan was over.

Their guide led the highborn and his companions back the way he'd come, up a narrow, spiral stairway that climbed past several more gallery levels until they emerged into a narrow room lit with pale witchlight. The transition from fire and shadow to the pale green light left Malus momentarily disorientated, a feeling that only deepened when the guide pushed open a tall door and led the men outside into the deep orange glow of the setting sun.

They exited through a portal built into the side of the fortress's thick wall, which emptied them out at street level at the end of a broad avenue lined on either side with some of the most palatial buildings Malus had ever seen.

Hidden behind the high walls of the temple fortress, the homes confiscated from the city's highborn by the order of the Witch King had not been transformed into dour vaults of worship. If anything, they had been made grander and more opulent than before. Long, roofed porches had been built along the fronts of most of the homes, with pillars of veined marble carved in the shapes of manticores, dragons and hydras. Windows had been broadened, and balconies built from soft stone instead of hard, ruthless iron. Malus saw door facings fashioned from gold and silver, wrought in intricate styles that could only have come from the hands of expensive dwarf slaves. The air was cool and smelled of incense. Priests and priestesses strolled casually along the street, wrapped in thick, red robes and kheitans of fine elf hide set with gold, rubies and pearls. The raw display of wealth and power nearly stopped Malus in his tracks. He'd known, like all druchii, that the temple of Khaine was universally feared. What he hadn't ever stopped to consider was that it was also very, very rich. Malekith's support had benefited the cult enormously.

The guide led them swiftly along the broad street, his eyes carefully downcast as he passed the high officials of the temple. He led them to the third house on the left, climbing a broad set of marble steps to a pair of gold-ornamented doors that slid open silently at his approach. Human slaves held open the doors and bowed from the waist as the druchii filed inside. Beyond was a spacious entry hall filled with expensive statues, some bearing the refined but effete style of the craftsmen of Ulthuan. They'd probably been tithed to the temple some time in the past by a noble seeking the elders' favour, Malus suspected.

They crossed the hall, the soles of their boots whispering across piled rugs, and climbed another flight of stairs. The druchii crossed another room lined with statues and hung with expensive tapestries, and were ushered into a small chamber set with a low table and half a dozen wooden chairs. A tray containing a plate of fruit and a bottle of wine sat on the table. The guide bowed to the men once more and left the room, closing the door behind him. Immediately the two zealots began a careful check of their weapons. Malus eyed the wine greedily, certain it would be a fine vintage and fighting the temptation to open it and find out.

He was still contemplating the bottle when the door swung open again and a small crowd of red-robed druchii bustled hurriedly into the room. The zealots immediately dropped to one knee, palms out, and Malus followed suit a moment later.

'Arch-Hierophant Rhulan will be along momentarily. In the meantime we shall hear your report,' a woman said in a harsh, businesslike voice. Malus looked up to see a tall, narrow-shouldered priestess striding purposefully towards him, walking with the aid of a slender, silver-chased staff. Her hair was white and bore the headdress of a witch elf, but she wore the heavy robes and ornamental kheitan of a temple dignitary. A short, broad man, also swathed in crimson robes came in behind her. A ring of gold glinted on each of his stubby fingers, and a pair of dark eyes glittered like chips of obsidian beneath a pair of jutting brows. A pair of temple novitiates bearing scribner's easels, ink and quills and sheets of parchment attended him.

'It would not be proper to begin without Rhulan,' said the last man to enter the room. He was of middle height and whipcord-thin, with a long, pointed face that reminded Malus of a fox. His red robes were not as heavy as the others, and his kheitan was noticeably devoid of ornamentation. To Malus's surprise, the man carried no obvious weapons, but he had no doubt that he was looking at the temple's master of assassins.

'In the absence of the Arch-Hierophant I am the voice of the temple,' the woman snapped, 'and I will hear what these men have to say.' The two druchii exchanged heated stares, but after a tense moment the man deferred with a bow. 'Now then,' the woman said, turning back to the assassins, 'we watched the heathens dispose of Veyl this morning,' she said, 'so we know your mission was a success. What I want to hear is why you are only now returning to the temple?'

Malus quickly took stock of the situation. The two temple elders and the servants were closer, but less dangerous than the man by the door. He would have to kill the master of assassins at once, and that would leave him in a position to cut off the others' retreat. Then they could lie in wait for this Arch-Hierophant to arrive and deal with him at their leisure.

Suddenly an idea occurred to Malus. He considered his circumstances for a second time, and then smiled within the depths of his hood. Yes, there was an opportunity here.

The female elder leaned in close to Malus, near enough for him to feel her hot breath. 'Answer me, hound! You were told to return at once. Why did you tarry, when there is still more of Khaine's work to be done?'

Malus looked up, meeting the elder's glare. He smiled a killer's smile. 'Please accept our apologies,' he said. 'We would have been here sooner, but it took hours to get the blood out of these robes.'

The elder's face twisted into a bemused frown. She opened her mouth to speak, but the words were lost in a torrent of blood. The elder staggered, dropping her staff and fumbling at the gaping cut in the side of her throat with one hand while clawing at Malus with the other. But the highborn was already on his feet, blood dripping from his sword, and he charged across the room at the man by the door.

For a split second, the temple elders and their servants were frozen in shock, just as the highborn hoped. The zealots leapt into action a fraction of a second behind Malus. There was a whickering sound, and one of the stocky elder's novitiates let out a startled cry and collapsed with a thrown dagger jutting from his chest. Malus saw the remaining novitiate draw a pair of long daggers from his belt, but the highborn knew the man wouldn't have them ready in time. He would be on the master of assassins in another three steps.

To Malus's surprise, the fox-faced druchii still hadn't reacted to the sudden attack. This is their master of assassins, he thought?

Then came the blow against the side of Malus's neck, clipping him beneath the ear. His vision disappeared in a burst of white pain and the highborn fell face-first onto the piled rugs. Both swords tumbled from his nerveless fingers. He realised, too late, that he'd made a fatal mistake.

Malus rolled weakly onto his side as the stocky druchii stepped back from the highborn's stunned body and met the rush of one of the black-robed zealots with his bare hands. The zealot's daggers were a blur of motion, but the master of assassins slapped them aside with contemptuous ease and drove his stiffened fingertips into his attacker's throat. Bone crunched and the zealot fell to the floor, writhing and choking for breath.

The surviving novitiate leapt at Malus, intending to finish the highborn off, but was intercepted in midstride by the last zealot. As the two druchii began a whirling dance of razor-edged steel, Malus tried to drive the numbing paralysis from his body by sheer force of will. He fumbled for his blades with leaden fingers, knowing that he had scant moments to spare before the druchii by the door regained his senses and raised the alarm.

His fingertips brushed the pommel of one of his swords, and the physical contact seemed to focus Malus's energies. Groping, he drew the weapon quickly into his palm and rolled onto his knees. There was a grunt and a crack of bone and the surviving zealot tumbled across the rugs, his right arm twisted at an unnatural angle. Malus straightened and saw the fox-faced druchii with his hand on the door latch. The novitiate was sinking slowly to the floor, blood pouring from a wound over his heart, and the master of assassins was turning to face Malus once more, the rings on his fingers glittering coldly.

Malus's thin lips compressed into a grim line as he reversed his grip on his short blade and hurled it at the fox-faced elder just as a pair of fearsome blows hammered into his chest. The next thing he knew he was bouncing off the far wall, his ribs afire with pain. Expensive statues crashed to the ground, snapping off delicate arms and sweeping dragon wings.

Move, move, Malus thought desperately, biting back a groan of pain as he lurched to his feet. The master of assassins was advancing on him slowly and deliberately, reaching for Malus with his small, lethal hands. Desperate, the highborn glanced around for a weapon. He snatched up a stone arm and hurled it at the master's head, and then followed it with a piece of broken wing and a length of barbed tail. The master of assassins batted them easily out of the air, closing inexorably on the highborn.

Malus dodged the first blow at the last moment, ducking behind the statue of a rearing griffon. The second blow shattered the statue into pieces, lashing the highborn's face with chips of razor-edged stone. The highborn stumbled, landing hard on a scattering of stone limbs and wings.

The druchii master yanked back the highborn's hood and seized Malus by the hair the moment he hit the floor. 'Your technique is disgraceful,' the master of assassins hissed, his free hand poised to strike. 'Your every breath is an insult to the glory of Khaine.'

'I'm… flattered… you noticed,' Malus grunted, his face contorted in a grimace of pain. 'What I lack in… skill… I make up for… in… treachery.'

The highborn rolled to the side, lashing out with the stone limb he'd snagged during his fall. Bone snapped like kindling as he struck the master in the left ankle, bringing the master of assassins to his knees. Shouting in rage and pain Malus struck again, lashing out at the hand that held him and breaking the stunned druchii's wrist. He tore himself free of the master's grasp and swung a backhanded stroke that caught the druchii against the side of the head. There was a sickening crunch, and the master fell lifelessly to the floor.

Malus staggered to his feet, gasping for air. He struck the master twice more for good measure, and then tossed the bloodied stone arm aside. The man might have been a master at killing victims through stealth and guile, but he wouldn't have survived ten seconds on the battlefield.

Across the room the surviving zealot had struggled to his feet, his broken right arm clutched close to his side. Malus glared at the man. 'You might have helped,' he hissed through clenched teeth. It felt as if at least one of his ribs was cracked.

The zealot's eyes widened. 'And deprive you of the honour of the kill?' he said, aghast.

'Ah,' Malus said. 'That. Of course.'

The fox-faced elder still leaned against the door, pinned there by Malus's sword. The highborn limped over and pulled the weapon free with a grunt of pain. Just as the elder's body slid aside the door swung inward, and Malus found himself face to face with a druchii in rich, crimson robes, overlaid with a brass breastplate studded with rubies and pearls. Upon the elder's brow was a circlet of gold inlaid with garnets in the shape of tiny, glittering skulls. Like the female elder Malus had killed, the man held a short staff, this one chased with red gold.

The elder's face went pale with shock. There was a faint rustle of woollen robes behind Malus. He took a deep breath, switched his sword from his right hand to his left, and spun just as he heard the sound of the zealot's approach and drove his short blade through the man's chest. The zealot doubled over at the force of the blow, and his life left him in a single, gurgling gasp. The highborn pushed the corpse away and turned back to the stunned elder.

'Step inside, Arch-Hierophant,' Malus said, indicating the far table with a sweep of his blood-spattered hand. 'Take some wine. You and I have much to discuss.'

Chapter Six
BALANCE OF TERROR

ARCH-HIEROPHANT RHULAN filled one of the brass goblets on the table to brim full with thick, plum-coloured wine and took a deep draught before turning back to face Malus. He had the face of an ascetic, with long, drawn features and a scrawny neck that bobbed furiously as he drank. The temple elder said nothing at first, surveying the room's grisly contents.

The highborn studied the man's reactions intently. Rhulan's eyes lit first on the female elder, lying close by in a spreading pool of dark blood. His thin lips pursed in a fleeting smile, and Malus could not mistake a smug gleam of satisfaction in Rhulan's brass-coloured eyes. The elder's gaze passed over the dead scribes and the contorted shape of the dead zealot, seeking out the slumped form of the fox-faced elder and grimacing in evident dissatisfaction. Malus could see the gears turning in the elder's mind as he took in the carnage, gauging new political equations within the temple. Judging by your reaction it would appear that I've handed you quite an opportunity, Rhulan, the highborn thought to himself.

It was only when the elder's searching gaze fell upon the battered form of the master of assassins that Rhulan was truly taken aback. Wine sloshed from the rim of his cup as he shot Malus a worried glance. 'You're not of the temple,' he said. 'Of that I'm certain. Who are you?'

'Who I am is not important,' Malus declared. 'My identity will not alter the situation you've found yourself in.' Unable to resist any longer, Malus walked stiffly to the table and helped himself to some wine. His ribs were aching madly, sending shooting waves of pain across his chest.

'And what situation would that be?' Rhulan snapped. The shock of what he'd seen was wearing off, and the elder was beginning to recover some of his composure.

'Save your bluster, holy man,' Malus shot back. 'The only reason you're still alive is because I'd rather bargain with you than kill you. Your city – nay, your very religion – is under siege by a small army of fanatics who believe you're denying Khaine's holy will, and they must be at least half-right, because you seem powerless to act against them directly.'

It was a feint, meant to upset Rhulan and get him talking, but Malus was inwardly shocked when the elder gritted his teeth and accepted the insult in silence. The highborn studied Rhulan intently. You truly are desperate, he thought. You suspect the zealots are right but you're trying to silence them. Why?

'How is it you bear the blessing of Khaine, but side with these heretics?'

Malus chuckled coldly. 'Rhulan, you shock me. How long have the zealots opposed the will of the temple? Did you honestly think that they could have survived as long as they have without the support of some among the priesthood? The temple fortress itself has been infiltrated, Arch-Hierophant. How else do you think I got in here?' It was another bluff, but judging by the look of terror that came over the elder's face, it was an allegation with bite to it.

'Who?' Rhulan stammered, his hand tightening on his cup.

This is almost too easy, Malus thought. He smiled. 'In due time, Arch-Hierophant. Let us first consider the crux of your problem. How are you dealing with Urial?'

The elder bristled. 'The man is deluded,' Rhulan snapped. 'We should have arranged for his death long ago. I knew that sooner or later he would try something like this.'

'Why then is he still within the Sanctum of the Sword if his claim is not legitimate?'

The knobbly muscles in the elder's jaw bunched tightly, like clenching fists. 'There is the matter of his sister,' Rhulan conceded, 'and his lineage. The situation is very complicated.'

Malus glanced at the thick liquid in his cup. He took a small taste and winced: too sweet by half. 'You accept that she is a living saint. The zealots know this.'

Rhulan shifted uncomfortably. 'Of that there can be no doubt,' he admitted. 'No one like her has been seen among the druchii since Nagarythe was lost,' the elder said, his voice tinged with wonder. 'There is much she could teach us once this... incident is resolved.'

'Is it your desire for Yasmir that keeps you from dismissing Urial's claims, or is he truly what he pretends to be? You must realise that the longer this draws out the more you play into the zealots' hands.'

Rhulan glared at Malus. It had been a long time since anyone had dared speak to him so brashly. 'His claim is compelling enough to demand exhaustive study before a decision can be made.'

Malus cut the man off with a sweep of his hand. 'The fact of the matter is that you think he might be right, but you don't want to hand him the sword, and I suspect your reasons have nothing to do with the will of Khaine.'

A tense silence filled the room. Rhulan had gone very still, his dark eyes narrowing warily as he studied Malus. The highborn took a sip of his wine contemplatively. I've hit a nerve, the highborn thought. What then was the temple's agenda?

'The temple keeps its own counsel in matters of the faith,' Rhulan said carefully. 'You said you had a bargain to make. I am listening.'

Malus fortified himself with a sip of the cloying wine and nodded curtly. 'Your position is untenable, Arch-Hierophant,' he said. 'Time is running out. You've been able to deny Urial so far, but his allies are preparing to take matters into their own hands.'

'How?'

The highborn shook his head. 'First things first. I can deliver the zealot leaders into your hands, but in return you will agree to grant me sanctuary in the temple fortress. Once we've dealt with the heretics inside the city, I can begin ferreting out their sympathisers within the temple fortress, leaving you to focus your efforts on Urial and his sister.'

Rhulan didn't reply immediately, contemplating the depths of his cup. 'I would need to discuss this with the council of elders,' he said.

Malus startled the man with a bark of laughter. 'Rhulan, ten minutes ago you were certain that the heretics couldn't possibly have agents within the temple fortress. Are you absolutely certain you can trust the elder council? The fewer people who know of this arrangement the more likely you are to turn the tables on the zealots.' Malus took a step towards the man. 'Choose, now.'

'All right!' Rhulan snapped. 'I accept your bargain. Woe betide you if you play me false.'

'I could say the same, Rhulan,' Malus replied, setting his cup aside. He searched for his second blade amid the bodies, and then held the weapon in his hand as he considered the two dead elders. 'Do not look at this as an adversarial arrangement, Arch-Hierophant. We both stand to benefit from this. When we're done the zealots will have been dealt a crippling blow, the temple will be cleansed of heretics and Urial will no longer be a problem.'

'And what of you? What do you stand to gain out of this?'

Malus smiled as he walked over to the body of the female elder. 'One thing at a time, Rhulan,' he said. 'Let's focus on you for the time being.' He grabbed the woman by the hair and pulled the head upright. The short blade flashed downward, biting into the corpse's neck, but it was too light for such butcher's work. Malus had to hack his way through the flesh and vertebrae, grimacing at the artlessness of the decapitation.

'What in the name of Khaine are you doing?' Rhulan gasped.

'I can't return to the zealots empty-handed,' Malus explained. Holding the grisly trophy by his side, he made for the fox-faced elder. 'For your part, I want you to stay here and help yourself to some more wine while I make my way back into the city. Wait half an hour before sounding the alarm, and then tell whomever you must that you arrived late to the meeting and found things as they are now.'

'Very well,' Rhulan said, uttering a sharp sigh as he reached for the wine bottle. 'How will we communicate? Will I find you skulking in my chambers tomorrow night?'

Malus chuckled. 'Nothing so dramatic. I still have some more enquiries to pursue among the zealots. When I have news worth sharing I will pass you a message through the shrine in the highborn quarter. Pick a trusted servant and have them check the offerings at the shrine each night.'

'And what will he look for?'

The highborn grunted in pain as he went to work again with his sword. 'Tell him to look for a head that's missing the tips of both ears,' he said, holding up the fox-faced elder's skull. 'I expect I'll have plenty of candidates to choose from in the coming days.'

SCREAMS AND THE clash of steel lingered in the air over Har Ganeth, echoing like the cries of ghosts beneath the gleaming moons.

It was less than a mile from the assassin's door to the house of the late Sethra Veyl, but Malus spent more than three hours getting there. Armed bands were prowling the streets with swords and axes in hand, looking for offerings to the Blood God. Armed and armoured highborn with retinues of well-armed retainers passed gangs of commoners wielding meat cleavers and knotted cudgels, each gauging the strength of the other like packs of hungry wolves. The night was still young, but many of the roaming bands already sported one or two bloody trophies. From what Malus could tell, there seemed to be an unspoken rule to prey on solitary travellers rather than engage in big street battles. It was certainly safer for the killers that way.

He moved with care, using his dark robes to melt into the shadows whenever he heard a group of druchii approach. There was no way to be certain if the marauders would spare even a temple assassin once their blood was up. Once, the highborn stepped into a shadowed alley and found himself face-to-face with a white-robed zealot. The true believer was splattered with gore, and half a dozen trophies hung from his broad leather belt. The zealot had glided silently towards Malus, raising his stained blades, but at the last moment he recognised the highborn's face and bowed deeply, stepping past Malus and resuming his own hunt along the city streets.

Malus didn't begrudge the delay. It gave him time to think. Now that he had a way into the temple, he had to make good his part of the bargain and deliver the zealots into Rhulan's hands. Once that was done, he could bend his efforts to penetrating the confines of the Sanctum of the Sword and locating the damned warpsword. As he crept through the confines of the highborn quarter he considered his options. There was still much he did not know, but for the first time Malus saw a clear path to his goal. For the moment at least he had the upper hand, and he intended to make good use of it.

It was near to midnight by the time he turned onto the narrow street outside Veyl's white door. A pile of torn and headless bodies lay in a heap in the middle of the lane and a single bloodstained zealot stood guard outside the door, his dripping blades crossed over his chest. He bowed to Malus as the highborn approached, and stood aside as Malus pushed the door open and disappeared into the courtyard beyond.

The small square was all but empty; clearly the zealots had been turned out into the night to reap offerings in the name of Khaine. To Malus's surprise, he found Tyran standing near the steps of the house, speaking to a small group of new arrivals. When the zealot leader caught sight of the highborn his eyes lit up with interest. 'Well met, holy one,' he said gravely. 'You return alone.'

Malus nodded, pulling back his hood. 'My companions died in glorious battle,' he replied. It seemed like the proper thing to say.

'And you did not,' Tyran observed, the unspoken question clear in the tone of his voice.

The highborn pulled aside his cloak. Moonlight glimmered on pallid flesh and dark, dried blood as Malus pulled his trophies from his belt and held them up to Tyran. 'Someone had to return with the good news,' he said.

Tyran took a step forwards, peering closely at the three bloodstained faces. 'I see Aniya the Harrower,' he said, pointing at the head of the female elder, 'and this is Maghost,' he said, glancing at the fox-faced man. He frowned at the pulped mess of the third trophy. 'And this?'

'The master of assassins, as you commanded,' Malus replied. 'He wasn't as accommodating as the other two.'

A slow smile spread across Tyran's face, his suspicions forgotten as he considered the news. 'The temple Haru'ann is broken, while ours is nearly complete,' he said. 'This is a great victory for the faithful.' He beamed at Malus. 'Truly you are blessed, holy one! You have hastened the day when the Swordbearer shall walk among us.'

'Such is my fervent hope,' Malus said with convincing sincerity. 'What is our next move?'

Tyran took the heads from Malus, smiling proudly into their vacant eyes. 'Now we can contest with the temple for the hearts of the people,' he said. 'The surviving elders will be in disarray, and the assassins will be paralysed until they choose a new master.' The zealot leader indicated the new arrivals with his free hand. 'More and more true believers arrive each day,' he said. 'We are strong enough to make our case openly in the city streets.' The zealot leader beckoned for the waiting druchii to join them. 'We can even count another blessed soul such as yourself in our ranks.'

Malus was scarcely listening. 'Good news indeed,' he said absently, pondering what the Haru'ann might be, and how that figured into Tyran's scheme.

Tyran bowed to one of the hooded figures. 'Holy one, this is Hauclir, a true believer from Naggor,' he said, indicating Malus. 'Truly, it is a powerful omen that two blessed souls from feuding cities should be brought together in the common cause for the glory of Khaine.'

The zealot reached up with a pale hand, drawing back his hood. His long, white hair glowed like a ghostly shroud in the moonlight, and his brass eyes shone like hot coins as he fixed Malus with an enigmatic stare.

'Truly the ways of the Lord of Murder are mysterious indeed,' Arleth Vann said, staring into his former master's eyes.

'PREPARE YOURSELVES, OH servants of Khaine! The Time of Blood approaches!'

The zealot stood on a block of dirty white stone, his twin swords glittering in the sunlight as he held them up to the afternoon sky. Twin pyramids of stained skulls rose to either side of the true believer, offering a welcome meal to a murder of nodding ravens that listened with cursory interest to the zealot's fiery speech.

Barely a handful of druchii paused to listen to what the true believer had to say, thinking at first that he was a novitiate of the temple preaching to the citizens outside the marble-columned shrine of the highborn quarter. A steady stream of men and women were passing through the small square in front of the low building, bearing offerings to be deposited before the altar at the far end of the shrine. A pair of true novitiates stood at the entrance to the dimly-lit building, fingering the ceremonial sickles hanging from their belts and glaring at the zealot across the square with naked contempt.

Malus had positioned himself at the mouth of a narrow street leading into the square, allowing him a clear view of both the shrine and the zealot's energetic sermon. The man had been at it for an hour. Not long after he'd begun, Malus caught sight of a messenger dashing down the steps of the shrine and heading north, towards the temple fortress. The highborn figured they wouldn't have to wait much longer.

For the past three days the zealots had sent men and women into the city, declaiming their beliefs to the people of Har Ganeth. Prior to today, the zealots had stayed on the move, wandering the city streets and spreading the word but not providing the temple with a stationary target to vent their displeasure upon. Today, Tyran had decided to give them their wish, sending a man to preach the true faith outside every shrine in the city.

'The Bride of Ruin awaits in the Sanctum of the Sword!' the zealot declared to his sparse audience. 'She waits for her mate, but the temple elders deny her. They defy the will of the Bloody-Handed God, and soon they will suffer his wrath!'

Malus surveyed the square, trying to spot the other zealots lying in wait for the temple's response. Dressed in typical robes and unadorned kheitans, they were invisible among the steady stream of servants and retainers traversing the square on their masters' business.

Malus knew that Arleth Vann was out there somewhere, and the thought made his blood run cold.

He'd nearly given himself away when the assassin had shown himself that night. For a moment Malus had panicked, thinking he'd walked into a devilish trap. Surprisingly, it was the daemon that had stayed his hand, banishing the cold terror with a voice of iron and bone. 'Look in his eyes, Darkblade,' Tz'arkan had commanded. 'Look! He is as shocked as you are.'

And it was true. For a fleeting instant they had eyed each other warily, but then Tyran invited the new arrivals to join him inside, and Arleth Vann had simply turned away, falling into step with the zealot leader and not giving Malus a single backwards glance. His mind reeling, Malus had staggered to the spare, unfurnished cell set aside for him in Veyl's house and sat with his back against the stout wooden door, his straight northern sword naked in his lap. He'd sat in the darkness for hours, sleep dragging at his exhausted mind as he tried to decide what was going to happen. Were they waiting for more of the zealots to return before they confronted him? His instincts had told him to run while he could, slipping into the city before Arleth Vann could betray his identity to Tyran. Except that the zealots were his bargaining chip with Rhulan. If he broke his agreement with the Arch-Hierophant he doubted he could get anywhere near the Sanctum of the Sword. He was entangled thoroughly in a web of his own making. So, he'd waited in the darkness, wondering how and when Arleth Vann would try to take his revenge. The next thing he'd known he was blinking at the first rays of daybreak, his eyes gummy from sleep, his charade still intact.

He'd seen little of his former retainer since then. Tyran spent the next few days sending the zealots into the city, sniffing for news of the death of the elders. Malus caught glimpses of the former assassin at dawn and dusk, coming and going from the house like one of the city's ubiquitous ravens. The highborn did not know where Arleth Vann slept, or even if he slept at all, but it was clear that when he was at the house he spent much of his time in Tyran's company. It was a situation that troubled Malus no end, but he hadn't the slightest idea what to do about it, not when the former assassin could betray him whenever he chose. So the highborn had kept his distance, passing cursory messages to Rhulan that did little more than state the obvious: the zealots were agitating the people of the city to force a confrontation with the temple.

It took two days before Malus realised he wasn't in immediate danger. No one had moved against him, indeed, Tyran treated him no differently than before. Belatedly, Malus realised that Arleth Vann might be just as wary of him. After all, he was a renegade himself, an assassin who'd broken his oaths and abandoned the temple in years past. The cult's treatment of prodigals was legendary. They never forgave nor forgot those druchii who betrayed their trust. They would spare no effort to capture or kill Arleth Vann if they knew he was in the city. A few judicious words spoken in one of the city shrines would be enough. It was a tenuous stalemate.

But why was he here, Malus wondered? Had he been a zealot all along, nursing his heretical beliefs in secret, or did he track me here, seeking to finish the job he'd begun in the Valley of Shadow? The only thing he knew for certain was that he couldn't wait for Arleth Vann to show his hand. He had to find a way to kill the man without betraying himself into the bargain.

Movement at the edge of the square caught Malus's attention. A trio of black-robed men were making their way towards the ranting zealot, sunlight glinting on the edges of their long, curved draichs. Malus straightened, reaching for his sword. The temple had heard Tyran's message and here was the answer the zealots had expected.

The three warriors were not merely swordsmen: they were Draichnyr na Khaine, peerless slayers of men renowned for killing foes with a single, perfect stroke of their huge swords. He had seen men like them at work when Urial had led the warriors of the temple into battle against their sister Nagaira. Their reputation was richly deserved. The highborn set off after the men, sliding his long sword from its scabbard and concealing it beneath his cloak. He noticed two other cloaked figures on the move as well, stalking after the temple executioners like lean, hungry wolves.

'Even now the cowards in the temple fortress set their dogs upon me!' the zealot cried from his pedestal, pointing at the approaching swordsmen. 'Why? Because they do not wish their lies to be known! They have deceived you, brothers and sisters! They have tricked you, and stolen from you, and twisted the words of the Blood God to feed their own greed! The Bride of Ruin has come! The Time of Blood is nigh, sons and daughters of lost Nagarythe! Will you stand tall before the Scourge or be swept aside?'

'Heretic!' the lead executioner thundered, causing the zealot's small audience to scatter. 'You blaspheme in Khaine's holy city and impugn the honour of his devoted servants.' He raised his sword. 'Even the Lord of Blood repudiates you. Your skull is not fit to lie at Khaine's feet. After we've split you like a steer you'll be thrown into the sea for the fish to eat.'

Malus was less than ten steps from the rearmost of the executioners. He reached up to his cloak clasp, unfastening it and letting it fall to the cobblestones. Out of the corner of his eye he glimpsed his compatriots readying themselves as well. The highborn's hand tightened on the hilt of his blade as he drew in a deep breath and shouted in a voice fit for a battlefield.

'The Swordbearer has come! Blood and souls for the Swordbearer!'

To their credit, the executioners reacted to the surprise assault with speed and deadly skill. The man in front of Malus whirled at his shout, his draich making a fan of reflected light as it spun in a defensive circle around the swordsman. To his left, Malus heard the sharp ring of tempered steel and then the sound of a man's death rattle. A body hit the cobbles with a muted thud, but the highborn didn't dare look away from the warrior facing him. One wrong move and the executioner would strike his head from his shoulders.

Shrieking a terrible war scream, Malus rushed at the warrior. The executioner's curved blade paused in its circling movements, and for a split second Malus was reminded of Tyran, standing frozen in the face of Sethra Veyl's furious assault. He means to let me commit myself, and then strike the killing blow, Malus thought. He held his blow as he rushed ever closer, dropping the point of his sword as he went. If the executioner didn't react quickly he would be run through.

At the last possible moment, the executioner exploded into a blur of motion, sidestepping the highborn's thrust and aiming a blow at Malus's neck. But as the warrior committed himself to the motion Malus checked his advance, planting his leading foot and pivoting into a short, vicious cut across the warrior's midsection. The heavy sword bit into the executioner's thick kheitan and the hard muscle beneath, spinning the druchii half around with the force of the blow and throwing off his attack. Before the warrior could recover Malus pulled his blade free and drove its point into the side of the man's throat. Bright blood jetted from the wound and the executioner staggered, choking on his own fluids. Eyes bright with hate, the warrior swept his long blade around in an off-balance strike to Malus's head, but the highborn tore his sword free and blocked the blow easily, before lashing out with a backhanded stroke that decapitated the mortally wounded man.

Malus stepped out of the way as the headless body toppled over, quickly taking stock of the situation. A second executioner lay dead, his torso split by a terrible wound that ran from his collarbone down to his waist. The headless body of the zealot who attacked him lay several steps away. The leader of the executioners and another zealot circled one another warily, each searching for a weak spot in the other's guard. Malus took a step towards them, thinking to strike the man down while his back was turned, but then remembered the true believers' strange sensibilities. Far be it from me to deny the man an opportunity to die, Malus thought sourly, and left the zealot to his fate.

The highborn turned back to the man he'd slain, snatching up his bloodstained head. Moving swiftly, he sheathed his sword and pulled out a short knife as he walked over to one of the trophy pyramids by the preacher's stone block. With his back to the rest of the square, he reached up and sliced off the tips of the executioner's ears, before putting away the knife and pulling a folded strip of oilcloth from his belt. The cloth note went between the executioner's teeth in a single, deft move, and then Malus ostentatiously set the skull atop the pile.

Just then the highborn heard the sound of a blade striking home, and turned to see the executioner staggering away from his foe, clutching at a terrible wound in his chest. His long draich fell from nerveless fingers as he stumbled towards the shrine. The novitiates at the top of the stairs looked on in horror as the warrior fell onto his face and died.

'The Time of Blood is at hand!' Malus said again, repeating the words that Tyran had told him to say. He eyed the city dwellers still standing in the square, his face alight with righteous wrath. 'Shake the temple doors and command them to hearken to the Sword-bearer! The Scourge is here, and he will strip the souls from the unworthy and fling them into the outer darkness!'

The people of Har Ganeth looked into Malus's dark eyes, and he saw that they believed him.

Chapter Seven
THE EXECUTIONER'S BLADE

THEY CAME FOR him that night.

It was well past midnight when the door to Malus's cell creaked open. His mind registered the noise, but it took precious seconds for him to force his exhausted body to awaken. By the time his eyes snapped open there was pale green light seeping into the room from the open doorway and he could see the shapes of men and women outlined in the corridor beyond. His hand closed on the hilt of his sword, but he knew instinctively that he was far, far too late. He was also so deeply exhausted that it was difficult to give much of a damn.

Malus lay there on his travel-worn bedroll, blinking stupidly in the witchlight for several long seconds. No one moved. 'If you've come to kill me, get on with it,' he growled. 'Otherwise let me sleep.'

Someone chuckled. 'Tyran sent us,' a woman's voice said. 'He wants to talk to you.'

Gods below, Malus thought, sitting stiffly upright. Did the bastard ever sleep? 'All right, all right,' he growled. 'Let me find my boots.'

He could feel them studying him as he collected his gear. Every inch of him ached, and his muscles refused to work as they should. He could sense their amusement as he fumbled clumsily with belt and sword. The zealots showed not the slightest sign of discomfort or fatigue.

For people who thought of themselves as the true worshippers of Khaine, the zealots had a strange notion of piety. Unlike the practices of the temple, with its devotionals and its catechisms, the only display of righteousness the zealots respected was the perfection of the killing arts. When they weren't out in the city ambushing temple warriors by day or collecting skulls on the blood-spattered streets each night the true believers were in the courtyard or the practice rooms of Veyl's house fighting with one another. Hour after hour, sparring with heavy wooden weapons or even live steel, the zealots devoted themselves body and soul to the craft of ending life as swiftly and irrevocably as possible. The temple's fearsome executioners were layabouts by comparison.

The more the zealots suffered the deprivations of hunger and exhaustion the more serene they became. They thrived on suffering, mortifying their flesh through exertion rather than by scourge or blade. Malus had thought himself a hard man before being thrust into the world of the zealots. Now he felt like an old, tired man trying to keep pace with a pack of lions. Give me the tender mercies of Slaanesh any night, he thought grimly. At least she expected her worshippers to sleep off their devotions.

Malus fell into line with the waiting zealots and followed them upstairs. The master's chambers were dark and silent. The highborn's tired mind registered fitful glimpses of dark hallways and turgid shadows cast by banked braziers. Before he knew it, he was climbing a familiar, narrow stairway and emerging onto the roof. A brisk wind off the sea blew salt mist into his face and banished the last vestiges of sleep. He took a deep breath of the briny air, looking out over the polished pewter surface of the Sea of Chill, and then to the west, where the moons peered bright and curious over the far mountains.

The zealots drew back their dark hoods and moved silently across the roof, settling down into a rough circle facing Tyran the Unscarred. The zealot leader's head was uncovered, his hair glistening with tiny drops of sea-spray. His draich lay across his folded knees, and he studied Malus thoughtfully. 'Come and join us holy one,' he said, 'we have much to discuss.'

Malus considered Tyran's words for signs of danger. It was possible the zealot leader was toying with him. If so, Malus thought, he would be made to regret it. 'A strange place for a meeting,' he mused, approaching the seated zealots.

Tyran shrugged. 'For a city dweller, perhaps. I've spent most of my life living under the open sky, moving from one city to the next or following armies on the march. This is as natural to me as a temple cell is to you,' he said. 'Besides, only a faithless heart hides itself behind walls of stone. We have nothing to fear from man nor beast, for the Lord of Murder is with us.'

The highborn bowed deeply. 'Well said.' He sat heavily on the slick roof tiles, wincing at the flare of pain from his stiff joints. Several of the zealots chuckled quietly, their faces hidden in shadow. Now fully awake, Malus surveyed his companions more carefully. There were six of them besides Tyran. He recognised nearly all of them, including the lone hunter he'd encountered on the streets on the way back from the temple fortress and the woman who'd first welcomed him into the house nearly a week ago. She returned his gaze with a frank, playful stare.

At the far end of the circle Malus found himself staring into a pair of brass-coloured eyes. Arleth Vann studied him with the expressionless interest of a rock adder. With an effort, Malus looked past the former assassin and focused on Tyran.

'Each day brings us closer to Khaine's triumph, brothers and sisters,' the zealot leader said with a fierce smile. 'Word of the Swordbearer and his bride spreads through the city, and the temple elders remain in disarray. Their assassins have gone into conclave, debating the choice of a new master, and the Haru'ann remains broken. The apostates have never suffered such setbacks before, and they are paralysed with fear: fear that the Time of Blood is indeed at hand and their lies are about to be exposed.'

Murmurs of approval rose from the assembled zealots. Tyran regained their attention with a raised hand. 'Their fear is so great that our allies within the temple fortress report that some of the apostates are considering recanting their decadent ways and joining with us for the greater glory of Khaine. One of them is a temple elder.'

The zealots glanced at one another, their eyes widening in surprise. One of the men snorted in disgust. 'They think to erase a lifetime of apostasy now that the hounds of Khaine are baying at their door? Let them offer their necks to the axe if they are so repentant.'

'Indeed,' Malus said. 'They knew all along what lies they were spreading. It's the fear of discovery that motivates them, not true faith.'

Several of the zealots nodded, muttering in agreement. In fact, it was fear of discovery that motivated Malus. Who was this elder? Was it Rhulan? What if the elder hoped to buy his survival by exposing the highborn's scheme?

'The ways of the Lord of Murder are mysterious and terrible,' Tyran replied, shaking his head. 'Like you, I have no mercy for those who turn aside from the holy path of slaughter, but there is a great opportunity here if we are bold enough to seize it.' The zealot leader folded his arms. 'So, after careful thought and prayer, I have decided to help this elder escape the clutches of the apostates.' He stared at each of the assembled druchii in turn, 'And I have chosen you to perform the rescue.'

Malus frowned. 'Entering the temple fortress so soon after our last effort will be very difficult,' he said. 'They will be watching for infiltrators at every door and gate.'

Tyran nodded. 'Of course. That is why the elder is going to come to us.' He met the zealots' confused expressions with a crafty smile. 'The confrontations across the city today have created an opportunity for us to exploit,' he said. 'Tomorrow, the temple elders will enter the city and appear at certain shrines to reassure the people and demonstrate their divine authority. The elder who wishes to join us has arranged to appear at the shrine here in the highborn district at noon.' Tyran smiled. 'Naturally, he will be under heavy guard, which itself provides us with another chance to demonstrate our righteous wrath. Your task is simple: slay the elder's bodyguards and escort him here, where we will test his devotion and plan our next move.'

Startled gasps rose from the zealots. Several prostrated themselves before their leader. 'This is a great honour,' the female druchii said, her eyes alight at the prospect of such a battle.

'If you succeed the rewards will be greater than you know,' Tyran said portentously. 'I believe Khaine has handed us this opportunity for a reason. If we prevail tomorrow, it will be a sign that our final victory is close at hand.' The zealot leader turned to Malus. 'Hauclir, I want you to lead this holy mission. Arleth Vann will be your lieutenant. You are both blessed by the Lord of Murder; together I know that you will prevail against the apostates.'

Malus felt his heart clench. He could feel Arleth Vann's reptilian gaze resting on him like the point of a knife. 'It… it's an honour to serve,' he managed to say.

The zealot leader nodded. 'After your exploits in the temple fortress, I have no doubt you will succeed,' he said, and then rose fluidly to his feet. 'You have ten hours, brothers and sisters. Prepare yourselves as your hearts dictate. Tomorrow the eyes of the Blood God will be upon you.'

As one, the zealots stood and took their leave of Tyran. Malus remained seated, lost in thought. Tyran was right in one sense; tomorrow would indeed present a golden opportunity, one that Malus could ill afford to ignore.

The question was, if he only had one chance to strike would it be better to kill Arleth Vann or the turncoat elder?

RAIN BLEW IN thin sheets across the small square outside the shrine, causing the passers by to huddle inside their oiled cloaks and making life thoroughly miserable for the crowd waiting for the elder's arrival. Word had gone out just after dawn, when well-escorted town criers had walked the city streets, announcing that the elders of the temple would come before the people to denounce the words of the heretics that blasphemed against Khaine's holy cult. The announcement made things somewhat easier for Malus and the zealots, giving them much-needed concealment as they waited for the elder to arrive.

The highborn glanced up at the weeping grey sky and frowned. 'He's late,' the highborn muttered.

'He's probably offering sacrifices to Khaine to stop the rain,' the female zealot replied quietly. Her name, Malus had learned that morning, was Sariya. She was very young, the daughter of a highborn family in Karond Kar. 'The Lord of Murder forefend that his chosen servants get their feet wet walking down the street.'

Malus grinned at the girl's acid tongue. The zealots all stood together at the edge of the crowd, waiting for the highborn's instructions. He'd told them that he wouldn't know what they would do until nearly the last minute. There were simply too many unknowns: how large would the elder's escort be? Would he stop to speak to the crowd, or march straight into the temple? How closely would his guards hem him in? Until he saw firsthand what he was dealing with, he had no idea how to respond.

Malus fingered the hilts of a pair of heavy throwing knives beneath his sodden cloak. Shortly before dawn he'd finally decided on their target.

'More likely he's being hampered by his escort,' the highborn muttered darkly. 'A large contingent would have a hard time getting organised and moving quickly down these cramped streets.' He slowly scanned the assembled druchii, looking for anything untoward. 'That, or they are waiting to hear back from their informants to see if the square is safe to travel through.'

Sariya gave Malus a sidelong glance. 'My, holy one, you're a font of cheery news.'

'The true faith is not an easy one,' the highborn replied with a wry smile, 'but it is realistic.'

He turned to Arleth Vann and caught himself just before he asked if the former assassin had seen anything. The druchii was looking away at the time and didn't catch Malus's startled expression. Sariya's banter had almost caused him to forget himself. He's no retainer of mine, the highborn thought angrily, quickly looking away.

The tramp of armoured feet carried across the rain swept square from the east. Heads turned. Malus stood on his toes to peer above the throng and caught sight of a rank of four executioners, their lacquered armour gleaming wetly in the weak light. They marched with their draichs unsheathed and raised before them like a hedge of razor-edged steel. Their faces were grim and their dark eyes fixed on the crowd as if viewing them from across a battlefield. Malus paid no attention to the executioners, instead straining his ears to gauge the weight of the marching feet echoing across the cobblestones. He bit back a snarl. It sounded like a full company of swordsmen, possibly as much as two hundred men. The temple wanted to send a very clear message to the people of the city.

'Damnation,' Malus muttered, considering his options. There weren't many to choose from. From where he stood, it looked as if the swordsmen were marching directly at the assembled crowd, evidently intending to create a cordon for the elder between the audience and the shrine. After a moment he thought he understood what the temple contingent was planning.

'All right,' the highborn said, turning his back on the crowd and addressing the zealots in low, urgent tones. 'Here's what we're going to do.' Malus took a deep breath. 'Arleth Vann, take Sariya and get inside the shrine as quickly as you can. The rest of us will work to the front of the crowd and attack the executioners once the elder shows himself. When the fighting starts, he'll retreat inside the shrine, where you'll be waiting for him. Kill his escorts and take him straight-away to Tyran. We'll keep the executioners distracted until you get away.'

Malus looked first to Sariya, and then at Arleth Vann, making certain they understood their instruc-tions. He met the former assassin's gaze and the druchii nodded curtly, acknowledging the order as he'd done countless times in the past. 'Go,' Malus said, and the two zealots headed swiftly away, circling around the edge of the crowd to get past the oncom-ing line of executioners.

The highborn turned back to his remaining men. 'Spread out and work your way up to the front of the crowd,' he said. 'No one acts until I give the order.' With that, he turned on his heel and started easing his way through the muttering throng.

Within moments Malus found himself fighting his way upstream against a press of people being pushed in the opposite direction. The executioners were using their blades to force the crowd to give ground, elicit-ing angry murmurs from the spectators. A long double line of armoured warriors was extending itself for twenty yards across the square in front of the shrine. A large block of troops was assembled near the mouth of the street the escort had emerged from, securing their line of retreat.

The tramp of feet fell silent, followed by the rattle of harnesses as the swordsmen adjusted their line. Malus stopped short behind the foremost line of spectators, first eyeing the warriors and their brandished blades and then trying to catch a glimpse of the steps to the shrine. He just caught sight of two hooded figures slipping inside the entrance to the building, and knew that Arleth Vann and Sariya were in position.

Movement near the mouth of the eastern lane caught the highborn's attention. All he could see over the line of troops was the tip of a gold-topped staff and a voluminous crimson hood. Was it Rhulan, he thought? There was no damned way to tell.

He watched the figure move along behind the line of executioners as he eased his sword from its scabbard beneath his cloak. Malus shifted slightly, taking up position almost directly behind a tall, scowling man who was glaring irritably at the temple soldiers.

Malus watched the elder begin to climb the temple steps, just as he'd anticipated – the man would need the extra height to address the crowd over the soldiers. The highborn took a deep breath and lowered his right shoulder. 'Blood and souls for the Swordbearer!' he roared, and shoved the unsuspecting man at the executioners as hard as he could. Taken by surprise, the spectator flew at the swordsmen with a startled shout, his arms flinging wide for balance, and the surprised executioner in front of him reacted out of instinct. A draich carved a flickering arc through the rain and the spectator screamed, blood rising in a fountain as the sword split him nearly in half.

The highborn struck at just that instant, while the executioner's blade was still deep in his victim's body. 'They mean to kill us all!' he shouted, stabbing his

sword into the executioner's exposed throat. The
swordsman reeled backwards, blood pouring down
the front of his armour. More shouts and the clash of
steel echoed up and down the line, adding to the pan-
demonium.

Malus leapt into the gap opened in the executioners'
line, hacking left and right with his heavy blade. He
struck the man to his left a heavy blow on the side of
his helmet and then cut open the hamstring of the
man on his right. The executioner collapsed with a
scream, clutching at his leg, and the rest of the swordsmen lost their self-control and attacked the shouting
crowd.

A draich swept down at Malus, but the swing had little real power and the highborn swept it aside with
ease. The tight ranks of the executioners made for an
imposing wall of men and steel, but it left the warriors
with little room to use their long blades properly. He
hacked at the man in front of him, feinting at his head
and then altering the course of the blow to smash his
heavy sword into the executioner's fingers. Two severed digits tumbled from the man's right gauntlet.
Malus half-knocked the draich from the man's grip
with a savage swipe and then smashed his sword into
the executioner's face.

In the space of an instant the square had become a
raging battlefield. The executioners lashed out at anything that moved, and spectators in the crowd were
fighting back in an effort to save themselves. Screams
and the stink of spilled blood filled the air. The executioner Malus had struck fell to his knees, his helmet
crumpled by the highborn's savage blow. He stepped

in and slit the man's throat with his sword, laughing like a madman in the ringing tumult. Malus felt the daemon respond to the terror and pain around it, writhing and squirming around the highborn's hammering heart. For a fleeting instant he was tempted to ask the daemon to share its power, just for the sheer joy of spilling blood. This was his element. He'd known it since the day he'd rescued the army of the black ark from the ambush at Blackwater Ford.

The line of swordsmen was disintegrating. Without orders, some men advanced into the crowd and others gave ground, splitting the force into isolated knots of struggling warriors. The cobblestones were black with pools of blood, men slipping and stumbling over fallen bodies or spilled entrails. As Malus watched, an executioner overbalanced and fell to the ground, only to be set upon by a trio of druchii who pounded his head and back with pieces of stone torn from the square itself.

A muffled shout drew his attention to the east where Malus caught sight of an executioner in ornate armour brandishing a rune inscribed draich and shouting orders to the block of swordsmen covering the eastern road. Once they entered the fight the battle would be over in moments. The highborn spun in place, looking everywhere for signs of Arleth Vann and the temple elder.

There! Malus saw a pair of dark-cloaked figures herding another druchii with a crimson cloak towards the lane on the south side of the square. No one was paying any attention in the chaos of the battle. This was the only chance he was going to get.

Drawing one of his throwing knives, Malus cut back through the seething mob, staying low and skirting struggling opponents as he closed the distance with the fleeing trio. A bloodstained man grabbed at Malus's arm, bleeding from a head wound and babbling incoherently. Malus stabbed him in the leg with an angry snarl and shoved the man away.

They were nearly at the mouth of the street. Malus picked up his pace, running up to the edge of the mob. It would be a long shot, he realised with a grimace. The highborn took a deep breath, drew back his arm and hurled the knife as hard as he could at the elder's retreating form.

The knife was just a dark blur against the grey mist as it arced towards its target. It struck the red-cloaked figure just beneath the left shoulder blade. Malus watched as his victim staggered under the force of the blow, and then took two more stumbling steps before falling face-first onto the cobblestones. Malus watched Arleth Vann turn at the sound. The two cloaked figures paused only a moment, staring at the fallen body. Then they turned and made good their escape.

A tremendous shout echoed from the other side of the square as the reserve block of executioners charged into the fray. Malus couldn't see what had become of the remaining zealots. Perhaps they had already broken free, or maybe they lay among the dead littering the cobblestones. Either way, they were no longer his problem.

Malus headed south, pushing aside other fleeing city folk as he fled the oncoming executioners. As he approached his fallen victim, however, he was gripped by overpowering curiosity. Was it Rhulan? Had he made the right choice? On impulse, he skidded to a stop beside the body and pulled his knife free, before rolling the corpse over to peer inside the depths of the hood.

His heart clenched. 'Mother of Night,' he cursed, looking into Sariya's lifeless eyes.

Chapter Eight
REVELATIONS

BLOOD FLOWED IN the streets of Har Ganeth, and the sounds of battle rang out all across the city as the warriors of the temple vented their fury on any druchii unlucky enough to be caught in their path. Men were chased down and hacked apart, their entrails spread for the ravens and their heads set aside as offerings to the Bloody-Handed God. Slaves were hunted and torn apart like wild animals. Market squares turned to charnel houses as the servants of the temple sought to drown their rage in rivers of blood.

An elder of the temple had been taken, so the rumours said, seized within the holy grounds of a city shrine while his bodyguards were slaughtered by a howling mob. Never in the history of the temple had such a crime been committed. It was an insult too great to be borne. Trumpets sounded from the temple walls all through the afternoon, and a flood of black-robed druchii streamed into the city streets with bared blades held in their hands, half-mad with anger and grief. The witch elves joined them late in the day, their muscular bodies painted with sweat and blood, and their eyes wild with murderous ecstasy. They sniffed the air and howled like wolves, their faces twisted in masks of bestial hunger, and when they could not find any more victims to kill on the city streets the brides of Khaine drove the temple servants to break down the doors of the lowborns' homes and flesh houses.

That was when the fighting began in earnest. For hundreds of years the people of the city had prospered under the terrible rule of the temple and bled for the Lord of Murder when necessary. The daylight was given over to the mundane needs of the city, but at night the streets were a place of holy communion, where sacrifices could be made to the Lord of Murder without fear of feud or reprisal. Highborn families would offer up clutches of slaves in hopes of a good flesh harvest or to call down a curse upon their enemies. Lowborn families, hungry for wealth and power, were forced to turn out their own kin in hopes of winning the Blood God's favour. One and all, they were prey to the armed bands that roamed the streets from dusk to dawn in search of victims to sate the eternal hunger of the temple.

The streets were given over to the Lord of Murder so that the houses of the citizens would remain inviolate by the unspoken rule that had allowed the city to survive for centuries. So when the servants of the temple tore down the doors of the lowborns' houses they did not find fearful victims waiting for the executioner's blade, but were welcomed with axes and spears like any other invader.

Malus Darkblade, the architect of the day's bloodshed, wandered the streets of Har Ganeth all through the afternoon, his face a mask of hate and his blade wet with blood. He staggered like a drunk and killed every living thing that crossed his path, furious with himself and with the city of madmen he found himself in.

Arleth Vann had anticipated him, forcing the elder to exchange his cloak with Sariya. Had it been a trap all along, designed to force his hand and show his true intentions to Tyran? Malus couldn't be sure, and wasn't certain it even mattered any more. The elder was doubtless safe at the house of Sethra Veyl, telling the zealot leader everything he knew. If Rhulan had told the elders of Malus's deal then he was certain to be exposed.

All this had gone through Malus's head as he'd crouched over Sariya's body. Then the fleeing mob surged around him, filling his ears with cries of anger and pain, and he let himself be caught up in it.

When he came back to his senses he was sitting in an alley surrounded by corpses. The sounds of battle raged in a small square just a few yards away. Malus listened to the clash of steel and the screams of the dying like another man would listen to the patter of rain or the whisper of wind in the trees. His robes were stiff with blood and his sword felt glued to his hand with layers of crusted filth. The stench of the battlefield filled his nostrils. His stomach rumbled and he recalled that he hadn't eaten all day.

A shadow passed over Malus's face, and he felt the beat of wings against his cheeks. The raven settled on the head of a man doubled over on the alley floor next to Malus. The bird studied him with one yellow eye and let out a croaking laugh. 'Blood and souls! Blood and souls!' the dreadful bird cried.

Malus took a half-hearted swipe at the damned raven, sending it squawking into the air. Exhausted, he slumped onto the bloodstained ground, rolling onto his back and staring up at a thin bar of cloudy sky between the alley's close-set buildings. He felt the daemon move within him, slithering against his ribs like a contented cat. The sensation repelled him.

His rage spent, the highborn wearily considered his options. There was a very real risk that his dealings with the temple had been exposed. Certainly Arleth Vann suspected him, but the former retainer might well have done that on nothing more than general principles.

The zealots were the key to the Sanctum of the Sword. He had to deliver Tyran and the other true believers into the hands of the temple, and that meant returning to the house of Sethra Veyl. Perhaps there were other ways to reach the warpsword, but they would take time to unearth, and time was one commodity he had in short supply.

I've got to go back, he thought grimly. I have to know what they're planning. Let Arleth Vann make his accusations. I've talked my way out of worse situations before.

Another shadow fell across Malus's vision. For a moment he thought the raven had returned, but then a bloodstained face and a pair of shoulders loomed into the highborn's view. A grimy hand reached for his hair, and a gore stained hatchet glinted in the fading light.

Malus rolled onto his side with a snarl and stabbed the man in the chest. The druchii, wearing the stained robes of a tradesman, groaned weakly and toppled onto his side. The man had a clutch of severed heads tied to his belt and a leather bag bulging with looted coin, gold earrings and silver bracelets. Malus had to admire the man's opportunism in the midst of chaos. The highborn helped himself to the bag and struck off the man's head for good measure.

A croaking laugh echoed down the alley. The raven looked up from its meal and eyed him knowingly. 'Gore-crow! Gore-crow!' the bird called mockingly.

Malus hit the bird squarely with the tradesman's head, sending it croaking angrily skyward in an explosion of greasy feathers. The damned skulls were good for something after all, he thought to himself.

THE HIGHBORN DISTRICT was relatively quiet after the bedlam of the lower quarters. Even in the depths of their anger the temple followers evidently knew better than to menace the city's well-armed nobility. Still, the tall houses were dark and tightly shuttered and the streets were largely deserted as Malus found his way to the house of Sethra Veyl.

There were no zealots standing guard outside the white door when the highborn arrived. Malus pounded on the door with the pommel of his blade, but got no reply. 'Open up, damn your eyes!' he roared over the wall, his previous anger returning. 'Since when do true believers cower behind stone walls?'

Within moments there was a rattle of bolts and the door opened. A white-robed zealot stood in the doorway, clutching his sword in a white-knuckled grip as he glared at Malus. 'No one enters tonight, holy one,' the man said, 'not even you. Tyran's orders.'

'If Tyran wishes to keep me out he can tell me himself!' Malus snarled, advancing on the man. The zealot raised his blade, but the highborn slapped it aside with his own and then shoved the man rudely in the chest. The true believer fell backwards onto the cobblestones and the men with him gave ground, stunned at Malus's bloody visage. To them he was the very image of the divine, anointed in the red wine of battle.

Malus raised his blade and levelled it at the astonished guards. 'Those of you who are ready to offer up your heads to Khaine need only stand in my path and I will give you gladly to the god.'

But the man Malus had struck wasn't so easily cowed. He sprang gracefully to his feet, a fierce expression on his face. 'Let us see who has the greater devotion, then,' he said, edging forwards with his sword held ready. 'I'll go to the Lord of Murder laughing with joy, knowing you'll soon be following me.'

'Enough!' cried a husky, female voice from across the small courtyard. 'Put aside your blades and let the man from Naggor pass. I can see the spirits of the dead that surround him. He has offered up a great bounty to our god this day, and punished the ranks of the blasphemers.'

The zealots reluctantly parted to allow Malus to pass. A woman waited on the steps leading up to the house, her pale face gleaming from the depths of a wide, black hood. The blood-witch studied Malus with a frank, predatory stare.

Malus made his way slowly across the courtyard, noticing for the first time that it was conspicuously empty. The zealots that had camped in the open space had all vanished, taking their meagre possessions with them. The highborn frowned up at the woman. 'Where is Tyran?' he asked.

'Elsewhere,' the blood-witch replied. 'When word of the elder's disappearance reached the temple the remaining leaders could not contain the fury of their servants. Once night has fallen and their bloodlust has been spent they will return to the fortress and the elders will send them against the houses of the true believers no matter where they lie.'

'And the elder who has joined us?'

The blood-witch smiled, showing her leonine fangs. 'He has proven worthy, holy one, and eager to witness the Time of Blood. Our Haru'ann is complete, while the temple remains in disarray.'

Malus paused, trying to puzzle out the full import of the blood-witch's words. If she knew so much and yet allowed him into the house then clearly the zealots still trusted him. Or perhaps they simply had no time to deal with him because something much more important was afoot. What was this damned Haru'ann everyone kept talking about?

'What would Tyran have of me?' he asked.

The blood-witch shrugged. 'When you did not return with the others it was assumed that you found a glorious death in the riots,' she said. 'Those of us who have no role in what is to come will take to the streets tonight and offer up tokens of devotion to the Bloody-Handed God.' She smiled again, her feline eyes glowing in the fading sunlight. 'I will dance with many men tonight, take many mates and bathe in their fluids. You may dance with me, if you wish.'

'That… that's quite an honour,' Malus managed to say, quite taken aback by the woman's feral gaze, 'but I am not worthy of your attentions. For one thing, I'm filthy.'

The blood-witch threw back her head and laughed. The sound both aroused and frightened Malus at the same time. 'Go then, as the Lord of Murder wishes,' she said. The blood-witch descended the steps, reaching up to gently trace a curved talon along the line of his jaw. 'Another night perhaps,' she said softly. 'Remember me, holy one. I might not recognise your freshly scrubbed face when we meet again.'

MALUS STRODE SWIFTLY down the deserted hall, his mind racing. Tyran was making his move tonight, of that he was certain, but what was his plan?

He reached the sparsely furnished cell that had been set aside for him and dashed inside, not bothering to shut the door behind him as he started gathering up his possessions. There was no way he was going to find the zealot leader before he set his plan in motion. The best he could do was to bluff his way into the temple and tell Rhulan what little he knew. Malus figured he could improvise the rest as the situation developed. It was not as if he had any other choice.

The highborn went to roll up his bedroll and realised that after everything that had happened he was still holding on to his sword. Malus stared at the long blade in irritation. Put the damned thing away, he thought. You wouldn't have made it this far if the zealots wanted to kill you.

Then a chill went down his spine as a dark shape moved through the light at his back. Malus whirled just as Arleth Vann struck.

The assassin was nearly invisible in the dimly lit room. The only warning Malus had was a glint of witchlight on metal as one of Arleth Vann's blades caught the light streaming in from the corridor beyond. The highborn raised his blade and narrowly parried a stroke that would have sliced open his throat. Pure, desperate instinct caused him to sweep his blade downwards and parry the assassin's second sword as it stabbed for his stomach.

Malus gave ground quickly, trying to circle around to the cell's doorway so he would be backlit by the corridor lights, but Arleth Vann anticipated this and darted swiftly to the side, aiming a flurry of blows at his former master's head and neck. The highborn parried stroke for stroke, but was forced inexorably backwards as he warded off the assassin's attacks. Malus fumbled for one of his throwing knives as the assassin shifted position again and melded back into the darkness.

The highborn pulled the dagger free as quietly as he could, reversing his grip on the blade with a flick of his wrist. He crouched low, sliding warily to the left. 'I continue to underestimate you, Arleth Vann,' he hissed. 'I never expected your little surprise in the Valley of Shadows, and here you nearly pulled the same trick on me again. Surely you realise that there's no honour left to reclaim by killing me. As far as the world knows, I died with the army outside Hag Graef.'

For a moment there was only silence. Malus waited, his ears straining for the slightest sound. Then there was a faint hint of movement and Arleth Vann spoke in a sepulchral whisper, like wind soughing through the cracks in a tomb. 'Would that I thought so as well,' he said, 'but in the absence of honour, the need for vengeance remains.'

Malus fixed on the source of the voice and hurled the dagger with all his strength, before bolting for the open doorway. He heard the discordant ring of steel behind him as Arleth Vann knocked the dagger aside and bit back a savage curse. He reached the shaft of light thrown by the hall lights and dashed for the relative safety of the corridor, only to be hauled roughly off his feet as Arleth Vann seized his bloodstained cloak.

The highborn crashed to the floor, swinging his sword wildly over his head. He felt the blade bite home, and Arleth Vann hissed a sibilant curse. Reaching up with his free hand, Malus undid the clasps of his cloak and rolled quickly to the side just as a curved sword thudded into the wooden floor where he'd been.

'What vengeance?' Malus spat, scrabbling backwards across the floor. 'I could understand such feelings from Silar or perhaps Dolthaic, even that rogue Hauclir, but you? I gave you a new life when you fled the temple. You owe me everything. It was you who was false. You swore fealty to me, when in secret your first loyalty was to these fanatics!'

There was a whirring in the air. A spinning shape passed through the weak light, and Malus caught sight of the hurled sword a moment too late. He moved to block the weapon but misjudged its trajectory. The back of the curved sword smashed into his right forearm. The highborn felt the bones break and cried out in pain. Then another blow knocked the broad sword from his nerveless fingers. Arleth Vann's hand closed around Malus's throat. His second sword hung poised above his head.

'My loyalty to you and to the temple was one and the same!' Arleth Vann snapped. 'I sought you out, across the length and breadth of Naggaroth. I served you for years, watching and waiting in secret because I was certain that you were the one. When the autarii foiled our attack in the Valley of Shadow I thought that it was Khaine's will, and I rejoiced.' The assassin bent lower, until Malus could see the anger and despair gleaming in his brass-coloured eyes. 'Then I returned to Hag Ganeth to find your brother Urial in the Sanctum of the Sword, and I was forced to admit my mistake. I'd found the right house, but chosen the wrong son.'

Malus wrestled with Arleth Vann's choking grip, but the assassin's fingers were locked around his throat like a vice. Slowly, remorselessly, Malus's former retainer lowered his sword and placed its point above his master's racing heart. 'I do not know how you gained Khaine's blessing since I last saw you,' Arleth Vann said, 'but whatever piety you may have found here, I know you for the deceiver you truly are. You destroy everything you touch, Malus Darkblade. For the sake of the faith, and for the sake of blessed vengeance, your life ends here.'

Sparks swam in Malus's vision. Desperate, he switched his grip to Arleth Vann's sword wrist, but the blade sank inexorably lower, driven by a ruthless engine of hate. The assassin's words rebounded in the highborn's brain. I served you for years, watching and waiting in secret because I was certain that you were the one.

Arleth Vann's blade pierced his skin. Icy clarity focused the highborn's mind. You know what to do. Act now or die!

'Tz'arkan!' Malus growled under his breath. 'I have need of your strength!'

His body spasmed as his veins burned with a torrent of black ice, driving Malus deeper onto Arleth Vann's blade. A wave of crystalline agony tore a strangled scream from Malus's lips as the bones in his right arm re-knit. The darkness receded as the daemon's energies kindled his vision, and the highborn saw the look of fear and wonder spread across Arleth Vann's face.

Malus put his right hand on Arleth Vann's chest and with a single shove the druchii flew across the small room. The highborn flew upright as if weightless, his limbs burning with foul energies. It tasted like wine on his lips. How had he gone for so many months without the daemon's touch? The power was intoxicating. Malus heard laughter ringing in his ears, and thought it was his own.

He advanced on his former retainer, gliding like smoke across the floor. His eyes were molten, gleaming in the faint light. Malus channelled the daemon's seething power into his voice as he spoke.

'It is you who were deceived Arleth Vann. Your faith deserted you in your time of trial and you doubted the Blood God's will. I am the Scourge, the anointed son of Khaine, and the Time of Blood is nigh.'

Arleth Vann looked up at Malus and cried out in awe. 'My lord!' he said, abasing himself at the highborn's feet. 'Truly I have failed you. My life is forfeit. Strike me down for my weakness and cast my soul into the Outer Darkness.' He drew a dagger from his belt with a trembling hand and offered it up to the highborn.

The gesture stunned Malus, rendering him speechless. What sort of madness was this religion that it drove men to offer up their lives like lambs? 'Put away your blade,' he snapped. 'I have no use for martyrs, Arleth Vann. If you would redeem yourself, then serve me as you once did, body and soul.'

Arleth Vann straightened, looking up at his master. Tears gleamed like gold in the reflected glow of Malus's blazing eyes. 'I swear it,' he said, 'body and soul, until death's release.' He bowed from the waist, pressing his forehead against the wooden floor.

Malus's eyes narrowed in triumph. Only then did he become aware of the laughter, still echoing within his mind.

'Now you accept your fate, Malus,' Tz'arkan said. 'I knew it was only a matter of time.'

'TELL ME OF the battle,' Malus said, peering out through the narrow window at the twin moons rising on the eastern horizon. 'What happened to you after the attack on my tent?'

Arleth Vann shrugged, the motion eliciting a grimace of pain as he dabbed at the cut oozing blood down the side of his left leg. 'There is not much to tell. The autarii nearly killed me. Had one of those bolts struck a finger's width more to the right it would have pierced my heart,' he said. 'I lost consciousness as I was being dragged from the camp. I awoke later, in a flesh house near the Slavers' Quarter. Silar had arranged for a chirurgeon to tend me, but it was many weeks before I was fully recovered.'

'What became of Silar and the rest?'

'Scattered like ravens, my lord,' Arleth Vann replied. 'They lost nearly everything when word came that you'd slain your father. All that treasure Silar had worked so hard to ferry from Karond Kar fell into Isilvar's hands when he seized your property. The new Vaulkhar was going to have us slain on the next Hanil Khar, but then he learned that you were heading for the city with an army from Naggor at your back. So we were given the chance to regain our honour if we returned to the Hag with your head.'

Malus nodded to himself, tasting bile in the back of his throat. 'I would have done the same, of course. It was by luck alone I survived.'

'We returned empty-handed, but Isilvar grudgingly credited us with causing enough of a diversion that the main attack was carried home successfully,' Arleth Vann said, wrapping a makeshift bandage around his leg. 'So we were given our freedom, such as it was. I think he wanted to seem magnanimous to the court, because he was still trying to win over many of the city's highborn. At any rate, Silar and Dolthaic left for Clar Karond, hoping to sign on with a corsair. Hauclir vanished. For all I know, he's still out there hunting for you.'

The highborn frowned. 'Did Isilvar not think me dead?'

'He said as much, but I doubt he truly believed it. We knew better. Scouts had turned up the body of Bale's only son, but you were nowhere to be found.'

'So how did you find my trail?'

Arleth Vann turned to face Malus, a bemused expression on his face. 'Your trail? I didn't come here looking for you, my lord. Word had spread among the true believers that Urial had appeared in Har Ganeth with the Bride of Ruin. The faithful were commanded to return to the Holy City and stand by his side as he petitioned the temple to perform the Swordbearer's Rite.'

Malus turned and approached the kneeling assassin, considering his words carefully. 'Arleth Vann, you have known me for many years.' He spread his hands and smiled sheepishly. 'You know I was never a worshipper at the temple. It was no accident that Khaine led you to me. I have need of a guide to illuminate the path I'm on.' He knelt beside his retainer. 'What is the

Rite of the Swordbearer, and why would the temple be loath to perform it for Urial?'

'The Warpsword of Khaine is bound within ancient, powerful sorceries, wards that can only be undone by a special rite, and only in the presence of the prophesied one,' Arleth Vann said. 'Only the Haru'ann can perform the rite itself, which is why the temple–'

'Wait,' Malus said, raising his hand. 'What is the Haru'ann?'

Arleth Vann looked shocked. 'The Haru'ann is the council of elders that serves the Grand Carnifex,' he said. 'There are five members of the council, each bearing a sacred duty to the temple.'

Malus remembered the blood-witch's words outside the house. *Our Haru'ann is complete, while the temple remains in disarray.* Suddenly he knew what Tyran was planning.

While the temple turned out its warriors for an assault on the houses of the faithful, the zealots were going to sneak into the temple and perform the Swordbearer's Rite themselves, delivering the sword into Urial's hands.

Chapter Nine
CITADEL OF BONE

THE PIECES ALL fell into place. Malus realised that Tyran had manipulated the elders of the temple masterfully. The zealot leader would call on his agents in the temple fortress to admit him and his zealot council while the warriors of Khaine fought the bulk of the true believers in the city streets. There would be nothing to prevent them from reaching the Sanctum of the Sword and performing the Rite of the Swordbearer for Urial.

Malus rose and began to pace the room, considering his next move. 'Where are Tyran and the elders now?' he asked.

Arleth Vann shrugged. 'I don't know, my lord. I brought the elder here and found Tyran waiting for me in the courtyard with a cadre of warriors. They took charge of the elder and left immediately.'

The highborn bared his teeth. 'Likely he's gone to ground somewhere close to the temple, waiting for the right time to make his move, or he could be inside the temple even now, having slipped inside with the returning warriors.' Malus took a deep breath. There was only one viable course of action to take. 'I have to speak to Arch-Hierophant Rhulan,' he said. 'Can you get us inside the temple?'

Arleth Vann cinched the bandage tightly around his leg and eyed Malus with a frown. 'You wish to speak to the blasphemers? Why?'

Malus steeled himself, wondering if what he was about to say would spark off another fight. 'Because we must sound the alarm and stop Tyran and his men before they reach the sanctum.'

The retainer stared at Malus for a long time, his expression unreadable. 'Why would we want to do that?' he asked at last.

'Because Tyran has thrown his lot in with Urial,' Malus replied, 'and my half-brother will stop at nothing to get his hands on the warpsword.'

The assassin shook his head. 'He isn't the chosen one. The rite will not work for him.'

'Do you think that will sway him?' Malus asked. 'He thinks that he stands upon the brink of everlasting glory. He believes Yasmir is his for the taking. When the rite fails he won't fault himself, but Tyran and his council. He believes that he is the prophesied one, and he will stop at nothing to fulfil his ambitions, even if that means destroying the cult in the process.'

Tz'arkan wrapped tightly around his heart, his voice rasping softly in the highborn's ear. 'Speak for yourself,' the daemon hissed.

Arleth Vann considered the highborn's words at length, his expression troubled. Finally, he nodded. 'There is a way,' he said. 'It's known to few people even within the temple, so we should be able to reach Rhulan's chambers unobserved. The path is long, however, and it will take time.'

'Then let's go,' Malus said, eyeing his half-packed possessions and deciding to leave them behind. His truly valuable items – namely the Octagon of Praan, the Idol of Kolkuth and the Dagger of Torxus – were buried in a saddlebag strapped to Spite's back. He could get another bedroll and water bottle later, if need be. Right now, every minute counted.

If they moved quickly they could catch the zealots' leaders all in one place, far from any hope of assistance, and he could hand the temple elders a great victory. In the back of his mind, however, Malus harboured an even more ambitious plan. If he could reach the sanctum as the zealots were performing the rite, his presence would allow it to conclude successfully. Then he could make his own play for the relic, perhaps with the daemon's help.

The highborn smiled grimly as he worked. It would be worth it just to see the look on Urial's face.

ARLETH VANN LED Malus out into the darkened streets, heading south and east away from the fortress. Malus kept pace with his retainer, sword in hand and scanning the streets and alleys with care. The sounds of fighting still echoed in the lower parts of the city, and he could see the flickering glow of fires on the horizon near the warehouse district. Based on what he'd witnessed over the course of the afternoon, when the temple warriors were unleashed on the zealot strongholds around the city, things would spiral rapidly out of control.

The assassin led Malus out of the highborn district, following a zigzag course through twisting lanes that led inexorably down the long hillside. Along the way the pair slipped past armed bands of city dwellers, spattered with dried gore and drunk on bloodlust, in search of more heads to hang from their belts. Each time Arleth Vann slipped silently from one pool of shadow to the next, moving like a ghost past the exhausted druchii.

They moved quickly through the city's entertainment district. The flesh houses were tightly shuttered and many of the ale rooms had been looted over the course of the day. Many of the looted buildings sported piles of fresh, severed heads outside their broken doorways and windows. Malus imagined the proprietors letting the looters drink their fill and then descending on the drunken thieves with clubs and meat cleavers, determined to recoup their loss in flesh if not in coin.

After almost an hour Malus found himself in the lowborn district, near the city's great warehouses and tanneries. The acrid stink of the tanners mixed with the smoke of burning buildings, causing his eyes to water. Malus thought he heard the call of a single trumpet from high up the hill, and imagined the great gates of the temple fortress gaping like a dragon's maw, ready to unleash the temple's wrath upon the city.

He was so focused on the distant sound that he almost walked right into Arleth Vann. The assassin had stopped in a pool of deep shadow a few feet back from the mouth of a narrow alley and was studying a dark, shuttered house across the street. Malus crouched beside the retainer, eyeing the building. To his eyes, it looked very old and decrepit. The witch-lamps over the door had long since expired, and at some point in the past one of the three iron balconies had given way, leaving only deep gouges in the stonework where the iron railings had once been. The door, Malus noted, was dark oak, and its iron hinges were thick and free of rust. 'What is this place?' he whispered.

Arleth Vann gave him a sidelong glance. 'This house is the reason why the temple chose Har Ganeth for their own.' He edged forwards and peered carefully up and down the street. 'I see no guards. Perhaps they were caught up in the fighting, or maybe the temple has grown lax over the years.' The assassin shrugged. 'Follow me.'

Moving quickly and quietly, the two druchii slipped across the moonlit street. At the door, Arleth Vann laid his hand on the dark wood and pushed. It slid open noiselessly, revealing abyssal darkness beyond.

Malus shot Arleth Vann a worried look. 'No guards and no locks?'

'No obvious ones,' the assassin replied, 'but the house is tightly warded, my lord. Be assured of that.'

The retainer stepped cautiously into the blackness. Malus followed, apprehension tickling his guts. As he crossed the threshold he felt a prickling sensation along his neck and scalp. Tz'arkan stirred. 'Old magic,' the daemon whispered. 'It tastes of rot and the grave. Be wary, Darkblade.'

Darkness, cold and dank, enveloped Malus. He stopped and waited for a moment, allowing his eyes to adjust. The entry hall of the old house was high ceilinged, like most druchii homes, and three narrow windows allowed only a trickle of moonlight past their grimy panes. Everything appeared to Malus in different shades of night. The ghostly arch of a stairway rose on his right, a fainter shade of black than the ebony surface of the floor. High overhead the perfect vault of shadow was smudged by a grey blob that Malus took to be an ancient witchlamp holder.

Arleth Vann turned back to Malus, his alabaster face hovering in the darkness like a disembodied spirit. 'There is a door at the base of the staircase. We'll follow it into the cellars,' he said, and disappeared into the gloom.

Malus lost sight of the assassin almost at once. Cursing to himself, he focused on the half-seen staircase, crossing the stone floor with care. After a few moments he reached the base of the stairs and worked his way along the wall until he almost bumped into Arleth Vann's nearly invisible form. Malus heard the creak of a door, and felt a gust of colder, wetter air against his cheek. He wrinkled his nose at the smell of damp earth and old rot. The doorway itself was a pool of darker shadow against the iron-grey of the wall. He sensed rather than saw Arleth Vann slip inside, and moved quickly in his wake.

Without warning, Malus's eyes were dazzled by an explosion of pale green light. He hissed a curse, trying to shield his eyes from the small globe of witchlight that burned in the palm of Arleth Vann's upraised hand.

'I never knew you were a sorcerer!' Malus exclaimed, blinking in surprise.

Arleth Vann shrugged. 'The temple teaches its assassins a few simple cantrips: how to make light, how to silence rusty hinges, things of that nature. Nothing like the knowledge possessed by someone such as Urial.'

They were in a narrow, enclosed stairway that led down to another ironbound door. Arleth Vann descended slowly, testing each of the stone steps with a tentative boot before proceeding. 'One of these steps activates a poison trap,' he muttered, 'so follow my moves exactly.'

'You seem to know a great deal about this place,' Malus said, attempting to follow in the assassin's footsteps.

Arleth Vann shrugged. 'This was how I escaped the temple, many years ago.' He paused at the third step from the bottom, testing the riser carefully with the point of his boot. 'This is the one,' he said, stepping carefully over the trap and continuing to the door. There was a grating of metal as he turned the iron ring and pushed it open, letting in a blast of frigid air that sank right into Malus's bones.

The doorway opened onto a stone landing lit by a flickering green glow. The assassin doused his witchlight and stepped through the doorway. Malus followed close behind Arleth Vann, watching his breath turn to vapour in the chill air. His boots skidded on the dark stones, which were rimed with glittering frost. Arleth Vann caught his arm at once, helping his master steady himself. 'Careful, my lord,' he said quietly. 'You wouldn't want to take a fall right here.'

Malus steadied himself and looked around. The landing was barely three paces square and looked out over a cavernous space at least thirty feet deep. From where he stood he could see that the upper half of the space was square shaped and bounded with finished stone blocks. Another narrow staircase descended from the landing, following the rough wall towards the chamber floor. The source of the light came from below, radiating upwards in a flickering, ghostly nimbus.

Malus freed his arm from his retainer's grip and carefully approached the edge of the landing. Below, he saw a wide ribbon of dark, glossy stone, wide enough for four men to walk abreast, leading to a tall archway set into the side of the great hill. The archway was at least fifteen feet tall at its apex, and appeared to be formed from huge, polished bones the likes of which he'd never seen before. It looked as if arch and roadway had been excavated from the cold earth. The piles of rock and soil cleared from the path formed raised banks to either side of the road, packed down to rock-like hardness over the passage of centuries. Four iron spikes, each twelve feet long, had been driven into both banks alongside the road, making a rough octagon pattern with the roadway passing through its centre.

Corpses were impaled on each of the iron spikes, their dark, shrivelled bodies stacked one on top of the other so that Malus couldn't tell for certain where one body ended and the next began. They had all been bound hand and foot, their limbs twisted in the throes of long, agonising deaths. They had hung from the iron spikes for a very long time, and colonies of grave mould covered the corpses, emitting the pale light that filled the eerie space.

Malus glanced in wonder at Arleth Vann. 'What is this place?'

'Hundreds of years ago, when the city was first founded, a druchii named Cyrvan Thel built this house,' the assassin said in a hushed voice. 'Several years after the building was complete, Thel decided to add a lower level for a wine cellar, and the workers uncovered the roadway. The paving stones resisted every attempt to remove them, including sorcery, so Thel ordered the workmen to follow their course and see how far they went. That was how they came upon the archway. When the workers broke through into the tunnel beyond a breath of foul wind rushed out that killed them in an instant. Thel, being a devout man, took this as an omen. When the air had cleared enough for a slave to survive without ill effects, Thel and a handful of retainers entered the tunnel to see where it led.'

'And what did they find?'

'The Vermillion Gate,' the assassin replied. He pointed to the arch. 'The passage leads deep into the heart of the hill, to a circular chamber that might sink all the way to the heart of the world itself. A flat-topped spire rises in the centre of that chamber, spanned by a bridge of ancient bone, and on top of that spire sits the dreadful gate. No one knows who built it or why, but it is old beyond all reckoning.' He turned to Malus, a fearful look in his eyes. 'It leads to the very heart of the Lord of Murder's realm.'

The highborn was taken aback. 'Khaine is a druchii god. How can that be, if the gate was made in a time before Nagarythe was lost?'

Arleth Vann spread his hands. 'Thel looked upon the gate and thought it had been set here in anticipation of our coming, a gift from the Blood God to his chosen people. He took word of his discovery to the elders of the cult, and they came from across Naggaroth to look upon the gate. When they beheld it for the first time, they knew that from that moment forwards the hill and everything upon it must belong to the cult. Shortly after, the Witch King gave Har Ganeth to the temple of Khaine.'

Malus stared at the archway of bone and a feeling of dread turned his guts to ice. 'Urial spoke of the Vermillion Gate,' he said, 'on the way back from the Isle of Morhaut. He used it to reach Har Ganeth.'

The assassin nodded thoughtfully, as if the highborn had answered a worrying riddle. 'Some of the texts in the temple library claim that a true disciple of Khaine can call upon the power of the gate no matter where in the world he may be. He can reach the cavern beneath the hill in a single stride, if he makes the proper offerings. Spirits guard the gate from the unworthy, and if they are not provided for they will exact a terrible price from those who cross the threshold.'

'He rewarded them amply,' Malus growled, thinking of the slaughter on the main deck of the battered corsair, 'and from what little I saw he timed his crossing so that there was a crowd of worshippers waiting on the other side.'

The assassin shrugged. 'Every new moon the temple elders gather at the gate to perform sacred ceremonies of veneration. If Urial had emerged from the gate – with Yasmir in tow, no less – it would have seemed most portentous indeed.' He turned and headed for the narrow staircase leading to the cavern floor.

Malus followed warily, picking his way across the landing and then down the long flight of stairs. The risers glittered with frost. When he reached out a hand to steady himself along the wall he found that it was covered in a thin layer of ice.

Malus felt a prickling along his skin as they made their slow descent. The chamber was thick with sorcerous energies.

The highborn cleared his throat. 'About Urial–' he began.

Arleth Vann cut him off with an upraised hand. 'Quiet,' he said, his voice barely a whisper, 'we are about to pass the guardians.'

The stairway ended at the edge of the roadway. Up close, Malus saw that the stones of the dark path were like blocks of obsidian, polished to a mirror hue. It looked as if every stone had a flaw to it: a faint, pale smudge in each stone's centre. When he bent a little closer, however, he saw that it wasn't a blemish on the surface: there was something within each of the stones. The shapes were blurry, but there was just enough play of light and shadow for the objects to take on the quality of living faces.

Puzzled, Malus started to bend even closer, but the daemon's voice rasped in his ear. 'If you value your sanity, mortal, look no further,' Tz'arkan said coldly. 'There are some things no druchii – not even you – were meant to know.'

The highborn straightened with a start. Arleth Vann was already some distance away, approaching the first of the iron poles with his head bowed and his hands tucked into his robes.

Malus moved as quickly as he dared, hurriedly following suit just as the assassin reached the first set of poles. Suddenly a chorus of thin wails filled the air, rising piteously from the blackened mouths of the bound corpses.

A thrill of terror coursed down Malus's spine. He had heard that sound once before, in the depths of Urial's tower.

The highborn glanced fearfully at the pole to his right. Pale mist was leaking from the slack jaws and gaping eye sockets of the impaled figures. The tendrils danced and wove about in a spectral wind, taking the shape of pale, spindly figures with long fingers and emaciated faces. Their eyes were orbs of purest jet, soulless and cruel. 'The maelithii!' Malus breathed.

'Be not afraid,' Arleth Vann hissed. 'Avert your eyes and walk the ancient path. They are bound to do no harm to those who bear the blessings of Khaine.'

Malus averted his eyes, focusing on the black stones at his feet. They would not be fooled by his magically altered eyes. He imagined the maelithii swarming over him, sinking their black fangs into his flesh and feasting on his life force. When they were finished with him his skin would be the colour of a deep bruise, the blue-black of a corpse lost for months in the snow.

The vengeful spirits whistled and howled above Malus's head, drawing ever nearer. His legs began to tremble. There was no way to fight these spirits: swords passed straight through them and left the arm numb and frozen to boot. He fought the urge to turn and run for the staircase, wondering how much further he was from the archway.

One of the maelithii let out a shrill cry and swooped close enough to Malus for him to feel veins of frost spreading through his black hair. Other maeliths began a cacophony of wailing in reply. They've found me out, he thought!

Malus felt a needle of ice pierce his cheek, and just as swiftly he felt the daemon uncoil in his chest like a startled viper. Tz'arkan howled a challenge at the maelithii that set Malus's teeth on edge and the baleful spirits withdrew, wailing plaintively.

The highborn quickened his pace, not caring if he trampled Arleth Vann in the process. The sounds of the maelithii receded behind him with every step. Then without warning he was surrounded in a flare of witchlight. When Malus looked up he found himself standing beside his retainer, just past the tall arch of polished bone.

Arleth Vann was looking back the way they'd come, eyeing the eight maelithii circling above the centre of the octagon. 'They seemed interested in you for some reason,' he told Malus, 'and then they cried out in fear. I've never heard the like.'

Malus looked back at the tormented spirits. 'They tried to claim something that belongs to another,' he said grimly.

The assassin frowned. 'I don't understand.'

'Count yourself fortunate,' Malus replied. He gestured down the dark passage. 'Let's go.'

THE PASSAGE SEEMED to go on forever. Arleth Vann's witchlight just barely reached the rounded walls to either side. To Malus's eyes they appeared to be made of dark, grainy stone, like granite, but worked in loops and strands as if the tunnel had been woven out of the stone rather than carved. He couldn't fathom how such a thing had been done, much less why. The strange patterns created many corners, niches and crevices among the coarse weave of the stonework, and over the centuries the worshippers of Khaine had filled those recesses with offerings to their god. Skulls by the thousand leered at the two druchii as they went deeper into the hill. Skeletal hands seemed to reach for them in the flickering aura of the witchlight. Malus saw leg bones and vertebrae, ribs and shoulder blades, all arranged to blend almost seamlessly with the fluid lines of the stonework. The dead pressed in on Malus from every side, setting his heart to race. He tried to focus on something else, and remembered the question he'd started to ask outside the archway.

'Why doesn't the temple want Urial to have the sword?'

Arleth Vann paused, turning to look back at his master with a rueful grin. 'Had you ever taken an interest in religion, my lord, you wouldn't have to ask such a question,' he replied. 'As far as the temple is concerned, they've already given the sword to another.'

'Another!' Malus exclaimed. 'Who?'

The assassin shook his head. 'Who else? Malekith, of course.'

'They think Malekith is the Scourge? How can this be?'

To Malus's surprise, Arleth Vann threw back his head and laughed. 'As clever a man as you are, my lord, I'm amazed you'd have to ask such a question. How do you think the temple of Khaine came to exist?'

Malus frowned. He didn't much care for the assassin's patronising tone. 'Malekith used the cult to consolidate his rule after Nagarythe was lost,' he snapped. 'They had every reason to hate most of the old houses, who worshipped Slaanesh and had persecuted them for hundreds of years. Malekith raised them up, made them the state religion, and in return they helped him break the power of the warlocks and assassinate any rivals to his throne.'

Arleth Vann nodded. 'Just so, my lord, but you must understand that the cult in those days was not like the temple as it is now. When you think of the temple, you envision people like your half-brother Urial, but back then they were true believers like Tyran. They were utterly devout, dedicated to the pure teachings of the Lord of Murder and the heirs of centuries of persecution.'

'They were fanatics,' Malus said, 'and I suppose they cared little for Malekith or his power plays.'

The retainer gave one of his rare smiles. 'Now you begin to see. The elders of the cult saw much to gain in Malekith's offer, however – power, legitimacy, wealth and influence – but they had to find a way to convince their followers that the alliance served the will of the Blood God.'

'So they claimed Malekith was Khaine's Scourge.'

'Indeed. For almost as long as the druchii have lingered in Naggaroth the temple has taught its followers that Malekith is their unquestioned master because he is the chosen Scourge of Khaine. When the time is right he will come to Har Ganeth and wed the Bride of Ruin. Then he will take up the Warpsword of Khaine and usher in the Time of Blood. Anything else is heresy.'

Chapter Ten
FAITH AND MURDER

MALUS STARED DUMBFOUNDED at his retainer. 'You mean to tell me that all of this is built on a lie? The temple followers sold out their faith for the sake of political favour?'

Arleth Vann nodded. 'Does this trouble you?'

The highborn cocked his head thoughtfully. 'Actually, it's rather reassuring. These motives at least make sense to me, but clearly not all of the faithful believed the elders' pronouncement.'

'No,' the retainer said. 'The elders built a compelling case, of course, pointing to numerous obscure prophesies that seemed to support their claim. A devious mind can make the words of an oracle fit anything he wants if he tries hard enough, but it wasn't enough. Several cult leaders and their disciples saw through the elders' arguments and refused to take part in the alliance, regardless of the benefits. The debates raged for years, but the nascent temple continued to grow and gain legitimacy. Finally, the true believers saw that their power was waning fast. If they didn't act soon, the elders and their blasphemy would be too deeply rooted to eliminate.'

'So they fought.'

The assassin nodded. 'They fought. At the culmination of a weeklong holy festival – the Draich na Anlar – the schism leaders gathered their followers and attacked the elders in the midst of their consecrations. Somehow, the attempt failed. Some scholars suggest that the schism leaders were betrayed, while others point to divine intervention. At any rate, the five true believers that entered the temple to kill the blasphemous elders were never seen or heard from again. Other confrontations across the city degenerated into a chaotic riot that killed thousands. Fighting raged through the city streets all through the night, and by daybreak the White City was stained with rivers of blood. Afterwards the temple elders tore the city apart looking for the schism leaders and their allies, dragging those they found into the street and decapitating them on the spot. This is how Har Ganeth came to be known as the City of Executioners.'

'And the survivors?'

Arleth Vann shrugged. 'They fled the city, spreading out all across Naggaroth and beyond to keep the true faith alive. They knew that one day the true Scourge would appear, and there would be another day of reckoning with the blasphemers.'

'So the zealots returned to their roots, worshipping in secret as they'd been doing since time out of mind.'

The assassin nodded, resuming his course down the long tunnel. 'It was the proper way, regardless. Khaine is not meant to be worshipped in a temple, but on the battlefield or by the side of the road. We are exalted by testing our strength against others and taking their lives with skill and daring.'

Malus fell into step behind his retainer, thinking back to the constant training and superlative skill of the zealots. 'So Khaine is actually a god of combat?'

'No, he is a god of death,' Arleth Vann replied. 'What is the greatest power a man can have in this world?'

Malus shrugged. 'The power of a king.'

The assassin let out a snort. 'A king can die on the field of battle like anyone else. Think again.'

'Damned sorcery, then.'

The retainer shook his head. 'No, it is simpler than that. The greatest power in this world is the ability to end life. The one thing every man shares, whether he is a slave or the Witch King himself, is a beating heart. The power to stop that heartbeat in a single stroke is what brings us closer to Khaine. We become gods, holding the lives of those around us in the palms of our hands. Do you see?'

'I believe so,' Malus said. 'That is the purpose of the executioners, I suppose?'

The assassin nodded. 'In the days before the temple, every worshipper of Khaine was an executioner: a Sword of Khaine. The true believer killed his opponents with a single, perfect stroke, making it a gesture of worship and enhancing his power with every foe he slew in battle. It was only after the temple was founded and the elders required acolytes to devote themselves to sinful practices like tithe collection that the executioners became an isolated sect.'

'And the temple witches?'

Arleth Vann cast a sidelong glance over his shoulder at Malus. 'They suffered the worst degradations of all. Once, they were Khaine's bloody oracles and the enforcers of the Blood God's divine will. They had the power to summon back the souls of the fallen and partake of their powers. And now? Now they are degenerates, aping the glories of their forebears with drugs and pitiful necromancies. You have seen true blood-witches, my lord. Can the witches of the temple compare to their terrible majesty?'

'No,' Malus admitted, 'certainly not. So what happened?'

The assassin shrugged. 'The blood-witches tried to stay apart from the fray during the early years of the schism. The brides of Khaine did not concern themselves with such petty conflicts. After the true believers were driven from the city and the elders hemmed the rest of the cult into temples, their prestige gradually diminished. There hasn't been a true blood-witch serving the temple for at least two thousand years.'

As they walked, Malus began to notice narrow doorways cut into the ropy stonework of the tunnel walls. The doorframes were made of glossy white marble and carved with intricate runes in archaic druchast. Next to the strangely flowing weave of the walls the newer construction still seemed crude and awkward by comparison. 'What are these?' he asked.

'Those? They are tombs,' the retainer said. 'The temple has always interred the faithful, despite the Witch King's edict of cremation. Perhaps the elders venerate the spirits of the dead in the hope they will intercede on their behalf when Khaine returns in his wrath.' He gestured at the doorways with a sweep of his free hand. 'The entire hill is honeycombed with tomb complexes, and they reach far into the earth.'

The two druchii walked on in silence for a time, journeying down the dark road past the doorways of the dead. Some quality of the stone swallowed their footsteps, and for a while it felt as if they had left the physical world behind, trudging like ghosts through some forgotten underworld. Malus considered the implications of everything Arleth Vann had told him. It did go a long way towards explaining the temple's odd behaviour… but his mind kept drifting back to his meeting with Rhulan, and the wary look on the elder's face. Urial's claim casts the entire history of the temple into doubt, the highborn thought, which was ample reason to keep him in seclusion and look for a way to silence him. However, that would be self-evident to anyone familiar with temple dictum. There's something more going on here, he thought. The elders have a secret that no one, not even the zealots, suspect.

Arleth Vann stopped. Malus looked around and saw that they had reached a point where two curving stairways – one ascending, the other descending

– were carved into the living rock to either side of the dark road. 'We'll go no further into the hill. The Vermillion Gate is close by, and it is always well-guarded by a cadre of witches and executioners.' He pointed to the climbing stairway. 'Here is where the journey becomes difficult.'

Malus eyed the staircase. 'More spirit wards?'

Arleth Vann shook his head. 'No. Just hundreds and hundreds of stairs.'

MALUS LOST ALL track of time as they trudged up the winding stairway. The journey passed as a blur of echoing steps and shadowy landings that opened onto ancient galleries and maze-like passageways leading to mouldy tombs. The temple hill was a labyrinth vaster and more convoluted than anything he had ever seen; even the tower of the mad sorcerer Eradorius seemed smaller and less complicated by comparison. The highborn mused between gasps for breath that crossing paths with Arleth Vann had turned out to be a great boon. Alone he might have been fumbling about the hill and its passageways until the seas ran dry. He breathed the dry, dusty pall of bone dust at every turn, as centuries of temple servants rotted to dust in the niches and alcoves beneath the great temple. The dust made his nose itch and left the taste of the grave in the back of his throat.

At last, they emerged into a well-lit chamber glowing with the green fire of witchlamps. They were in a large space with low, vaulted ceilings, practically an underground plaza compared to the tight passageways and the narrow, enclosed staircase they'd travelled. Malus fought the urge to rub the ache from his trembling legs. 'Where are we?' he asked quietly.

'We're in the vaults beneath the temple proper,' Arleth Vann replied, eyeing the many passageways leading off from the chamber. 'From here we can reach almost every major building within the fortress, including the elders' private chambers.'

Malus nodded, gritting his teeth against the burning ache flaring from his knees. 'All right. Where are we likely to find Rhulan at this point?'

'When the elders are not conducting their rites, they typically retire to their chambers,' the assassin replied. 'No doubt to reflect on matters of the faith,' he said with a sneer.

'Yes, but this is no typical night. An elder has deserted the temple. The story on the street might be that the man was kidnapped, but I imagine the rest of the elders know the truth of the matter. Their warriors have taken to the streets to fight the true believers, and their sacred council remains broken. Where do the elders normally go when they meet in conclave?'

'The council chambers within the Citadel of Bone,' Arleth Vann replied, 'but if the elders are meeting there they will be well-guarded.'

'I thought the temple assassins were supposed to be invisible,' the highborn snapped.

'When the situation demands,' the retainer answered coolly. 'Can my lord say the same?'

Malus gave the man a hard stare. 'Just get us as close as you can. We'll improvise from there.'

'You mean we'll kill whoever gets in our way.'

'That is what I said, yes.'

Arleth Vann gave another of his ghostly smiles. 'It is good to know some things never change. Follow me, my lord.'

THE ASSASSIN QUICKLY led Malus out of the well-lit tunnels beneath the temple and into noisome passageways dripping with slime and tangled with dense layers of cobwebs. He made no effort to relight his sorcerous lamp, forcing Malus to crouch low and follow the almost undetectable sound of the retainer's footfalls. From time to time their path crossed better-travelled corridors, and once or twice the highborn caught snatches of whispered conversations as the servants of the temple went about their nightly tasks. Each time, Arleth Vann would pause at the junction and listen for several moments, gauging the servants' movements, before darting silently across the passageway into the darkened tunnel mouth opposite. Malus felt like a rat inside the walls of some vast city house, scuttling from shadow to shadow to avoid the master's house serpents.

After nearly half an hour, Arleth Vann stopped a few feet shy of the end of the passage and drew his twin blades. He turned to Malus. 'From here on out, I go ahead,' the assassin whispered. 'Wait three minutes and then follow after me.'

Malus frowned. 'Three minutes? How will I know where you've gone?'

The assassin looked at Malus over his shoulder. 'Look for the trail of bodies,' he said in a hard voice. Then he stepped out of the corridor and slipped off to the right.

Malus drew his own sword. His limbs felt leaden after the long climb through the heart of the hill, and the prospect of more fighting filled him with a weary kind of dread. I should drink of the daemon's power, he thought. Just a little, to lend me strength and take away this damned fatigue.

No sooner had the thought occurred to him than a wave of trembling wracked his body. His insides twisted with need as he thought about the glorious, icy vitality of the daemon's power. 'Mother of Night!' he breathed, dropping to one knee. The hunger felt bottomless, and his mind recoiled in terror from it.

It was several minutes before the trembling passed, leaving Malus feeling even weaker than before. His face and neck were bathed in cold sweat, and his guts felt tied in knots. The highborn clenched his sword tightly, focusing on the strain of his knuckles and the hard weight of the sword hilt digging into his palm. With an effort of will, he forced himself back onto his feet. A terrible sense of foreboding pressed down upon him. Had the daemon's recent silence been nothing more than the infinite patience of a predator, knowing its prey was but a single step away from ruin? Blessed mother, have I gone too far, Malus thought? Am I now beholden to the daemon, body and soul?

The daemon slithered across his ribs. 'Are you unwell, Malus?' Tz'arkan's voice slid into his ears like sweet poison. 'The temple elders await. Do you wish my aid?'

Yes, Malus thought. He bit his lips to keep the words from slipping past them. His mind roiled with horror and revulsion. Another wave of trembling passed through his taut frame.

'Come now, don't be proud,' the daemon whispered. 'I can feel your weakness, little druchii, your need. If you go before the elders like this they will see how weak you are. Let me make you strong again.'

Malus tasted blood on his tongue. He bit deeper into his torn lip, letting the pain kindle the fires of his hate. With hate all things are possible, he told himself. 'I… want nothing from you,' he gasped, sending a trickle of blood coursing down his chin. 'Nothing, you hear?'

The daemon chuckled, his manner smug and easy. 'That's an easy thing to say when you're alone and in the dark,' Tz'arkan said. 'You have no idea how pitiful you look. If the elders see you like this they will laugh in your face. Is that what you really want?'

Growling like a wounded beast, Malus forced his body to move: one step, and then another. Hate seethed in his heart, a weak fire compared to the icy torrent of the daemon's power, but it propelled him nonetheless. He bared red-stained teeth and spat onto the stone floor. 'They will see what I choose to show them,' the highborn said, feeling a little of his old strength return, 'nothing more or less.'

'Of course,' the daemon said in a patronising tone. 'I should have guessed you'd say such a thing. Perhaps you can manage a little longer without my help, but mark me: there will come a time very soon when you will find yourself in dire need of my power. Ask, and it will be yours.'

Malus staggered from the dark passageway, blinking owlishly in the light of the corridor beyond. Not ten feet to the right a temple servant lay on his face in a pool of spreading blood. The man had died without the slightest sound.

The highborn drew a shuddering breath, horrified that suddenly he felt unequal to the task before him. He'd thought he'd gained the upper hand over Tz'arkan, and the whole time the daemon had simply bided its time, like a spider sitting in the centre of its invisible web.

All is not lost just yet, the highborn thought. I still live. I still have my sword and my mother's ring; and my hate, always my hate. Dark Mother, let that be enough!

Licking bitter blood from his lips, Malus set off in the assassin's wake.

ARLETH VANN WAS true to his word. The assassin left a trail of slaughter that a blind man could have followed. Malus passed more than a dozen temple servants in corridors and at junctions, each laid out on the floor as if slain in mid-stride. At one point he passed a trio of corpses propping one another upright, and Malus was struck with the image of the pale-faced assassin weaving his way through the close knit group and slaying them so quickly that they fell almost as one. The man's supernal skill filled Malus with admiration even as it reminded him of his own wretched state.

Finally Malus found himself at the end of a long corridor built from pale marble that glowed beneath globes of witchlight. An open doorway waited at the other end, beyond a pile of armoured guards. The highborn picked his way through the tangle of steel-clad bodies, his boots making tacky sounds as he crossed an enormous puddle of congealing blood.

Beyond lay a narrow chamber, dominated by a short ramp that led upwards to a large, echoing chamber. Arleth Vann waited at the base of the ramp, surrounded by half a dozen dead servants. The assassin was pausing to clean his twin blades with a cloth rag appropriated from one of the corpses. His pale face was spotted with blood and eerily serene. The roar of scores of angry voices rolled down the stone ramp from the chamber beyond, washing over Malus in seething waves.

'Where… where are we?' Malus stammered, raising his voice to be heard above the cacophony.

'Just beneath the council chamber,' Arleth Vann replied. 'This is the room where they remove claimants who fail to persuade their case before the council.'

At that moment a projectile hit the top of the ramp with a wet thud and bounced down the slope past the assassin. Malus caught the furious expression on the face of the severed head as it rolled across the floor.

The retainer looked up from his work. 'Are you well, my lord? You look–'

'I expect I look as if I'd crawled from a tomb, considering the route you took us through,' Malus snapped. 'It's a wonder I can see after all the webs I walked into.' He looked down at the grisly trophy and gave it a savage kick. The spiteful gesture heartened him a little. 'I'm fine,' he said, injecting a touch of steel into his voice, 'merely vexed at the foolishness of priests.' Without another word he moved past his retainer and climbed the ramp, his sword held at his side.

For a moment Malus was certain Arleth Vann had led him wrong. He found himself near the point of an oval chamber, ringed by a gallery that rose in tiers for at least twenty feet. Men and women crowded the tiers shouting and shaking their fists at the brawl that raged on the chamber's floor. The air stank of blood and shook with the inchoate thunder of an arena in the city's entertainment district. Not ten yards from where Malus stood more than a score of druchii pushed, pummelled and slashed at one another. At the centre of the fight two older men grappled with each other, their faces twisted with bestial hate. Broad bladed knives trembled in their white knuckled fists as they wrestled for the advantage. Each man wore rich, red robes and kheitans of fine leather studded with gold and precious stones. Their retainers were only slightly less bedecked themselves, their struggles having left a fortune in gilt and gems scattered across the marble floor. Wounded men stumbled or crawled away from the raging fight, clutching at their wounds and screaming encouragement to their respective sides. A handful of corpses lay forgotten underfoot.

Malus looked up at the gallery, realising that the shouting throng was made up of still more richly attired elders and their servants. Six large thrones were set around the perimeter of the chamber at the lowest gallery tier. Three of the seats were empty, although they were surrounded by elders and their retinues like hounds standing over a freshly killed deer. At the apex of the oval chamber, in a throne that surpassed all the rest in size and extravagance, sat an ancient druchii in vestments of hammered brass inlaid with diamonds and rubies. A mask of gold worked in the shape of a leering skull concealed his features, but his gnarled fists shook as he leaned forwards in his chair, shouting encouragements or curses upon the men fighting below. Malus caught sight of Rhulan sitting on the throne to the elder druchii's right. Of all the assembled elders, he seemed least interested in the fight. A gold mask lay in his hand as he leaned to one side and conferred with one of his followers.

The highborn looked over at Arleth Vann, who emerged from the ramp behind Malus. 'This is how the temple council conducts its affairs?' he shouted.

Arleth Vann shrugged. 'You must admit it's more entertaining than any drachau's court,' he shouted back.

The highborn shook his head irritably. 'To the Outer Darkness with this,' he snarled. He pointed at the reeling brawl. 'Make me a hole,' he said to the assassin.

Arleth Vann nodded grimly, raising his short blades. He glided swiftly towards the fight with Malus close behind and cut his way through the crowd like a thresher harvesting grain. Men fell away to either side, struck down by the assassin's flickering blades, and the rest recoiled in shock from the sudden assault. Within moments Malus reached the battling elders, each man lost in his own single-minded struggle. The assassin stepped aside with a bow. Malus walked up to the two men and swung his heavy blade, decapitating both elders in a single stroke.

Blood erupted in a bright fountain from the two slain men, their bodies falling against one another in a grisly embrace. The severed heads bounced audibly on the stone floor in the sudden, shocked silence.

Gore dripping from his blade, Malus turned, regarding the assembled elders with cold, brass eyes. 'Now that I have your attention,' he said, his voice echoing in the council chamber, 'I've come to bring a warning to the council. You must sound the call to arms and hurry to the Sanctum of the Sword. While you squabble here like dogs over a corpse, Urial and his supporters are closing their hands around the Warpsword of Khaine.'

Murmurs of shock and snarls of derision echoed from the assembly. At the far end of the chamber the Grand Carnifex of the temple rose portentously to his feet. To his right, the Arch-Hierophant turned pale, his dark eyes shifting from Malus to the leader of the temple and back again.

The Grand Carnifex's voice was a liquid rasp, bubbling up from old lungs thick with corruption. 'Who are you?' he said, his words carrying across the chamber in spite of the mask he wore.

'A servant of Khaine,' Malus answered. 'A man with a dire warning, and beyond that, what does it matter? Your enemies are on the verge of destroying you, Grand Carnifex: you and this house your predecessors have built. Will you act, or shall we sit here and waste precious time with introductions?'

The entire chamber resounded with a single intake of breath as the audience recoiled in shock at Malus's words. Steel rang as swords leapt from gilt scabbards, and a number of the temple elders barked at their retainers to make a way for them to reach the chamber floor. Then Rhulan leapt to his feet, calling out in a carrying voice. 'How do you know this?' he asked, looking meaningfully at Malus.

The highborn met the elder's gaze and nodded respectfully. 'Because I have spent the last four days at the feet of Tyran the Unscarred, the leader of the zealots who oppose you,' he answered. 'I have sat in their councils, and I know that they have agents within the temple itself.' He surveyed the outraged elders coldly. 'They have been in close contact with Urial since the moment they entered the city and everything they have done has been in preparation for this very night.' He raised his bloodstained sword and pointed at each of the empty thrones in turn. 'Do you think this was all some sort of accident? A stroke of cruel luck? No. They struck directly at the Haru'ann, sowing confusion and discord while they formed a learned council of their own. Now, with all your warriors pounding at the gates of empty houses across the city, they have slipped inside the temple and are performing the Rite of the Swordbearer even as we speak!'

'Let them!' A woman shouted. Her voice was an angry rasp, cutting jaggedly through the tense atmosphere. Malus saw a young priestess in the third tier of the gallery face the Grand Carnifex. 'We know Urial is not the Scourge. The ritual will fail, and we will have the opportunity we've been waiting for to denounce him!'

'If the rite fails the heretics will find fault in the men performing the rite, not in their would-be saviour,' Malus shot back. 'This can only end in death,' he snarled, looking to the Grand Carnifex. 'You know this.'

'I say this is the work of the heretics!' said an older druchii to Malus's left, leaning over the first tier railing and pointing a long finger at Malus. 'They've already sent assassins against us once. Perhaps they sent this loudmouth to draw us to the sanctum so they could slay us all!'

Malus gave the elder a cold stare. 'If you fear for your life, elder, then by all means run and cower beneath your overstuffed bed.' He met the Grand Carnifex's dark gaze. 'This is a matter for warriors.'

'This is nothing of the sort!' snapped the young priestess. 'If this is true, the zealots have handed us an opportunity! Let them try to complete their ritual. When it fails they will return to their followers and fall upon one another, looking for someone to blame. This crisis can solve itself in a single stroke.'

Malus watched the Grand Carnifex glance at the priestess, and for a brief moment he caught a flicker of uncertainty in the ancient druchii's eyes. He is afraid, Malus thought with a start.

'I have heard enough,' the Grand Carnifex declared. 'Summon the guards. We will march to the sanctum and offer prayers to the Lord of Murder for a bloody deliverance from the works of heretics.' He held out his hand and a retainer appeared from behind the tall throne to press a huge, rune carved axe into the Carnifex's palm. 'If there are trespassers within the sanctum we will offer them up as sacrifices to our lord.'

The Grand Carnifex rose to his feet. Ropy tendons stood out taut as steel wires beneath the skin of the elder's neck and arms as he levelled the axe at Malus. 'If not, I will strike off your head and pour your blood upon the sacred stone,' he declared. 'As you said, stranger, this can only end in death.'

Chapter Eleven
WARPSWORD

THE SKY OVER Har Ganeth was the colour of blood as the doors to the Citadel of Bone yawned open and Malus followed the elders of the temple into the battle torn night. More buildings were burning in the city below, sending towering plumes of cinders into the sky, and the air reverberated with the distant clash of arms. Malus knew that the streets would be choked with corpses come the dawn, but the madness and slaughter in the city was nothing more than a mummer's show. The true battle would be fought between a few score men and women within the towering structure barely thirty yards from the council chambers.

Witchlight globes swung from long, iron poles as a vanguard of temple executioners led the way, their bared blades glittering coldly as they fanned out into the deserted lane outside the gleaming citadel. Behind them came the temple elders, led by the Grand Carnifex in his grinning skull mask. The remaining officials and their retainers jockeyed for position behind their leader, brandishing broad knives and ornamented axes at the prospect of reaping fresh skulls for their hungry god.

All except for Rhulan. The narrow-faced elder had dutifully slipped on his skull mask, but let the mob sweep past him until he fell in among the guards escorting Malus and Arleth Vann. The executioner escort eyed Rhulan curiously as he paced along beside the highborn, but made no move to intervene.

'Why didn't you warn me?' the elder hissed. Unlike the Carnifex, his voice was muffled beneath the weight of his mask.

'There was no time,' Malus replied. 'The zealot leaders guarded their plans with care. No one was told until late this evening.'

Rhulan said nothing for a moment, staring into the night. Then the death's head turned back to Malus. 'If Tyran and his lieutenants die tonight, then their agents must be slain as well. We must sweep them all up in a single stroke. You understand?'

I understand that our arrangement is at an end, Malus thought grimly. 'I suspected as much,' he said coldly. It was unavoidable. Tyran had forced his hand, just as he'd forced the elders' hand.

If Tyran and Urial were stopped, Rhulan would force him to reveal what he knew about their network within the temple. Once they realised he was bluffing, he was finished.

Malus eyed the white stone of the temple rearing into the flame-shot sky like an upraised blade and thought he could sense the sorcery at work within. Somehow, in the midst of battle, he would have to make his move.

'Once you have the sword, what then?' the daemon whispered. 'Will you cut your way through the elders of the temple and into the city beyond?'

'First things first,' muttered Malus. Rhulan shook his head, thinking the words were meant for him.

'Fear not,' the elder said. 'However many agents this Tyran has, he could not have slipped into the temple undetected with more than a token force. There are nearly a hundred of us. We can bury the heretics in bodies if we have to. The zealot uprising ends tonight.'

'And Urial?' Malus asked. 'Surely you knew he would attempt this, sooner or later. The temple thought he was marked by Khaine from the moment he emerged from the sacrificial cauldron.'

'We knew nothing of the sort,' the elder snapped. 'Yes, clearly he was blessed by the Lord of Murder, but none of the witches could divine his destiny. Certainly no one believed that Khaine would anoint a cripple as his Scourge. His ambition has got the better of him.'

The highborn cocked his head at the quaver in Rhulan's voice. He studied the elder with narrowed eyes. 'You aren't so sure.'

'Do not presume,' Rhulan said archly. 'You heard me. He is a cripple. It's inconceivable that he could be Khaine's chosen one.'

'Then why do you sound so afraid?'

Just then a howl of challenge, fierce and joyous, rang out from the front of the great temple. 'Weep, unbelievers, for the great reckoning is at hand! The faithful stand in the presence of the sword and the Time of Blood draws nigh! Your wickedness will soon be revealed for all the people to witness, but see the gift of Khaine's mercy we bear in our hands. Come and redeem yourselves on our hungry blades!'

The procession of elders stumbled to a halt in a welter of angry shouts and bellowed curses. Seeing his chance, Malus nodded his head at Arleth Vann and quickened his pace, diving into the milling press of the elders and working his way towards the Grand Carnifex. Rhulan shouted something that Malus didn't catch. Then there was a rush of pounding feet as the highborn's escorts swept wide of the crowd and ran ahead to join the semicircle of warriors forming a cordon between the Carnifex and the five white-robed zealots that stood in his path.

They seemed like living shards of the shimmering, blade shaped tower that rose behind them. Moonlight shone on their unbound hair and glinted on the edges of their fearsome draichs. The zealots' dark eyes were alight with holy purpose. They were ready to shed their blood in holy sacrifice to the Lord of Murder. Malus thought he'd never seen five more dangerous warriors in all his life.

The Grand Carnifex however was not impressed. He raised his enchanted axe skyward and his voice trembled with rage. 'Be silent, unbeliever! Your every breath defiles this sacred place!' The elder spread his arms wide and commanded the executioners. 'Split their bodies asunder and cleanse this holy earth in libations of blood!'

With a shout the temple guards raised their long swords and charged at the waiting zealots, who met them with triumphant shouts and an intricate dance of death.

Malus watched in horrified wonder as the five zealots wove their way among four times their number of foes. Their swords were a gleaming blur as they rushed, ducked and spun, seeming to glide past a flurry of fearsome sword strokes and bypass their opponents' heavy armour with swift, precise blows. Executioners collapsed, clutching at the stumps of severed arms or hands, or doubled over from disembowelling strokes that slipped beneath the edge of their breastplates. Screams of anger and pain reverberated in the red tinged air, some cut short with a ringing note of steel.

The fight was over in moments. With a clatter of steel plates the last executioner stumbled away from the pile of fallen bodies, one hand outstretched towards the gleaming temple of Khaine. His draich tumbled from his fingers as he fell to his knees, and then toppled lifelessly to the ground.

One of the five zealots lay among a score of fallen temple guardsmen. The rest were streaked with splashes of gore, but their white robes made it plain that none of the blood belonged to them. Their leader raised his dripping blade to the Grand Carnifex and smiled.

'Your men are forgiven,' the zealot said with a smile. He'd just killed four men in as many seconds and wasn't even short of breath. 'Why do you hesitate, Grand Carnifex? Do you fear that the Bloody-Handed God has no cold mercy in his heart for one such as you? I assure you that he does.'

To Malus's surprise, the Grand Carnifex threw back his head and laughed. It was a terrible, bubbling sound, full of hatred and black fury. The Carnifex reached up and pulled away his ceremonial mask, revealing a ruin of broken bone and deep, twisted scars. The master of the temple was ancient, marked by hundreds of years of brutal war. The fearsome blow of a battle-axe had caved in the right side of his face, twisting his mouth into a feral, gap-toothed sneer. The tip of his nose was nothing more than a nub of ragged flesh, and his forehead was a patchwork of ancient scars, one on top of the other. The zealot leader met the Carnifex's baleful gaze, and Malus saw the briefest flicker of fear.

The Grand Carnifex hefted his enchanted axe. 'My god knows nothing of mercy, you moon eyed fool,' he hissed. 'He does not forgive. He cares nothing for redemption. He simply hungers, and I live to see him fed.'

That was more like it, Malus thought. He drew his sword. 'Blood and souls for Khaine!' he roared, and the elders took up the shout just as the Grand Carnifex charged the zealot leader.

Malus glanced at Arleth Vann. 'Stick close,' he shouted, drawing one of his throwing knives.

The assassin shook his head. 'You can't possibly expect to fight these men, my lord. They are the best warriors Tyran has, and they have no fear of death. Their skill–'

'I'm not going to fight them, you fool. I'm going to kill them,' Malus snarled, and charged into the melee.

The zealots had resumed their deadly dance, reaping a red harvest among the elders and their retainers. They were constantly in motion, whirling and cutting with their long, curved swords as they wove among the howling mob. Their skill was transcendent and glorious in its purity and lethality. They were living works of the killer's art. Anyone who stepped within reach of their whirling blades was dead in seconds.

Malus watched the nearest zealot decapitate a howling acolyte and then spin gracefully on his heel to eviscerate a charging priestess. When he did the highborn struck the swordsman dead from fifteen paces away, burying his throwing knife in the back of the zealot's skull.

Shaking his head, the highborn peered through the melee for his next victim. Five yards away the Grand Carnifex fought the zealot leader in single combat. The master of the temple was already wounded in half a dozen places, but the speed and ferocity of his attacks was undiminished. Knowing better than to intercede, the highborn turned away and spotted a third zealot, hemmed in by a circle of wary elders. They pressed the swordsman from all sides, like wolves surrounding a mountain lion. When the zealot attacked they gave ground, providing him no opening to employ his deadly blade, but giving the druchii behind him a chance to strike at the swordsman's back.

Malus timed his move just as the zealot made another fierce rush. The elders fell back as before, but the highborn came up behind them and caught one of the men by the scruff of the neck. The elder let out a cry as Malus shoved him onto the zealot's blade. The razor edged sword sank deep into the man's chest and Malus continued to push the dying elder forwards, trapping the draich beneath the man's collapsing form. The zealot had just enough time to shout a bitter curse before the highborn split his skull like a melon.

A savage howl rang though the air. The highborn turned to see the priestess who had gainsayed him in the Citadel of Bone raise a bloody axe and a zealot's severed head to the burning sky. A deep wound scored her left shoulder, but her face was lit with a savage grin.

That left the zealot leader. If he knew his companions were dead the fanatic gave no sign. The swordsman held his draich before him, its point aimed at the Carnifex's throat. His body was taut, like a steel trap wound and ready to strike. The temple leader glared forbiddingly at the young warrior, flexing his two-handed grip on the haft of his great axe and shifting slightly from foot to foot. Blood flowed freely from deep wounds in his arms, chest and legs.

The two warriors faced each other for long moments, neither one presenting an opening to the other. No one moved. The temple elders observed the fight with reverent silence. Malus stole a glance at the temple and suppressed a snarl. His hand strayed to the other throwing dagger at his belt. 'Get it over with, for the Dark Mother's sake,' he muttered under his breath. 'I don't have time for this.'

It was the zealot who lost the test of wills. Thinking his foe was weak from blood loss and perhaps coveting the glory he'd gain from slaying the master of the temple, the swordsman exploded in a blur of motion, aiming a fearsome blow at the Carnifex's neck. The temple master was anything but weak, however, and as the long sword sang through the air he struck it with a backhanded blow from his axe. The enchanted steel broke the sword in three pieces. Then the Carnifex's return stroke sliced the man's head from his shoulders.

The temple master bent and plucked the zealot's skull from the ground. 'Take the heads of the others,' he ordered, tying the trophy to his belt. 'When this is done we will pile them high on the temple altar.'

Malus surveyed the grisly remains of the battle. Nearly two score of their number lay dead or dying, and he knew the worst was yet to come.

'Let us be swift,' the highborn said. 'We can catch Tyran and his heretic council as they attempt to perform the rite.'

'Blood and souls!' cried the axe wielding priestess, and the rest of the elders took up the shout. Their blood was up, and they rushed towards the temple in a ragged mob, eager to show their devotion to the Lord of Murder. The mob quickly left the Grand Carnifex behind as they swept up the white steps of the temple and through the tall, narrow doorway. Malus paced along behind them, checking to make sure that Arleth Vann was close by. He nodded to himself. This was going to work.

The temple was built from the same alabaster stone as the rest of the city, but there the similarities ended.

The work of dwarf slaves – scores, perhaps even hundreds of them – was evident in the intricate design. The building centred on a single, narrow spire that rose like a sword into the burning sky, built from a broad, octagonal base supported by a cunning network of graceful buttresses that soared more than thirty feet into the air. The white marble was fitted with joins so precise that the whole structure looked more like a sculpture than a building, carved from the summit of the hill by the hands of a god. The temple was a symbol of wealth and power that could humble a drachau, much less a man such as Malus. He stared up at the great spire and could not help but feel a surge of black-hearted avarice.

The highborn raced up the temple steps, listening to the cries of the elders echoing angrily in the cavernous space beyond. Doors of dark oak plated in brass had been swung wide, providing a glimpse of the red shot blackness beyond.

Malus crossed the threshold and tasted blood in the air. Sorcerous energies pressed against his skin, pulsing in time to a rhythm he could not hear. Tz'arkan writhed in his chest, reacting hungrily to the power reverberating through the temple.

The space beyond was cavernous, lit by dozens of braziers that painted the walls and ceiling with leaping crimson shapes and menacing shadows. Pyramids of skulls, hundreds of them, were arranged in complex patterns across the black marble floor. Overhead, a red-tinged haze of smoke spread the bloody glow of the fires. The air reeked of rot and the sweet smell of cooking flesh. Malus's eyes burned and his throat ached, and for a moment it was as if he had been cast back in time, and was struggling through the red tinged realm of Urial's tower in the Hag.

At the far end of the chamber Malus saw another broad staircase, rising to another narrow doorway. He turned to Arleth Vann. 'Where do we go?' he asked.

The assassin nodded at the stairs. 'The temple has three sanctums. This chamber is reserved for acolytes and visitors. Up the steps yonder we will come to a smaller chapel where the temple priests and the elders make sacrifice and worship. Beyond that lies the Sanctum of the Sword.'

Malus nodded and started loping towards the stairs. 'When we reach the sanctum, I'll need a clear path to the sword. Do whatever you must.'

'I understand,' the assassin replied grimly. 'Khaine's will be done.'

The air grew thicker as Malus neared the steps to the second chapel. He felt a buzzing in his ears, like the distant shouts of a multitude. Again, he found himself reminded of Urial's tower, and steeled himself for what might lie ahead.

'You will need my power,' the daemon whispered. 'Take it, or you will die.'

The highborn paused, halfway up the broad stairway. 'No,' he hissed.

'Now is not the time for pride, Malus. You are weak. You know this. I can help. If you do not partake of my power you will be defeated. They are much too strong for you.'

A shudder wracked Malus's body. All at once he felt shrunken and starved, his muscles shrivelled and his bones aching from fatigue. Unbidden, he thought of Urial and his sorcery, and of Tyran's fearsome sword-play.

'I have my hate,' he whispered. 'I have my wits. They will suffice, daemon. They always have.'

'You know that isn't true. How many times would you have been lost had it not been for me?'

Malus bared his teeth, forcing doubt and fear from his mind by sheer, bloody minded will. The he heard the war screams and the shrieks of dying men coming from the chapel at the top of the stairs, and ran towards the sound.

The chapel was a smaller, oval-shaped chamber some eighty paces across, surrounded by roaring braziers that sent columns of scented smoke spiralling upwards to the peak of its arched ceiling. Between each brazier were deep, arched niches filled with stacks of gilded skulls, and a pile of similar, unadorned trophies lay in deep drifts around the raised dais at the far end of the room. A pall of shifting, reddish steam hung above the marble platform, rising from the brass mouth of an enormous cauldron sunk to knee height within the dais itself. Terrible power seethed from the vessel, its bubbling liquid hissing and spitting as if stirred to life by the desperate battle being fought nearby.

Another, narrower stairway rose beyond the dais, climbing towards a towering sculpture of the great god Khaine on his terrible brass throne. A doorway lit with crimson light gleamed at the base of the fearsome statue, and a fierce melee raged within feet of the glowing portal.

Another rearguard, Malus thought angrily. The crowd of temple elders and their retainers had swept up the short flight of stairs and swarmed around the fight just before the doorway. He couldn't see much of what was happening thanks to the haze of boiling blood rising from the cauldron, but he could clearly hear the clash of steel and the screams of the dying.

The air hummed with power. Malus felt pains shoot through his insides and a hot tear trace its way down his cheek. The drop broke over his lip and he tasted blood. Almost there, he thought. Just a little closer!

Malus pushed his way through stragglers on the near side of the dais and clambered onto it. He found himself looking down into the seething surface of the cauldron, where small skulls and delicate bones rolled in the dark, boiling liquid. He caught Arleth Vann climbing up beside him and shook his head. 'Go around the side,' he ordered in a rough voice. 'I'll draw the attention of the rearguard. You come in and attack them from the rear.'

The assassin nodded and dropped back off the dais. Malus turned back to the cauldron, took a deep breath, and leapt into the pall of steaming gore. Sword held ready, the highborn cleared the gaping maw of the sorcerous vessel and landed in a crouch on the other side.

He found himself looking over the heads of shouting elders as they tried to force their way up the narrow staircase and join in the fight. Figures pushed and stumbled over the bodies of the dead, and pale hands dragged bloody corpses away from the battle, leaving them to fetch up against the foot of the dais.

Malus stood, peering intently at the swirling fight near the top of the stairway. A single figure spun and stabbed within a raging circle of temple elders. He caught sight of a long, tight braid of glossy black hair, and slim, alabaster arms moving in a swift, steady rhythm of slaughter.

Then the crowd recoiled under a fierce onslaught, and it seemed that the entire front rank of the elders simply collapsed like threshed wheat. A pale, blood spattered face appeared, and Malus found himself staring into Yasmir's violet eyes.

She wore the ritual garb of a temple witch: a long crimson loincloth of silk held by a girdle of golden skulls that wrapped around her slender hips. Her torso was bare, decorated with streaks and loops of sticky blood, as were her long arms and her long, delicate fingers. A torc of golden skulls surrounded her slender throat and bands of gold and rubies gleamed at each wrist. Beneath the angular headdress of a temple witch her oval face was serene and achingly beautiful, like a flawless sculpture animated by the breath of the Blood God himself. Two long, needle-like daggers flickered in her dripping hands, licking through the air like adders' tongues to turn aside stabbing blades and pierce deep into yielding flesh.

When her eyes met his he felt a cold shock transfix him. It was like looking into the eyes of death itself, and at that moment he wanted nothing more than to sink into her embrace.

The crowd of elders surged back up the stairs, only to lose three more men to Yasmir's flickering blades. As they fell she extended a small foot and took a single step forwards. Her eyes never left his.

'She is coming for you, Malus,' Tz'arkan whispered. 'Accept my power, or she will kill you!'

If she reached him he would die. Her eyes told him that. He could feel her desire like a cold breath against his skin. Malus's hand tightened on his sword, but it felt no better than a bar of lead.

Three more elders leapt at Yasmir, striking at her almost simultaneously. They died before the blows were halfway to their target, stabbed through throat, eye and heart. She took another small step as the dead fell at her feet.

Malus couldn't take his eyes off her. Another few steps and she would be almost close enough to touch. Yet he could not move, transfixed by her violet gaze like a bird before the gliding serpent.

'Hear me, Darkblade, this is the moment of truth! The Bride of Ruin approaches, and without me you cannot prevail. Take what I offer you! Take it!'

A terrified cry went up from the elders, and they fell back before the onslaught of the living saint. One man realised he could not escape and simply sank to his knees before Yasmir, accepting a dagger point in his eye with a prayer upon his lips. Others at the base of the stairs turned and ran.

Less than ten feet separated them. Suddenly the very air resounded as if struck by the hammer of a god, and Malus sensed that the Rite of the Swordbearer had been completed. Somewhere beyond the red-lit doorway he knew that Urial was reaching for the Warpsword of Khaine, and the thought of being thwarted so close to his goal kindled a spark of bitter hate in his breast.

Death approached, bearing her dark knives, and damnation lay coiled in his breast. What could he do?

With a cry of despair three elders fell and poured out their blood on the marble steps, and Yasmir leapt like a deer onto the edge of the dais. Malus drew a shaky breath, gazing into her face. 'Hello sister,' he said.

That was when Arleth Vann appeared, crying out the name of the Blood God as he leapt at Yasmir's back. Quicker than lightning his short blades jabbed at her throat and arms, but she whirled with uncanny speed, flowing like water around his strokes and stabbing the assassin once, twice, thrice. Her long braid uncoiled like a whip, brushing Malus's cheek.

Without thinking he seized that thick rope of hair, and the spell was broken. His hate blazed like a furnace and he pulled with all his might, twisting into the motion and dropping to one knee. Yasmir was pulled from her feet, crashing into and over Malus and falling headfirst into the seething fluids of Khaine's cauldron.

Tz'arkan writhed and screamed in rage, raking along the inside of Malus's ribs, drawing an involuntary shout of pain from the highborn even as he bared his teeth in triumph. Arleth Vann sank against the side of the dais, one arm pressed tight against his chest. A trickle of blood leaked from the corner of his mouth. 'The will of Khaine be done,' the assassin gasped.

The way to the sanctum was clear, and Malus knew that speed meant everything now. Tyran and his ritual mates would be nearly spent from the exertions of the rite. He would deal with Urial now, and claim the warpsword for his own.

With a howl of bloodlust he leapt over Arleth Vann and charged up the stairs, his sword held ready.

A shadow loomed in the doorway just as he reached it. He felt an icy shock transfix him as his half-brother Urial stepped through the portal, clad in gleaming black armour. His brass-coloured eyes gleamed with triumph and his thin lips were drawn back in a savage smile.

Malus tried to raise his sword, but his body refused to obey. He staggered slightly, still off-balance, but something held him upright.

The highborn looked down at the length of dark, gleaming steel that pierced his chest. A thin line of blood ran down the surface of the warpsword, filling the runes etched along its surface.

'Looking for this?' Urial asked, and plunged the blade deeper into Malus's chest.

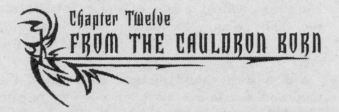

Chapter Twelve
FROM THE CAULDRON BORN

MALUS FELT HIS heart clench in agony as the long blade slid between his ribs. His chest spasmed and he gasped, coughing up blood. Urial's sepulchral laugh rang in his ears.

'Glory to Khaine, greatest of gods!' Malus's half-brother shouted, his pale face alight with triumph. 'Truly it is a gift to find you here at the moment of my exaltation.' The former acolyte stepped closer, his twisted left foot dragging slightly across the polished marble. His withered right hand was tucked against his breastplate, its deformity hidden within a shell of dark steel armour. Urial's gaunt, hawk-like face was lit with a savage grin and his thick, white hair spilled unbound around his shoulders. He looked like a sorcerer prince out of the ancient legends, radiating icy cruelty and implacable power.

'It is fitting that you be the first to die,' Urial said, his voice almost a whisper. 'After all you and that whore Eldire have done to me, this will be sweet indeed.' He smiled, flexing his good hand on the warpsword's hilt. 'I'm going to split you from crotch to chin and let you bleed out on these steps. Then I'll command the blood-witches to call you back, and I'll look you in the eye as I feast upon your liver.' His grin hardened into a sneer. 'Once I've eaten of your spirit Darkblade you will be no more. I will take your strength – such as it is – and what is left will be lost to the Abyss forever.'

With a single, fluid motion, Urial jerked the warpsword free from Malus's torso. A wave of pain spread like ice through the highborn's body, so great it took his breath away. Blood leaked from his gaping mouth as he swayed on his feet. Then his knees buckled and Malus fell backwards, landing on his back and sliding limply down the marble steps. His sword, clutched in a death grip, rasped and rang as it was dragged along in his wake.

Malus fetched up at the base of the dais, his labouring heart sending cold waves of pain rippling through his chest. Tz'arkan stirred, and for a brief moment the agony subsided. 'I'm here, Malus,' the daemon whispered. 'Ask, and I shall heal you. The wound is deep, and you will die unless I intervene.'

It was hard to think and harder still to breathe. 'Not… possible,' Malus rasped, bloody froth collecting at the corners of his mouth. 'The prophecy…'

Urial looked out over the temple elders and raised the bloodstained sword, savouring their cries of dismay. Behind him came a slow procession of white-robed zealots, stiff and exhausted from their labours. Tyran led the way, his draich unsheathed by his side. He looked down at the crowd of elders and gave them the serene smile of an executioner. 'The Time of Blood is at hand!' the zealot leader proclaimed. 'Weep for the end of your world, you faithless curs! Khaine's truth gleams from the edge of the Scourge's blade. Prostrate yourselves at his feet and beg for his forgiveness!'

'Yes. Plead for a clean death to wash away your sins,' Urial hissed at the stricken throng. He brandished the warpsword at the crowd like a burning brand. 'When the cauldron spared me you knew that I was blessed by the Lord of Murder. You knew the prophecies of old, and yet you refused to believe the signs that were before your very eyes, because I was a cripple,' he spat, 'a bent and twisted man, unfit to wield a dagger, much less this sacred blade!' Urial took another slow step down the stairs. His face was taut with murderous rage and his eyes gleamed with savage glee.

'I say to you that these withered limbs were a warning, revealing your blindness and lack of faith! You chose the pleasing lie over the grim truth of Khaine's will, and you will reap the bitter fruit of your faithlessness!' The Swordbearer gave a bloodthirsty laugh. 'I have claimed the sword, and soon I shall take my magnificent bride. Then the world will burn – oh, how it will burn! – and we shall rise on a tide of blood as high as the stars themselves.' Urial levelled the warpsword at the temple elders. 'But these glories are not for the likes of you. The blood-witches will call you back and we will feed your guts to the ravens!'

'Be silent, heretic!' thundered the Grand Carnifex.

The crowd of elders fell away to either side from the fearsome master of the temple as he strode into the chapel and climbed onto the dais beside the bubbling cauldron. The Carnifex's face was a mask of fearsome, righteous rage, and fresh blood dripped from the long blade of his rune carved axe. The severed heads of the zealots slain outside the temple were clenched in his left fist, and his gold covered kheitan was smeared with dark splashes of gore. He was the image of an avenging hero, anointed in sacred blood, and the ferocious glare he laid upon Urial stopped the Swordbearer in his tracks.

'You are an abomination, Urial of Hag Graef,' the master of the temple proclaimed. 'You claim that the cauldron gave you back as a gift from Khaine, but I say the Lord of Murder spared you to test our beliefs, not fulfil them!' The Grand Carnifex surveyed the assembled elders, fixing each one with a stern glare. 'The will of the Bloody-Handed God is clear to the faithful: Malekith is his chosen Scourge, who will lead the faithful to glory!' He cast the severed heads into the cauldron and raised his axe to Urial. 'You are a deceiver and a false prophet,' he declared. 'You have defiled the holy sanctum and laid hands on the sacred blade of the Scourge.' The master of the temple stepped from the dais onto the steps, taking his axe in a two-handed grip. 'I condemn you and repudiate you, and it is my joyous duty to slay you in the Blood God's name!'

To Malus's surprise, Urial smiled and shook his head. 'The first man that dies by this blade is my half-brother. You aren't fit to bleed on my boots, you fraud.'

'Slay the blasphemer!' Tyran cried, and two zealots answered with a lusty roar, charging down the steps past Urial and brandishing their deadly blades. The Grand Carnifex met them with a howl of righteous fury, his axe whirling in deadly patterns as he advanced on Urial.

The charging zealots reached the Carnifex first, their blades flickering like lightning. The master of the temple gauged their advance, and with skill born of countless battles he shifted his stance and sidestepped to the left, meeting the left-most attacker blade to blade. The zealot's sword snapped as it met the temple master's ensorcelled axe, and the Carnifex responded with a lightning return stroke that split the man's torso crosswise, just beneath the ribs. His sudden dodge threw off the rightmost attacker's stroke just enough to spoil the man's killing blow, but not enough to fully escape the reach of the long blade. Malus felt the hot droplets of the old druchii's blood as the zealot's sword tore a deep cut through the Carnifex's side.

A torrent of blood and spilled organs tumbled down the steps around the temple master's feet as the two halves of the slain zealot emptied their contents onto the stairway. 'Blood and souls for Khaine!' the Grand Carnifex shouted, pivoting smoothly to meet the remaining zealot's charge. The old druchii parried a deft swing at his upper thigh and struck back with a reverse stroke at the zealot's head, but the robed warrior ducked nimbly beneath the blow. The zealot stepped into the temple master's guard with a blurring backspin, aiming an eviscerating cut at the Carnifex's midsection, but the old druchii gave ground and parried the blow against the long haft of his axe. The swordsman skidded slightly in the thick blood coating the stone steps, but with preternatural agility he checked his motion and leapt backwards, getting swinging room for his two-handed blade and chopping downwards into the Carnifex's right leg. The long sword bit deep into the meat of the temple master's thigh, but like an old, grizzled boar the Carnifex bellowed in rage and pressed the attack. Twisting slightly to trap the sword in the wound, the old druchii lashed out one-handed with his axe and hacked off the zealot's right arm just above the elbow.

The zealot let out a sharp hiss of pain, blood pumping from the severed limb, but his left hand tore the draich free from the temple master's leg and the swordsman got the long weapon into a defensive stance as the Carnifex lurched forwards. Drops of hot blood scattered like rain as the old druchii unleashed a barrage of blows against the zealot's faltering guard. On the third, ringing stroke the rune-carved axe snapped the draich just above the hilt and the curved blade buried itself in the zealot's face. Drunk on pain and slaughter the Grand Carnifex pulled the axe free and rounded on Urial. Laughing like a madman he ran his tongue along the edge of the gore-stained blade. 'The blood of slain warriors is sweet,' he proclaimed, 'but cowardice is bitter! I can smell your blood curdling to vinegar, Urial. The true Scourge of Khaine would not cower and leave others to fight on his behalf.'

The elders of the temple shouted their approval and the zealots responded with a maddened cry as the two sides threw themselves at one another. Robed figures poured around the dais like a black wave, surging up the stairs alongside their master as white-robed zealots rent the air with bloodthirsty howls and rushed to meet them. Blades flashed and rang and more blood poured down the black stairs as the battle was joined in earnest.

Amid the mayhem Malus felt strong hands grab his shoulders and try to pull him upright. Crying out in pain and coughing up more blood, the highborn tried to twist in the unseen grip and came round to find himself staring up into Arleth Vann's bloodstained face. 'Let go of me!' he croaked. 'Let go! You have to get to the Grand Carnifex. When Urial falls, you must claim the sword and bring it to me.'

The former assassin shook his head. 'It's hopeless,' he said in a dull voice. 'Urial has the warpsword. Not even the master of the temple can prevail against him.'

'But you can,' Tz'arkan whispered in Malus's head, 'with my help. Take it, Malus! Quickly, before it's too late!'

The highborn shook his head angrily. 'I don't need your damned help!' he gasped. His knees weakened and he slumped against Arleth Vann, who struggled to hold him upright. The ache in his guts belied his defiance. His lungs felt heavy, as if a great weight was pressing down on them, and a numbing coldness was spreading across his chest. Hissing in frustration, he tried to push himself back upright and catch a glimpse of Urial among the swirling melee raging on the stairway.

Urial and the Grand Carnifex raged at one another like demigods less than fifteen feet away, their sorcerous weapons striking showers of angry sparks as they clashed again and again in a flurry of artless, brutal blows. The master of the temple lashed at Urial relentlessly, but the former acolyte wielded the warpsword one-handed and blocked the Carnifex's two-handed blows with ease. Still, the Swordbearer was giving ground, falling back towards the sanctum one slow step at a time. Malus would have taken this as a good sign were it not for the vicious smile on Urial's gaunt face.

The master of the temple was weakening. Bleeding from deep wounds, any of which would have been enough to kill a lesser man, the old druchii was slowing a little with each murderous stroke. Whatever strength the Grand Carnifex had stolen from his foes was nearly spent, and Malus realised that with every step he took towards Urial he became more isolated from his fellow elders. He was already a solitary black figure in a surging sea of white.

With a bloodthirsty howl the old druchii feinted at Urial's waist, and then checked his swing and made a vicious, backhanded blow at the Swordbearer's knees. Again, Urial blocked the heavy blow with frightening speed, as if he was swinging nothing more than a willow-switch. The Grand Carnifex stumbled slightly, and Urial flicked his blade across the temple master's face, scattering a thin spray of blood. The old druchii barely flinched from the blow, redoubling his attack with a swipe at Urial's sword arm. Laughing, the former acolyte swayed back, letting the axe blade whistle through empty air. Then he straightened and slashed open the temple master's left arm from wrist to elbow.

Urial was toying with him, Malus realised, his heart sinking. He fumbled at his belt for his remaining throwing knife, but the hilt of the blade was slick with his own blood and slipped from his fingers. His bitter curse was lost amid the cacophony of screams and clashing blades echoing in the steamy air.

The Grand Carnifex reeled as Urial raked his blade across the old druchii's forehead. Another stroke sliced off the temple master's left ear. The wounded elder swayed on his feet, his chest heaving. Blood had soaked through his robes, making them gleam dully in the reddish light. Malus saw Urial say something to the Carnifex, but the words were lost in the tumult. The temple master responded with an angry shout and aimed a powerful stroke right at the centre of the Swordbearer's chest.

Urial blocked the blow easily, a smug expression on his face; one that turned to a look of horror as the canny old druchii hooked the blade of the sword with the beard of his axe and pulled the former acolyte off his feet. The Swordbearer crashed against the Grand Carnifex, his mouth gaping like a gaffed fish as the old druchii closed a powerful hand on Urial's narrow throat. The axe rose heavenward, trembling in the temple master's hand, and then plunged downwards into the former acolyte's left shoulder. Urial screamed in pain and fear as the sorcerous blade pierced his black armour and bit into flesh and bone.

For a moment, Malus thought Urial had dropped the sword. He saw the bloodstained blade dip, but then it flashed upwards, piercing the temple master's midsection and rising underneath the ribs until the point erupted from the elder's right collarbone. Both men froze for several long moments, and then the old druchii sagged, sinking to his knees.

A cry of horror went up from the temple elders as they saw their master fall, turning to wails of terror as Urial gritted his teeth and levered his blade upwards, splitting the old druchii's chest open like a slaughtered steer. The bloodstained axe fell from the temple master's lifeless hands, his ruptured body toppling onto its side.

'Blessed Mother of Night,' Malus hissed, as the zealots redoubled their attack and the temple elders recoiled in horror. He saw Urial searching the melee intently, and knew who his half-brother was looking for. The highborn looked to Arleth Vann. 'This is about to become a rout,' he snarled. 'We've got to get out of here!'

The former assassin nodded and without warning heaved Malus back onto the dais. Groaning in pain, the highborn pushed himself across the black marble, close enough to brush the lip of the brass cauldron in passing. He heard an exultant shout over the din: had Urial seen him? Fighting against waves of crushing pain he forced himself to crawl across the dais and into the crowd on the other side.

Shouts of panic and the frenzied cries of the zealots rang out behind Malus, and he felt the crowd around him surge backwards, like a black tide receding towards the far doorway. He let himself be borne along in the press, until he realised that the shouts of the dying were spreading around the sides of the dais like fire through tinder. Tyran and his men were closing in like a pack of wolves. Snarling angrily and spitting streams of dark blood, the highborn threw himself forwards, using the blade of his sword to batter his way through the panicked elders. He stumbled and kicked his way through piles of weathered skulls. 'Stand fast!' he managed to shout. 'Avenge your master and slay the unbelievers!'

If his words had any effect on the panicked elders and their men he could not say, but the men and women in front of him gave way rather than feel the bite of his sword. Arleth Vann appeared at his side, swords bared and facing back the way they'd come in case the zealots pressed too close.

They had forced their way through the far doorway within moments. Malus paused at the threshold and risked a backwards glance just as a great wail of despair went up from the servants of the temple. He saw that the zealots had swept past the dais and were wreaking a terrible slaughter among the panicked and demoralised elders. On top of the marble platform, shrouded in crimson steam, Urial the Forsaken stood before the great cauldron where he'd been sacrificed as a crippled babe, only to be reborn as one of Khaine's chosen. He held the Grand Carnifex's severed head over the mouth of the great vessel, letting streams of dark blood fall into its hissing brew. The Swordbearer's eyes were fever bright with divine madness, and his hateful gaze was fixed hungrily on Malus.

Then the contents of the cauldron erupted, showering Urial and the zealots with a rain of steaming fluids as Yasmir burst from the cauldron's depths. Heat shimmered from her naked form, and blood ran like quicksilver from her alabaster skin. Her raven hair had gone snowy white, and when her eyes opened Malus saw they were luminous and golden. They transfixed him, sinking like hooks into his labouring heart.

Yasmir smiled, revealing curved, leonine fangs. Long, black talons gleamed in the ruddy light as she gripped the edge of the cauldron and climbed gracefully onto the dais. The newborn blood-witch extended her sleek arm and beckoned to Malus, summoning him to her side.

Malus was already fleeing, stumbling like a child into the lesser sanctum with his own eyes screwed fearfully shut. He could still feel her stare upon him, like hot metal searing his skin.

He felt someone grab his arm as he stumbled on the broad stairway. After a dozen steps he dared open his eyes again and saw it was Arleth Vann at his side. Rhulan eyed him fearfully from the centre of the room. The Arch Hierophant stood next to a slender female elder with a shaven head, her scalp tattooed in myriad intricate patterns that seemed to shift restlessly in the firelight. He had a fleeting memory of her in the Citadel of Bone, sitting in a throne almost directly across from the seat of the Grand Carnifex. She had to be the fifth member of the temple's Haru'ann. Malus suddenly realised that with the death of the Carnifex she and Rhulan were the only senior temple leaders still alive. They were surrounded by a thin cordon of temple retainers under the watchful eye of the young priestess that Malus had seen earlier.

'What has happened?' Rhulan asked, although from the look on his face it was clear that the elder already suspected the worst.

'We've failed,' Malus said bitterly. 'The Grand Carnifex is dead, and we're next if we don't get out of here.'

The tattooed woman gave Malus a look of contempt. 'You expect us to surrender the temple to a gang of heretics and thieves?' she snapped, her voice thick with a rustic northern accent.

'That's not a matter of debate,' the highborn shot back. 'You've already lost the temple. Your only choice is to stay here and throw your lives away or retreat and find another way to strike back.' He looked to Rhulan. 'We need real troops, and quickly. Are there any warriors left here at the fortress?'

Rhulan shook his head. 'We sent every swordsman and witch into the streets, hoping to overwhelm the zealots. If we sound the recall, the troops in the highborn district could be here within the hour.'

'By then it will be too late,' Malus snarled. He turned to ask something of Arleth Vann, but the question died on his lips. The highborn glanced back at Rhulan. 'What about the temple assassins?' he asked.

The Arch-Hierophant frowned. 'They have withdrawn into their tower to select a new master,' he said. 'After that they will swear vengeance upon the man who killed their former master and will not rest until he has been slain.'

Malus grinned. 'Is that so?' he asked. 'Well, then, I've got a proposition for them. If they want their

vengeance they'll have to stop Urial from getting his
first. Let's go.'

Chapter Thirteen
AMONG THE DEAD

AT THAT MOMENT a chorus of terrified wails erupted from the inner sanctum as the temple elders' courage finally gave out. The stream of wounded and demoralised temple servants pouring into the outer sanctum suddenly became a raging flood as scores of panicked druchii fled before Urial and his fearsome bride.

'Go!' Malus shouted at Rhulan. 'Gather your retainers and make for the temple doors.' Then he turned to face the tide of retreating temple servants and raised his bloodstained sword.

'Stand fast!' he roared, his face a mask of implacable rage. The shout was almost lost in the surf-like roar of the rout, but the leading rank of fleeing druchii saw the highborn's furious expression and pulled up short. He took a step towards the fearful elders. 'Turn and face the enemy! Defend your elders and the sanctity of the temple, for Khaine is watching!'

Each word was like a dagger, digging into Malus's chest. His lungs felt thick and swollen, and they couldn't seem to hold enough air. The daemon was right, Urial had wounded him badly. His chest heaved and he turned his head to spit a gobbet of blood onto the marble floor, but instead of fear, Malus felt only a black, boiling rage.

He stepped fearlessly into the press, forcing frightened men to either side. 'Skulls for the Blood God!' he cried, bloody foam flecking his thin lips. The front rank of temple servants turned with him, raising their weapons as Malus forced his way through the crowd towards the narrow door.

He knew that if he could reach the door they could hold it almost indefinitely. The battered temple retainers could form a tight ring around the portal and slay the zealots one at a time if they tried to fight their way through. The doorway was less than twenty feet away, but the path was crammed with thrashing, black-robed figures that contested each and every upward step. Malus snarled like a trapped wolf, laying about the men before him with the flat of his sword and eyeing the doorway with mounting dread. If the zealots could reach it before he did then all would be lost.

'Stand fast!' Malus shouted again, and succeeded in rallying the men closest to him. 'Drive for the door!' he ordered, and the men around him tried to force their way upwards, against the tide. The fleeing druchii pushed back, yelling and cursing. A temple retainer in front of Malus stabbed wildly at the highborn, and Malus split his skull without a moment's hesitation. He stepped into the gap the fallen man left behind and continued to press forwards. 'Hold them at the door!' he repeated. 'We'll stop them here!'

Had they been soldiers, accustomed to following orders amid the chaos of battle, the plan might have worked, but these were elders and temple acolytes, many of whom had not spilled another's blood except in temple rituals. The death of the Grand Carnifex and the slaughter visited upon them by the vengeful zealots had ground their courage to dust. Malus was halfway to the door when a chorus of thin cries rose to challenge his shouted commands.

'The Swordbearer is come! All hail Urial, the Scourge of Khaine!'

Men screamed as their fellow temple brethren turned on them, crying out Urial's name and stabbing their kin in hopes of saving themselves. The throng pressed with renewed vigour against Malus and his handful of rallied troops, but this time it was with knifepoints and axe-blades as well as elbows and fists.

The highborn heard the brittle snap of bones as the man in front of him was struck in the back by a retainer's axe. He fell with a gurgling scream, and his assailant pulled his weapon free with both hands and set upon Malus with a fevered gleam in his dark eyes. Malus blocked the frenzied axe-stroke with his upraised blade and then smashed the man in the face with the round pommel of his sword. The retainer staggered, fetching up against the men behind him, and Malus chopped his sword deep into the turncoat's neck.

A dagger lashed out from Malus's left, scoring a narrow track along his left bicep. He coughed and spat more blood, his breath coming in wet, rattling gasps. A short sword chopped at him from the right and Malus blocked the clumsy strokes without conscious thought. The crowd at the top of the stairs surged forwards. A man fell towards Malus, and he stabbed the druchii in the chest, unable to tell whether he was friend or foe. Then he saw it: a white sleeve spattered with red, holding up a bloodstained draich in front of the doorway to the inner sanctum. The zealots had seized the doorway to the sanctum, and there was no holding them back.

Another dagger reached for Malus. Unable to discern who held it in the tangle of bodies he took a swipe at the man's hand and severed a pair of fingers. Something sharp jabbed at his lower leg, causing him to shout in surprise. He stole quick glances left and right and saw the men beside him putting up a fight, but the weight of numbers had shifted against them. If they stayed where they were they would be overcome within minutes.

Malus gathered in as much breath as he could. 'Warriors of the temple!' he cried. 'One step back!'

The elders and their men eyed Malus with bewilderment, but their ragged line fell back a step. Several of the oncoming druchii overbalanced and fell at the feet of the retreating temple loyalists, and Malus was heartened to see his men despatch the turncoats with swift, merciless blows. The highborn risked a quick glance over his shoulder and saw Arleth Vann right behind him, his swords held low and to either side of his body. Malus noticed the rivulets of blood running from beneath both of the assassin's sleeves and dripping from his clenched fists, but the highborn had no doubt that his retainer could still fight and kill on command. 'We're retreating to the door!' he shouted. 'Watch our backs and keep the bastards from flanking us once we're off the stairs!'

Arleth Vann nodded grimly and turned his back on Malus, surveying the chapel floor.

'Warriors of the temple! One step back!' Malus commanded, and the retreat began in earnest.

The eighty paces back to the doorway were the longest steps of Malus's short life. Every loyal temple servant between Malus and the doorway was dead within moments and there was nothing in front of him but a bloodthirsty mob howling for his head. A man charged headlong at him, brandishing an axe, and the highborn dropped to one knee and stabbed the turncoat in the groin. Another rushed in and slashed for his face with a short sword. Malus pulled his sword from the axe man and blocked the sword stroke, forcing his assailant backwards with a jab to his face. He regained his feet and stepped backwards, taunting the men in front of him to try their luck against his blade.

And so it went: step, parry, kill and step again. As the temple loyalists came off the steps the mob spilled onto the chapel floor and lapped around the ends of the ragged line, slowly forcing the retreating fighters into a tight knot of weary men. The piled skulls on the chapel floor were a boon to the loyalists, breaking up the turncoat attacks so that they couldn't press the defenders from all sides. True to his word, Arleth Vann kept the line of retreat open, slaying every turncoat who crossed his path.

When they were slightly more than halfway to the doors, Malus was panting like a dog. Red spots swirled at the corners of his vision as he struggled for breath. He'd picked up a dagger from a fallen turncoat and fought on two-handed, blocking with the heavy northern sword and stabbing foes with the knife. He'd lost track of the number of men he'd killed. The rest paced in his wake like wolves, sensing that he was weakening and waiting for the right moment to strike. The highborn gasped like a landed fish, hardly daring to glance away from his opponents to see how well the rest of the loyalists were faring.

With each, halting breath he felt the daemon shift inside him, saying nothing but reminding him of its presence. Malus caught himself with the daemon's name on his lips, more than once, knowing that a single word could fill his lungs with fresh air and turn his blood to deadly ice. Each time he pushed temptation away with a snarl, although whether from fear or sheer, bloody-minded spite he could not say.

It was only when the turncoats redoubled their attacks that Malus knew they were nearly to the door. He heard the tempo of fighting increase to either side of him, and the three men who had been testing his defences for the last few minutes decided to rush him all at once. Two men held short, stabbing swords, while the druchii on the far right hefted a large, single bladed axe.

The axe man nearly got him, rushing forwards just as Malus tried to blink a swarm of bright spots from his eyes. He sensed more than saw the looming shape of his assailant and on instinct alone he leapt forwards and to the right, placing himself within the arc of the axe man's swing. Malus's attacker tried to adjust his aim by pivoting further to his right, but the move was a second too slow and his aim was poor, and the weapon struck one of the swordsmen in the back of the head instead. Before the axe man could recover Malus stabbed him twice in the chest and neck. Then he threw himself at the last swordsman, who was stepping over his fallen mate and thrusting his weapon at the highborn's throat. The turncoat's shorter blade meant he had to overextend himself in order to reach his target and the highborn made his foe pay dearly for it, sidestepping the thrust and chopping his sword deep into the side of the man's neck.

Malus risked a quick look backwards and saw the doorway only a few paces distant. Someone – probably one of Rhulan's men – had pulled the doors partly shut, so only one or two men could slip through at a time. Already there were only a bare handful of loyalists led by Arleth Vann remaining on the interior side of the door, barely keeping the escape route open. The highborn would have laughed out loud if he'd had the wind for it. Instead he turned back to the bloodthirsty turncoats, and found himself face to face with one of Tyran's zealots. The swordsman held his gore-crusted draich at the ready, a rapt smile on his face.

I can't beat him, damn it. I can barely breathe, he thought. Still, he leapt at the man with a rasping shout, holding his dagger close and feinting at the zealot's face to gauge his prowess. The swordsman was clearly spent from his exertions performing the Swordbearer's rite, because his killing stroke was just barely slow enough for Malus to block the blow with the flat of his dagger. Malus retreated from the swordsman, chest heaving, and the zealot glided after him, his expression hungry and intent.

Malus angled his course to head for the doorway, hoping his memory and blurred eyesight hadn't deceived him. He threw another short jab at the zealot's eyes, and pulled back just in time to avoid having his sword arm taken off at the elbow.

The zealot laughed. 'You disgrace yourself, blasphemer,' he said. 'I had hoped you would be a worthy foe, but you puff and stumble like a drunkard. Why don't you throw down your swords and accept Khaine's cold mercy?'

A ghostly grin came and went from Malus's bloody lips. 'Because I know something you don't.'

The zealot frowned. 'Such as?'

'Such as my retainer is about to stab you in the side of the neck.'

The swordsman whirled, raising his blade in a blurring defensive move. Malus leapt at the same time, catching the zealot's left arm at the crook of his elbow and shearing straight through it. The zealot staggered, but before he could regain his senses the highborn finished him off with a thrust to his neck.

Arleth Vann finished off the turncoat in front of him and took a step back, reaching Malus's side. He gave his master an accusatory look. 'I heard what you said,' he declared sternly, 'suggesting I would interfere in a sacred duel!'

'I'm a bit surprised he fell for it myself,' Malus replied. He grabbed the assassin by a blood soaked sleeve and pulled him back through the doorway. Wide-eyed druchii stood to either side of the threshold, their hands gripping the edges of the tall, oak doors.

'Shut them! Hurry!' Malus ordered. 'They're almost upon us!'

The retainers leapt to obey, pulling hard on the heavy panels. Frantic, bloodstained faces appeared in the narrowing gap and hands pounded fearfully on the closing doors. A pale hand shot through the gap, reaching desperately for Malus. With a curse the highborn stepped to the side and brought his sword down on the offending limb, severing it in a spray of blood. The loyalist's agonised shriek was lost in the heavy thud of the doors slamming shut.

Malus turned and sought out Rhulan, who stood ashen faced at the foot of the temple steps. 'Can you seal it?'

The temple elder started at Malus's voice, as if lost in a reverie. 'Seal?' he asked, blinking owlishly.

'The door, damn you!' the highborn snapped, his voice so sharp that Rhulan and his retainers flinched at the sound. 'Do you know some sorcery to lock the doors?'

'Oh, yes. Of course.' Rhulan strode forwards, raising his right hand. 'Step away from the doors,' he said.

Malus and Arleth Vann cleared the steps, and the rest of the temple servants scattered to either side. The heavy doors began to swing open almost immediately, giving vent to a chorus of fierce cries and pounding fists. A severed head rolled through the widening gap, bouncing wetly down the wide steps to stop at Malus's feet.

Then Rhulan straightened to his full height and spoke a single word of power that crackled in the air like the lash of a whip. He made a fist with his upraised hand and the twin doors slammed shut with a thunderous boom.

Malus nodded in weary satisfaction, revising his opinion of the frail looking Rhulan somewhat. He quickly took stock of the motley band of loyalists who'd escaped the debacle within the temple. Rhulan had six men and women standing in a loose circle around him, and Malus saw the tattooed elder standing a short distance away, surrounded by her own coterie of retainers and hangers-on, including the axe-wielding priestess he'd seen fighting earlier. Four more loyalists stood near Malus at the foot of the steps. They were all that remained of the meagre force he'd led out of the building.

Out of the hundred druchii who'd followed the Grand Carnifex from the Citadel of Bone, less than twenty remained. Malus shook his head bitterly and tried to curse, but all he could manage was a wet, wracking cough that sent spasms of pain through his chest. He swayed on his feet, but Arleth Vann steadied him with a bloodstained grip.

'Are you well?' Rhulan asked, his face paling further.

With an effort, Malus bit back a sharp-tongued reply. He spat another mouthful of blood onto the ground and took a strangled breath. 'Well enough,' he managed to say.

'We haven't long,' the elder said, his voice hollow. 'What do we do?'

The daemon stirred. 'Listen to him,' Tz'arkan whispered. 'Time is running out for you, little druchii. You must choose.'

A sharp spike of pain lanced through Malus's chest, almost doubling him over with its intensity. Again, Arleth Vann's grip steadied him, but Malus jerked his arm away. With nothing but bitter rage to sustain him, he forced himself upright.

'We go talk to these assassins of yours,' he said through clenched teeth, 'and then we put an end to these fanatics once and for all.'

AFTER THE IVORY eminence of the Citadel of Bone and the dwarf-wrought glory of the temple, Malus had no idea what to expect from the sanctum of the temple's holy assassins. A razor-edged keep wrought entirely of steel? A palace of ruby and garnet? Many fanciful visions passed through his mind as Arleth Vann shepherded him across the temple grounds.

It turned out to be a hole in the ground.

More accurately, it was accessed by a long, spiralling path, almost a hundred and twenty paces across, that wound its way deep into the earth. Large witchfire globes surrounded the perimeter of the wide spiral, throwing shifting patterns of light across the narrow pathways. The path was wide enough for only one traveller at a time, and it was formed of dark, crimson glass that glimmered like fresh blood in the sorcerous light.

Rhulan took the lead. The temple retainers – even the fearsome priestess with her bloodstained axe – looked to one another apprehensively as they fell into line behind their masters. Even Arleth Vann seemed hesitant to begin the descent, although Malus suspected that he had very practical reasons for avoiding his former comrades. He didn't expect that the silent knives of Khaine nurtured any compassion for those who broke their oaths and deserted the order.

The descent seemed to go on forever. It was fully five minutes of slow, methodical pacing before they'd completed the first circuit and began to sink below the earth. Malus gritted his teeth, one hand pressed against the wound in his chest, and expected to hear the sounds of pursuit at any moment. He couldn't imagine that Urial would be delayed overmuch by Rhulan's ward, nor would he waste a single moment in setting the hounds on his trail.

It was almost another five minutes before they were fully below ground. What in the Dark Mother's name was taking so long, he wondered? Were there traps for the unwary? Poison needles or voracious spirits? Everyone ahead of him seemed to be studying the path at their feet with intense interest. Concentrating on keeping his breathing even, Malus followed suit, watching the gleaming red stones for telltale pressure plates or tripwires.

On and on they went. The smell of damp earth filled his nostrils, and when they had passed beyond the light of the braziers their path was lit with the faint effulgence of grave mould, glowing from niches on the glistening stone walls.

He soon lost track of time. One step led to the next, their pace neither speeding up nor slowing down. A tight band of pain began to constrict around his chest, and from time to time a drop of blood would slip past his lips and fall heavily to the pathway. His breath bubbled in his throat, as if he was caught in the grip of a terrible ague. He heard the daemon whispering in his ears, but the sound was strangely faint, like the murmur of the tides, and he paid it little heed.

After a time Malus began to sense that their curving path was shrinking, drawing tighter and tighter with each revolution. He took heart, realising that they must be close to their destination, but he was careful not to get complacent and take his gaze from the perilous floor.

Not long afterwards he watched his steps glide across a narrow threshold, and looked up to see that they had reached a small, circular chamber carved from dark stone. Globes of witchlight gleamed from the walls, worked into carvings of dragons and leering daemons. Double doors stood on the opposite side of the circle. Rhulan gave the party a single backwards glance, his expression clearly indicating that they should wait here, and then went to stand before the doors. He spoke not a word, nor rapped upon the wooden panels, but nevertheless one door swung silently open, allowing him to slip inside.

After Rhulan was gone many of the loyalists sank wearily to the stone floor. Some checked their injuries, while others slumped into an exhausted stupor. The tattooed elder drew apart from the rest and sat with her back to one of the curving walls, closing her eyes as if to meditate or pray. The axe-wielding priestess sat, and then stood, and finally began to pace like a caged lion, her expression distant and vengeful.

Malus declined to sit as well, not so much out of nervousness, but because he wasn't certain he could get up again if he did. It was bad enough that Arleth Vann had to see him in such a weakened state; he would be damned if anyone had to carry him. The assassin leaned against the wall beside the entryway, resting his head against the carved stone. His gaunt features were scabbed with dried blood, and the front of his sleeves and kheitan were stiff and dark with gore.

The highborn glanced back the way they'd come. 'All that caution, and not a single trap or alarm,' he said. 'It appears that the assassins are less fearsome than their reputation suggests.'

Arleth Vann looked up at him, a bemused expression on his face. 'What are you talking about?'

Malus pointed back at the curving path. 'All that checking for traps,' he said, 'totally unnecessary.'

'Traps?' the retainer said. 'That was a labyrinth, my lord. A journey of meditation. Who lays traps in a labyrinth?'

The highborn blinked. 'Oh, well, no one, I suppose.' He frowned. 'What assassins' order forces you to walk a labyrinth to reach them?'

Arleth Vann studied his master for several moments, uncertain whether or not he was being mocked. 'We are not mere cutthroats, my lord,' he said at last. 'The Shayar Nuan are a holy order, much like the executioners or the temple witches.'

Malus raised an eyebrow at the name. 'The Blessed Dead? Is that what they call themselves?'

'That is the name we call ourselves,' the assassin said. He gave Malus one of his ghostly smiles. 'Now that you've heard it I have to kill you, of course.'

The highborn glowered at his servant. 'You speak as if you are still one of them.'

Arleth Vann shrugged. His brass-coloured eyes were haunted. 'We are Shayar Nuan when we emerge from the cauldron, my lord. Nothing can take that away.'

'I don't understand. I thought the cauldron was reserved only for sacrifices.'

The assassin sighed, trying to find a way to explain. 'Yes and no, my lord. The witches of the temple bathe in the cauldron. It is the source of their terrible allure and ageless vigour,' he said. 'That power is indeed born from sacrifice: prisoners, criminals, the weak and the crippled, as well as every neophyte assassin. It is the final rite of passage. We die, yet live on in service to Khaine.'

Malus peered closely at the assassin. 'You don't mean to say you're actually dead?'

'It's a metaphor, my lord. You're familiar with the term?'

'Don't get flippant with me,' Malus snarled weakly. 'In case you've forgotten, I was stabbed with a sword not too long ago, and I'm not in the mood.'

'Your pardon, my lord,' the retainer replied.

'Besides, with everything else I've seen in this damned city, I wouldn't be at all surprised.'

'No, I suppose not,' Arleth Vann replied. 'All right, consider this: how do you kill a man who is already dead?'

Malus considered the question. 'Cut off his head and limbs and burn the bits. It's the only way to be certain.'

The assassin's brow furrowed. 'I begin to see why your father never considered sending you to the temple,' he said. 'Let me be blunt: the greatest power a man can have is the ability to take the life of another. That is the central tenet of the executioners. If a man is already dead, however, not even the blessed swords of Khaine can touch him. He is a ghost, fearing nothing of this world or the next.'

Malus grunted, touching off a spasm of coughing. 'Interesting,' he said, wiping his mouth with the back of his hand. 'If I recall, you said that the order was a recent invention, not originally part of the Lord of Murder's cult.'

Arleth Vann eyed the other Khaineites warily. 'That is so,' he admitted softly. 'The Witch King needed a way to eliminate threats to the state without risking open war with the noble houses, and the temple needed a new reason to justify its authority after the last of the warlocks had been killed.' He shrugged. 'In the past, those who survived the depths of the cauldron were taken by the witches and trained in the ways of the cult. Many became priests, and others lived as exalted oracles or scholars. The temple elders gave them a new calling: the art of stealth and silent murder, a combination of the witch's magic and the executioner's skill.'

'And Urial was trained in these arts?'

The assassin shook his head. 'No, according to all reports, he was a voracious scholar and a potent sorcerer, but that was all. His deformities precluded him from mastering the arts of combat. As far as I know, he was never considered for inclusion into the order, nor could he truly be considered a priest, for even elders like Rhulan must be ready and able to march to war. Honestly, I don't think anyone quite knew what to do with your brother.'

'It's a pity they never asked me. I could have offered a number of pointed suggestions.' Malus studied the closed doors. 'Do you think they will help us, now that Urial has the sword?'

Arleth Vann shrugged. 'Truly, it's hard to say. Like the blood-witches of old, the order professes to take no interest in the affairs of the temple. Indeed, much of the witches' prestige and authority has been ceded to the assassins over the centuries. They may see Urial as usurping Malekith's role as the Scourge, or they may not care who wields the warpsword so long as Khaine's will is done.'

Another sharp jolt of pain stabbed through Malus. His breath was coming in shallow draughts, and shadows crowded at the edges of his vision. He knew that time was running out. Where was Rhulan? What was taking so long?

'It appears they need some persuading,' he said grimly, and lurched towards the doors.

Arleth Vann let out a startled shout, but Malus was at the doorway before anyone could react. He placed his hands against the cold, damp oak and pushed.

The doors opened easily, giving way to cave-like darkness. Without hesitation, Malus plunged through. He walked blindly forwards, expecting any moment to smash into a wall or plunge off the edge of a pit. He dimly heard Arleth Vann shouting his name, but he paid no mind.

After only a few moments he saw a dim light up ahead. A few steps later he could make out three figures, two standing and one kneeling before them. Malus guessed that the kneeling figure had to be Rhulan, and a dozen strides later, his suspicions were confirmed.

The Arch-Hierophant knelt in a circle of faint luminescence that seemed to emanate from the very air itself. Two robed figures stood before him, their faces hidden within deep hoods.

Rhulan glanced back fearfully at Malus's approach. His eyes widened as he recognised who it was. 'Blessed Murderer! What are you doing here? You were supposed to wait!'

'Time is more precious than gold at the moment,' Malus seethed, 'and we are growing poorer by the second.' He faced the hooded men. 'Are you among the elders of the order?'

One of the figures stepped forwards. 'The elders are in conclave,' a young man's voice replied. He reached up and drew back his hood, revealing the boyish features and dark eyes of an initiate.

Malus pointed at Rhulan. 'Do you not know who he is, boy?'

'Of course,' the initiate replied, 'but he has brought no blood tithe and nor have you. Not even the Grand Carnifex may speak to the elders without a suitable offering. The commandments of the order are clear–'

The highborn's hurled dagger struck the initiate in the forehead with a meaty thunk. The boy's body quivered for a moment, his mouth frozen in mid-sentence, and then the corpse collapsed to the floor.

Malus turned to the second hooded figure. 'All right,' he said coldly. 'There is my blood tithe. Take me to the elders.'

Rhulan let out a strangled gasp. The hooded figure considered the dead acolyte for a moment, and then faced Malus. 'Your tithe is... acceptable,' he said, 'but the elders are choosing a new master. They will speak to no one until their sacred duty is complete.'

'Do you not realise that a usurper has stolen the Warpsword of Khaine and killed the Grand Carnifex? If we do not move against him quickly he will seize the temple and then the city beyond!'

The figure said nothing.

Furious, Malus tried another tack. 'Are you not bound to avenge the death of your fallen master?'

'Yes,' the figure replied.

'Well it was I who slew him!' the highborn declared. 'I beat the fat oaf's brains out with a hunk of broken marble. If your damned elders don't get off their arses and do something about Urial, he'll kill me and rob them of their revenge.'

Someone shouted angrily. Malus couldn't be certain who it was. The room started to spin. A fierce jolt of pain shot through him, but with a shout of rage he fought to stay upright. The highborn groped for his sword, but powerful hands seized his arms and pulled him from his feet.

Malus never felt himself hit the ground.

* * *

HE WAS FLOATING through darkness. A hot wind hissed across his face and strange sounds echoed in his ears.

Visions came and went in brief, red flashes. He saw stone walls and robed men, twisting passages and narrow stairs. After a time he realised he was being carried, but he could not guess where or why.

Sometimes the sounds resolved themselves into voices, echoing in close, dark spaces. Sometimes they whispered, sometimes they shouted. He tried to answer them, but no words would come.

The next thing he knew, he was cold. No, he was laying on something cold. He tasted blood. There was another red flash, and Malus flinched, blinking in the sudden glare. Arleth Vann loomed over him, his pale face mere inches from Malus's own. Brass-coloured eyes peered deep into his.

Malus tried to speak. The sounds that came in response to his efforts were barely recognisable. 'Where… are… we?'

The assassin's face receded. The torchlight painted a wall of rock to Malus's right, revealing deep niches set at regular intervals from floor to ceiling. Skulls and piles of bones shone dully in the flickering light.

'Among the dead,' Arleth Vann replied. Then darkness closed in once more.

Chapter Fourteen
CONTEMPLATING THE ABYSS

A HOT WIND blew over Malus, tangling his unbound hair and blowing fine, rasping sand across his face. Flat plains stretched for miles, lifeless and inimical.

He lay on his chest, facing north, staring at the broken line of iron dark mountains that reared up from the edge of the burning world. Malus knew that one of the mountains had a cleft in it, as if it had been split by the axe-stroke of a god. At the foot of that mountain, in a dead and withered wood, there was a road of dark stones that led to an ancient temple.

He'd tried to do his part. He had tried to gather up all five of the lost relics, but in the end he'd failed. It was too much: too much for any one man to do.

Now the sands were running out. They were stolen from him by the desert wind, streaming away into the pale white sky.

He tried to rise to his knees, but his body refused to obey. A hot pain burned like a coal beneath his skin, stealing his breath away. He'd crawled for miles upon miles, trying to reach the temple and beg the daemon to release his tainted soul. Terror gripped him as the hour drew near, when Tz'arkan would claim his soul for all time.

A hand, cool and strong, gripped his shoulder. Sharp, writhing pain made him cry out as he was turned onto his back. Harsh, white light burned through his clenched eyelids. Then a shadow covered him, blotting out the merciless sun.

He felt a caress along the line of his blistered cheek. The skin was rough, calloused at fingertip and palm.

'Do you suffer, my lord?' her voice, throaty and deep, reminded him of the slave cruise, and the time before the daemon's curse.

'I have to get to the temple,' he croaked, his breath coming in bubbling gasps. His clumsy fingers pawed at the ragged tear in his robes. 'I'm hurt,' he said, bitter tears carving tracks through the grime caking his face. 'There is a daemon inside me–'

'Hush, my lord,' she said, 'the corruption has made you mad. I shall not let the daemon have you. Do not fear.'

Gentle fingertips probed at the tear. Malus opened his eyes and looked up into Lhunara's face. She smiled, causing the blood-filled orb that had been her right eye to bulge from its ruined socket. Blood and vile fluids seeped from the terrible wound in her skull and maggots writhed in the rotting brain matter, disturbed by the terrible heat.

Her fingers wriggled into the tear and then the open wound beneath. He felt the cold digits grasp the inside of his ribs and he screamed as she flexed her arms and pulled his ribcage apart. Flesh and bone parted with a rotten, tearing sound.

She lowered her face to the gaping hole and started to feed, tearing at his organs like a wolf, and it was all he could do to open his mouth and scream.

HANDS SHOOK HIM, gently at first, and then insistently. 'Wake up, my lord. For the Murderer's sake, wake up!'

Malus awoke, his rising scream silenced by a spasm of wracking coughs. His body was cold and damp, and his joints ached from lying on unyielding stone. He rolled onto his side, spitting clots of blood and phlegm from his mouth and struggling for a decent breath.

He lay on a mortuary slab in a small, rectangular cell. Its previous occupant, some withered temple elder from centuries past, had been dumped unceremoniously on the rough-hewn floor. Long niches lined the walls, filled with the tattered skeletons of favoured retainers and allies. A small oil lamp guttered from one of the higher niches, shedding a dim yellow light onto the ancient crypt. The air was dank and thick with dust, coating the back of his aching throat.

Strong hands gripped his shoulders, touching off a thrill of terror as he relived the last moments of his nightmare. He tried to fight back, but a fist of agony clenched around his left lung, leaving him near senseless with pain. Arleth Vann pulled his master back down onto the slab, studying him with concern.

'You had a nightmare, my lord,' he said quietly. 'It must have been a terrible one. I don't think I've ever heard you scream before.'

Malus wiped his face with a trembling hand. 'That's just because you haven't spent much time with me lately,' he replied, attempting a half-hearted smile. 'I've had occasion to hone my vocal skills over the last several months.' He pushed aside the retainer's hands and tried to sit up. 'Where in the Dark Mother's name are we?'

'Deep in the tombs,' the assassin replied. 'By the time we'd emerged from the assassin's sanctum Urial had already broken through the temple door and was well on his way to seizing the entire temple fortress. The great gates had been opened and a large force of zealots had slipped inside, reinforcing Urial's small band. They were killing every slave they could find and rounding up all the remaining acolytes. It was all we could do to sneak past their hunting parties and lose ourselves in the catacombs.'

Malus winced as another stabbing pain shot through his chest, but he refused to lie back down again. 'How long have I been out?'

'You've been in and out for most of a day,' the assassin said. He nodded to the narrow doorway over his shoulder. 'Rhulan and the rest are in the antechamber beyond. They haven't stopped bickering since we got here.'

The highborn muttered a curse. 'An entire day,' he said bitterly. 'Urial grows stronger with every minute. Do we know what is happening on the hill?'

Arleth Vann shrugged. 'I made a trip to the surface a few hours ago, hoping to get some food and water from the kitchens and maybe some hushalta,' he said. 'Urial is in complete control of the temple, and he's closed the fortress gates to the temple warriors still out in the city. Much of Har Ganeth continues to burn, and I could hear sounds of fighting in the high-born district.'

Malus nodded thoughtfully. 'A damned brilliant plan,' he admitted. 'Urial holds all the advantages.' He tried to slide his legs off the slab, grimacing in pain. 'If we don't do something very soon, all will be lost.'

Arleth Vann reached for the highborn. 'My lord, I'm not sure you should be moving,' he said. 'Your wound…' He paused, his face troubled.

Malus stopped. 'What about my wound?'

The retainer considered his words carefully. 'The warpsword pierced between your ribs and punctured your left lung,' he said. 'There was bloody froth on your lips, and you were gasping for air. Most men die from such a wound, even with the aid of a chirur-geon. Indeed, there were times during the morning when I was certain that you were about to take your last breath.'

'But?' the highborn enquired.

Arleth Vann started to reply, but words failed him. Helplessly, he pointed to the cut in Malus's robe.

Malus looked down, realising for the first time that his kheitan had been stripped off and his robe loos-ened. He felt a twinge of dread as he reached up with tentative fingers and pulled the dark cloth aside.

Arleth Vann had evidently used some of his plundered water to clean Malus's wound as best he could. The skin on the left side of his chest was mottled with dark, indigo-coloured bruises from his breastbone all the way to his navel. The puncture was a neat line almost as long as his finger, running between his fifth and sixth ribs. The ache in his back told him that a similar wound was present there as well.

The skin around the puncture was almost solid black. The injury itself was sealed shut, bound by a rope of thick, black tissue that wept a pale, foul smelling liquid.

Mother of Night, Malus thought, his blood running cold. What has Tz'arkan done to me?

Arleth Vann pointed hesitantly at the highborn's wound. 'I... I've never seen anything like that, my lord,' he said. 'What is it?'

Corruption, he thought, remembering Lhunara's words. The daemon's grip on his body was far worse than he'd imagined possible. Suddenly he remembered the stab wound he'd received in the battle on the Slavers' Road. He ran a hand over his thigh, finding not so much as a scab or scar. It was all he could do not to cry out in fear.

I'm teetering on the abyss, he thought. One more step, and I'm lost!

Belatedly, Malus realised that Arleth Vann was watching him, his expression growing more disturbed with each passing moment. He groped about for an explanation. 'It's... it's the blessing of Khaine,' he said. 'Am I not his Scourge?'

A cruel chuckle echoed in Malus's head. It was all he could do not to clench his fists and try to beat that sound out of his skull. 'What of you?' Malus asked, eager to think about something else. He studied his retainer's filthy, tattered robes and bloodstained skin. 'I saw what Yasmir did to you with her knives.'

The retainer averted his eyes, apparently willing to accept Malus's explanation, although his expression remained troubled. 'The wounds in my arms will heal,' he said simply. 'The witches teach us techniques to speed the healing process and knit torn flesh. As for the rest...' He reached up and pulled back a flap of his own robe. The faint light gleamed off polished rings of fine, close-set mail stitched to the inside of the assassin's clothes. 'They weren't as bad as they looked.'

Malus hazarded a weak chuckle. 'I thought you and your kin had no fear of death.'

The assassin shrugged. 'I don't fear death, my lord, but that's no reason to make things easy for my foes.'

Suddenly a heated exchange of words echoed from the antechamber beyond the tiny crypt. 'Speaking of making things easier on our foes,' Malus said. He drew as deep a breath as he could manage, and was both surprised and frightened to discover that he was breathing much easier than before. Then slowly, painfully, he pushed himself off the stone slab. His legs threatened to give way beneath him. Arleth Vann leaned forwards, reaching for him, but Malus waved him away. Another deep breath, and a measure of strength returned. The highborn adjusted his robes, cinching them tight, and then headed for the doorway.

Two more oil lamps threw fitful light on a rectangular chamber some thirty paces long. More crypt entrances, many still sealed by thin wooden doors, lined both of the long walls of the room, while larger entryways opened onto subterranean darkness at either of the short ends of the chamber. Alcoves had been carved into every free space on all of the room's walls and piled with skulls and cloth-wrapped bones. Ancient statuary lay in broken, moss covered piles in each of the four corners, their original appearance long lost to the mists of time.

Rhulan stood in the centre of the room, glaring hotly at the young priestess who'd fought so well in the battle at the temple. Her hands were open in supplication, but Malus could see a steely glint in her eyes. There was a hint of anger and desperation in her voice. 'We deserve answers, Arch-Hierophant,' she said. 'If Urial is not the Swordbearer, how could this have happened?'

All eyes were on Rhulan. Every one of the temple loyalists sat on the bare stone floor, watching the exchange with hope and dread in equal measures. Even the tattooed elder had taken keen interest in the argument, sitting with her back to one of the piled sculptures, a pair of broad bladed knives lying naked in her lap.

'Does the writ of the temple not teach us that Malekith, lord and Witch King, is Khaine's chosen Scourge?' the priestess continued. 'Was the blade not bound by chains of sorcery, warding it so that only the Swordbearer could draw it forth?'

Malus saw a glimmer of fear in Rhulan's eyes. His lip trembled as he struggled for an answer. It looks as if he's living his worst nightmare, the highborn thought.

'No ward is perfect,' Malus interjected, causing everyone to jump. Startled faces turned to regard the highborn as if he'd risen from the dead.

'Urial is a potent sorcerer in his own right,' Malus continued, leaning against the doorframe for support, 'and has he not spent years studying the temple's lore? He's had plenty of time to uncover a means to circumvent the magic protecting the sword.'

'But the sword is meant for the Scourge alone.'

Malus studied Rhulan carefully. The elder was clearly very nervous. He knows that the sword has passed through many hands over the centuries, the highborn thought. Have they told the faithful it was passed directly from Khaine to the hands of the temple? 'The sword may be meant for the Scourge, but cannot others bear it? Wield it, even? After all, how long had the elders kept it before they came to Har Ganeth?'

The priestess glanced at Malus, her brow wrinkling in thought. 'Are we certain he is not the Scourge?'

'I am,' Malus said with utter conviction. He eyed Rhulan. I'm not so certain about the Arch-Hierophant, though.

'Malekith is the chosen one,' Rhulan said weakly, 'so it is written.'

'Then you had best get the blade out of Urial's hands before the Witch King learns of this,' Malus said.

'Why is that?' the tattooed elder asked, fixing Malus with a penetrating stare. 'This is a matter for the temple to resolve.'

Malus shook his head. 'Not if word of this coup makes it to the other cities,' he said. 'Malekith cannot see it as anything less than a challenge to his authority. He will have to take the sword from Urial, if only to prove that it is his by right. If other members of the temple decide that Urial is the true Scourge, the resulting feud could tear Naggaroth apart.'

'Blessed Murderer!' Rhulan said, placing a trembling hand over his mouth. 'What are we going to do?'

'We're going to fight them,' Malus said grimly. 'You should have been out in the city hours ago, rallying the faithful behind your banner. In a battle like this, the side that seizes the initiative will triumph, and I guarantee that Urial has already started moving against you.'

The priestess frowned. 'Urial can't possibly stop us,' she said. 'He has his zealots, but we have a small army at our command.'

'Urial has more than just his true believers,' Malus said. 'He has an entire city to call upon. Everything the zealots have done up to this point is to turn the citizens of Har Ganeth against the warriors of the temple. They goaded the temple into a campaign of fire and slaughter, and then they locked them out of their safe refuge, leaving them at the mercy of the people they savaged. Once Urial shows the people that he has taken up the sword and condemns the warriors of the church for their crimes, the streets will run red once more.' He pointed to the two elders. 'You must escape the fortress and rally the faithful. Denounce Urial and blame yesterday's bloodshed on the zealots, and then hunt down the heretics remaining in the city and turn your attention to retaking the fortress.'

The elder gave Malus a stricken look. 'We can't fight Urial,' he said.

'Why not?'

'The bearer of the warpsword cannot be defeated in battle,' the elder replied. 'So it is written.'

Malus started to argue, but then he understood. You think Urial really is the chosen one, he thought. You know the truth about the prophecy, and you're trapped between the Witch King and the man you believe is the true Scourge.

'Leave Urial to me,' the highborn said. 'I will remain behind with a handful of volunteers and strike the usurper directly while your forces hold his attention at the fortress gates.'

Rhulan said nothing for a moment, his dark eyes narrowing as he considered Malus's plan. Finally, he nodded. 'So be it.' He turned to the assembled loyalists. 'Mereia and I must join our brothers and sisters in the city. Who will remain behind and take the battle to the usurper?'

'I want no more than a dozen,' Malus said. 'We will have to strike hard and fast. Even then, there is little chance that many of us will survive.'

The priestess turned to the highborn, raising her chin haughtily. 'I will stay,' she said. Other druchii rose to their feet, singly or in small groups. Malus counted only ten, but he wasn't going to press the issue.

Rhulan surveyed the volunteers and nodded. 'The blessings of the Lord of Murder be upon you, brothers and sisters,' he proclaimed. 'Khaine's will be done.'

'Khaine's will be done,' the faithful answered.

Mereia, the tattooed elder, rose smoothly to her feet. 'How will we escape from the fortress?'

Malus looked to Arleth Vann.

'Take the winding staircase and follow the ancient road to Thel's house,' the assassin said. 'Even if there are guards watching the passage, you could still slip past them in the darkness. You could even call the maelithii down on them if you could fight your way to within sight of their iron anchors.'

Rhulan nodded. 'Then let us go. Every moment is precious.' As Mereia and their escorts gathered up their weapons, the Arch-Hierophant stepped close to the highborn.

'Are you certain you are capable of this?' he asked, studying Malus's face intently. 'Your wounds are grave.'

'I have suffered worse,' Malus said evenly. 'Never fear, Rhulan. I will fulfil my part of the plan. See that you do the same.'

'The fate of the temple – perhaps Naggaroth itself – rests in your hands. So far, Urial has yet to put the sword to the test, and if we can deal with him before he reveals the sword to the people then no one ever has to know this happened,' the elder said quietly. 'How will you separate Urial from the sword?'

Malus shrugged. 'I don't know for certain, but I expect it will involve a bit of bloodshed.'

'Remember what I said,' Rhulan whispered. 'Everyone knows the sword cannot be defeated in battle. You must find another way to best Urial and take the blade from him, and once in your possession it must never be used, by you or anyone else. Swear it!'

The highborn gave the elder a bemused look. 'As you wish, Arch-Hierophant.'

Rhulan nodded. 'Good. Very good. When you have the sword, bring it to me, and you will be well rewarded.'

Malus fought to keep his expression neutral. What are you playing at now, he wondered?

Before he could inquire further, a faint sound echoed from the dark passageway to Malus's left. Everyone in the antechamber froze upon hearing it.

'What is that?' the priestess whispered, clutching her axe.

The sound faded, but the echoes still lingered in Malus's mind. Setting his jaw, he slowly drew his sword.

'It sounded like a howl,' he said.

Chapter Fifteen
THE ABODE OF THE DEAD

THE CRY CAME again – a thin, almost despairing sound that wound faintly down the corridors of the crypt. The Khaineites shared apprehensive looks.

Malus looked to Arleth Vann. The assassin drew his twin blades, his expression tense. 'Whatever it is, it's coming this way,' the retainer said.

'Could it be a wight or a guardian spirit?' the highborn asked.

Rhulan answered, a quaver of fear in his voice. 'We built these tombs to contain the dead, not give them free rein.'

'Then I believe Urial has come looking for us,' Malus growled.

Mereia rose gracefully to her feet. 'What do we do?'

'You and Rhulan get out of here. Now.' Malus said. 'We'll buy you as much time as we can.'

The howl echoed down the eastern passage once again – then dissolved into a chorus of shrieking, gobbling cries that seemed to draw nearer by the moment. Galvanized by the horrific sounds, Rhulan, Mereia and their escorts dashed for the western corridor. The tattooed elder gave Malus a comradely nod as she passed. 'Kill one for me,' she said, drawing a vicious grin from the highborn.

Rhulan's parting look was far grimmer, as he paused at the mouth of the passageway and turned his gaze on the highborn. 'Remember what I said,' he said. 'The future of the temple depends on it.'

'I'll do what must be done,' Malus said gravely. 'Count upon it.' *Providing I live through the next ten minutes,* he thought.

He was in no shape to fight, of that alone he was certain. The wound in his chest ached when he moved, and his limbs felt clumsy and weak. Unbidden, he thought of the daemon. A taste, just the merest taste of Tz'arkan's power would make all the difference.

Could he take one more sip from the font of corruption without losing himself forever? He could bargain with the daemon. He could ask for just enough to get through the next battle, and no more. He could do that, couldn't he? If he died here, in the depths of this goddess-forsaken crypt, his soul would belong to the daemon anyway. Was it not better to live in corruption than to die and be enslaved forever?

The cries of the hunters drew nearer, and Malus felt all too keenly just how trapped he'd become.

More sounds emanated from the darkness: wet, slithering sounds, punctuated by the dry scrabbling of claws. One of the loyalists let out a frightened cry and shrank from the passageway. 'Blessed Murderer deliver us,' he said, his voice cracking with strain. 'We're all going to die!'

The words sent a tremor through the assembled Khaineites, but the axe-wielding priestess let out a derisive snort. 'Speak for yourself, wretch,' she said, spinning the haft of her weapon in her hands. 'I'm going to live long enough to make the bastards pay for what they've done.'

Arleth Vann chuckled. 'Never underestimate the power of sheer, bloody-minded spite,' the assassin said. 'Isn't that right, my lord?'

Malus thought it over. A wolfish smile spread across his face. 'Truer words were never spoken,' he said, hefting his sword. 'We'll meet them at the threshold,' he said, the words coming briskly as a plan of action took shape. 'Whatever's coming, I'd rather face them one at a time.'

The loyalists took heart from the highborn's fierce demeanour, readying their weapons and rushing to form a tight semicircle around the open doorway. The sounds of the approaching hunters stalking down the narrow passageway grew louder and more terrible: a cacophony of slithering, galloping, clawing madness that sent chills down the highborn's spine. Suddenly he was reminded of the twisted Chaos beasts that he fought in Urial's tower, many months past. As bad as those things were, this sounded a great deal worse.

The roiling tide of unnatural motion swept down on them in an avalanche of unsettling noise. Then it suddenly stopped. The druchii stared vainly into the cave-like darkness, more unsettled than ever.

An eerie stillness hung in the air, setting Malus's nerves on edge. He glanced at the man on his right. 'Fetch me one of those lamps,' he whispered, barely loud enough to be heard. The loyalist nodded and quickly snatched a lamp from the base of a broken statue. The brass vessel was hot to the touch as it was pressed into the highborn's hand.

'Let's see what we're dealing with,' Malus said, hurling the lamp down the passageway.

The palm sized lamp tumbled end over end, its tiny flame guttering until it struck the stone floor and broke apart. Orange fire whooshed into life as the wick ignited the spreading oil, revealing the hunters in all their horror.

There were three of them, their bulk so great that they could not stand side-by-side in the narrow, bone strewn corridor. Firelight shone on glistening, gelatinous flesh, shot through with thin, black veins and throbbing with unnatural strength. They had lean, powerful bodies similar to those of lions, their broad paws tipped with glossy, black claws, but their heads were like bloated octopi. The closest one to the fire reared back on its paws, its soft, bulbous skull pulsing with rage as it lashed the air with eight long, whip-like tentacles. Hundreds of suckers lined each tentacle, each one fitted with a barbed hook for trapping and shredding prey. At the centre of the mass of tentacles a cruel, glossy beak snapped furiously at the offending flame, unleashing a torrent of thin shrieks and gobbling cries.

The man beside Malus screamed like a child, and the Chaos beasts attacked.

The lead hunter bounded over the pool of flame and leapt for the screaming man, as if drawn by the sound. Its tentacles made a whirring sound in the air as they lashed at the terrified druchii. One slashed across the man's face, shredding the skin and muscle beneath as if they were rotted cloth. The stench of brine and rotted meat filled Malus's nostrils, making him gag. More tentacles wrapped around the hapless druchii, in the blink of an eye, enfolding him and pulling him from his feet. Wet, tearing sounds emanated from within the writhing web of fleshy ropes, and the druchii's frenzied screams of agony made Malus's blood run cold.

'Kill it!' Malus cried. 'In the Dark Mother's name, kill the thing!' He slashed at the beast's shoulder with his sword, but the creature's gelatinous flesh was deceptively strong, and his blade rebounded as if he'd struck solid oak. Arleth Vann darted at the thing, unleashing a flurry of stabbing blows. The blades sank barely an inch into the creature's flank, producing thin streams of clear, foul-smelling ichor.

Blows rained down on the creature from all sides. The priestess aimed a fearsome, two-handed blow at the creature's bulbous skull, but the axe blade left only a shallow cut in the heaving flesh. Undeterred, the Chaos beast continued to rip its victim apart. Blood poured from between the thrashing tentacles.

More tentacles whirred through the air, this time from the left side of the doorway. Malus heard a strangled scream and turned to see another man lifted from his feet by a second Chaos beast that clung to the wall of the passage like a spider. One broad paw had reached around the edge of the threshold and flattened itself against the wall of the chamber for support, and Malus saw that the base of the creature's feet were also lined with hooked suckers. The beast lifted its victim off the ground as if he was a child, wrapping one tentacle around the druchii's sword arm and ripping it off in a spray of hot blood.

'Mother of Night!' Malus cursed fearfully. They didn't stand a chance against these things. 'Run!' he shouted to his dwindling band. 'We can't stop them!'

The loyalists needed no convincing. They broke and ran for the western passage with barely a backward glance. Malus, Arleth Vann and the priestess were the last to break away, leaving the creatures to consume their prey. Though powerful, the beasts didn't seem to be much smarter than hunting hounds, easily distracted by the smell of blood, which suggested that their handlers were probably somewhere close by.

They were barely halfway across the antechamber when the third beast raced along the right wall of the passage and bounded heavily into the chamber, its tentacles waving sinuously as if it was tasting the air for prey.

The priestess let out a defiant scream and the beast oriented on her at once. Thinking quickly, Malus let out a war scream of his own and the beast turned to face him, spreading its tentacles wide and showing its clashing beak. The highborn raced for the nearest wall as the beast gathered itself and leapt with a keening wail.

It landed less than five paces from Malus, reaching for him with a blur of fleshy whips just as the highborn grabbed up the second of the three oil lamps and flung it at the creature's head. The lamp burst apart, covering its bulbous skull with blazing oil, and the beast recoiled with a tortured shriek as its wet flesh sizzled in the flame. The highborn took no time to savour the hurt he'd caused. The moment the beast was distracted he ran for the western passage as fast as his feet could carry him.

Malus plunged into near-total darkness without the faintest idea where he was going. He sensed he was in another narrow corridor, the twin of the passageway to the east. Somewhere up ahead he heard faint shouts, so he gritted his teeth and ran towards the sound. His feet struck a pile of spilled bones and he stumbled through the remains, cursing under his breath. Thin howls echoed behind him as the hounds began sniffing for new prey.

He reached a crossroads lit by patches of grave mould and paused, his heart hammering in his chest. The shouts seemed to be coming from everywhere at once, overlaid with the unsettling cries of the Chaos beasts. Thinking quickly, he glanced at the stone floor and saw hints of wet tracks following the passage to the left.

The highborn ran on, swallowed once again by suffocating darkness. The passage curved before he knew it and he bounced along the wall for several feet before it straightened out again. A piercing cry rang out behind him. It sounded as if one of the hounds had reached the crossroads, just a dozen yards or so away. Malus broke into a run, not caring if he ran headlong into another wall.

After another dozen yards the passageway opened into a larger, broader antechamber, bordered by half a dozen crypts and connecting three other passageways. Malus's heart leapt when he saw a small globe of green witchfire glowing at the mouth of the southern corridor. Arleth Vann beckoned to him urgently. 'Hurry, my lord! They're right behind you!'

An impertinent reply rose to his mind, but Malus elected to save his laboured breathing for more important work. Sharp daggers of pain shot through his chest as he struggled to breathe, and whenever he stood still it felt as if the chamber would start to spin. Focusing his will, he took the deepest breath he could and ran on.

The assassin took the lead, racing down the twisting passageway as fleet as a deer. Arleth Vann pulled steadily away from Malus, even as the sounds of the pursuing hounds drew closer. He could hear their wet, slithering strides and the click of their claws on the stone as they bounded steadily closer.

Malus could only utter a breathless curse as the retainer darted around a sharp corner up ahead, taking the faint light with him. The sounds of pursuit echoed all around him, and he found himself dreading the whip-like touch of the hounds' lashing tentacles against his back.

He was so focused on the sounds behind him that he missed the turn ahead, crashing against the wall hard enough to lose what meagre wind he had. He rebounded from the stone and reeled like a drunkard with the gobbling cries of the hunters punishing his ears.

He staggered a handful of steps around the corner, and found another long corridor glowing with patches of mould. A broad, jagged fissure ran across the passageway.

Arleth Vann was nowhere to be seen.

Grunting against the pain and loss of air, Malus lurched down the hall. He could hear the whirring of the tentacles. The hounds were just around the corner.

'My lord!'

Malus started at the sound. The assassin's voice was coming from the fissure. 'Down here!' The retainer said. 'Quickly!'

There was no time to argue. The first hunter rounded the corner with a wailing roar and Malus threw himself at the fissure. Fierce pain bloomed in his chest as he hit the stone floor and half-slid, half-rolled into the jagged opening. Clawed tentacles scraped the stone just a hand span behind him.

Malus felt a powerful sense of vertigo as he tumbled over the edge. The fissure was no mere cleft in the ground. It was a narrow crevasse, plunging deep into the earth. Arleth Vann let out a warning shout as Malus flailed desperately at the close-set, irregular walls. Pain bloomed in his knees and elbows as he managed to wedge himself tightly enough to stop his fall. His boots hung over empty space, leaving Malus giddy with fear.

'My lord!' the assassin cried from above. 'Are you all right?'

'Just fine,' Malus snarled. 'These jagged rocks managed to break my fall.'

A sharp howl echoed in the darkness and clawed tentacles lashed against the sides of the crevasse as one of the hunters tried to reach its prey. 'Keep going down!' the assassin shouted. 'The beasts won't be able to reach us.'

A tentacle slapped the wall of the crevasse less than a hand span from Malus's head. The highborn frantically groped about with the toes of his boots, trying to find some kind of foothold, but nothing gave him enough purchase.

Then Malus felt a sharp impact as one of the beast's tentacles struck him in the cheek. Another tentacle brushed against his neck. With a desperate shout the highborn relaxed his limbs and plummeted into blackness.

STRONG HANDS PULLED at Malus's shoulders, rolling him onto his back. His eyes fluttered open, and then snapped shut as a jagged pain lanced through his chest. The highborn bit back a tortured groan, hearing the sound echo in the space around him.

'My lord?' Arleth Vann said. The assassin bent close, examining Malus's chest. 'You're bleeding again. I think you tore your wound open in the fall.'

'Where in the Dark Mother's name are we?' he panted, forcing his eyes open again and peering around in the subterranean gloom. Faint witchlight played on smooth walls and square beams, hewn from living rock. The stone ceiling of the passage was split crosswise by a ragged cleft, its edges still spilling a faint spray of earth from his long, uncontrolled plunge.

'We're safe, for now,' the assassin said. 'The hunters can't fit into the cleft, and their handlers won't abandon the beasts to come after us alone. They might even think we're dead.'

Gritting his teeth, Malus tried to sit upright, but another flare of sharp-edged pain forced him to abandon the effort with a frustrated snarl. He pressed his hand to his left side and it came away sticky with fresh blood. 'They may not be all that far wrong,' he snarled, 'but that doesn't answer my question. Where in the Dark Mother's name are we?'

'We're outside the Lodge of the Delvers,' Arleth Vann said, reaching his hands under Malus's arms. Slowly, carefully, he pulled the highborn upright. 'There may be only a handful of people left in the temple who even know this place exists.'

Biting back waves of pain, Malus allowed himself to be pulled to his feet. The passageway was low ceilinged, brushing the top of his head. The corridor itself ran as straight as an arrow, receding into blackness to the right. To the left, it ran for thirty paces and ended at a pair of stone doors hung on hinges of gleaming iron.

Arleth Vann helped Malus down the passage, towards the waiting portal. As they came closer, Malus could see that the surfaces of the doors were elaborately carved with underground scenes. Short, stout figures with braided beards came and went in fantastic scenes of subterranean splendour, bringing riches from the deeps and crafting them in works of cunning and art in a wondrous city chiselled from stone. It was like nothing the highborn had ever seen before.

He reached out and touched the surface of the doors, and the massive stone slabs swung inward on perfectly balanced hinges, revealing a broad, low-ceilinged room. A number of bare stone tables stood inside the chamber, each one short and broad. Four were arranged on each of the long sides of the room, their feet facing another, more ornately carved table in the room's centre. Another set of double doors stood at the chamber's opposite end.

Malus frowned. 'This is where the temple keeps its dwarf slaves?'

'In a manner of speaking,' the assassin replied. 'This is where the builders of the temple were entombed.'

The retainer helped Malus into the room, leading him to the central table and leaning the highborn against it. 'The elders entombed their dwarf slaves?' Malus asked, unsure at first if he'd heard the assassin correctly.

Arleth Vann nodded. 'It was a singular honour, a reward for their labours. Surely you noticed the crafts-manship of the building?'

'I had rather a lot on my mind at that point, but, yes, I noticed,' Malus replied irritably.

'That was just after the schism,' the assassin said, sur-veying the room appreciatively. 'With the dissenters driven out or slain, the first elders began work on the great temple in earnest. Over a hundred and twenty dwarf slaves laboured to build it, and construction took almost half a century. When the building was complete and the warpsword installed in its sanctum, the elders had the dwarfs build this splendid mau-soleum for themselves. They told the delvers that their work had earned them a place of everlasting honour among the faithful, and that their spirits would be venerated for all time.'

'And then?'

Arleth Vann paused. 'Once they had completed the crypt the elders had them all killed and interred within.'

'Mother of Night,' Malus gasped. 'A hundred and twenty dwarfs, cut down in their prime?' The waste of so much valuable chattel staggered the imagination. A highborn could build and outfit a raiding ship for the cost of just one dwarf slave. Short of dragon eggs there was no more expensive commodity in all of Naggaroth.

The assassin shrugged. 'Bad for them, but good for us. The lodge was built deep below the hill – deeper even than the Vermillion Gate – and no one has come here for millennia. Only a few records of the place remain in existence, buried in the archives of the temple library.' He nodded to himself. 'It's a perfect base of operations, really: defensible and difficult to reach, but close enough for us to reach the passage leading to Thel's old house and communicate with the loyalists in the city if we need to.' He sighed. 'Now I've just got to get back up into the tunnels and lead the rest of our people down here past those damned beasts,' he said. 'This could take time. Will you be all right until I get back?'

Malus had nothing to say. When Arleth Vann looked over at his master he found the highborn had passed out once more.

Chapter Sixteen
DARKNESS AND DOUBT

'The wound is grave, my lord.'

Malus's eyes fluttered open. He was lying on the stone slab in the antechamber of the dwarf tombs. Someone had stripped away his kheitan and robes, and gooseflesh raced along his bare shoulders and back.

Firelight danced along the walls and limned a robed and hooded figure at work beside one of the long tables at the highborn's right. Malus heard the sound of metal ringing faintly on stone as the figure laid out a series of small tools. The voice he'd heard was familiar, but he couldn't place it.

He tried to rise, fearful that the figure would see the daemon's taint upon him, but ropes pulled tight at his wrists, shoulders and forehead. Memories of his days in his father's tower sent a cold thrill of panic racing up his spine. 'What is going on?'

'There is an infection,' the figure said. 'Your lung has collapsed, and the wound is… corrupted. Something must be done quickly, or you will die.'

A shiver of fear wracked his body. He knew what the figure was trying to say. 'You are going to have to cut the infection away,' Malus said, unable to keep a note of dread from his voice. Have you any hushalta?'

'No,' the figure said, holding a small, curved blade up to the light. 'You must brace yourself for what must be done, my lord. It is the only way.'

The figure turned towards him, reaching for his chest with a long-fingered hand. Orange light shone on the blade's razor edge. Malus could feel the wound in his side begin to throb and his heart quicken in fearful anticipation.

'I will work very quickly,' the figure said. Fingers played across Malus's ribs, fluttering like spider's legs over the raw, bleeding wound. 'You may scream if you wish. It will not trouble me.'

Malus opened his mouth to reply, but the words were lost in a terrible groan as the figure's bare fingers pressed into the cut and spread wide, enlarging the tear. Hot blood welled up in the wound, flowing down his side as the knife went to work. A spear of white-hot pain lanced again and again into his chest, stealing his breath away. Just when it seemed he could take no more he saw the figure straighten, holding up a lump of pink, glistening meat in its hand. The hooded face looked down at him.

'You see? Almost the size of a fist. As I said, very grave.'

A shudder passed through Malus. 'I feel… cold…'

'Of course,' the figure replied, tossing the flesh onto the floor. 'That is to be expected, but it is a small price to pay for your health, is it not?'

The figure raised the knife again, but this time its bloodstained hand pulled at the hem of its own robes. With a flick of its wrist it pulled its robe open and revealed bare, gleaming ribs stained black with corruption. Nearly all of the internal organs were missing, save for a wrinkled sac of flesh pulsing close to the breastbone.

'Nearly done,' the figure said. As it spoke, it reached up into its chest cavity and cut away the tattered, oozing remnant. 'The wound is painful, but it will heal, and then you and I will be stronger than ever.'

Malus tried to move, but the bonds held him fast. He screamed, shouting curses at the figure as it bent low and pushed the corrupted tissue into the highborn's gaping wound. At once, he felt the alien flesh wriggle and squirm inside him – and worse, he felt his organs heave and rise up to meet it.

The hooded head turned, close enough for Malus to see the face sheltered within. It was *his* face, pale and perfect, devoid of any daemonic taint. Only the eyes – black orbs like shards of the Outer Darkness itself – suggested the depths of the corruption that seethed within.

Tz'arkan smiled, showing jagged, obsidian fangs.

'You'll be a new man before you know it,' the daemon said with a gruesome chuckle.

'CAREFUL! CAREFUL! HOLD him tight!'

Malus awoke with a shout, struggling against the grip of the four druchii who held him pinned to the stone slab. Arleth Vann loomed over him, pressing a hand to his clammy forehead and forcing a small vial between his lips. 'Drink,' he said, his voice hard and unyielding.

The taste of burnt copper flooded Malus's mouth. He gagged and tried to spit the hushalta out, but the assassin cursed fiercely and covered the highborn's mouth. Glaring at the retainer, he reluctantly swallowed the healing draught and forced himself to relax.

Arleth Vann studied Malus's eyes closely for a moment, and nodded in satisfaction. 'All right. You can let go,' he told the druchii, and the loyalists withdrew. They eyed Malus fearfully as they returned to sentry positions on either side of the dwarf lodge's entryway.

Malus raised a trembling hand and pressed it against his side. The wound ached fiercely. He pulled open his grimy robe and peered at his ribs, discovering the cut scabbed over and beginning to shrink. The black bruises remained, however, giving him the look of a week-old corpse. His mouth still tingled with the sharp taste of copper, and his joints creaked like dried leather. 'Water,' he said hoarsely.

The retainer lifted a leather water bottle to the highborn's lips, and Malus drank greedily. It was warm and brackish, but he savoured it like rare wine. When his fierce thirst abated somewhat, he glared at the grim faced assassin. 'You've been drugging me,' he croaked.

'You were going to die otherwise, Scourge or no,' Arleth Vann replied.

Malus drew a deep, slow breath, his eyes narrowing as he tested the extent of his injury. 'How long have you kept me out?'

'Three days.'

'Mother of Night!' Malus seethed, grabbing a handful of his retainer's robe. 'Have you any idea what you've done? Rhulan has been waiting outside the wall all this time! You may have damned us all!'

'Rhulan is not at the wall,' the assassin replied. 'In fact, I can't say for certain that he's even in the city any more.'

The highborn's anger faded. 'He hasn't rallied the warriors of the temple?'

Arleth Vann shrugged. 'If he tried, they evidently didn't listen,' he said gravely. 'I made my way out through the house of Cyrvan Thel the night after we reached the lodge, hoping to locate some food and other supplies,' he explained. 'The city had gone mad. Bloody riots were raging in the streets and much of the city was burning. From what I could discern, the temple warriors are holed up in scattered pockets all across Har Ganeth, cut off from one another by the raging mob. Certainly no one is directing their efforts to regroup and reach the temple.'

Malus took his hand away from Arleth Vann and slowly, painfully, he forced himself upright. The pain gave him something to focus on beside the rising tide of dismay that lapped at his brain. 'So Rhulan and Mereia ran afoul of the riots,' he said.

'It is possible. There are bodies everywhere,' the assassin replied. 'Or they might be trapped with one of the isolated war bands and can't find a way to communicate with the rest.'

The highborn gave his retainer an appraising stare. 'You don't think so,' he said.

Arleth Vann weighed his reply carefully. 'If he isn't dead, I think he's escaped the city,' he said with a sigh. 'Perhaps his courage failed him. Who knows? You heard him in the crypts. He thought Urial couldn't be beaten.'

'Damnation,' Malus spat. 'I thought at least Mereia would have been made of sterner stuff. We needed that diversion to help us reach Urial.'

The assassin straightened and set the water bottle on a nearby table. 'In a way, the temple warriors may be serving us better in the city than they would outside the temple gates,' he said. 'As long as the fighting continues, Urial must divide his forces between the temple fortress and the riots in the streets. He doesn't dare ease up on the pressure and allow the war bands to link together.'

Malus considered this. 'How easily can you move about the catacombs?'

'I can come and go as I wish, so long as I'm careful,' the assassin replied. The tunnel network is just too vast and interconnected to patrol effectively. I still hear Urial's hunters prowling through the crypts, but in truth they are poor trackers. So long as one is patient and quiet, they can be circumvented.'

'All right,' the highborn said with a sigh. He suddenly felt completely drained, as if the mere effort of sitting upright had consumed every ounce of his energy. 'How many of us are left?'

'Eight, counting you and me,' Arleth Vann replied. 'After the flight from the crypt I was able to find out where six of the volunteers were hiding and led them down here one at a time. Khaine alone knows what happened to the other two.'

The highborn nodded. His eyelids were getting heavy. He realised that it was because of the damned hushalta. 'No more mothers' milk,' he mumbled. 'No time to waste. Find where Urial is hiding... how he's being guarded...'

Arleth Vann said something in reply, but the assassin's voice seemed to fade into the distance as the healing drug pulled him under.

WHEN HE AWOKE again, Arleth Vann was gone.

Malus was ravenous. He took that as a good sign. The highborn lay on the stone slab in the centre of the dwarf lodge for several long minutes, gauging the stiffness of his limbs and the degree of pain in his chest. Finally, he summoned his resolve and swung his legs off the side of the table.

His knees nearly gave way beneath him when he slid to the stone floor. The sentries at the door stirred as Malus caught himself on the edge of the table. 'I'm all right,' he said, waving them back to their places. In point of fact, he felt anything but.

Malus looked around the chamber. Several small oil lamps flickered on three of the long side tables, and the assassin's water bottle still lay nearby. The door opposite the lodge's entrance stood open, and he thought he heard faint sounds echoing from beyond.

He reached for the water bottle and took several deep draughts, wincing at the vile taste. 'What time is it?' Malus asked the sentries.

The loyalists looked to one another and shrugged. 'Night time, I think,' one of them said. 'I no longer know what the hour is.'

Malus nodded thoughtfully. Then, gritting his teeth with effort, he walked towards the open doorway.

Beyond the low threshold he found himself in a long, irregular chamber that stretched off to his right. The features were a strange mixture of square-cut pillars and straight walls connecting small, rounded niches that had been carefully shaped to resemble natural caverns. In each niche the stone floor rose up to form a squat, rectangular tomb, inscribed with angular dwarf runes and overlaid with arcane magical sigils that glittered in the lamplight. There was no gilt-work or precious gems, no grave goods or mummified slaves, but the sheer scope and craftsmanship of the crypt was staggering. The caverns and their connecting passages had been hollowed out of solid rock, and the crypts constructed with surpassing skill.

Malus could see that the four tombs closest to him were open. He limped slowly to the nearest one, noticing a name inscribed at the foot of the stone coffin in druchast. *Thogrun Hammerhand*, it read, *Stonemaster*. A broad-shouldered dwarf clad in a slave's simple woollen robes lay in the coffin. His red beard was thick and stiff as wire, and his skin was the colour of granite. Only the faintest signs of decay could be seen around the stonemaster's seamed eyes and rounded nose. It was as if he'd been laid in the coffin only a few days before. The edges of the gaping cut that bisected the stonemaster's throat were only just beginning to shrivel. A veritable pall of sorcery hung over the figure, encasing it in a tight weave of magical energy.

More sounds echoed through the chamber from its far side: the scrape of stone, mutters, and faint, tired sounding curses. Frowning, the highborn sought out the source of the noise.

The room curved slightly to the right, following a logic that perhaps only a dwarf could appreciate. Malus walked past nine more crypts before the walls of the room narrowed to form a short, broad entryway into a connecting chamber. Two loyalists worked in front of the entryway, hauling heavy, rectangular stone panels into place to form a kind of defensive breastwork facing back the way Malus had come. They looked up at the highborn's approach and paused in their labour, wiping their faces with grimy rags.

Malus reviewed their work and nodded appreciatively, noticing that the stone panels were the thick lids used to seal the dwarf tombs.

'I see my retainer has been keeping everyone busy,' he said.

One of the men nodded. 'This is the last of them, my dread lord,' he said, a little breathlessly. 'There are more like this going all the way back to the prime chamber. We didn't have much to work with, since this place is practically built like a fortress already. A handful of people could hold off an army down here if they wanted to.'

Malus considered the crude fortifications and had to agree. With multiple, well-protected bastions to retreat to, they could take a fearsome toll of Urial's zealots if discovered. His half-brother's Chaos-spawned monsters were another matter, but he didn't think it wise to point that out. 'Where is our camp?' he asked.

The loyalist gestured over his shoulder. 'Five chambers further back, my lord,' he said, 'just outside the prime chamber. There's some food and water there if you're hungry. Your man brought in supplies a couple of days ago.'

Malus nodded again and carefully picked his way over the defensive barriers. 'With luck, we won't have to put these to the test,' he said, 'but carry on, all the same.' The men went back to work as the highborn disappeared into the chamber beyond.

The grave lodge wound back and forth through the rock beneath the hill like the track of a serpent. Each burial chamber was slightly curved, running away at an angle from the one before it. Possibly it was a technique to allow such a large number of tombs to fit within the stone confines of the region, but Malus suspected there was a ritual purpose to the layout, as if the curving lines of the chambers formed a sigil or sacred rune carved into the undying rock. At each entryway the druchii had built a defensive position using the lids of the tombs found nearby. One or two oil lamps sputtered in each chamber, providing just enough light to travel by.

By the time he'd passed through the second burial chamber the sounds of work behind him were swallowed by the stone walls, leaving Malus wrapped in funereal silence. For a brief time he felt truly alone, passing from shadow to shadow like a ghost amid the broken tombs, and it soothed him after a fashion.

'Did you have pleasant dreams?' whispered the daemon inside his head.

Malus paused at the entrance of the next burial chamber. Was it the fourth, or the fifth? He hadn't been keeping track. 'I dreamt of stuffing you into a chamber pot and throwing you into the deep sea,' he growled.

Tz'arkan chuckled. 'Dreams of vengeance and spite. I should have expected no less.' The daemon uncoiled itself within the highborn's breast. 'What of your wound? Are you healing well, little druchii?'

Malus's hands clenched into fists. 'You should know better than I, daemon. Soon I'll be no better than the wretches confined in these tombs, infused with so much sorcery that not even the worms will touch me.'

Obscene laughter raked along the inside of Malus's ribs. 'Such childishness! Such vanity! Your body has recovered from a mortal wound in less than a week. There are men who would think that an awesome gift, one worth almost any price.'

The highborn entered the next chamber, picking up his pace. 'The difference is that I see through your deceptions,' he replied. 'Every time I open myself to your power I let you increase your hold over me.'

'I have your soul, Darkblade.' The daemon sounded genuinely amused. 'What greater hold over you do I need?'

'Then why this?' Malus pulled open his robes, revealing the glossy, black scabs on his chest and the deep bruises in his flesh. 'Your gifts are making me into an abomination!'

Tz'arkan sighed. 'No, they are making you worthy of the fate that awaits you. Do not dissemble, Malus. I know your heart's deepest desires. You crave power.

You dream of the day when all of Naggaroth bows before you.'

Malus continued on in silence, stalking angrily past the dwarf tombs.

'Did you think that mere treachery and cunning would be enough to supplant one such as the Witch King? You will need power beyond that of the greatest druchii heroes. That is what I offer you, yet you reject it at every turn.'

'I don't feel stronger, daemon. I feel... hollowed out.' Malus said. 'I feel twisted and diseased. You're corrupting me.'

'To what purpose?'

'To enslave me! What else?'

The daemon laughed. 'Stupid, stupid Darkblade! Why would I do such a thing? I know your fate. I laid its foundations millennia ago. In that sense, you were a slave to my wishes from the moment you were born. For the sake of argument, let's assume you are right. Let's say that I am subverting your will with each touch of my power. Tell me then: how is it you continue to resist me, even as your body weakens and your foes gain in strength? Have you lost one whit of your obstinate personality since you entered my temple in the north?'

Malus held his tongue. Part of him hungered for the daemon's power, like a drunkard ached for the taste of wine. If Tz'arkan didn't know it, he wasn't about to volunteer the information.

'Nothing to say? I thought not,' the daemon replied smugly.

The highborn crossed the dimly lit burial chamber and entered the next. Things were different here. More lamps burned along the curving chamber, outlining a meagre camp of bedrolls and cloth bags lying haphazardly in a dense cluster in the centre of the room. The priestess and a druchii novitiate lay wrapped in their cloaks, sleeping soundly on the stone floor. It struck Malus that after all this time he still didn't know the young priestess's name.

'So what will you do, Malus?' Tz'arkan asked. 'Will you continue to suffer needlessly, or will you allow me to renew your strength?'

Moving silently, the highborn picked his way among the snoring loyalists and sought out the far end of the room. Another set of defensive barricades had been placed there, but Malus also saw that a large stone door sealed this portal. Runes had been carved into the door's surface and inlaid with molten silver. Powerful charms and spirit wards radiated from the barrier, tingling across the highborn's skin.

Malus climbed over the barricades and carefully pushed the door open.

There were no oil lamps within. He pushed the stone door wide, letting the illumination at his back flow into the small room before him. It was similar to the burial niches he'd passed along the way, fashioned like an artificial cavern and containing a single tomb. Unlike the rest, the stone coffin was still sealed, and its surface was covered in a profusion of layered sigils and spells. *Gothar Grimmson*, the inscription read, *Ironmaster*.

Malus stepped inside the prime chamber and, after a moment, pushed the door closed. Darkness and silence swallowed him whole.

'How do I know you're telling me the truth?'

The daemon chuckled. 'Lies are for the weak and the stupid, Darkblade. I have little need of them. I have said this before, and I will say it again: I have never lied to you, ever.'

'You haven't told me the entire truth, either.'

'That, Malus, is a very different thing,' Tz'arkan replied archly. 'I've told you everything you needed to know at the time.'

'So what aren't you telling me now?'

The daemon paused. 'Nothing of import, I assure you.'

Malus smiled coldly. 'Then you'll understand if I look for answers elsewhere.'

'What does that mean?' the daemon hissed.

Wrapped in concealing darkness, Malus raised his hand and felt for the cold silver band that circled the finger of his left hand. The sentry had told him it was night outside, and as near as he could reckon the moon would be waxing bright.

Of course, Eldire hadn't bothered to explain to him how the damned ring actually worked. Lacking any other ideas, he clenched his fist and focused his will into a single word.

Mother.

Malus felt a ghostly breeze touch his face. He smelled the faint scent of ashes. Suddenly the daemon wrapped tightly around his heart, making him wince.

'Malus, what are you doing?' Tz'arkan asked sharply. 'What foolishness is this?'

The daemon's grip was relaxing and its voice fading. A strange, silvery glow, like faint moonlight, began to fill the small chamber. Malus felt his aches diminish, yet at the same time his body turned leaden and cold.

The light intensified, pushing back the shadows and drawing the sharp outline of a figure standing next to the ancient tomb. From one moment to the next the figure took on more and more solidity, swelling from little more than a silhouette to a tall, square-shouldered woman wearing the black robes of a seer. Long, white hair hung in a thick braid to below her waist, bound at the tip with a band of gold. She was statuesque and regal, with a face that was both beautiful and coldly forbidding. Wreathed in pearlescent light, she studied her surroundings with detached interest, entirely unfazed by his sorcerous summons.

'Eldire,' Malus said, inclining his head respectfully.

She turned at the sound of his voice. 'Hello, my son,' she replied. Her voice sounded clearly in the room, although it had a curious echo to it, as if she was speaking from the bottom of a well. Eldire's body remained somewhat ethereal, like a ghost's, and he could see the faint outline of the dwarf tomb through her vaporous form.

'It has been some time, Malus,' Eldire continued. 'I had begun to fear the worst.'

The thought made Malus chuckle. 'As if a seer of your power would have any need to worry.'

'Nothing is ever certain, child, especially where divination is concerned,' she said coolly. 'We deal in possibilities. Where you are concerned, the threads of fate are more tangled than most.'

The highborn frowned. 'That doesn't sound encouraging.'

'On the contrary, it means you are finally attempting to create your own fate instead of having one shaped for you,' she said. 'Of course, this necessarily means that things are less certain than they were before.'

'So you're saying I'm flirting with disaster.'

'More so than usual, yes,' Eldire said. Her lips quirked into the briefest of smiles.

'I'll try to take heart from that.'

'Good,' she said, turning to regard the tomb beside her. 'Now perhaps you can explain what you are doing in a dwarf crypt when you should be at Har Ganeth looking for the warpsword.'

And so he explained as best he could, describing how he'd finally gained entrance to the City of Executioners and then found himself caught up in the holy war waged between the temple loyalists and Tyran's zealots. He told her of the debacle in the sanctum and their retreat into the catacombs.

Then he spoke of the wound he'd been given, and the power of Tz'arkan's hold over him.

'He claims to be strengthening me,' Malus said bitterly. 'It makes some sense, come to think of it, but is it the truth? What other reason can there be, if not to enslave me completely?'

Eldire considered all that Malus had said. 'The daemon speaks the truth, as far as it goes,' she said carefully. 'It is true that Tz'arkan has stolen your soul, and that corrupting your body would not gain it any more influence over you than it already has, but I do not think it seeks to control you at this point. It intends to *become* you.'

A chill coursed down the highborn's spine. 'What do you mean?'

'Tz'arkan is transforming you, slowly and surely, to become a daemonhost,' the seer replied. 'Normally such a process takes a great deal of time, but your case is hardly normal, is it?'

'So the daemon seeks to… what? Wear me, like a glove?'

'In a manner of speaking, yes. Your soul will be destroyed, and Tz'arkan will take its place.'

Malus looked down at his chest. 'If the daemon's energies can heal me like this, how far gone am I?'

Eldire glided silently forwards and reached a ghostly hand towards the wound. Her expression darkened. 'You walk a knife's edge, my son,' she said. 'Chaos energies seethe within your flesh, but you have not yet been wholly consumed. Your will remains strong, and while it does you can keep the daemon at bay a little longer.'

Malus nodded, even though he felt anything but strong. Did he dare tell her how his limbs trembled at the thought of the daemon's power? He craved the icy rush of Tz'arkan's gifts, and he feared, deep in his bones, that he could not beat his half-brother without them.

'The battle ahead will be difficult,' he said. 'How will I be able to confront Urial alone and defeat him when he wields the warpsword?'

'How should I know?' Eldire asked irritably. 'I'm hundreds of leagues away. I've never set foot in Har Ganeth, much less examined the sword. You will simply have to find a way.'

Malus sighed, folding his arms tightly across his chest. 'Why couldn't you simply turn up and solve everything with a bit of arcane insight, like the sorcerers in all the legends?'

She leaned close. 'If we could truly do that, my son, we wouldn't have need of people like you,' the seer replied. 'Find a way. Your soul depends on it.'

'With hate, all things are possible,' he said, wishing the saying still had the power to reassure him.

Eldire smiled, brushing an insubstantial hand against his cheek, and then stepped away. She studied the tomb once more. 'Why so much effort for dwarfs?' she asked.

'It was a reward for building the temple,' Malus said sourly. 'A hundred and twenty prime dwarf slaves. Such a waste of very expensive flesh.'

The seer extended a long finger, tracing the sigils inscribed into the tomb. 'Dead, but their spirits remain,' she said. 'These are powerful wards of binding. A great deal of sorcery was invested in these tombs.'

'Who can fathom the wisdom of priests?' Malus asked with a shrug.

'Indeed,' Eldire admitted with a sigh.

'Has word reached the Hag about Urial?'

'No, not yet,' she said. 'If the priestesses at the temple know it, they are keeping the news to themselves. You are right of course, once Malekith learns that Urial has the sword, he will march on Har Ganeth. A fast rider could reach the Hateful Road from Har Ganeth in less than a week.'

Malus imagined Rhulan galloping down the Slavers' Road for all he was worth. 'And Isilvar?'

Eldire looked back at Malus. 'The Drachau has proclaimed him a hero for saving the city,' she said. 'His power grows by the day.'

'As powerful as Lurhan?'

'No, but powerful enough, in time,' she said. 'Forget him and Hag Graef, my son. Your future lies elsewhere.'

'My future is mine to decide, mother,' Malus said. 'You told me that. When the time is right, I will return to the Hag. I have unfinished business there.'

Eldire opened her mouth to respond, but thought better of it. She shrugged. 'As you wish, child. First, however, you must deal with Urial. That, I fear, will be challenge enough.'

With that, she was gone. There was no gesture of farewell – Eldire simply faded like a ghost, taking the penumbral light with her.

Malus was swallowed in darkness and doubt.

Chapter Seventeen
SECRETS OF THE SWORD

WHEN ARLETH VANN returned to the lodge he found Malus sitting on the tomb of Gothar Grimmson, picking at a few scraps of stale bread and a piece of stringy meat spread out on a greasy cloth in his lap. An oil lamp sputtered on the top of the stone coffin, near the dwarf's feet.

The highborn glanced up as the assassin slipped quietly into the small crypt. 'Where did you find this awful stuff?' he asked, grimacing in distaste. He pulled a thread of the dark, stringy meat from the cloth and reluctantly put it in his mouth. 'If I didn't know better I'd say you robbed the temple kennels.'

'Nothing so fancy,' Arleth Vann replied.

Malus paused in mid-chew. 'Do I want to know?'

'Almost certainly not.'

The highborn eyed the rest of the food with dismay. 'Damnation,' he muttered wearily, and forced himself to continue eating.

'How are your injuries, my lord?'

'Better,' the highborn answered, hoping he sounded sincere. 'Or well enough for me to get out of this damned mausoleum, at any rate. What have you learned?'

The assassin glanced back into the chamber beyond, checking to see if anyone might be listening. Apparently satisfied, he sank to his haunches and steepled his fingers under his chin while he collected his thoughts.

'It's getting harder to move around the temple grounds,' he began. 'The zealots have killed most of the temple novitiates and slaves, and converted the rest. Those that remain have been given a brand in the centre of their foreheads in the shape of a sword. I think Tyran has done this to make infiltrators easier to spot.'

Malus considered the news. 'Are there still zealots in the fortress grounds?'

'Yes. I'm not certain how many, but most of them know one another on sight at this point.'

'I see,' the highborn replied. He pulled out his dagger and began sawing at the stale bread. 'Any news of the temple assassins?'

Arleth Vann shook his head. 'Incredibly, they remain in conclave. I suppose Urial's move has complicated their decision somewhat.'

'That doesn't sound good. If they were solidly for Rhulan and the loyalists they would have made up their minds by now.'

The retainer shrugged. He drew his own stained cloth parcel from the folds of his robe and unwrapped it across his knees. There was a piece of flatbread inside and a handful of small, dried fish. 'That's true, but at least they aren't actively opposed to us yet.'

'True enough,' Malus said. He stopped sawing at the bread and inspected his work, surprised that he'd barely made an impression on the stale lump. Frowning, he set the bread on the top of the tomb and hammered at it with the pommel of his knife. The blows made no mark at all. He held the lump up to the lamplight. 'If I could put a strap on this I'd use it as a shield,' he muttered darkly.

Arleth Vann pulled a small bottle of water from his belt and set it by his knee. Then he reached into the voluminous folds of his left sleeve and produced a small, clay jar. The assassin broke the wax seal around the lid of the jar and pulled off the lid, sniffing experimentally. Satisfied, he dipped one of the fish in the jar and popped it into his mouth, chewing contentedly.

'What have you learned about Urial and Yasmir?'

The assassin frowned, switching back to business. 'Nothing good, I'm afraid. It appears that your half-brother has taken his bride-to-be and retreated back into the Sanctum of the Sword. Only Tyran and a few other zealots are allowed inside to confer with him, and the temple is heavily guarded.'

Malus leaned back against the foot of the coffin. 'How heavily guarded?'

'I can only guess based on what I was able to overhear, but I would say at least a dozen zealots stand guard at the entrance to the sanctum, and twice that number on the stairs leading from the chapel on the ground floor.' The assassin shook his head. 'We can't fight our way through all that without raising an alarm.'

The highborn stared at the stone floor. He knew that there was a way. With the daemon's help he could carve through the true believers like a whirlwind, but Eldire's words dogged him. *You walk upon a knife's edge.*

'Surely there are secret passageways leading into the sanctum? Every other building on the hilltop seems riddled with them.'

Arleth Vann shook his head. 'The sanctum was created specifically to safeguard the sword and serve as the site for the temple's holiest rites. There is only one way in and out.'

Frustration gnawed at Malus, setting his teeth on edge. He leaned his head back and knocked it lightly against the tomb. 'There has to be another way in. Think, damn you!'

'Not unless you know a way to dig through dwarf-crafted stone,' the assassin replied grimly.

Malus froze. 'What did you say?'

The assassin frowned. 'I wasn't trying to be impertinent. I just said that unless you know a way to dig through dwarf-crafted stone–'

'That's it!' Malus said leaning forwards intently, 'Dwarf-crafted stone.' The highborn tapped his lower lip thoughtfully. Slowly, he turned and looked back at the tomb. 'Blessed Mother of Night,' he whispered in wonder.

Arleth Vann eyed his master warily. Surreptitiously, he picked up the jar of yellow sauce and sniffed it suspiciously, before setting it down again. 'Is everything all right, my lord?'

Malus stared thoughtfully at the foot of the coffin. 'Why is this room called the prime chamber?' he asked.

The assassin shrugged. 'That's not its real name. Dwarf burial rites are very secret affairs. Bodies are prepared in the antechamber yonder, away- from the prying eyes of all but their kinsmen, and then laid to rest in their crypts.' He looked around the small room. 'I called this the prime chamber because there's just one tomb in here, unlike the others.'

'So this slave was someone important?'

'Most likely. A master of his craft, perhaps.'

Malus nodded, feeling his heart quicken. 'And the sanctum is made of stone? All of it?'

Arleth Vann could not help but give his master a condescending stare. 'Of course, my lord. Dwarfs don't build with wood. Every bit is cut stone, cunningly fitted together. What *are* you driving at?'

Once again, Eldire's words echoed in Malus's ears. *Why so much effort for dwarfs?*

The highborn reached up and touched the inscription on the tomb. 'Tell me,' he said, looking back at his retainer with a dawning smile, 'if the temple was built entirely of stone, what did the elders need with an ironmaster?'

Arleth Vann's eyes narrowed warily. 'I don't understand.'

'Gothar Grimmson here is an ironmaster, not a stone carver,' Malus said. His mind raced as he began putting the pieces together. He rose to his feet and began to pace the small room. 'What if the sword Urial took from the sanctum isn't the actual Warpsword of Khaine?'

The assassin was too stunned to speak for a moment. 'That's absurd,' he sputtered.

'Is it?' Malus asked. 'You said that the sanctum was built to safeguard the sword, but from what? The relic had been in the possession of the elders for centuries. Why the sudden need to enshrine it under layers of sorcerous wards?'

'I…' The retainer's voice faded as he wrestled with the notion. 'I don't know. Perhaps the elders feared the schism leaders would try to steal the sword at some point.'

'Or perhaps they already had!' the highborn exclaimed. 'You said that the five zealots who volunteered to kill the temple leaders were never heard from again. Doesn't that seem odd to you? If they had been caught or killed, wouldn't the elders have wanted to make a public spectacle of their deaths?'

'I suppose so.'

'Then it's reasonable to assume they weren't caught. So what happened to them?' Malus spun on his heel, his stride quickening along with his thoughts. 'What if they realised that their assassination attempt was doomed to fail, and decided on another course of action? Perhaps they couldn't kill the elders, but they could deprive them of the cult's most prized relic! So they took the sword and vanished.' The highborn nodded to himself. 'That's why the elders sent their warriors rampaging through the city afterwards. They weren't looking for the zealot leaders so much as they were looking for the warpsword itself!'

'But we know the assassins never returned from the fortress,' the retainer said. 'So where did they go?'

'Where else? Through the Vermillion Gate.'

Arleth Vann froze, a rebuttal dying on his lips. 'Blessed Murderer,' he swore softly. 'Of course.'

'One can imagine how frantic the elders were when they learned the sword had been taken,' Malus said. 'How could they claim to be the true servants of Khaine without the blade in their possession? What would become of their alliance with the Witch King? The elders may have survived the assassination attempt, but the zealots had dealt them a mortal blow all the same.

'Then a very strange thing happened. Days turned to weeks, and weeks into months, and nothing more was heard about the sword. If the zealots had it, they would have used it to discredit the temple publicly. So the elders realised they'd been given a sort of reprieve. For the moment, no one in Naggaroth knew of the warpsword's fate, so they hatched a desperate plan to save themselves.'

'They made a copy of the blade,' Arleth Vann said, his voice tinged with wonder.

'Exactly,' the highborn said. He patted the foot of the tomb. 'They had Gothar here make a perfect copy of the relic, and then made a grand show of installing it in the temple. The sanctum wasn't built to safeguard the sword at all, but to protect the temple's darkest secret.'

'That's why they killed the dwarf slaves,' the assassin said. 'They had to silence Gothar so he couldn't betray them, and murdered the rest to camouflage the act.'

'The elders even went so far as to bind their spirits into these tombs so that no sorcerer could question them later,' Malus said with admiration. 'That's why the elders kept Urial at arm's length all this time. Even if he had been the true Scourge, they couldn't give him what they didn't have.'

'So Rhulan and the other elders knew the truth?'

'Yes. That's why he told us we couldn't fight Urial directly – because the legend says the bearer of the warpsword can't be defeated in battle. If we put the lie to that claim, the rest of the deception would have begun to unravel.'

The assassin nodded thoughtfully. 'It all makes sense,' he said. Although from the sound of his voice he was loathe to believe it. Suddenly he straightened. 'Do you think Urial knows he doesn't have the real sword?'

'Honestly? I don't think so,' Malus said. 'Not yet, at least. Until the blade is put to the test he has no reason to think it is a replacement.'

'That's why Rhulan hasn't rallied the temple warriors. He doesn't dare spur a real confrontation with the zealots, despite the fact that he knows he has a good chance of defeating them.' The assassin shook his head ruefully. 'What madness!'

'Indeed,' Malus said. He continued to pace, tapping his chin furiously. 'Mother of Night,' he swore. 'The sword could be anywhere in the world. How are we going to find out where the assassins took it?' The rush of triumph he'd felt as all the pieces of the puzzle clicked into place turned to bitter frustration. For a moment he thought he'd found a way to cheat the

daemon and claim the sword without having to confront Urial or Yasmir at all. He struggled with a flood
of hopeless fury, so preoccupied that at first he didn't
notice Arleth Vann had spoken. Malus caught the
questioning look in the assassin's gaze and paused in
mid-stride. 'What?' he asked.

'I said that I think I know a way,' Arleth Vann
replied.

THE ASSASSIN'S RIGHT hand shot up and the small party
froze in place. Malus and three of the surviving six loyalists settled onto their haunches, hands tightening on
their weapons. Darkness flowed towards them as
Arleth Vann closed his left hand, muffling the small
globe of witchfire he'd conjured.

For several long moments Malus heard nothing but
the sound of his own heart labouring in his ears. Then
he heard a faint, keening wail, skirling out of the
blackness somewhere up ahead of them. Two of the
druchii behind Malus shifted nervously at the ominous howl. One let out a fearful moan.

'Hsst!' Malus whispered threateningly. 'Not a
sound!'

No one moved. Malus caught himself holding his
breath, straining to hear the telltale signs of discovery.
A minute passed, and then another.

Finally Arleth Vann relaxed, opening his hand and
filling the narrow tunnel with cold light. He turned
his body slightly so he could glance back at Malus.
'The Chaos beasts are hunting somewhere up ahead,
but they don't seem to be in our path,' he whispered
to the highborn.

Malus nodded. He hadn't the faintest idea how the assassin could tell, but he knew better than to argue with the druchii's keen senses. 'How far to the citadel?' he asked.

'Another few minutes, if all goes well.'

'Let's go, then.'

The retainer rose silently to his feet. Malus followed suit. Behind him, the axe-wielding priestess – whose name he'd finally learned was Niryal – and two more loyalists made ready to move. They had been working their way through the tunnels beneath the hill for more than an hour, climbing from the deepest levels where the dwarf lodge was located and taking a circuitous route to the subterranean chambers of the Citadel of Bone. They had been forced to crouch in the darkness and hold their breath many times, while Urial's hunters prowled nearby, but so far the assassin had succeeded in leading them away from the horrific beasts. Arleth Vann's assessment had been correct; the monsters were fearsome killers but very poor trackers. Had the zealots turned a pack of nauglir loose in the tunnels the loyalists would have been in serious trouble.

Not for the first time, Malus wondered how Spite was faring in the war-torn city. Was he still being fed and boarded in the highborn district's nauglir pens, or had hunger or misadventure driven the cold one into the streets? He had no real fear for the nauglir's safety – the warbeast was more than a match for any but the most heavily armed war bands prowling Har Ganeth's streets. It was the safety of the relics in the cold one's saddlebags that gave the highborn cause for concern.

He was haunted by visions of the cold one clawing its way through the doors of its pen and tearing its saddlebags off in the process, or having them ripped open in a fight and spilling their contents onto the street.

One thing he was coming to realise about sorcerous relics was that finding them was only half the challenge. *Keeping* them for any length of time was just as hard, if not harder.

If the zealots had stolen the sword and escaped through the Vermillion Gate hundreds of years ago, Malus hadn't the faintest idea how to track them, but Arleth Vann knew of a library in the Citadel of Bone that might contain some useful clues. All they had to do was slip past Urial's hunters and zealot patrols and infiltrate one of the most important buildings in the temple fortress undetected. As ever, the assassin volunteered to make the attempt alone, but Malus had insisted on sending a small party instead. There was simply too much at stake to risk sending a single man, even one as skilled as Arleth Vann. If anything went awry and Urial guessed their interest in the library, the would-be Scourge could place it under such heavy guard that they wouldn't be able to get anywhere near it – or worse, lay a sorcerous ambush to catch them unawares the next time they tried to reach it.

Holding the globe of witchlight over his head, Arleth Vann set off down the narrow, bone-strewn corridor. Many of the crypt passages had been thrown into disarray by the passage of the Chaos beasts. Skeletons had been scattered from their shelves and crushed to powder beneath the hunters' leonine paws.

Some of the fresher ones even had the skulls and long bones split open in a vain search for meat. The assassin picked his way carefully among the drifts of bone and rotted cloth, leaving Malus and the loyalists to follow in his footsteps and watch every dark niche and side passage with a growing feeling of unease. No one spoke, but everyone shared the same sense of dread. The longer they spent in the tunnels, the greater the chance that the hunters would catch their scent. Sooner or later their luck would run out.

Arleth Vann moved unerringly through the maze of tunnels, pausing only occasionally to check his bearings at corridor junctions or antechambers. From what Malus could tell Niryal and the other temple servants were just as disorientated as he was. All he knew for certain was that they were close to the surface. The corridors showed signs of frequent traffic and were largely free of cobwebs and layers of dust. The highborn was surprised at how eager he was to get above ground, even for a short time. It had been almost six days since he'd been out in the open air, and the claustrophobic weight of the catacombs was beginning to tell on his nerves.

Long minutes passed, and Malus's impatience grew. One passageway led to another and every sound set the highborn's teeth on edge. They heard no more hunting howls echoing in the blackness. Did that mean the beasts had moved further away, or were they creeping stealthily closer, waiting until the very last moment before rushing at their prey in a cacophony of terrible, whistling shrieks?

Finally, Malus could take no more. He quickened his steps slightly, enough to catch up to Arleth Vann and pluck at a corner of his robe. The assassin stopped.

'You said just a few more minutes,' Malus whispered.

'We're nearly there,' the retainer replied. He pointed into the darkness ahead. 'There is a chamber just a few more yards that way. Beyond it will be a ramp leading up into the citadel's lower rooms.'

Malus took a deep breath, forcing himself to relax. 'All right,' he said, 'lead on.'

The assassin slipped quietly along the corridor, and within a few minutes more Malus saw the glow of the witchlight expand to fill a broad chamber just ahead. It was a rectangular room almost twenty paces across on its long sides, and its walls and corners were piled with skeletons and crumbling skulls. Passageways led off to the left and right, and a long, sloping ramp led upwards from the opposite side of the chamber. Arleth Vann stepped to one side as he entered the room, and Malus rushed past with the loyalists hot on his heels.

'Wait, my lord!' the assassin hissed in warning. 'Something's not right–'

Frowning, the highborn turned to ask what he was talking about, but his question went unasked as a chorus of high-pitched screams shattered the dank air.

Chapter Eighteen
INTERROGATING THE DEAD

FOR THE BRIEFEST instant, Malus froze in horror as the high-pitched shrieks reverberated across the dimly lit chamber. The attackers charged from the shadowy passageways, but instead of the rapacious Chaos beasts they expected, their foes were in the shape of men. They wore grey robes and kheitans beneath long shirts of blackened mail, and their skin and hair were smeared with a thick layer of soot or ash. Each man carried a short, cruelly hooked spear or a short, stabbing sword with a serrated edge, and their expressions were contorted in snarls of feral bloodlust.

Malus knew that these were not sorcerous monsters that shrugged off the touch of sharpened steel, and the knowledge filled him with murderous vigour. The highborn raised his sword and met the enemies' charge with a bloodthirsty laugh. 'Blood and souls for Khaine!' he cried, and rushed at the oncoming men.

The first man he reached lunged at Malus with his spear, his eyes widening in surprise at the highborn's reckless charge. Malus slapped the spearhead aside with the flat of his blade and then smashed the heavy sword into his attacker's face with a backhanded strike. Bone crunched as the keen edge struck the man just beneath his nose and split his skull in half. The corpse lurched on past the highborn for several more steps before collapsing to the floor.

The clangour of battle filled the air as the loyalists threw themselves at their foes. An ashen-faced attacker screamed as Niryal ducked beneath his spear thrust and hacked off his right leg just below the knee. Arleth Vann drew one of his blades and danced through the onrushing foes sweeping in from the left, toppling two men in a spray of bright crimson.

Two druchii rushed at Malus, holding their saw bladed knives in an underhand grip. Still laughing furiously, he charged the first man, driving him back with a swipe at his face. The second man saw an opportunity and lunged in from the right, bringing up his blade in a disembowelling thrust, only to find he'd fallen into the highborn's trap. At the last moment Malus pivoted away from the thrust and severed the man's knife-hand with a short, powerful stroke. Hot blood sprayed across Malus's face as the maimed warrior reeled backwards, but the highborn had already turned his attention back to the second knife wielder. The druchii slashed at Malus's throat, but the highborn blocked the knife stroke easily, deflecting the smaller weapon away with his heavier blade. Before the druchii could recover Malus planted his left foot and lunged, driving his double-edged sword into the man's throat. The point of the blade grated against the druchii's spine and the mortally wounded man dropped lifelessly to the floor.

Suddenly Malus felt something curved and sharp circle his left ankle. He glanced left just in time to see one of the druchii leering triumphantly at him before hauling back on his spear. The weapon's curved billhook pulled Malus off his feet. Instinct and battle-hardened reflexes made him rotate in midair, letting him take the fall on his back instead of his sword arm, but the spearman was a quick and cunning fighter, stepping in swiftly and smashing his billhook against Malus's sword-hand. The highborn roared in pain and rage as his sword was sent spinning end over end across the room.

The spear swept around again, this time angling for Malus's neck, but the highborn caught the haft with both hands and pulled the druchii towards him. As the man stumbled forwards, Malus kicked the druchii hard in the groin and then smashed a heel against his attacker's left knee. The man fell hard, his face locked in a grimace of pain, and Malus pulled the spear from his hands. The highborn reversed his grip on the weapon and buried the spear's point in his foe's temple, and then crawled clear of the twitching body and scrambled for his lost blade.

Men were running past him. The ashen-faced attackers were in full retreat, demoralised by the ferocity of their foes' counterattack. There was a whirring of steel through the air and then a meaty *thunk*, and one of the fleeing druchii let out a strangled gasp and fell to the floor with Arleth Vann's sword buried in his back. Malus reached his sword and lurched to his feet, but by then the rest of the attackers had vanished, their footfalls receding swiftly into the darkness.

Arleth Vann dashed to his victim and pulled his sword free with a muttered curse. Malus took stock of his party and found that none of the loyalists had been injured in the brief fight. He turned to his retainer. 'Who in the name of the Outer Dark were they?'

'Beastmasters,' the assassin replied. 'The temple employs them to provide animals for festival games and to train its warriors.' He glanced down the left passageway, concern on his face. 'We must have surprised them as much as they did us, but they'll be calling the hunting beasts to them at any moment. We need to get inside the citadel, now!'

'Lead on,' Malus said, and Arleth Vann darted up the ramp without another word.

The ramp ran up through a series of large storerooms, switching back upon itself with each new level. They passed dusty crates and cracked clay urns that had once held expensive ink, bales of rotting cloth and sheaves of incense sticks that thickened the air with cloying, spicy scents. They saw no one as they raced for the upper levels of the tower, although in places Malus noticed a line of fresh boot prints running ahead of them through the layers of dust.

After several long minutes they reached the chamber and the top of the ramp, their noses clogged with dust and strange scents. A pair of broad, iron-banded doors stood at the other end of the room, and one of the heavy panels was slightly ajar. Arleth Vann rushed down an aisle of crates and pulled the door wider, as if he feared it might slam shut at any moment. Malus glimpsed a large, dimly lit room, beyond, piled high with more supplies. Stairs rose along the high, stone walls into the tower proper.

The assassin breathed a sigh of relief and doused his sorcerous light. 'We're in luck. The fools didn't think to bar the door. Quickly now!'

Malus and the loyalists filed through the doorway and Arleth Vann pulled the heavy door shut behind him. A broad, wooden wheel was mounted on a spindle set into the stone wall next to the doorway. The assassin grabbed the wheel's spokes and leaned against it, pushing with all his strength. Bemused, the highborn joined him on the wheel's opposite side and pulled, grimacing at the flare of pain in his chest. At first the wheel refused to budge. Then, inch-by-inch, it began to turn. There was a building screech of rusted iron, and then the doors trembled with a muted *thud*.

'That's it,' Arleth Vann said breathlessly, leaning against the wheel. 'The dwarfs built this to secure the citadel in times of war.' He pointed at the top of the threshold. 'Iron rods can be lowered into slots on the top of the doors, fixing them in place. The beasts can't get to us now.'

'How are we supposed to get back to the lodge?' Malus asked.

To his surprise, Arleth Vann gave him one of his ghostly smiles. 'Honestly, I have no idea. I'm more or less making this up as I go.'

Malus winced. 'Ah, well, that's comforting.'

'Would it help if I told you that it may not be a problem?'

'And why is that?'

'There's a good chance we'll all die once we reach the library.'

The highborn stared balefully at his retainer. 'I think you spent too much time with Hauclir back at the Hag. He's been a bad influence.'

Arleth Vann straightened. 'Really? That's interesting.'

'Why?'

'He said the same thing about you.'

Malus frowned. 'Impertinent wretch.'

'That's funny. He said the same thing–'

'Enough!' the highborn growled. 'Let's go see this damned library!'

Arleth Vann gave Malus a sketchy bow and dashed off, heading for a staircase on the far side of the room.

They climbed two more floors before they emerged into a corridor lit with globes of witchfire. The air smelled fresh, and Malus drank it in like wine. They were finally above ground.

Muted shouts echoed from one end of the corridor. Malus turned to Arleth Vann. 'What's that?'

'Urial must have men guarding the citadel,' the assassin said. 'The beastmen are raising the alarm.' He glanced down the opposite end of the passageway and seemed lost in thought for a moment. 'We'll take the servants' stairs,' he said after a moment. 'This way!'

Malus and the loyalists raced after the assassin, dashing through a maze of corridors before reaching a set of tightly curving stairs that led up into the higher levels of the tower. They climbed for a long while, their panting breaths echoing hollowly in the dark, cramped space. The highborn expected a wave of screaming zealots to sweep down on them from above at any moment, but many minutes later they left the staircase and emerged unchallenged into a brightly lit hallway. Arleth Vann raised his hand in warning, crept silently to the end of the passageway and peered into the space beyond. He motioned for the group to join him a moment later.

They crept from the passage into a large, open room not unlike a highborn's entry hall. A sweeping staircase rose to a gallery overlooking the room, and a circular platform sat in the centre of the chamber, piled high with severed skulls. Incense hung heavy in the air, attempting to mask the stench of rot rising from the putrefying trophies. A pair of heavy, gilded doors stood shut in a shadowed alcove beneath the gallery, opposite an open archway that led to an antechamber on the far side of the tower. The marble floor was covered in scraps of cheap brown paper. Malus frowned and stirred a pile of papers with his toe. Each sheet was covered in fine, archaic script. 'What's all this?' he asked quietly.

'Petitioners' writs,' Arleth Vann replied. 'Members of the temple may petition the Haru'ann for access to the libraries, and if their request is granted they are given a scrap of paper marked with the elder's signature and a verse or two from the *Parables of Sundered Flesh*. Then the petitioners are left here to wait and meditate upon the verses until the librarians call their names.' He gestured at the pile of grisly trophies. 'Many petitioners bring offerings in hope that the librarians will expedite their access, but the keepers of the sacred texts are rarely impressed.' The assassin pointed to the double doors. 'This level contains nothing more than histories and copies of sacred texts,' he said, indicating the gallery overhead. 'What we want is up there.'

Arleth Vann crossed the chamber and climbed the staircase two steps at a time. Malus went after him, noting that Niryal and the other loyalists followed with considerable reluctance. Priestesses and mere novitiates were not welcome in this place.

The gallery was furnished with thick rugs and plush, high-backed chairs arrayed in twin ranks before a single door of blooded oak. Side tables set off in the far corners were set with silver goblets and bottles of wine, clearly meant for the pleasure of the temple elders. Arleth Vann turned to Niryal and the loyalists. 'Wait here,' he said.

To Malus's surprise, Niryal glared at the assassin. 'We know our place,' she said. 'It is you who overstep your bounds. This is not proper!'

'You are welcome to complain to the Grand Carnifex,' the assassin said coolly. He pushed the door open and stepped into the room beyond as if he belonged there. Malus followed close behind.

The upper library was huge, its curving walls lined with bookshelves that stretched as much as three storeys high. Long ladders of blooded oak ran on tracks of polished brass that circled the towering shelves, allowing apprentice librarians to scurry up and retrieve volumes for their patrons. Thick rugs were piled on the stone floor around ranks of wooden carrels, their working surfaces brightly lit by a cluster of large witchlight globes suspended on a chain from the centre of the vaulted ceiling. The air was thick with the smell of dust, old leather and ancient paper. It reminded Malus of his half-sister Nagaira's former library back at the Hag. 'These places are nothing but trouble,' he muttered darkly.

Arleth Vann moved quickly to the far side of the room. There, beyond the furthest rank of work carrels, the rugs abruptly stopped at an expanse of polished black marble. A large circle of arcane sigils was carved into the stone, and beyond that stood a series of tall, wooden cabinets arrayed in a rough semicircle. The assassin studied each cabinet in turn before settling on the fourth in line and pulling its wooden doors open.

There were dozens of polished skulls inside, resting on shelves lined with black velvet. They all looked very old, and many were bound together with intricate nets of gold and silver wire.

'What is all this?' the highborn asked.

Arleth Vann looked over his shoulder at his master and smiled faintly. 'These are the real treasures of the library,' he said. 'Sacred texts are well and good, but the temple has always placed its greatest faith in the wisdom and insight of its elders. These cabinets contain the skulls of more than four hundred of the greatest men and women of the temple, stretching back for more than four thousand years. Their spirits remain tied to their skulls with powerful spells, so that they can continue to serve the faithful long after their deaths.'

The assassin reached into the cabinet and reverently lifted one of the skulls from its resting place. Malus noted that several spots on the shelves were empty, and thought of the skull that Urial had showed him in his quarters on the *Harrier*. A thought occurred to him. 'Why didn't Urial forsake the temple like the other zealots? He had to have known that the temple elders didn't dare acknowledge him even if he had been the true Scourge.'

Arleth Vann shrugged. 'I suppose it was greed. You've seen the wealth and luxury that the temple elders enjoy here. I suspect that Urial kept the zealots at arm's length for years, knowing he would need them when the time came to make his play for the sword, but looking to build his influence in the temple at the same time. Perhaps he seeks to reconcile the two in some fashion, letting him have the best of both worlds.'

Malus gave a cynical grunt. 'So much for the purity of faith,' he said. 'At least the Slaaneshi are honest about their appetites.'

The assassin shot the highborn a warning glare. 'Don't blaspheme,' he said, 'especially not in the presence of four hundred very pious, very savage ghosts.'

'Point taken,' Malus replied, watching his retainer carry the skull into the magic circle. 'For an assassin you seem to know a very great deal about the temple and its history,' he said.

Arleth Vann paused, staring down at the skull. 'I never wanted to be an assassin,' he said quietly. 'This is where I wanted to be, among the books and the old bones.'

'You wanted to be a librarian?' Malus said, not bothering to hide his disdain.

The retainer shrugged. 'I grew up here. My parents gave me to the temple when I was just a babe, like so many others. I grew up in the cells near the Assassin's Door, and when I was five I was given to the librarians to carry books and run errands. I took to letters well and could write by the time I was seven.' He looked up at the shelves. 'I was also good on the ladders, which the elderly librarians appreciated. I prided myself on getting up and down as quickly and quietly as possible.' His expression darkened, 'and that was my undoing, in a way. The librarians assigned me to a temple witch who was working on an important project, and she thought my skills were going to waste fetching books and picking up rubbish. So she spoke to the master librarian and at ten years old I began my tutelage with the temple assassins.'

Arleth Vann knelt and gently laid the skull in the centre of the circle. 'Once I entered the assassins' order, I was forbidden to enter the library, of course. So at night I would sneak into the crypts and slip back into the citadel, where I would spend hours poring through the old tomes. That's how I learned about the schism, and the deception the elders have practised for millennia. The truth is here, scattered in vague references and small details spread through scores of unrelated books.' He stood and pointed to one of the carrels near the back of the room. 'I was sitting right there the night I put all the pieces together. That was both the best and the worst night of my life. Nothing was the same after that.'

'So you threw in your lot with the zealots.'

The assassin gave Malus an indignant look. 'We're not talking about some petty highborn intrigue, where one's allegiance shifts with the wind. I was a servant of Khaine, and I had been practising heresy from the moment I entered the temple. So what other choice did I have but to leave Har Ganeth and seek the wisdom of the zealots?'

'That's why they sent you to Har Ganeth in search of the Scourge?'

'No,' the assassin replied, 'for all that you have seen of Tyran and his schemes here in the city, the true cult is not as dogmatic and rigid as the temple. Masters wander the land, practising their devotions and perfecting the killing arts, and aspirants to the cult must seek them out for instruction. When the master deems the student worthy, he or she is sent out into the world alone to worship the Bloody-handed God and wait for the coming of the Scourge.' The assassin smiled faintly. 'Unlike most true believers, I wasn't content to simply wait for the Time of Blood to announce itself. I began searching for signs of the Scourge in every city I came to.'

'Why?'

The assassin shrugged. 'Redemption, I suppose, or revenge against the temple. At any rate,' he said with a sigh, 'that was how I found myself in a seer's hut outside Karond Kar several years ago, wagering my soul in a game of Dragon's Teeth in exchange for a divination. The woman was utterly mad, but her visions were true. She told me that the Scourge would be born of a witch in the City of Shadow, and would dwell in the house of chains.' He shook his head ruefully. 'The old wretch tried to serve me poisoned wine afterwards. The city folk had warned me she was a poor loser.'

Malus considered this and tried to hide his discomfort. He'd never inquired about Arleth Vann's beliefs when the assassin had served him at the Hag, and now he found all this talk about service and devotion more than a little disturbing. 'I hope you aren't expecting some kind of divine forgiveness from me,' he said, 'because I don't do that sort of thing.'

The assassin shook his head and chuckled softly. 'Khaine forfend!' he said. 'No, I simply serve, my lord. If the Lord of Murder wills it, I will find my own redemption. Speaking of which,' he said, drawing a deep breath, 'we're wasting time. Urial's men could be searching the citadel as we speak, and I don't know how long this summoning will take.'

'I thought you said that the assassins' order only taught you minor sorceries,' Malus said.

Arleth Vann nodded. 'That's right, but I've observed similar rituals many times in the past.'

'Meaning you've never done this before.'

The assassin hesitated. 'Strictly speaking, yes.'

'Mother of Night,' Malus cursed. 'What happens if the summoning goes wrong?'

'Well,' Arleth Vann said carefully, 'there is a very small possibility that I could lose control of the magical forces and cause a minor explosion.'

'Ah,' the highborn said, 'in that case, I'll wait in the gallery.'

'Very well, my lord.'

Malus turned on his heel and strode swiftly from the room, pulling the oak door shut behind him. Niryal and the two loyalists stood at the gallery's edge, peering over the rail at the space below. The priestess turned at his approach. 'Did you find what you were looking for?' she asked.

'My man is still searching,' the highborn replied. 'It shouldn't be long.' He joined her at the rail. The two temple servants stepped away, retreating to the top of the stairs.

Niryal resumed her watch, her expression troubled. She was tall and lean, with weathered skin stretched taut over hard, cable-like muscles. Faint scars marked the backs of her hands and the side of her thin face and neck, and her small mouth was set in a hard, determined line. 'How am I to address you?' she asked.

Malus gave her a sidelong look. 'What?'

Her dark eyes met his. 'You have a retainer – a man with the blessing of Khaine upon him and the swords of an assassin, no less – but for Rhulan, none of the other elders had any idea who you were. You know next to nothing about the temple, but you know things about the warpsword and about Urial that no one else does.' She looked him up and down. 'You dress like a beggar but shout commands like a high-born, and somehow you spent several days in the company of Tyran and his zealots, and then arrived unannounced in the council chambers to deliver an anonymous warning to the Grand Carnifex.' She cocked her head inquisitively. 'So, who... or what... are you?'

The highborn spread his hands and managed a smile to mask his concern. 'As I said to the council, I'm a servant of Khaine. What else matters?'

Niryal arched a whip thin eyebrow. 'I can think of a great many things, but let's start with this: how can you be so certain that Urial is not the Swordbearer after all? The more I think about it, the more trouble I have believing that he found a way to circumvent Khaine's will and claim the blade for himself.'

Malus hesitated. 'Malekith is the Scourge of Khaine, so it is written.'

'Yes, but written by whom? All I know is that the Witch King is in his tower at Naggarond, and Urial is here with the warpsword in his hands. I saw it with my own eyes, just as I saw him slay the Grand Carnifex in single combat. The Grand Carnifex! How can that be possible if Urial isn't Khaine's chosen one?'

The highborn's eyes narrowed warily. 'Because Urial is a sorcerer of fearsome power, and he has coveted the warpsword for many years. The Arch-Hierophant realised this. Why can't you?'

Niryal leaned close to Malus. 'The Arch-Hierophant has fled the city,' she whispered. 'I heard your retainer say so.'

Malus stiffened. 'Rhulan is a coward,' he hissed.

'Or he has no faith in you, and if he does not, then why should I?'

Out of the corner of his eye, Malus saw the loyalist sentries watching from the stairs drop into a crouch.

He caught the warning movement a moment too late. Before he could react he heard shouts of alarm from the chamber below. The highborn gave a silent snarl as he saw a trio of temple beastmasters standing just inside the room. One of them locked eyes with Malus and levelled a short spear at his face.

'Damnation,' Malus cursed quietly, and the air shook with hoarse war screams as the beastmasters charged for the gallery stairs. Five of Tyran's zealots followed hot on their heels, their gleaming draichs held high.

'Stop them on the stairs!' the highborn shouted to the loyalists. The stairway was just wide enough for two men to walk abreast. If they could keep their foes off the gallery floor the zealots would be at a disadvantage with their long blades. As he raced past Niryal, Malus shot a nervous glance at the door to the upper library, but there was no hint as to what was happening on the other side. All he could do was hope Arleth Vann learned what he needed quickly. They couldn't hold out for long.

The beastmasters flung themselves at the loyalists, jabbing fiercely with their spears in an effort to drive them back. One of the men started to give ground, but Malus reached the top of the stairs and grabbed a fistful of the retreating man's robe, forcing him back. The highborn stood close, just above and behind the two loyalists, looking for an opportunity to strike.

One of the beastmasters blocked a spear thrust with his sword and then drew a ragged cut across his opponent's weapon arm. Seeing an opportunity, the second beastmaster feinted at the man in front of him and then threw a lightning quick thrust at the overextended swordsman, but Malus's sword flashed down like a thunderbolt, biting deep into the beastmaster's forearm. Bones snapped with a brittle crack and the beastmaster's howl of pain turned to a choked gurgle as his opponent recovered from the feint and stabbed him in the throat.

The dying beastmaster sagged to his left and tumbled off the stairs. His companion stepped forwards into the gap, aiming a low blow at his foe's legs. The loyalist tried to block the thrust, but the stroke was ill timed and the steel spearhead dug a deep gouge along his thigh. Screaming in pain, the temple servant slashed wildly at the beastmaster's head, but the warrior ducked beneath the blow and drove his spear deep into the loyalist's abdomen. Malus saw the sharp, steel point burst from the man's back and the loyalist died with a terrible groan.

Growling like a wolf, Malus kicked the dead loyalist in the back, sending the corpse crashing into his killer. The beastmaster shouted angrily and pushed the corpse off the stairs, but as he tried to pull his spear free of the falling body Malus swept down the stairs and split the man's skull. The beastmaster collapsed, blood spilling down his shattered face, and the highborn pivoted on the ball of his foot and drove his blade into the third beastmaster's chest.

The second blow nearly got him killed. Just as Malus pulled his sword free from the dying man he caught a flash of steel, and instinct caused him to fall backwards, away from the draich's blurring strike. The sword flashed through the space where his head had been, continuing downwards to slice across the high-born's forearm. He grimaced at the sudden flare of pain, but there was no time for concern – the zealot continued to press his attack, reversing his curved sword and slashing upwards at Malus's neck. The highborn rolled right, feeling the razor edged steel hiss through the air a finger's breadth from his jaw-bone. Then there was a meaty *crunch*, and hot blood sprayed across his face. He opened his eyes in time to see the zealot fall off the stairs, the top of his head shorn away by the stroke of Niryal's axe.

Legs pumping furiously, Malus scrambled back-wards up the stairs. The zealots pressed forwards. On the highborn's left the surviving loyalist was also retreating, blood flowing from a deep wound in his shoulder. Niryal stood over Malus, her bloody axe swinging in vicious strokes to keep the enemy at bay. Then movement on the floor below caught the high-born's eye. Zealots and black robed temple converts were streaming into the room and adding their weight to the group pushing up the stairway.

'Fall back!' Malus shouted angrily. 'Back to the library!'

The wounded loyalist stole a glance at Malus upon hearing the order, and the mistake cost him his life. His opponent leapt forwards with a shout and brought his powerful blade down at the juncture of the man's neck and shoulder. The blow chopped through collarbone and ribs, splitting the breastbone and tearing through his vitals. Blood burst from the man's open mouth and he fell without a sound. Whether by luck or design the loyalist's body collapsed against the front rank of zealots, slowing their advance long enough for Malus to scramble to his feet and race for the library door.

The door latch was icy cold to the touch. Malus pulled the door open and a blast of freezing air lashed at his face. Frost glittered on the inside of the door, and the chamber was suffused with a shifting blue glow. At the far end of the room, Arleth Vann stood before the elder's skull, which floated in the air several feet above his head. Blue flames burned from the skull's eye sockets, and it was attached to a wispy body that twisted and writhed as it hung in the air.

Malus raced across the room, feeling the invisible tension of the sorcerous struggle seethe across his skin. Arleth Vann's back was arched and his head was thrown back, his mouth working silently as he waged a battle of wills against the elder's spirit. Niryal stumbled through the door behind Malus, her eyes going wide at the scene playing out before her.

'Into the circle!' Malus shouted to her as he stepped across the mystical lines. Power surged and crackled around him. He felt a wave of freezing cold against his face, and his hair stood on end. A seething crackle filled his ears. The highborn turned to find the priestess right on his heels. As she stepped into the circle they were buffeted by a cyclone of unstable energies. Arleth Vann's head snapped forwards, his face etched with strain and his eyes wide.

'Release the energy!' the highborn shouted into the building storm. 'Let it go!'

The door to the library burst open as the first of the zealots charged in. In half a dozen strides the swordsmen were halfway across the room. Malus started to shout at the assassin again when he heard Arleth Vann howl in agony and the world exploded in a blast of bluish flame.

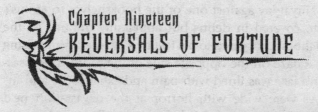

Chapter Nineteen
REVERSALS OF FORTUNE

A CLAP OF thunder smote Malus's ears and he was yanked off his feet by the power of the blast, like a leaf caught up in the wake of a raging wind. He heard screams and the sound of splintering wood, and then he crashed into something hard and unyielding, knocking him senseless.

When his vision finally cleared, long moments later, he found himself sprawled beneath a pile of shredded, smouldering books at the base of one of the library's many bookshelves. The ringing in his ears began to fade, replaced by the groans of wounded men.

A hazy, bluish light hung in the air, seeming to emanate from the very stones of the floor, walls and ceiling. The witchlight globes had shattered in the blast, and drifts of shredded paper hung like fine ash in the unearthly glow. Everything caught in the blast had been destroyed. The study carrels had been smashed to pieces like a ship's rail hit by a catapult stone, and the hundreds of books lining the shelves around the room had been mulched by a storm of wooden shrapnel. The tall cabinets containing the skulls of former elders were likewise crushed, spilling a rain of bone fragments onto the floor.

Niryal lay against one of the bookshelves to Malus's left, covered in debris but apparently unhurt. As the highborn staggered to his feet he saw Arleth Vann rising in a daze on the opposite side of the room. The assassin's face was lined with pain and exhaustion, and his eyes were wide with horror at the devastation he'd wrought. The arcane circle laid in the floor was gone, its lines of silver obliterated by the release of magical energy. Malus reckoned that the only reason he and his companions were still alive was because the destructive force radiated outwards from the edge of the circle and dragged them along with it.

Their foes had not been so fortunate.

The zealots closest to the circle could not even be said to resemble men. Their swords had shattered and their clothes had burned away, but their bodies had simply melted like candle wax, leaving nothing but piles of steaming, red mush behind. The next rank of men had caught the full fury of the blast's shrapnel, riddling and slicing their bodies into tattered, dripping rags. Only those closest to the narrow doorway had escaped death, although the door itself had been torn to flinders and hurled into the gallery beyond. Bodies writhed on the floor, clutching seeping wounds or mangled limbs.

His breath turning to vapour in the unnaturally cold air, Malus cast about for his sword and found it imbedded in a pair of thick, leather-bound tomes still resting on their shelf at roughly chest height. The highborn yanked the blade loose, spilling the torn contents of the books onto the glowing stone, and stumbled through the debris towards the wounded men with a grim look on his face.

'Blessed Murderer,' Niryal gasped, her face pale and furious as she surveyed the desolation. 'What have you done?'

'What was necessary,' Malus snapped, reaching the first pair of wounded men and despatching them with short, vicious strokes. Steaming sprays of blood arced heavily through the blue tinged air with each upswing of the double-edged blade. 'Would you rather have let these blasphemers kill us?'

'Of course!' the priestess cried. 'Our lives mean nothing compared to the knowledge within these walls–'

Malus rounded on her, levelling his dripping sword at her face. 'Don't start,' he warned. Nearby, a zealot rolled onto his stomach and began crawling towards a nearby blade. The highborn caught the movement and fell upon the wounded man, hacking remorselessly at his head and neck.

'None... of... this... is... yours!' Malus said, emphasising each word with a vicious sword stroke. The zealot collapsed, and the highborn searched for another victim. 'Every book, every damned skull, all of it belongs to Urial. Do you see?'

'What I see is another bloody disaster!' the priestess shot back. Somehow she'd managed to keep her grip on her axe during the explosion, and she pointed the curving tips of its twin blades at Malus. 'Everywhere you go, you leave death and ruin in your wake.'

Malus stepped over to an unmoving form and studied it. Quick as an adder he stabbed the man in the throat and was rewarded with a bright fountain of blood. The man began convulsing, and the highborn grunted in satisfaction. 'Didn't I say I was a servant of Khaine?' he replied, giving her a challenging stare.

'What servant of Khaine would leave his god's temple in ruins?' she said.

'One fighting a war,' the highborn replied. He pointed through the doorway with his sword. 'If you think that usurper in the sanctum is the true Scourge, then go to him and see how he rewards your misguided beliefs.'

The two druchii exchanged furious stares: Niryal trembling with anger, and Malus cold and still as stone.

A pile of debris shifted, revealing a badly wounded zealot. A bloody groan bubbled from the warrior's lips.

Niryal's face twisted in a bitter grimace. Hefting her axe, she took three swift strides and buried the heavy blade in the wounded man's chest. The priestess pulled her weapon free, spattering the surrounding books with spots of bright crimson, and then stalked from the room with a single, hateful glare. Moments later Malus heard the wet, butcher's sound of her axe cleaving into the survivors in the gallery.

Malus turned to Arleth Vann. The assassin's gaze still wandered through the ruins of his childhood, drifting from one devastated pile of books to another. The highborn joined him, picking his way carefully through the wreckage.

'Do not mourn,' the highborn said softly. 'You did what had to be done.'

Arleth Vann seemed to notice him for the first time, peering out of his bleak reverie. 'She was right,' he said, his voice hollow. 'You can't imagine what has been lost, my lord: so much knowledge... so much history!'

Malus took his retainer by the throat, pulling him close. 'Knowledge is illusory,' he growled. 'History is but prologue. Everything kept in this room was meant to shepherd the temple to this point in time. It served its purpose, Arleth Vann. The Time of Blood is nigh.'

The assassin stared at Malus, a stricken expression twisting his pale features. He nodded slowly. 'Yes, of course. You have the right of it my lord.' Arleth Vann spoke intently, as if trying to convince himself. 'What's past is past.'

'Well said,' Malus replied. 'Did you learn anything from the elder?'

Arleth Vann glanced at the ruined circle. The elder's skull sat upright at its centre, miraculously unharmed by the blast. 'It was harder – much harder – than I expected,' he admitted, 'but, yes, the elder finally shared some of his knowledge.'

'And?'

The assassin breathed a misty sigh. 'There is no way to track the zealots through the gate,' he said. 'To do that would require a personal connection with one of them, like the blood of kinship or the power of a sorcerous oath.'

Malus growled deep in his throat. 'That is not helpful.'

Arleth Vann interrupted the highborn's protests with a raised hand. 'We have no tie to the zealots, but we do have a powerful connection to the sword itself.'

'What tie?'

'Why, you, of course,' the assassin replied. 'You're the Scourge. The blade is fated to be wielded by you during the Time of Blood. That destiny binds you to the warpsword, and with it you can navigate your passage through the Vermillion Gate.'

Damned fate! Malus thought bitterly. He imagined he felt the daemon swell with pleasure inside his chest. 'Then we shall leave at once,' he said brusquely, 'provided we can get back into the crypts.'

'We can't go back the way we came, obviously,' the assassin replied, his voice slowly regaining its strength as he shook off the strain of the ritual and its cataclysmic end, 'but if we move quickly we can slip out through the ground floor and find another entry point in one of the nearby buildings.'

'What about the guards?'

The assassin managed a faint chuckle. 'They're all up here and more will be coming any minute. Urial could not have helped but sense what happened here.'

'I shouldn't be surprised,' Malus said. 'Let's get out of here. Once we've reached the lodge, however, I've got another errand for you.'

'As you wish, my lord,' the retainer replied, stifling a weary sigh. 'May I ask a question?'

'Make it quick.'

Arleth Vann nodded in the direction of the gallery. 'Would you have let her go to Urial if she'd wished?'

Malus didn't dignify such foolishness with an answer.

THE FOUR REMAINING loyalists filed silently from the prime chamber, all of them casting troubled glances over their shoulder at Malus and the tomb of Gothar the Ironmaster. Niryal was the last. She hadn't said a single word since leaving the Citadel of Bone, but Malus could plainly see the anger and doubt warring behind her eyes. The conflict had only deepened when he'd told them his theory about the warpsword.

He could tell that they wanted to believe him, because it meant that there was still a chance to restore the rightful order in the temple and gain some vengeance in an otherwise hopeless situation. The fact that the temple elders had lied to the faithful about the sword for centuries hadn't made much of an impression yet, but that would come in time. Providing that any of them survived.

There was no telling what they would find on the other side of the gate. Malus had wracked his brain, trying to deduce where the zealots would have taken their prize, but he couldn't think of a single place that made any sense. He wanted some idea of what they would be up against when they emerged on the other side of the gate.

A shiver passed through Malus, making him cast a worried glance at the chamber door. Fortunately, the temple servants were gone, having been told to gather up their meagre camp and make ready to depart. The highborn wrapped his arms tightly around his chest and breathed deeply, trying to keep his knees from trembling.

Malus ached for a taste of the daemon's power. The need had come upon him as they slipped from the citadel and crept across the temple grounds. Maybe it had been the brush with sorcery in the library, or the after-effects of the battle, but as he'd walked he felt his muscles shrivel like old roots and his guts turn to ice. It was by sheer willpower alone that he forced himself to complete the long journey back to the lodge. He'd told the loyalists his plans while leaning against the tomb so they wouldn't see his body tremble.

Just a taste, he thought. Just a small taste. Eldire said all wasn't yet lost. My will is still strong.

Another wracking shudder passed through him. He felt his knees buckle and couldn't get his hand out in time to keep himself from landing hard on the stone floor. Malus bit back a stream of vicious curses, appalled at his own weakness.

'It will only get worse, little druchii,' the daemon whispered, sliding like oil across his brain. 'This is but a taste of the ordeals to come, unless you let me help you.'

'You're corrupting me,' the highborn growled wearily, 'chewing out my guts from the inside, like a rat. Do you think I can't see what you're doing?'

'Malus, you brought this on yourself,' the daemon replied, 'the ordeal in Lurhan's tower, and all those times afterward, when we returned to Naggaroth from the sea. You were too greedy, taking too much of my strength at once.'

'Don't put this on me!' the highborn shouted angrily. 'I did what I had to in order to survive! I took nothing but what I needed at the time.'

'If that's the way you insist upon looking at it, then I can't make you think otherwise,' Tz'arkan replied, 'but all that is in the past. You are what you are, and nothing can change that. Why make yourself miserable, and risk your continued existence into the bargain, by wallowing in this wretched state? Let me restore your strength. You're going to need it for what lies ahead.'

Malus clenched his fists. It all sounded like sweet reason. Why bother fighting it when he was already so far gone? What would be the point? If you're already damned, better to go out in a blaze of glory than shivering and whimpering in a corner. 'What does lie ahead?' he asked, desperate to change the subject. 'What do you know?'

'I know there will be struggle, of course, hard, desperate fighting and rivers of pain. It is your fate, little druchii.'

'Fate,' Malus spat, feeling a little of his old hatred flare to life. Mentally, he huddled around its wan flame. 'You mean the grand trap you built for me.' Suddenly, a thought occurred to him. 'How does Khaine fit into all this?'

'What are you talking about?'

'Your plan,' the highborn said. 'What does a daemon of Slaanesh have to do with the Scourge of Khaine? And how is it that one of the five relics used to bind you just happens to be the talisman of Khaine's chosen one?'

The daemon didn't respond at first. Malus took that to be a sign he was on to something.

'The sword has not always been called the Warpsword of Khaine,' Tz'arkan said. 'It is very, very old, and has had many names in its time.'

'What was it called when it was being wielded by the Chaos lord who bound you?'

'What's the point? You don't have the mouth parts to pronounce it properly anyway.'

The highborn put that unpleasant mental image aside. 'My point is that the relic wasn't handed down to the cultists by Khaine himself. It fell into their hands sometime after you were bound in the far north.' Malus's mind began to race as he considered the implications. 'They were meant to keep it until the day I would come and claim it. So, is the prophecy of the Scourge also part of your plan? Did you plant that seed as well as the sword?'

Tz'arkan chuckled gleefully. 'Who can understand the machinations of fate, Darkblade? Certainly not you. How could I possibly manipulate so much while trapped in my crystal prison hundreds of leagues distant?'

'I don't know. I was hoping you would tell me.'

'Then you are destined for disappointment, I fear.'

Malus relaxed a little. With his mind fully engaged, the aches in his body seemed to abate. 'All right. Let us suppose that Khaine handed down the prophecy of the Scourge, and you somehow inserted this relic into the legends, knowing that one day I – or some other misbegotten bastard like me – would come along to claim both. Aren't you courting Khaine's wrath in all this?'

The daemon sighed. 'Such a clever little beast you are sometimes. All right, as a token of pity for the sad state you are in, I will tell you this much: the Blood God does not care who spills blood in his name, or why, only that it flows.'

Malus considered this. 'Then, in truth, anyone can wield the blade.'

'Anyone? Hardly.'

'Obviously it isn't meant solely for the Scourge of Khaine, which means that I have no more a tie to the damned thing than anyone else.'

'No, but I do,' the daemon said. 'I have felt its bite, and it remembers the taste.'

The highborn's eyes widened. 'Then you knew that the sword in Urial's hand was a fake.'

'Of course. I knew it from the moment he stabbed you.'

'And it never occurred to you to tell me?'

'Certainly it did,' the daemon purred, 'but where would be the fun in that?'

Malus bared his teeth at the daemon's gleeful laughter, huddling against the stone tomb of the ironmaster as he felt another of the tremors begin.

HE WAS DOZING fitfully when Arleth Vann finally returned.

Malus awakened to a gentle tapping on his boot. The highborn opened his eyes to find the assassin crouching a polite distance away. Arleth Vann's pale face was smudged by soot and mottled with spots of dried blood.

'Where have you been?' the highborn asked, trying to rub the exhaustion from his face.

'In the city, of course,' the assassin replied wearily. 'Things have taken a turn for the worse.'

'Worse for us, or for them?' Malus winced. 'Never mind, the answer's obvious.' He tried to stand. 'Help me up.'

Arleth Vann pulled him upright, a worried frown creasing his face. 'Is it the old wound?'

'That and more, but I will survive,' the highborn said. 'Now tell me what's happened.'

The assassin nodded and headed for the doorway with Malus following close behind. 'Sometime this morning – most likely just after dawn – the temple warriors abandoned their holdouts and tried to fight their way out of the encirclements Urial threw around them.'

The highborn shook his head, bemused. 'Why now, of all times?'

Arleth Vann shrugged as they passed through the first of the burial chambers. The two temple loyalists resting there saw Malus on the move and rose to their feet, picking up cloth bags containing their supplies and falling into step behind the highborn.

'There are rumours on the street. Most people think that the holdouts ran out of food several days ago, so they had the choice of breaking out or starving to death. Others say that penny oracles in the merchants' district have had visions of a terrible army bearing down on Har Ganeth from the west.'

Malus hissed thoughtfully. Could the Witch King already be on the move, he wondered? 'Anything's possible,' he admitted. 'Were the breakouts success-ful?'

'Eventually,' Arleth Vann said. 'The fighting lasted all day, and there are rumours that hundreds of warriors and witches were slain. What little of the warehouse district hadn't burned before was put to the torch, it seems. Over the course of the day the isolated warbands managed to link up and fight their way to the city gate.'

The highborn stopped in his tracks. 'The *city* gate? Not the fortress gate?'

Arleth Vann nodded. 'They retreated about half a mile up the Slavers' Road to the west and they're building a camp by the shore.'

'Those fools,' Malus spat. 'Urial controls the entire damned city! It will be a hundred times harder to dislodge him now. Unless...'

'Unless perhaps those penny oracles were right and the temple witches have foreseen that Malekith is on the way.'

'Damnation,' Malus said. 'If it's true, then we're nearly out of time. If Urial is still in control of the city when the Witch King arrives, the die will be cast and there will be no stopping the war that will follow.' With a muted growl he leapt back into motion, speeding though the succession of chambers with long, impatient strides.

'Honestly, my lord, I'm surprised you care,' Arleth Vann said, moving swiftly to keep pace. 'Would a holy war not serve Khaine's purposes?'

The highborn gave his retainer a hard look. 'Under the circumstances, I believe that's for me to decide.'

'Of course, my lord.'

Malus continued on, rushing through the last of the crypts and coming to the open doorway of the lodge's antechamber. A familiar, acrid reek filled his nostrils, and he heard one of the accompanying loyalists let out a surprised curse at the smell. A sharp, drawn-out hiss sounded from within the antechamber, like steam whistling from a cracked kettle.

Though small for its breed, Spite took up nearly a third of the large, rectangular antechamber. Arleth Vann had left it resting on his haunches just inside the lodge's main doors, and even with its powerful tail tucked along his side, the nauglir was long enough to brush the ends of the long tables on either side of the room.

Malus raised a warning hand. 'Wait here,' he said to Arleth Vann and the loyalists. Spite, hearing his voice, rose onto its clawed feet and turned its huge, blocky snout in his direction. Nostrils flared wide as Spite tasted his master's scent.

The highborn slowly crossed the room, studying the cold one carefully for signs of danger. Before he'd sent Arleth Vann into the city to fetch Spite he'd applied a fresh coat of vrahsha to both his and his retainer's skin from a small vial tucked into his robes. The salve disguised a druchii's scent, but not the daemonic corruption that Malus knew was spreading through his body.

Spite's nostrils flared as it tasted Malus's scent. A low grumble rose from its chest.

'It's all right, you great, dumb beast,' Malus said lightly, 'it's me.'

The cold one lowered its head slightly. Venomous drool fell in long, ropy strands from its huge jaws. Spite growled threateningly as the highborn took another step forwards. Scales grated over stone as the nauglir uncurled its tail. The powerful, cable thick muscle brushed the room's centre table in passing and smashed one of the corners into powder with a sharp *crack*.

Malus stopped where he was, suddenly wary of getting within the cold one's reach. 'Where did you find him?' he asked.

'In the stables where Tyran's men left him,' the assassin replied. 'He'd broken out of the pen days ago and just seemed to be settling there.'

The highborn looked the nauglir over and noticed a number of recent wounds on the warbeast's armoured hide. None looked remotely life threatening. To his great relief, the saddle and bags on the cold one's back still looked intact. 'Has Spite been fed?'

'Oh, it's eaten well,' the retainer assured him. 'There were bits of flesh and pieces of broken bone all over the pen. It probably ate the attendants first, and then started hunting the locals over the last few days.'

Malus nodded. If Spite was well fed, this was as safe a time to approach the beast as any. Taking a deep breath, he took another step forwards.

The cold one settled slightly onto its haunches, assuming a defensive stance, another bad sign.

'What do you think you're doing?' Malus said to the warbeast. 'It's me, and I don't have time for your nonsense. There's hard riding to be done.'

He took another step forwards. Spite's jaws began to open, one slow inch at a time.

The highborn realised that Spite was getting ready to attack, and felt an overpowering rush of frustration. 'Now you listen here, you great lump of scales,' Malus snapped, levelling an angry finger at the one ton war-beast, 'I didn't come all this way to get made a meal of by my own mount. Now *stand*, and let me look at you!'

Malus's commanding shout rang from the chamber walls, startling the cold one. Spite jerked back, nostrils flaring, and snapped at the air with a bone-jarring crunch of dagger-length fangs. For an instant the high-born feared that the warbeast would turn and dart out of the antechamber into the tunnel beyond, but then it paused, blew steam from its nostrils and settled obediently onto its haunches.

Inwardly the highborn breathed a sigh of relief. 'That's better,' he said, and walked up to the nauglir. He circled the cold one and looked him over, check-ing talons, teeth, eyes, flanks and tail. Once he was convinced that the beast was essentially unhurt, he moved to check his possessions. 'Help me with this armour,' he called out to Arleth Vann.

Moving warily, the retainer joined Malus at Spite's side and helped remove the leather bags containing the highborn's plate harness. Arleth Vann worked quickly and efficiently, unwrapping the armour plates from their oiled cloths and then helping Malus into his old kheitan. Within minutes the highborn was buckling his sword belt over his mail fauld and almost feeling like his old self again.

'You said that fighting in the city lasted until around sunset,' Malus said, pulling on his armoured gauntlets, 'what time is it now?'

'About two hours past sunset, my lord,' the assassin replied.

Malus grimaced. The first light of false dawn had been paling the sky over the fortress when he, the assassin and Niryal had escaped the Citadel of Bone. 'We've lost a great deal of time,' he said. The highborn glanced at the lodge's main doors. 'Where's Niryal? She and one of the other loyalists were standing watch.'

Arleth Vann frowned. 'I didn't see anyone when I came in, my lord.'

Malus froze. A cold knot of dread tightened in his guts.

Suddenly, Spite turned, pointing his snout towards the tunnel outside and growling threateningly. At once, a chorus of gibbering howls answered.

Chapter Twenty
BLOOD AND SOULS

'BAR THE DOOR!' Malus shouted, grabbing Spite's reins and leading the cold one deeper into the room. Arleth Vann and the loyalists leapt to obey, giving the hissing nauglir as wide a berth as possible. The three druchii reached the doors and pushed them shut. Then they picked up wedge-shaped pieces of stone they'd broken from the dwarf crypts and began jamming them as tightly as they could into the narrow space beneath the stone panels.

'What did you see?' the highborn asked his retainer as he guided Spite around the far end of the room's central table.

'I saw at least one of the hunting beasts,' the assassin replied, using a hammer looted from one of the tombs to drive the wedges home. Flecks of stone flew with every sharp blow. 'Worse, I saw witch-lights.'

'How many?'

'At least a dozen,' Arleth Vann said grimly.

'Mother of Night,' Malus whispered. That many lights could mean fifty men or more. 'Any sign of Niryal or the other sentry?'

The retainer shook his head. 'If the assassins finally decided to join Urial they could have taken both of them and left no one the wiser. They probably let me through because I had Spite with me.'

'And they know we're trapped,' the highborn said grimly.

Something heavy smashed against the doors with a thunderous crash, causing even Spite to jump. Stone dust puffed through the doorjamb, and a gibbering howl echoed outside. Malus heard the scrape of thorny tentacles lashing against the stone.

'Get back,' Malus ordered, drawing his sword. Arleth Vann and the two loyalists retreated behind Spite. The nauglir was back in a defensive pose, growling ominously, its long tail extended. The highborn patted the cold one's neck as his companions drew their weapons and formed a small semicircle behind him.

They heard another fearsome crash, and a sharp crack of breaking stone.

'That won't hold for long,' Arleth Vann muttered.

'I don't suppose there's a secret passage out of here that you haven't told me about?' Malus asked.

'If there was, don't you think the dwarfs would have taken it?'

'Good point.'

Another blow struck the doors, and this time the druchii could see a pair of cracks spreading upwards and downwards from the centre of the leftmost panel.

Malus tried to think past the frantic sound of his pulse pounding in his ears. 'Perhaps we could hide in the tombs? Pretend we're dwarfs?'

Arleth Vann shook his head. 'It wouldn't work, my lord, Spite's too tall for a dwarf.'

'There is that,' Malus deadpanned. 'I suppose we'll just have to find a way to kill the bastards then.'

With a thunderous *crack*, the leftmost door exploded in a shower of dust and fragments, and the lean form of one of the Chaos beasts came tumbling into the chamber. Dust caked its damp, gelatinous hide, and its claws raked across the stone as it skidded to a halt. Tentacles lashed the air hungrily and one of the beast's fist sized eyes focused on the highborn, only a few yards away.

Spreading its fearsome, barbed whips and hissing through its glossy beak, the hunter gathered itself to leap. Malus slapped his hand against the nauglir's neck and shouted 'Hunt, Spite! *Hunt!*' just as the creature pounced.

The Chaos beast was swift as a hunting cat, but the nauglir let out a bellow that shook dust from the ceiling and met the fearsome creature mid-leap. The hunter was huge, but Spite's body was a third again larger and much more massive. The two creatures crashed together and the hunter was propelled backwards, its tentacles lashing furiously at Spite's armoured hide as the cold one dug its claws in and tore at the beast's throat. They landed with an earth shaking crash, smashing two of the side-tables to pieces just as a wave of screaming druchii charged through the broken doorway.

They were a mismatched band, armed with an apparently random mix of weapons and armour. Black-robed temple servants brandished short swords and heavy axes next to knife wielding druchii in plain robes. One woman with the leather jerkin of a butcher hefted a gore-crusted cleaver beside a highborn wearing full armour and wielding paired swords. The only thing the mob had in common was the sign of the Blood God branded on their foreheads and the mindless look of bloodlust that burned in their dark eyes.

Their savage charge ran headlong into the path of the two wrestling beasts. Spite's lashing tail smashed three city folk off their feet, hurling their broken bodies back onto their companions. Lashing tentacles cut like saws through the enemy ranks, the barbed hooks ripping off hands, legs and faces with indiscriminate fury. Showers of blood and torn flesh burst among the charging druchii, but the survivors paid the carnage little heed. They saw Malus and his men across the room and scrambled past the thrashing creatures, their faces alight with the prospect of slaughter.

Malus bared his teeth at the oncoming mob. 'If they want a battle we'll give them one,' he said, raising his sword. 'Blood and souls!'

'Blood and souls!' the warriors of Khaine shouted, and the slaughter began in earnest.

The attackers were largely unskilled, making mistakes in their frenzy that no experienced soldier would have. Howling zealots raced around to either side of the large, central table that Malus had situated his men behind, thereby breaking the force of their charge, but some were so eager for bloodshed they scrambled atop the table itself. The highborn let them come, ducked low out of the reach of their shorter weapons, and hacked off their legs at the knees. Three city folk died that way, spilling huge gouts of blood onto the flat stone as they toppled off onto the heads of their compatriots.

To Malus's left, Arleth Vann slew every foe that came within reach, blocking with one sword and coolly despatching each opponent with a single thrust or cut from the other. To the highborn's right, the two surviving loyalists staggered against the frenzied assault of the zealots, but grimly held their ground, lashing at their foes with red stained swords.

With the tabletop clear Malus turned his attention to his right, using the corner of the table to keep the zealots at a distance where their knives and axes couldn't reach him. It was like slaying cattle. The frenzied city folk rushed at the loyalists, clashing blades, and Malus stabbed them in the throat or chest, dropping them to the ground. Whatever had robbed the attackers of their reason served to blind them to the murderous efficiency of the highborn's tactics.

The thrashing struggle of the huge beasts continued near the door. Spite's neck and flanks were crisscrossed with countless furrows from the hunter's barbed scales, but the nauglir had the Chaos beast by the throat, keeping its fearsome black beak at bay. The two creatures struggled to overbear one another, but Spite's greater bulk and long tail gave the cold one a powerful advantage. The nauglir found its feet and bore down with its jaws, forcing a strangled screech from the hunter. Its thick skin was more than enough to stave off sword and axe blows, but could not resist the fearsome might of the cold one's powerful bite. Runnels of clear ichor flowed off Spite's jaw as the warbeast lifted the hunter off the floor and shook it like a terrier shakes a rat. Tentacles flailed and bones snapped. Then Spite jerked his head and flung the creature across the room. It smashed into another of the long preparation tables, shattering it beneath its weight, and the hunter went limp.

Spite's bellow of victory shook the antechamber, drowning out even the zealots' frenzied screams. Barely a handful of attackers were left, out of the score or so who had charged into the room, and Malus felt his spirits lift. If this was the best the zealots had available, then Malus and his followers could easily fight their way out to the gate.

The druchii woman with the two-handed cleaver charged at one of the loyalists with a piercing, bestial shriek, foam flying from her thin lips as she swung her filthy blade at the man's neck. The loyalist tried to parry the blow, but the heavier weapon knocked his blade aside and deflected into the man's shoulder. Before the butcher could pull her grisly weapon free Malus leaned in and took off the top of her head with his long sword. Bone and brain sprayed into the air, but the highborn looked on in shock as the frenzied druchii jerkily pulled her weapon free and tried to strike another blow before collapsing to the ground.

There were only two attackers left on Malus's right. On the left Arleth Vann duelled with the armoured highborn, blocking the noble's clumsy, frenzied attacks and darting in to strike at unprotected joints or exposed gaps in his plate harness. Leaving the assassin to finish the highborn, Malus edged in beside the wounded loyalist and took the battle to the zealots.

A man rushed at Malus with a bloody woodsman's axe held high. The highborn pivoted on his left foot as the blow fell, allowing the blade to pass harmlessly by, and stabbed the onrushing zealot through the heart. Sneering in disdain, Malus pulled his sword free and rounded on the second man, who was raining blows on the uninjured loyalist with a knotted club in one hand and a short sword in the other. The zealot was so intent on his victim that he never saw Malus step up beside him and split his skull from back to front, spraying the loyalist fighting him with bits of blood and bone.

On the other side of the table the armoured highborn slumped against the flat surface with a groan, succumbing to blood loss and a score of deep wounds. Arleth Vann stepped close, slicing his swords across the noble's neck in a scissoring motion, and the man's head went bouncing across the floor.

Malus himself leaned back against the other side of the table, panting like a hound and trying to ignore the dull pain throbbing in the side of his chest. Bodies were heaped everywhere, bleeding out onto the floor. The fight had lasted less than half a minute.

The loyalist who'd been struck by the cleaver was bleeding badly, the shoulder and sleeve of his robe

already soaked and dripping. The other man appeared
unhurt, as did Arleth Vann. All things considered, it
could have gone much worse, the highborn thought.

Malus pushed himself away from the table and
walked over to the body of the Chaos beast. The creature's neck was ripped open, revealing strange,
yellowish muscles and a backbone that looked as if it
belonged in a shark rather than a lion. Stepping carefully through the spreading pool of gluey ichor, the
highborn raised his sword and began hacking at the
flesh, working from the inside out. It was tough going,
but within a few minutes the large, octopus-like head
rolled free. He bent and picked the thing up by its tentacles, and walked to the shattered doorway. Grunting
with effort, he took two quick steps and hurled the
trophy through the doorway.

'We'll let them think on that for a bit,' the highborn
said grimly. He turned to Arleth Vann. 'You check that
one's arm. I'll look over Spite.'

They worked quickly, unsure what awaited them
outside the lodge. A cursory check showed that Spite
had dozens upon dozens of shallow cuts from the
beast's tentacle hooks, but nothing that the nauglir's
legendary constitution could not handle. Malus had
moved on to check the state of his saddlebags when
Arleth Vann joined him. 'The man's wound is deep,'
he said quietly, 'and I've no means to close it. He'll die
in a few minutes, maybe less.'

'Then we'd best get this over with quickly,' the highborn said. 'Let's take a look outside.'

The two druchii crept up to the doorway and peered
into the tunnel beyond. Globes of witchlight filled the

wide passage with ghostly luminescence, forcing Malus to squint into the cold glare. What he saw made his heart sink.

There were scores of white-robed zealots filling the tunnel, their robes and blades stained with smudges of soot and streaks of old blood. They stood in a packed group behind two more of the terrible Chaos beasts, which lashed at the air with their tentacles as if angered by the sight of their mate's severed head. A handful of beastmasters circled the creatures, holding their short spears and prods ready. They threw black looks at the broken doorway of the lodge, as if anticipating their own measure of revenge for their slain kin.

'Mother of Night,' Malus cursed softly, 'they must have pulled every zealot from the city back into the fortress.'

'With the temple warriors gone, why not?' the assassin replied, his face grim. 'They sent in those city folk just to take our measure and keep us occupied.'

'Well, what are they waiting for?'

As Malus said the words, a ripple of motion passed through the packed ranks of the zealots. Men stepped aside, bowing their heads as Urial moved through the crowd. A trio of blood-witches attended the usurper, and Urial carried the copy of the warpsword in his hand. The mere sight of the weapon seemed to leach the strength from Malus's limbs, reminding him of the wound he'd been dealt and of the daemon's poisonous touch.

The would-be Scourge of Khaine reached the front rank of the men and stopped. Urial eyed the head of the dead Chaos beast and laughed.

Malus fought a black tide of despair. He looked upon the assembled zealots, and the merciless arithmetic of the battlefield showed him the future as clearly as any seer could. There was no way they could prevail against such numbers, to say nothing of the sorcery of Urial and the blood-witches.

'We'll have to fall back,' he said. 'We can't possibly hold them here. We'll use the fortifications at each burial chamber to slow them down, bleed them–'

'No,' Arleth Vann said quietly.

'What?' Malus demanded, his expression incredulous.

'Don't be a fool, my lord,' the assassin said. 'You know better than that. We could fight them all the way back to the prime chamber, trade ten lives for each one of ours – twenty if you count Spite – and they would still have men left over. That's without counting your half-brother, much less the blood-witches.'

'Have you any better ideas?' Malus snarled.

The assassin nodded. 'When they attack, you mount Spite and ride straight through them. We'll cover your back as long as we can.'

'You can't be serious,' Malus said.

'Of course I am!' Arleth Vann said hotly. 'You have to escape and find the sword, for Khaine's sake! Otherwise the temple – even Naggaroth itself – could well tear itself apart.'

'Why would you do such a thing?' the highborn asked, torn between revulsion and awe. 'The temple owes you nothing.'

Arleth Vann turned away, eyeing the crowd of zealots and the leonine blood-witches. 'Do you remember what I said about seeking redemption, about a good death outweighing a bad life? What better chance than this to cleanse the taint from my honour?' He looked back at his lord. 'There's no glory in living as an outlaw, my lord, no matter what the bards say.'

Malus was surprised at how much the comment stung. 'You've been a highborn retainer for the last five years,' he growled.

'That didn't change who I was,' the assassin replied, 'but this will.'

The highborn bit back his anger. Fleeing the battle felt like cowardice, but the assassin's logic was unassailable. He could either stay and die – or worse, fall into Urial's clutches – or he could fight his way free and locate the sword. 'Damnation,' Malus snarled, and then turned and made his way to Spite.

Nearby, the two loyalists watched Malus intently. The wounded man was pale and shaky, using his left hand awkwardly to press a soaked bundle of cloth against his wounded shoulder. Their expressions were bleak.

'We're breaking out,' Malus told the men as he grabbed Spite's reins. 'I'm going to provoke the zealots into charging us, and then I'll counter charge with my nauglir and open a hole in their ranks. Stay close behind and keep our flanks clear, and we'll fight our way through. Understand?'

Both men nodded. The look in their eyes said they understood completely.

Malus nodded, and then headed Spite towards the doorway. The zealots hadn't moved. Urial appeared to be speaking to the assembled force, but Malus couldn't hear what his half-brother was saying. He's probably ordering his men to take me alive, he thought. I expect he and the blood-witches have something special planned.

The highborn turned to Arleth Vann. 'Are you ready?' he asked.

'I suppose I've been waiting for this for a long time,' the assassin said calmly. 'Farewell, my lord. When the Time of Blood comes, perhaps you and I will meet again.'

Malus didn't know what to say. He shook his head fiercely. 'If you see the Lord of Murder before I do, you march up to his throne and tell him I'm coming. Tell him that when I get there I'm going to kick his brass teeth straight down his throat.'

Before the assassin could reply, the highborn drew a deep breath and shouted into the tunnel. 'What are you waiting for, brother? More men, perhaps? I think these dead bakers and butchers had more courage between them than you and all your ilk!'

Malus heard Urial laugh. 'Is that you, brother?' the usurper asked. 'I was certain you'd died. The last time I saw you, that man of yours was dragging your limp body away from me as fast as he could.'

'What can I say, brother? He's a very pious man, and was afraid I'd hurt Khaine's Scourge.' Malus said, his voice dripping with contempt. 'Fear not, I set him straight. I told him all about the night on the *Harrier*, and what that damned skull of yours told me. Say, did the skull ever speak to you alone, or did you just forget to mention that to the temple elders? That was part of the prophecy, correct?'

'Shut your blasphemous mouth!' Urial snapped, the heat in his voice so strong that Tyran and the closest zealots gave the usurper questioning looks.

'How are things with your new bride? Is she still spurning you? I expect so,' Malus said, smiling despite himself. 'The Bride of Ruin is not meant for the likes of you, brother. She will never think of you as anything but a withered, pitiable man.'

The highborn's taunts were drowned by Urial's wordless shriek of rage.

Arleth Vann chuckled, readying his blades. 'You always did have a way with words, my lord.'

Malus swung into the saddle. 'Perhaps I'd have made a decent priest after all.'

The assassin smiled ruefully. 'I don't know if I'd go that far–'

A roar shook the tunnel as the zealots charged. Blades glinting, they flowed in a furious tide past the Chaos beasts, charging for the dwarf lodge at the command of their lord.

'Now?' Malus said, looking to Arleth Vann.

The assassin shook his head, peering into the tunnel. 'Not yet.'

Shouts of bloodlust echoed in the antechamber. The sounds of pounding feet filled Malus's ears.

'Now?'

'Not yet.'

Malus could make out individual voices in the thunder of the war shouts. He could hear the slap of boot heels on stone.

'We did decide to fight them in the tunnel, correct?' the highborn said pointedly.

The assassin looked at Malus and nodded solemnly.
'Go, my lord, and Khaine be with you.'

'Not if he knows what's good for him,' Malus
growled. He put his boots to Spite's flanks. 'Charge!'

The warbeast leapt forwards with a bone jarring
roar, its shoulder striking the edge of the right door
and smashing the heavy panel from its hinges. Malus
ducked at the last moment as they crossed the threshold, feeling the top of the doorframe scrape along his
backplate.

When he looked up again he saw that they were
rushing at the front rank of zealots, less than ten yards
away. The charge of the white-robed druchii faltered
as the nauglir bore down on them, its blunt jaws
clashing together as it smelt the blood on the zealots'
robes. Malus howled like a wolf as they plunged into
the press, his blade falling left and right as he lashed
out indiscriminately at the bodies flashing past.

Zealots screamed, flung like bloody dolls into the
air by the nauglir's jaws or smashed aside by the
beast's armoured shoulders. A blade struck Malus on
the left thigh and glanced from the steel plate. On his
right, the highborn slashed down at an upturned face,
splitting the druchii's skull like a melon. He twisted
his waist and cut to his left, knocking aside a bloodstained draich and slicing open another man's
forehead.

The cold one plunged on, leaving torn and broken
bodies in its wake. Zealots struck at the nauglir from
all sides, opening deep wounds in the beast's muscular flanks, but the pain only enraged the cold one
further. A zealot leapt for the nauglir's face, aiming a

lightning thrust at Spite's left eye, but the cold one's training took over and the beast snapped at the flickering motion. The huge jaws bit off the swordsman's right arm at the elbow and spat his twisted sword onto the tunnel floor.

Malus looked over his shoulder to see how Arleth Vann and the others were keeping up. The wounded loyalist was already dead. His headless body lay only a few yards from the lodge's broken doors. The assassin and the last remaining warrior fought side-by-side close to the cold one's lashing tail.

Roars of rage turned to screams of anger, pain and fear. Men fell back to either side of the thundering cold one, stunned by the ferocity of the sudden attack. A tight semicircle of zealots formed between the nauglir and Urial. Malus smiled fiercely and aimed Spite directly for them.

The swordsmen held their ground, ready to die to protect their lord. Malus did everything in his power to give them their wish.

Spite let out a bloodthirsty roar and lunged at the man to his right, catching the swordsman's right arm and torso and biting them in half. The zealot to the cold one's left saw his opportunity and slashed with all his might at the nauglir's bent neck, but Malus anticipated the move and blocked the stroke with his sword. Hearing the sound, Spite jerked his huge head and smashed the zealot to the ground, where the beast crushed the screaming man beneath a clawed foot.

Malus caught a flicker of movement in the corner of his eye and instinctively dodged to his left. The movement saved his life, a draich glancing from his right pauldron as a zealot leapt onto Spite's flank and grabbed hold of Malus's saddle. Snarling, the highborn elbowed the man in the face, and then slashed open his throat as he reeled from the blow.

More zealots were closing in on both sides as the attackers recovered from the surprise charge. Urial stood just five yards away, surrounded by the fierce blood-witches. Letting out a battle scream, the highborn kicked Spite's flanks and charged.

Zealots were thrown left and right by the lunging warbeast, and Malus raised his sword for a decapitating stroke as he bore down on Urial. The blood-witches scattered, hissing curses, but the usurper stood his ground. With less than two yards between them, Malus saw his half-brother smile.

Suddenly Urial raised the sword in his left hand and shouted a word that smote Malus like a physical blow. Spite stopped dead in his tracks, roaring in pain and confusion. It took all of Malus's skill as a rider not to be thrown from the saddle by the force of the sudden stop.

'Forwards, Spite! Forwards!' the highborn roared, but the warbeast could only shake its head and bellow in pain, as if pressed against a wall of fire.

Urial laughed. 'He won't move, not if his life depends on it,' he said. 'Did you think me a fool, knowing you had your damned cold one with you?'

Malus shouted in impotent rage. Men were closing in from behind the nauglir and to either side, like wolves closing in for the kill.

Then there was a flash of movement and Urial ducked, catching Arleth Vann's hurled knife on the side of his head rather than in his throat. The knife scored a bloody line through the usurper's scalp, and in an eye blink, the spell was broken.

'Go, my lord!' Arleth Vann shouted, racing up beside Malus with the last surviving loyalist close behind. The assassin charged at Urial, blades reaching for the man's throat.

Zealots roared their bloodlust as they closed in on Spite. Malus gritted his teeth and once again spurred the nauglir forwards. 'Run, Spite, run!' he yelled, knowing that Urial could renew the spell at any moment.

Arleth Vann was determined not to give the usurper a chance. His short swords wove a pattern of death before him, stabbing at Urial's face and neck. Urial parried the attacks with unnatural agility, wielding his large sword as if it was a willow wand. Though no warpsword, it was clear that the dwarf ironsmith had imbued the weapon with considerable power.

Swallowing bitter bile, Malus spurred his mount past Urial. A lone voice cried 'Blood and souls!' as the last temple warrior charged at the witches. His sword sliced at one blood-witch's head, but she dodged the blow with unnatural speed, and her two compatriots fell upon the man from either side. His fierce shouts turned to a gurgling scream as their talons slashed open his throat. The witches bore the struggling man to the ground, and like lionesses, began to feed.

The last Malus saw of Arleth Vann, he was trading blows with his half-brother, circling and stabbing, leaping and slashing within a closing ring of zealots. Cursing venomously, he turned away and tried to guide his mount past the waiting Chaos beasts.

Unlike the zealots, the beastmasters knew very well how dangerous a charging cold one could be. They scattered like quail at the thundering nauglir's approach, shouting commands to the hunters in a strange, savage tongue. The air filled with the hunters' obscene, gibbering cries as they were unleashed upon Malus and Spite.

There was no point trying to fight. Malus knew all too well how useless his sword was against the monsters' hide. He bent low in the saddle and cried, 'Race like fire, beast of the deeps! Show these slugs how you can run!'

Rumbling like a cauldron, Spite obediently lowered his head and stretched his legs into a full, earthshaking gallop.

Malus angled their flight to pass the beasts on their right. The closest hunter flared its tentacles and screeched at the nauglir, but the cold one lunged at the Chaos beast and struck the creature a powerful blow with its shoulder. The hunter was knocked sideways, tentacles lashing, and the highborn was slapped on the side of his head by the back of one of the beast's fleshy whips. The blow nearly took his head off, throwing him hard to the left and almost pitching him from the saddle. Another tentacle brushed against his leg, the barbs scraping against his armour.

Suddenly, Spite lurched and bellowed in pain. The cold one's body slewed to the left, struck on its rear flank. Blinking tears of pain from his eyes, Malus glanced back and saw another of the hunters sinking its claws into Spite's powerful rear leg, much as a lion would pull down a gazelle. The highborn looked into the creature's right eye and heard the whirring of its tentacles as it reached up to pluck him from the saddle.

Malus hauled on the reins and planted his right heel in Spite's side, and the obedient warbeast slashed its tail to the left. The powerful motion flung the clutching Chaos beast over the nauglir's back, smashing it against the side of the tunnel. 'Go!' Malus shouted, spurring his mount forwards once more.

With the howls of the hunters echoing behind them, Malus and Spite raced down the broad passage. Darkness engulfed them, and the sounds of battle faded.

He gave Spite his head, trusting the cave born nauglir's senses as they raced down the passageway. Arleth Vann had shown him where the tunnel ran, and he knew that after a hundred yards it ended in a large, empty chamber that once housed the dwarfs while they worked on their tomb. A spiral ramp at the west end of the chamber led up to the road of black stones that would take Malus to the Vermillion Gate.

When the echo of Spite's footfalls suddenly stopped, Malus knew he'd entered the housing chamber. He slowed the warbeast's pace and guided him to the left, allowing the nauglir to pick his way through the debris-strewn room. When he felt a breath of moving air against his cheek, he nudged the cold one's flanks. 'Climb the ramp,' Malus said, trusting it was there even though he couldn't see it. 'Up!'

With a grunt, the cold one padded forwards and sure enough, Malus felt them begin to climb. The ramp was just broad enough for the cold one to work its way up, and the highborn lay flat against the nauglir's back and tried to stay out of the way.

After several long minutes, Malus found he could see vague outlines of the ramp around him. They were almost at the top, where the road's glowing fungus shed a modicum of light. Two turns later Spite edged out into the main passageway, and the highborn breathed a sigh of relief.

He turned Spite's nose to the left, heading deeper into the hill, and let the warbeast lope down the tunnel. They rode on in silence for some minutes, until Malus began to feel the tingle of eldritch power against his skin. They were drawing close to the ancient gateway.

Moments later Malus found himself riding through a long, underground plaza, its ceiling lost in darkness high overhead. Worn stone statues flanked the long chamber, their features worn smooth over uncounted millennia. A heavy silence hung in the enormous chamber, and even Spite seemed to feel its weight.

The plaza led them to a large, semicircular gallery at the edge of a wide, natural pit. Here, statues of beautiful, fearsome blood-witches bore lamps of witchlight and robed executioners carried elegant swords of white marble. A slender bridge of stone ran from the gallery to a circular spire of rock that rose from the centre of the pit. The top of the spire was flat and capped with paving stones of glossy, black marble, and upon those stones rose an arch of seamless, reddish stone.

Taking a deep breath, Malus led Spite onto the bridge. He had no idea if the span would support the cold one's weight, and it was just barely wide enough to accommodate it. A cold void yawned beneath the bridge, leading perhaps to the heart of the world itself.

'Easy, Spite, easy,' he said. The nauglir seemed to understand, taking one slow step at a time as it edged its way across the abyss.

Nearly five minutes later they were just over halfway across the span, and Malus was starting to breathe easier. Then he heard the sounds of pounding feet behind him and turned just in time to see the Chaos beast leap at Spite with a chilling howl.

Chapter Twenty-One
RED SKIES

THE CHAOS BEAST landed square on Spite's back, its talons sinking deep into the nauglir's hindquarters. The cold one roared in surprise and pain and instinctively turned to bite its attacker. The nauglir's right hind leg slipped from the bridge, and to Malus the world seemed to lurch vertiginously to the right. He threw himself to the left, away from the bottomless chasm, just as the hunter lashed at him with a pair of tentacles.

One of the barbed whips wrapped around his left arm and another wound around his waist. Screaming in fear and rage, Malus hacked at the tentacles with his sword, but the rubbery skin was barely marked. With no apparent effort the beast dragged him out of the saddle.

Malus looked down and saw nothing but emptiness and shadow. Then Spite's jaws snapped at the hunter and caught the tentacles in his fearsome maw.

The cold one's teeth parted the whips like thread, splashing Malus with sticky ichor. Still screaming, he fell like a stone, hitting the edge of the span and tumbling over it face-first.

By an equal mix of pure luck and desperation, Malus caught the raised edge of the span with his left hand and seized it like a drowning man. His legs swung past and he rocked like a pendulum over the pit as the two beasts raged above him. He heard the sounds of talons on stone as he fought for purchase, clawing at the other side of the bridge with his hind leg in an effort to force himself back onto the span. A stream of broken stone trickled into the blackness, and Malus heard an ominous crack.

His ichor covered hand and arm slid across the stone. With a thrill of terror, he realised he was slipping. The highborn threw his other hand over the edge of the bridge, hoping to stop his fall without losing his sword, but he hadn't reckoned on the slickness of the foul ooze coating his arms, and the sudden motion caused his left hand to slip.

Malus's stomach lurched as he dropped. Then he felt a heavy weight cover his arm and jerk him to a stop. He hung over the pit for an instant, his legs swinging uselessly. Then the mind numbing panic subsided and the highborn had the presence of mind to let go of his sword and try to find some kind of purchase with his right hand.

The weight on his left arm shifted slightly, and Malus distinctly felt the armoured shell of his vambrace bend beneath the pressure. Pain began to build at his forearm and wrist as they took the mounting strain. Gritting his teeth, Malus pulled himself upwards with his sword hand until he was able to get the crook of his arm over the bridge's rounded edge.

A clawed hand the size of his torso slashed past him, missing his head by inches. Spite had managed to regain his footing and was reaching back to claw and bite at his attacker. In doing so the one-ton warbeast had stepped on Malus's arm.

The Chaos beast still clung to Spite's hindquarters, tearing at one hip with its cruel beak and lashing at the warbeast's face with its remaining tentacles. The nauglir's clashing jaws had bitten off several more, and the stumps sprayed the cold one with gouts of clear, briny ichor. Spite roared and lashed his tail, hoping to dislodge the hunter from his back, but the Chaos beast only dug its claws in deeper and held on. The nauglir's foot ground down as it swung its tail, and the pain in Malus's arm intensified. He threw a leg over the edge of the bridge and pulled most of his body over. Then he grabbed up his sword and slapped at Spite's leg with the flat of the blade. 'Get *off*, you great lump of scales!'

Whether by accident or design, Spite lifted his leg and Malus yanked his arm free. The vambrace was crumpled, and a thin stream of blood leaked past the edges of the steel halves from where the armoured parts had bitten into his skin, but the highborn was not in any position to complain.

Spite shifted again, and Malus heard his jaws snap shut on empty air just above his head. A surge of terror shot through the highborn as he saw a shadow spread like a stain on the bridge around him, and out of pure instinct he rolled as far to the left as he could, just as a smothering weight of stinking flesh smashed against him.

He couldn't breathe for a moment, much less see, but then the Chaos beast drew back from its lunge and Malus saw how horrifyingly close he'd come to being impaled by the thing's beak. The shroud of flesh surrounding its mouth slid away from Malus, and without its weight to pin him he fell back over the edge of the span. Screaming, he flailed his hands and grabbed the first thing he could: a bleeding stump of wriggling tentacle. The highborn felt the clenching barbs of the thing's suckers scraping against his armoured glove as the creature screeched in his ear and tossed its head, flinging Malus high into the air.

The highborn held on for dear life as he was whipped about by the hunter's thrashings. More tentacles lashed around Malus, wrapping his legs and trying to pull him closer to the creature's rending maw. He groped at his belt, desperately trying to find some weapon he could use against the thing. The beast's strength was enormous, drawing him inexorably towards the great beak, and he had no illusions that his armoured breastplate would give the beast a second's pause before it tore him to pieces.

The monster's lunge had left it overextended, however, and Spite saw his chance. He darted forwards, closing his jaws around the hunter's neck. The Chaos beast shuddered and screamed, spraying Malus with spittle and gobs of sticky ichor.

He heard the creature's thin bones crunch as Spite bit deeper, and he knew what was soon to happen: the nauglir would break its neck with a savage shake and hurl the beast aside, just as it had down in the crypt. Frantically, he started to kick and thrash in the monster's grip, praying to the Dark Mother that it would start to weaken as its wounds began to tell.

With a fierce kick, Malus managed to pull his left leg free. He felt the beast begin to shift as Spite found his footing and started to lift. Acting on impulse, the highborn drew back his armoured leg and kicked the monster on the side of its beak. To his surprise, the monster howled and let go of his other leg.

Spite rumbled deep in his chest, lifted the hunter into the air, and started to shake. Malus heard bones crunch and felt the beast go limp. As the nauglir was wrenching the hunter back over the bridge the highborn took a deep breath and let go.

For a horrifying moment, Malus was certain he'd miscalculated. Rather than being thrown back onto the bridge, it seemed as if he was being hurled along its length, his arms flailing wildly as he began to plummet downward. At the last moment his left hand struck the edge of the bridge and he grabbed hold, his shoulder flaring in pain as it took the brunt of the impact. Without hesitating, Malus kicked up his feet and swung roughly over the edge of the span, just in time to see Spite hurl the broken body of the Chaos beast into the abyss.

Panting and giddy with terror, Malus rolled carefully onto his back and savoured the sensation of lying on something that wasn't writhing or clawing at him.

Further back on the bridge, Spite lifted his snout and roared in triumph, and the highborn felt the curved bridge start to shift.

'Damn me,' Malus breathed, rolling onto his knees. He could see wide cracks spreading along the length of the bridge, racing towards him from the weakened section where the nauglir still stood. 'Spite!' Malus cried, waving his arms. 'Go! Move!'

The cold one looked curiously at his master. It blew a gobbet of ichor from its nostrils and shifted its weight, edging its way towards him.

'No! Not this way, you thick lizard! Back! Go back that way!' he yelled. He scrambled down the bridge, waving his hands wildly at the heavy cold one. Grumbling, the nauglir finally got the message and turned around, walking ponderously towards the Vermillion Gate.

The bridge groaned and crackled with each hair-raising step, but Malus managed to recover his sword and creep onto the spire without further incident. He fell to his knees beside the cold one, trembling with exertion.

'Well, I think it's safe to say we won't be going back that way,' he gasped.

The nauglir rumbled and turned to sniff at the red stone arch. After a moment, Malus managed to catch his breath and staggering back to his feet, he went to check on his cold one's injuries. He counted more than a dozen deep gouges torn by the hunter's beak, and applied a healing salve from his saddlebags to each before climbing back into the saddle.

No sooner had he taken up the reins than he heard a commotion at the gallery behind him. Malus turned in the saddle to see about a dozen zealots standing at the foot of the bridge, glaring angrily at him. Apparently they'd seen the damage to the middle of the span, and had no interest in testing its strength.

The highborn gave the zealots a mocking salute with his sword, and then nudged Spite towards the arch. Taking a deep breath, he addressed the daemon. 'I don't suppose you know anything about this gate?'

'I know a bit,' Tz'arkan admitted.

Malus bit back an angry curse. 'Well, why don't you tell me how it works?'

The daemon shifted within his chest. 'There's little to tell. Cross beneath the arch and fix your destination firmly in your mind.'

'I don't have a destination, as you damned well know,' Malus snapped.

'Don't be churlish, little druchii,' Tz'arkan sneered. 'I will guide us to where we need to go.'

They rode towards the archway. Malus studied it closely as they approached. There was not a single rune or sigil anywhere along its length. Whatever magic worked upon it was invisible to his uneducated eye. He could feel its power though, washing over him in pulsing waves that made his ears ring and set his teeth on edge.

As they passed beneath the arch, the highborn expected to see a portal of smoke or light, but nothing appeared. 'Are you sure you know how this works?' he said.

Then the world turned the colour of blood, and Malus felt himself twisted inside out.

Tz'ARKAN HAD NEGLECTED to mention the pain.

Malus was blind, plummeting through howling darkness, and it felt as if ravens were feeding on his organs. The highborn felt their sharp beaks tear at his heart and lungs, worrying out little pieces and pecking thoughtfully at his quivering flesh as if savouring a fine meal. He could not move, could not scream. All he could do was suffer the ravages of the carrion birds for what felt like an eternity.

Then there was a clap of thunder, a hot wind smote Malus in his face, and Spite was stumbling down a shallow hillside of loose stone and parched dirt.

The nauglir bellowed in confusion and pain. Malus reeled in the saddle, feeling sticky moisture on his face. His stomach heaved, and for a terrifying moment it felt like something was trying to force its way out.

Spite skidded to a stop at the base of the hill and Malus all but fell from the saddle. He landed hard on his knees and vomited a fountain of dark blood and glossy, black feathers onto the lifeless ground.

'Mother of Night,' he groaned, wiping his mouth with the back of his gauntlet. The armoured glove came away slick with blood. Gasping for breath, he straightened and tried to see where he was.

The hillside behind him emptied onto a dry and desolate plain under a swirling sky the colour of blood. Towering black mountains reared above the northern horizon, their iron flanks painted with chiaroscuros of jagged yellow lightning. The hot wind seemed to blow from every direction, shifting crazily around the compass at the whim of some lunatic god. It moaned and whispered in his ears with a susurrus of strange voices, hinting at things that he only dimly grasped, but the pieces he understood turned his guts to greasy ice.

A city of black iron and blasted stone sat on the plain like a vast, black spider. Tall, blade-like towers reared hungrily into the crimson sky behind ruined walls and craggy battlements. Pillars of inky smoke rose here and there across the cityscape, wreathing the ancient buildings in a pall of suffocating fumes and ash. Off to the east, huge, hulking shapes the size of citadels writhed and lumbered along the horizon, reaching skyward as if to grasp the fickle lightning, and bellowing in madness and rage.

The gate had sent him into the far north, into the Chaos Wastes. Nowhere else in the world could such a vision of torment exist.

Why had the zealots brought the warpsword here, he wondered? What had possessed them? Was it fear of discovery by the temple, or had the blade itself chosen its resting place?

'Where is the sword, daemon?' Malus croaked, his throat ravaged by his ordeal. 'Enough with your damned games. Just tell me where to find it so we can quit this accursed place!'

'It is yonder, I think,' Tz'arkan said. Malus knew the daemon meant the foul city on the plain.

'You *think*?'

'What am I, a hound that sniffs out swords?' Tz'arkan spat. 'The gate is not so precise as I imagined, or else my control was not quite as perfect as it might have been. We are in the proper area, and I feel a source of great power to the north. What else could it be?'

'Here? In the Wastes? It could be a great many things.' Before Malus could expound further, however, Spite looked back the way they'd come and sniffed the hot air warily.

The highborn looked back over his shoulder. Up the long, rocky hillside, perhaps two hundred yards away, a knot of horsemen regarded him from the hillcrest.

Malus glared sidelong at the nauglir. 'You and your damned bellowing,' he muttered, climbing to his feet. As he did so, the horsemen kneed their mounts forwards, walking them carefully down the treacherous slope.

'Time to be going,' the highborn said, reaching for his saddle. He swung himself onto Spite's back and kicked the nauglir into a trot. His mind racing, he led the warbeast out onto the plain.

The cold one's feet kicked up puffs of grey dust as the nauglir trotted across the wasteland towards the ruined city. The horsemen easily kept pace with the cold one, fanning out expertly into a semicircular formation once they came down off the hillside. Malus studied them intently as they rode, but he could make out few details except for the spears that rose above the riders' heads and the skill with which they rode. As near as the highborn could reckon there were at least a score of them. That either meant a large patrol or a small raiding force. Malus wasn't certain which possibility he preferred.

Spite made good time at first, but as the minutes wore on the highborn noticed that the great beast began to tire. His gait became uneven, and Malus let out a curse. The nauglir was going lame from the deep wounds in his hind legs. It was much harder to lame a nauglir than a horse, but with only two legs to drive it along, when it happened the effects were often much worse. The highborn snarled. He didn't dare stop to let the beast rest, but if he didn't slow down the cold one would eventually collapse. Having little choice, he reined in and slowed Spite to a walk.

The riders gained ground steadily, although they did not seem especially eager to get within spear distance of the lone druchii. The closer they got, however, the more they hemmed Malus in to left and right. Soon their intentions were clear: they were herding him closer to the city on the plain.

Malus considered his options as they rode on. As far as he knew, the sword was somewhere in the city, and it was entirely possible that whoever led those riders might know where it was. However, he doubted that anyone in this goddess-forsaken wasteland would have any interest in helping him. It was far more likely that they were herding him along like a prize cow for slaughter. That left fighting or running, and at the moment he couldn't manage either, unless he called upon the daemon.

With Tz'arkan's help he could wipe out the riders to the last man, with or without Spite, but at what cost?

Do I have a choice any more, Malus thought?

Behind him, the riders blew a strange, skirling horn. Malus's heart quickened, thinking the riders were about to charge, but when he looked back they were still keeping their distance a few hundred yards away.

They were only a few miles from the city. The high-born knew that he had to act soon. He had no intention of becoming a prisoner to these Chaos twisted savages. The more he thought about seeking the daemon's help the more he felt his body ache for the taste of Tz'arkan's power. How much more potent would it be here, with the energies of Chaos raging through the very skies? How like a god he could be!

Malus had the name of the daemon on his lips when they crested a gentle rise in the landscape and saw the riders waiting ahead of him.

There had been no warning of their approach, no horns or telltale dust clouds. They had mastered the terrain with devilish cunning, using its folds to manoeuvre directly into his path. Just like that, the trap closed shut around him. Horsemen from the trailing patrol had already reached the rise to either side of him, cutting him off from escape. The riders in front were less than a hundred yards away, waiting patiently.

He studied the men awaiting him as he guided Spite down the shallow slope. They were broad shouldered, powerful men, wearing animal furs and bits of ragged chainmail. Bracelets of silver or hammered brass adorned their arms, and steel helmets with mail skirts rested on their shaggy heads. Their skin was swarthy, almost like brown leather, and their bodies had been twisted by years of living beneath the boiling sky.

Malus saw ram's horns sprouting from the forehead of one warrior, while another stared at the highborn with a single, catlike eye set in the centre of his forehead. Another man had two heads upon his neck, one broad and flat-nosed and the other shrivelled, scaly and bestial. Even their horses showed signs of terrible mutation, with cloven hooves and mangy bodies thick with cable-like muscles. Fangs protruded from their slack mouths, and their lolling tongues were long and forked like serpents'.

As he drew nearer, three of the riders kneed their mounts forwards upon some unspoken command. Each drew weapons that glinted in the bloody light. The man with one eye readied a long, curved sword and a steel buckler, while the two-headed man brandished a pair of long handled axes. A third man with piercing blue eyes and a ragged, drooling hole where his mouth should have been, uncoiled a long whip in his left hand and hefted a short, stubby mace in his right.

None of the other riders moved. Malus looked back at the men behind him, and saw them observing the scene from the rise many yards away. The highborn questioned whether this was some sort of challenge. He'd heard that some tribes of marauders favoured trials by combat, pitting their champions against those of their enemies. If that was their intent, he was happy to indulge them and see where it led. At worst, he could call the daemon's name and fight his way free if he had to.

The three riders spread out, edging their mounts forwards. Spite, smelling horseflesh, quickened his pace and let out a hungry roar, but the mutated animals were unfazed by the nauglir's hunting cry.

Malus realised that they were all going to attack him at once. He guessed that was supposed to be some sort of compliment. He drew his sword and decided to change the rules of the game.

Kicking his heels into Spite's flanks, Malus turned the nauglir hard right and charged at the two-headed man. The cold one closed the distance in an eye blink, but the horseman reacted with amazing speed, kicking his mount into a gallop and dodging nimbly out of the nauglir's path. Then he darted back at Malus, slashing at him with both deadly axes. Caught by surprise at the deft manoeuvre, it was all the highborn could do to get his sword up in time to block the flurry of strokes. Even so, the rider's last blow rang hard against Malus's pauldron, drawing a hiss of pain from his lips.

Malus reined Spite around, but already the two-headed man was darting away, his horse responding to his commands as if they were of one mind. The highborn started to lunge Spite after the horseman when a blur of motion to his right caught his eye. The one-eyed swordsman was charging at him from the flank, his sword gleaming redly. Malus cursed and twisted in the saddle, blocking the horseman's blow, but the attack had tremendous power behind it, nearly knocking his sword from his hand.

The one-eyed rider swept past, and Malus felt something wrap around his sword arm and haul backwards, wrenching the limb painfully in its socket. The blue-eyed man was behind Spite, hauling on his own reins and trying to pull the highborn from his saddle.

Gritting his teeth with pain, Malus wrenched his reins and applied his left boot, and Spite lashed out with his powerful tail. The blue eyed man had just enough time to comprehend his mistake before the muscular appendage slammed into his horse's side, splintering ribs and shattering the man's leg. The horse collapsed with a strangely human scream, but the wounded warrior held onto his whip with both hands, still drawing Malus with him towards the ground.

Hot pain lanced from the highborn's shoulder across his narrow chest as he heeled Spite around. He looked over his shoulder and saw the one-eyed swordsman sweeping in on his left flank, while the two-headed axe man was coming up fast just behind and to the right. He yanked at the whip wrapping his arm, but the braided rawhide bound him fast.

Facing the prone marauder, Malus kicked Spite into a trot. The blue-eyed warrior tried to roll aside, but the whip trapping the highborn worked against him as well. The marauder let out a terrible, gobbling cry as the nauglir crushed him underfoot.

Hooves thundered to Malus's left as the one-eyed swordsman swept in, aiming a mighty stroke for the back of the highborn's neck. Malus gauged the man's approach, and at the last moment he kneed Spite hard and threw up his left arm. The nauglir sidled towards the onrushing horse, closing the distance faster than the swordsman expected and throwing off his aim. The flashing sword smashed into the back of Malus's shoulder, hard enough for the highborn to hear the pauldron bending. Then Malus closed his hand around the marauder's wrist and dropped his arm, trapping the sword against his chest.

The one-eyed swordsman let out a savage curse and tried to ride past, but he was far too close to the cold one to escape. The nauglir's jaws closed on the horse's head and crushed it like an egg. The animal collapsed, throwing its rider forwards, and Malus let the man go. He rolled admirably with the fall, tumbling to a stop more than a dozen feet away. Spite leapt at the man like a cat upon a mouse. The swordsman barely had time to scream before the nauglir's bloody jaws clamped down and bit him in half.

Malus was just turning to look for the third rider when a pair of blows struck him from behind. One hit square between his shoulder blades, rocking him in the saddle, while the other struck a glancing blow against his head. Pain bloomed behind Malus's eyes and his body went slack. The next thing he felt was the jarring shock of hitting the dusty ground.

Vague noises came and went as he slowly regained his senses. He heard the sound of hooves and the roar of the cold one, both noises reverberating oddly in his head. He opened his eyes and saw the two-headed man swinging wide of the cold one and angling back towards him.

He tried to sit up, shouting as a spike of pain lanced through his skull. He felt hot blood running down his cheek and the back of his neck. Malus saw a glint of metal on the ground nearby and dimly recognised it as his sword. He rolled over and crawled towards it as the two-headed man kicked his horse into a gallop, bearing down on him. The ground shook as the horse drew closer, and Malus knew that there was no way he was going to reach the weapon in time.

As the thunder loomed over him Malus threw himself flat and rolled onto his back, looking up at the marauder leaning down out of his saddle to strike with his axe. The blade blurred through the air. Malus reached up and crossed his arms, forming an X, and the haft of the long blade crashed against them. The highborn grabbed the leather wrapped haft and held on for all he was worth. The marauder, already at the limit of his balance, came out of the saddle and hit the ground hard, close to Malus.

Malus yanked hard on the axe, pulling it from the marauder's hands, and then rolled drunkenly to his feet. His opponent was on his back, still clutching his second weapon. Without hesitation the highborn charged at the man, bringing his axe down on the marauder's head. The two-headed man brought up his axe and blocked the highborn's blow, but Malus twisted his weapon and hooked the beard of the axe around his opponent's haft, pulling it out of the way. He rushed in, hammered an armoured boot into the marauder's groin, and then broke several of his ribs. Grabbing his axe with both hands, he twisted the weapon out of his stunned opponent's grip and methodically cut away both of the warrior's heads.

The highborn straightened, his chest heaving, and looked for someone else to kill. The knot of riders at the base of the depression had not moved during the fight. Now one of their number slid gracefully from the saddle and approached Malus. He was a huge, broad shouldered warrior, with dark tattoos spiralling across his powerful chest. His skin was the colour of polished mahogany, and one of his eyes glowed a nacreous green, like trapped witchlight. Two large broadswords hung from a wide leather belt at his hips, but the man made no move to draw them.

A trickle of blood ran down Malus's cheek and touched his lips. He spat it into the dust. 'If you don't want to die empty-handed you'd best draw one of those blades,' he growled.

To his surprise, the warrior halted and addressed him in passable druhir. 'You were magnificent, holy one. Whom do I have the honour of addressing?'

The highborn frowned. This was just about the last thing he expected.

'I am Malus, of Hag Graef, a warrior of the druchii.'

The man bowed deeply. 'You bear the blessing of the Lord of Murder in your eyes.' He straightened and said gravely, 'You have come for the sword.'

The frankness of the question stunned Malus. 'Yes. Yes I have. How did you know?'

'It was foreseen,' the warrior said with a dreadful smile. His teeth were filed to jagged points. 'You are the Scourge. We have been waiting for you for a very long time.'

Chapter Twenty-Two
THE AGELESS KINGS

THE DARK-SKINNED warrior turned to his companions and shouted something in a foul, debased tongue. The warband erupted in cheers and savage howls that were echoed by the riders at the crest of the rise.

Malus frowned thoughtfully, considering what he'd heard. 'Who are you?' he asked.

The tattooed marauder bowed again, in a passable impersonation of a druchii retainer. 'I am Shebbolai, the chieftain of the Tribe of the Red Sword. We serve the Ageless Kings in the City of Khaine, yonder.'

At first Malus wasn't sure he'd heard the man correctly. The City of Khaine, he thought. 'Who are these Ageless Kings?'

'Servants of the Bloody-handed God, who brought the great sword out of the hands of the blasphemers and kept it safe for many centuries, awaiting the day when Khaine's Scourge would walk out of the wasteland to claim his due.' The chieftain gave Malus another sharp-toothed smile and beckoned to him. 'Come, we must waste no time. The kings will want to see you at once.'

Malus was taken aback. Was it possible that the five assassins still lived after all this time, guarding the sword until the coming of the Time of Blood? It seemed incredible, but who knew what strange forces were at work here in the Wastes?

Slowly, painfully, the highborn recovered his sword. He looked at the bodies of the men he'd slain. 'Who were these warriors?'

'The champions of the tribe,' Shebbolai said proudly. 'Not even I could have defeated them all at once.'

Malus didn't think that spoke very highly of Shebbolai or the rest of his tribe, but the highborn judiciously held his tongue. On impulse he went to each of the men, struck off their heads, and carried the trophies over to Spite. The marauder chieftain watched, nodding in approval.

The highborn stuffed the heads into one of the empty sacks that had held his armour, and hung it from his belt like any zealot pilgrim. He took Spite by the reins and looked the cold one hard in the eye. 'Hunt, Spite,' he said. 'See what you can eat in this damned wasteland and wait for my call.' Then he slapped the nauglir on the neck and sent it loping off to the east. Whoever these Ageless Kings were, he wasn't about to trust them completely, not with his cache of Tz'arkan's relics at stake.

Malus turned back to Shebbolai. 'I'll take his mount,' he said, pointing to the two-headed man's horse.

The warrior nodded. 'He's yours,' the chieftain said. 'The horse and all three men's wives. It is your right.'

'Just the horse will do,' the highborn said, fighting to suppress a look of pure horror.

SHEBBOLAI LED THE party through a ruined gate at the southern edge of Khaine's city, past towers of bleached skulls that rose more than thirty feet into the crimson sky. The city itself was huge, easily the size of Hag Graef, and looking at the sleek, black stone of its construction Malus couldn't help but see the hands of elves in its making. Certainly the Ageless Kings hadn't built it. The crumbling structures groaned under the weight of ages, perhaps going back as far as the Great War against Chaos or even earlier.

Malus and the marauders rode down deserted streets piled with broken stone. He found himself catching movement out of the corner of his eye more than once, but when he turned to look, he saw only a shadowy alley or an empty doorway. Piles of ancient skulls stood at every corner, reminding the highborn of Har Ganeth, hundreds of leagues distant.

'How did your tribe come to serve the Ageless Kings?' Malus asked.

Shebbolai chuckled, letting his horse find its own way along the avenue beside Malus. 'By conquest, of course. Long, long ago my tribe wandered these plains like the other tribes, but the Ageless Kings came from the cold lands and slew our chieftain and nearly all of his warriors with the power of the red sword. Then they took the wives and children of the tribe and brought them here, to the City of Khaine. We have served them ever since.' The marauder twisted in his saddle and pointed back to the plains from whence they had come. 'We rule all the land from east to west, and many tribes pay us tribute in flesh and treasure to cross our territory.' Shebbolai smiled proudly. 'Other tribes must journey for many leagues in search of wealth and glory to heap at the feet of the Old Gods, but we need only stretch out our hands and the tribes bury their faces in the dirt and give us all they have. There is no tribe more powerful or more favoured by the gods than ours.'

'A tribe's glory is wrought in battle, is it not?' Malus asked.

Shebbolai's smile faded. 'We fight from time to time, but few of the tribes dare to challenge the power of the sword. The Ageless Kings tell us to bide our time and wait for the coming of the Scourge, and then we will drown ourselves in hot blood!'

The highborn nodded thoughtfully. 'The Ageless Kings are wise,' he said. 'Tell me, how many of them are there?'

'The legends say there were five at first, but now only three remain,' the chieftain said. 'Once they rode alongside the tribe, bearing the red sword before them, but for many hundreds of years they have kept to the god's temple here in the city.' Shebbolai extended a hand. 'There it is, yonder.'

Malus saw a squat, square tower rising from a pile of ruins just ahead. Perhaps it had always been a temple or a citadel for one of the city lords. Now its sloped flanks were adorned with thousands upon thousands of skulls. The sheer scale of the offerings stunned the highborn. Not all of the temples in Naggaroth combined could equal it.

The closer they drew to the temple the more people Malus saw: hideous, twisted wretches, clothed in rags and bits of fur, who watched the passage of the chieftain and his retinue with hard, feral stares. Many of the buildings near the temple were inhabited, but few were in good repair. Whatever wealth the tribe had accumulated, it hadn't gone towards providing the marauders with luxury or comfort. As they rode through the more populated streets Malus could sense an undercurrent of tension rising out of the squalor, and wondered how he might turn that to his advantage.

Before they reached the temple the riders passed through a broad plaza. Princes and generals in ages past might have reviewed their armies in such an expanse. Now, however, it was a forest of iron poles bearing the rotting, headless corpses of thousands of sacrificial victims. The stench of decay was immense. Malus gritted his teeth and tried to keep his expression neutral as they worked their way through a miasma of death.

Malus studied the bodies closest to the narrow path. 'Many of these look quite fresh,' he observed. 'It seems you've been fighting recently.'

Shebbolai's expression darkened. 'Just the killing of dogs,' he said gruffly, and spoke no more.

Beyond the plaza of corpses the riders reached a broad flight of stone steps leading up to the tower. As they reined in, a pair of towering doors at the top of the steps groaned open, and a mob of cowering, naked human slaves spilled out. Their bodies were thin and sallow, covered with scars and weeping sores, and they raced to the bottom of the steps to take the marauders' horses and see to their needs. Malus slid gratefully from the saddle, happy to be rid of the mangy, stinking beast, and tossed its reins to one of the trembling humans before following Shebbolai up to the open doorway.

The chieftain ushered Malus across the threshold with a bow, and then returned to his fellows. A long, broad corridor stretched beyond, lit by globes of flickering witchlight. The highborn composed himself before striding swiftly down the long passageway. Tall figures in ornate, archaic brass armour stood sentinel along the corridor. The men were inhumanly strong, their bodies swollen to hideous proportions, and they held huge, double-headed axes in their broad, scarred hands. The highborn studied them as he walked past, feeling the weight of their gaze, but unable to see the expressions behind their helmets' ornate faceplates.

Malus stepped into a large, dimly lit space at the end of the passageway. A single shaft of light speared down into the centre of the chamber, falling upon a small stone altar carved of dark marble. Its square sides were anointed in fresh blood, and two grinning skulls rested upon it, their surfaces stained nearly brown by centuries of bloody libations.

Malus approached the ancient bones, noting that they were free from mutation and perfect in form. The cheekbones were sharp, the jaw lines angular. The two dead kings,' he murmured, reaching out to touch the remains of one of the five lost assassins.

'You are not worthy to touch the bones of the Ageless Kings!' hissed a voice from the darkness. The sound was eerie, like a keening wind whistling through bare branches and forming words Malus could understand. It echoed in the vast chamber, seeming to come from every direction at once. 'You defile this sacred place with your presence!'

Malus turned, seeking the source of the frail voice. 'Are you wraith or man?' he called out. 'Show yourself!'

Another voice spoke. Like the first, it was chillingly unnatural, like the groan of glacial ice. 'We are ageless,' it said, 'and we rule here, not you.'

The imperious tone in the groaning voice annoyed the highborn. 'You rule here? I thought you were waiting, serving the will of Khaine and guarding the warpsword until the arrival of the chosen one.'

A third voice answered, thin and creaking like old leather. 'Who are you to question us so?'

Malus took a deep breath. 'I am the Scourge,' he said. 'Your vigil is ended, for I have come for the sword. The Time of Blood is nigh.'

The echoes of his voice faded into the stillness. Malus waited, straining to locate the aged assassins in the depths of the room. After a moment he caught the faintest sound of movement to his left: a dry rustle of robes.

'Impossible,' the first voice said. 'You cannot be the chosen one.'

Malus turned to the source of movement. 'Can I not? Am I not druchii, like you? Do I not bear the blessing of Khaine upon my face? I have followed you here through the Vermillion Gate, drawn by the tie I have with the sword. How else could I have found you here in the Waste?' He held out his hand. 'Will you bring me my sword, or will you dishonour your long vigil here at its end?'

More faint hints of movement whispered in the darkness. The second voice spoke. 'You come from the temple,' it groaned.

'So did you, once upon a time,' Malus answered. 'The true believers count you among the dead. The heretics in the temple concealed the theft of the sword and have ruled unchallenged for centuries.'

'That is of no matter to us,' creaked the third voice. 'Let them rule atop their filthy hill. It will all be swept aside when the Time of Blood arrives.'

The voices were drawing closer. Malus was certain now. 'Why conceal your triumph from your fellows?' he asked. 'They might have swayed the people of the city to the true faith had they known.'

Faint shapes resolved themselves at the edges of the light. Malus saw the outlines of robed and hooded figures regarding him from the darkness. 'We are the true faith,' the first voice replied.

'Prove it,' Malus said. 'Give me the sword.'

'The sword is not here,' the second voice groaned, 'and you are not worthy.'

'You dare deny me?' the highborn snapped. 'I am Malus of Hag Graef, born in the city of shadow to the house of chains. My mother was a witch and I slew my father with my own hands. The skull of Aurun Var spoke to me through my sister, a living saint of the

Lord of Murder. Have you forgotten your duty after so many centuries, or has your lust for power turned you into the very heretics you once rebelled against?'

All three voices shouted at once. 'Blasphemy!'

'A man blasphemes against the gods, not cowardly figures hiding in the shadows of a ruined temple,' Malus shouted. 'Did you steal the sword to keep it from the hands of the temple elders, or did you secretly covet its power? What are you but pathetic mockeries of the very heretics you once railed against?'

'Seize him!' the first voice shrieked. Malus reached for his sword, but huge figures loomed silently out of the shadows to either side of him. There had been more of the armoured guards standing a silent watch in the darkness of the room, and they grabbed Malus's arms and lifted him from the ground as if he was a child.

The robed figures crept slowly into the light, drawing back their hoods, and Malus looked upon them and cried out, horrified at what the assassins had become.

Their bodies were impossibly ancient, shrivelled and dried like mummies over thousands of years in the hot air of the Wastes. Two males and a woman – her paper thin lips framed a pair of yellow fangs that told Malus she had once been a blood-witch – little more than living skeletons with parchment skin stretched over sharp bones.

The man in the centre of the trio stepped close to Malus, studying him with cold, reptilian orbs that bore little resemblance to living eyes. 'You are young and strong,' the creature said, its voice whistling from the depths of dried lungs and past cracked lips. 'The people here are faithful, but their spirits are weak. We have lived on thin gruel for far too long,' the withered druchii said. 'You are blasphemous, but in a sense you are also a blessing from Khaine. Tonight we will kill you, so that tomorrow we may call back your spirit and consume it. Your energies will restore us and lend us strength for a very long time to come.'

'You would dare take the life of Khaine's chosen Scourge?' Malus raged.

The withered creature looked up at Malus and shook his head. 'The true Scourge would not have been taken so easily,' he said, and gestured to the guards.

'Take the heretic to the plaza and crucify him,' the Ageless King said.

Chapter Twenty-Three
THE BURNING BLADE

MALUS ROARED LIKE a trapped animal, thrashing and kicking in the guards' iron grip as they began to remove him from the altar room. Consumed with rage, he used their strength against them, twisting at the waist and kicking the man to his left in the side of the head. The highborn's armoured shin rang like a gong off the polished brass helmet and the guard staggered, allowing Malus to pull his arm free.

The guard on his right reacted quickly for a man of his immense size, reaching for Malus's throat with a wide, spade-like hand. Snarling, Malus ducked beneath the guard's lunge and tried to grab the bone handle of a dagger sheathed at the man's waist. The highborn's hand closed on the hilt and he drew the blade free, just as a clawed hand grasped the side of Malus's cheek and every nerve in his body exploded in icy pain.

Malus convulsed beneath the witch's agonising touch. His body arched, taut as a bow, and his face locked in a rictus of torment. Malus dimly heard a sharp, brittle *crack* near his waist and realised that the bone hilt had snapped in his clenched, quivering hand.

Armoured hands grabbed him roughly, tearing the dagger away and lifting him from the ground. His gaze was fixed. He could not move, could not breathe, could not even blink. The pain was so intense that he could barely think. Tz'arkan's name rose unbidden to his mind, but he had not the power to speak it.

The blood-witch recoiled from Malus with a frightened groan, her black eyes glittering with shock and horror as the guards dragged him away. The last thing he saw as darkness enfolded him was her white, withered face, its leathery features twisting into an expression of despair as the witch reeled from the glimpse she'd been given into Malus's soul.

In time, the pain began to recede, like a slow tide ebbing from his tortured frame. Visions of red slowly resolved into a crimson sky, painted with twisting shapes of black smoke and ashen clouds. Thunder rumbled in the distance.

Long shapes loomed at the edges of his vision. He lay on his back amid a forest of dying men, their ravaged bodies impaled upon iron stakes as tall as saplings. His body was contorted awkwardly on the wide paving stones, like a statue tumbled from its plinth. Figures moved slowly past the limits of his eyesight, their movements perceived as no more than shifting shadows playing across his contorted form.

He thought he heard a voice rise in anger, and moans of defeat and despair. Malus could not tell if they were real or part of a dream, and his mind wandered as he stared into the shifting, crimson sky.

Once he thought he saw the blood-witch standing over him, a curved knife trembling in her shrunken hand. Shrieks and groans echoed in the turgid air, and when he looked into her eyes she wailed like a ghost and shrank from his sight. He tried to laugh but managed only a low, tortured moan.

The sky darkened. Thunder rolled like war drums, and drops of blood mixed with gritty ash fell heavily against his face. Hands gripped him around his arms and lifted him. He rose into the air, wondering if he was being offered up to the storm.

Then he was falling again, being lowered onto a frame of rough wood in the shape of an X. The hands pulled at him, stretching his contorted limbs and laying them flat against the crossbars. His head sagged between the cross-posts, sending drops of dark red streaming down into his ears and hair.

He felt his gauntlets being pulled away. Something cold and sharp pressed against his right wrist. His mind drifted, unable to make sense of what was happening.

Then the first hammer blow struck, driving the spike deep into his wrist, and Malus began to scream.

THUNDER CRASHED, VIBRATING his armour like a struck gong and startling him awake. His body jerked, and he cried out in the grip of raw, jagged pain as his broken wrists and ankles grated against the nails pinning him to beams. Agony caused his stomach to clench, and he vomited blood and bile onto the paving stones.

Darkness had fallen since the guards had nailed him to the wood and left him in the plaza to die. Lightning raged overhead, playing a nightmarish pantomime of shadows across the stones of the plaza. Blood and ashes had dried on his cheeks, forming a brittle death mask that lent a daemonic cast to his angular face.

Had it not been for his armour he would have been dead already, suffocated by his own ribcage as he hung from the upright wooden posts. As it was, the interlocking plates kept his body from sagging too far downwards, taking some of the weight off his mutilated wrists. He'd swum in and out of consciousness for hours, delirious from pain and loss of blood.

His mind was clearer now. Perhaps the last vestiges of the witch's touch had faded, or else his nerves no longer had the power to communicate the awful truth of his injuries. It was enough that he was able to notice the solitary figure outlined by the flash of lightning only a few yards away.

Grunting in pain, he managed to raise his head slightly and peer at the motionless figure. 'Sh… Shebbolai,' he whispered, his voice little more than a thready rasp.

The figure stirred. 'I thought you dead,' the chieftain replied. He stepped closer. Another flicker of lightning etched his dark skinned face in sharp relief, revealing an expression of anger and torment. 'How can this be?' he asked. 'You are the first warrior of Naggaroth to come here since the arrival of the Ageless Kings.

You bested my finest warriors, and you bear the mark of Khaine in your eyes. You must be the Scourge!'

'The Ageless Kings have forgotten their duty to the Lord of Murder,' Malus rasped. 'They have been seduced by power and wealth. Long ago they ruled this land to safeguard Khaine's sword. Now they rule for their sakes alone.'

'Do not blaspheme!' Shebbolai snapped.

'You know it's true!' Malus said. He tried to look up at the bodies hanging nearby. 'On the way here you told me that your tribe rarely fought any more. Where, then, did all these men come from? They have the look of warriors, but were they foes taken in battle or members of your own tribe who rebelled against the Ageless Kings and their inglorious rule?'

'You're here now,' the chieftain said, 'and The Time of Blood is at hand! How can they deny you?'

'Because this is all they have,' Malus said. 'They've clung to life and power for so long that the struggle is all they know. They cannot return to Naggaroth, not as they are, and once I claim the sword, who will fear them? The centuries have made them mad, Shebbolai, and weak. Their time is at an end.' Malus met his eye. 'It's your time now. Of all the hundreds of chieftains who have led the red swords, it is you who will ride to battle beside Khaine's chosen Scourge.'

An expression of awe transformed Shebbolai's scarred face. 'What would you have me do?'

'Tell me where to find the warpsword.'

'It... it is not here,' the chieftain said. 'Long ago, when the kings first came here, the sword passed between them at the turning of each moon, so that all of them would share the burden of safeguarding it. One day the king who kept the sword refused to give it up, and they fought among themselves. The struggle lasted for centuries, or so the legends say.' Shebbolai turned and look back at the temple. 'Two of the kings died during the feud. You saw their skulls in the reliquary chamber.'

'And the sword?'

'They agreed to place it beyond their grasp except in the direst of circumstances, so that they would never feud amongst themselves again. They took the sword north, into the mountains, and hid it in a cave, so goes the legend,' Shebbolai said grimly, 'as it has been passed down through the line of chieftains. It is part of our pact with the Ageless Kings, to keep their secret from the rest of the world.'

'That's all very fascinating,' Malus wheezed impatiently, 'but how am I to find this cave?'

'Follow the skulls,' the chieftain said. 'They will lead you through the gullies to the cave and its guardian.'

'Guardian,' Malus spat, 'what sort of guardian?'

The chieftain shrugged. 'The legends do not say: something powerful enough to guard the warpsword for ages and not be tempted by it as the kings were.'

'Delightful,' the highborn snarled. The pain in his wrists was starting to build once more. Gritting his teeth, he tried to take some of the weight off of them, prompting a groan of torment as he bore down on the spikes penetrating his feet just below the ankles.

When the agony subsided and his vision cleared he focused his gaze on Shebbolai once more. 'You must pass the word to those of your tribe you can trust,' the highborn said. 'When I return with the sword the reign of the Ageless Kings will end. Do you understand?'

The chieftain nodded. 'I understand.'

'Good. Now get me down from this damned cross,' Malus groaned.

But Shebbolai was unmoved. He looked Malus in the eye. 'If all you say is true, and you are the Scourge of Khaine, you should be able to free yourself.' He backed away from the cross. 'I will await your return,' he said, and disappeared into the darkness.

Malus stifled a vicious curse. He had a plan for Shebbolai and his warriors, so for the moment he needed the chieftain on his side. Plus, he thought bitterly as he tried in vain to close his fists, there was not enough mothers' milk in the world to heal him from the guards' iron spikes.

Lightning flared overhead and arced among the iron poles of the plaza. Malus heard screams and smelled the sweet odour of burning flesh. He drew a deep breath.

This would not be any mere taste. He stood at the edge of an abyss. The next step he took would be into darkness.

Thunder crashed. 'Tz'arkan!' he screamed at the bleeding sky, and his veins burned with the daemon's icy touch.

Power coursed through him in an icy torrent, banishing fear, weakness and pain. The strength of a god flowed through him. Clenching his fists, he tore them free of the iron spikes and laughed like a madman as shattered bone and torn flesh re-knit. Reaching down, he pulled the lower spikes loose with his bare hands and fell to his knees upon the gore slick stones. Malus squeezed the spikes between his fingers as if they were half-melted wax, and threw them high into the air.

He felt the lightning coming before it flared overhead. He heard the heartbeats of the men slowly dying among the forest of iron poles. He could taste the scent of each and every living thing in the city, and see the peaks of the mountains to the north despite the roiling darkness overhead.

It was like nothing he had ever felt before. The daemon did not merely strengthen and heal him. He *was* the daemon, and the daemon was him.

HE'D FOUND THE cold one a mile outside the city, tracking it through the darkness by its peculiar, acrid scent. It had growled threateningly at his approach, lowering its blocky head and snapping its fearsome jaws, but he had met its red eyes and bent his will upon the beast. The nauglir struggled against him but a moment, and then recoiled with a cry of pain. He advanced on the beast, lashing it again and again with his power, until it lay on its belly and allowed him to climb into the saddle.

Malus led Spite around the ruined city under the cover of darkness and up into the broken foothills to the north. His razor-keen senses banished the darkness and allowed him to traverse the narrow, labyrinthine gullies as if it was broad daylight.

Shebbolai had spoken true. He began to see the bones almost at once: smashed skeletons of men and horses, the long bones snapped and sucked clean of marrow and the skulls split open to get at the brains. Shorn armour and broken swords lay rusting in the dirt, enough to equip an army. For the first hour he'd amused himself by counting the skulls, trying to gauge how many souls had gone into the narrow defiles in search of Khaine's sword. Before the hour was up he'd counted a thousand, and didn't bother to continue from there.

Spite's broad feet were wading through drifts of old bones before long, crushing them and kicking them underfoot. They led unerringly upwards, many times branching off into twisting side paths, but Malus kept to the primary trail, knowing where it must eventually lead.

'Whoever lives here, daemon... has quite an appetite,' he said.

'Then let's hope he's sleeping, Malus,' Tz'arkan replied. The voice reverberated through his skull no differently than the highborn's own, as if he and the daemon were simply two spirits bound to the same body. 'Somewhere in these gullies lies the lost Warpsword of Khaine. We're not leaving until you've found it.'

The tone in the daemon's voice angered Malus, as if he was nothing more than a slave going about his master's business. For the moment, he chose to hold his tongue. Tz'arkan's power had subsided somewhat, but still flowed freely, infusing him with strength and power such as he hadn't known for months.

Up ahead the gully widened, forming a broad V that pointed to the mouth of a large cave. The gully floor outside the cave was literally carpeted with bones and the detritus of the dead. After many long months, he'd reached his goal at last.

Malus reined in Spite and slid carefully from the saddle. The nauglir shied away from him at once, retreating further down the length of the gully. He shot the beast a warning glance. 'I found you once, dragonlet. I can find you again,' he warned, and then turned his attention to the drifts of old bones that blanketed the rocky ground. It was a crude but effective alarm, providing the sword's guardian had sharp ears.

Choosing his course very carefully, Malus began to pick his way through the multitude of fallen treasure seekers. He tried not to think about the fact that many of them had probably attempted the very same thing.

'Quietly now, Darkblade,' Tz'arkan said, 'let's not wake anyone.'

'Your concern is touching,' the highborn murmured, slowly drawing his sword.

Lightning flickered silently overhead, making the landscape of bones appear to shift and slide. Disorientated, Malus tried to step over a yellowed skull directly in his path, and came down directly on it instead. The aged bone collapsed with a hollow *crunch* that seemed to echo like thunder between the gully walls.

Malus froze, not even daring to breathe. A moment passed, and then another. Still he waited, straining his ears for any signs of movement.

Two minutes passed. Only then did Malus relax, cursing his foul luck.

That was when the night air shook with an ear-splitting roar and an enormous figure emerged from the depths of the cave.

The guardian of the sword was huge. Its lower body alone was larger than a cold one, covered in scales of indigo and dusky red. Large legs, like those of a dragon, propelled it in a thunderous charge down the slope towards Malus, kicking up clouds of powdered bone with every ponderous step. Above the set of clawed forelegs where a dragon's neck and head would normally be there was instead a broad leather belt, decorated with scales of gold and a buckle shaped like a skull. Above the belt, towered the upper torso of a fearsome ogre, clad in crude armour that protected its midsection and capped its powerful shoulders. Tusks thick enough to disembowel a boar jutted from the shaggoth's thick lips, and its ice blue eyes gleamed beneath a craggy brow and a round steel helmet. In its platter sized hand, the guardian held a sword that was longer than Malus was tall, and the creature raised it angrily as it bore down on the stunned highborn.

'Mother of Night!' the highborn cursed.

'Malus, under the circumstances I think I'll let you run, now!'

The terrible sword whickered through the air. Galvanised by the daemon's shout, Malus hurled himself to the left, just out of the weapon's reach. The blade struck a pile of bones and sent shattered fragments spraying into the air. Still bellowing in rage, the dragon ogre charged past, quickly changing course to come around for another charge.

The creature was between Malus and his cold one. Frantically he cast around for other avenues of escape, but the walls of the gully were steep and sheer. 'There's nowhere to run!' he exclaimed.

The dragon ogre bore down on Malus again with a terrible crunching of bones. The highborn raised his sword warily. There was no way he could trade blows with something so massive. He would have to wear the monster down with lightning-fast strikes, much as he'd seen Arleth Vann kill the highborn in the crypt.

He crouched low as the beast charged into reach. Its sword swept down at an angle, aiming to cut the druchii in half from shoulder to hip. At the last second, Malus dodged to the left, cutting across the dragon ogre's path and fouling his swing. The creature let out a furious cry and the highborn answered with a druchii war scream as he put all his strength into a powerful cut aimed just below the shaggoth's belt.

The heavy northern sword, backed by the daemon's terrible strength, struck the monster dead on, and the steel blade shattered with a discordant clang. Malus barely had time to register his shock before the dragon ogre lashed out with a clawed forelimb and struck him a backhanded blow that sent him flying head over heels into the air.

Had the limb struck his chin it would have taken his head clean off. As it was, the shaggoth's paw had glanced off his chest and dented his thick breastplate. He felt as if he'd been kicked by a nauglir, and he gasped for breath as he hit a pile of old skulls near the side of the gully wall.

Malus rolled off the pile of bones, glaring helplessly at the monster. He tried to subdue it by force of will just as he'd done to the nauglir, but the dragon ogre was unfazed. Furious, he grabbed a skull and hurled it at the beast with all his strength. 'Curse you, creature!' he roared. 'Curse you back to hell!' The projectile struck the beast in the side of the head and shattered into pieces, leaving not a mark on the monster's thick skull.

Terror and despair raged through Malus. The daemon's gifts were useless. Had he surrendered the last vestiges of himself for nothing?

Bellowing like a bull, the dragon ogre came about, readying its massive sword.

Malus could feel Tz'arkan's strength pulsing through him. He could hear the blood rushing in his veins and feel the fury of the storm raging overhead, but not a bit of it mattered. In the next few moments the shaggoth would cut him apart.

As the dragon ogre trotted towards him, Malus's eyes turned to the dark mouth of the cave. I'll be damned if I'm going to die empty-handed, he thought.

The highborn pushed himself to his feet and sprinted up the gully. The dragon ogre bellowed angrily, surprised by the sudden move. Tz'arkan was surprised as well.

'Malus, where are you going? You're running towards the cave!'

'We still have a job to do, remember?' the highborn countered.

'You fool! It's right behind us!' the daemon said. 'You'll trap us in there!'

'I need a weapon,' Malus snarled. 'The warpsword is in there. That will do.'

Malus reached the entrance to the cave. A cacophony of pounding feet and crunching bone rose behind him as the shaggoth charged headlong up the gully.

'The Warpsword of Khaine is no pig stick to be used in brawling!' the daemon raged. 'It is a talisman of glorious power–'

'It's still a sword,' Malus said. 'Shut up, daemon!'

Malus rushed into the cave. He expected a long, carrion choked passageway, leading back into darkness. Instead he found himself in a broad, high-ceilinged cavern. The space was piled with bones and rotting bodies nevertheless, save for a cleared area near the centre of the chamber where the dragon ogre evidently slept. A plain stone altar stood on the other side of the cleared area, and upon that altar rested a sword.

The Warpsword of Khaine was a double-edged blade nearly as long as a draich, slightly wider at the point than at the hilt to give the weapon extra power to cut with. Its blade was sheathed in a scabbard of black lacquered bone, chased with gold and ornamented with fiery rubies. The weapon's hilt was long and slim, built for two hands and wrapped with dark leather. A large cabochon ruby, like a dragon's eye, gleamed at the point where hilt met blade. It glimmered with power, radiating from the entire blade in waves of invisible heat.

Malus looked upon the sword and saw the potential hidden within its depths. He saw red battlefields and toppled towers, looted cities and fallen kings. With such a blade a druchii could conquer the world.

'Malus, I forbid this!' the daemon snarled. Was there an edge of fear in Tz'arkan's voice?

The highborn dashed across the chamber. The shaggoth burst into the cavern just behind him, shaking the dank air with its furious cries.

'Then we die here,' Malus replied. 'The choice is yours.'

In truth it wasn't. Nothing the daemon could say or do would keep Malus from placing his hand upon the warpsword's hilt and drawing the weapon from its scabbard.

The hilt was hot to the touch, as if the ancient steel was still fresh from the forge. The warmth sank into his skin, suffusing his muscles with power. He drew the weapon in a single, smooth motion, marvelling at the blade's black finish. Its edge shone like fire in the gloom.

With a stentorian bellow the dragon ogre charged. Malus felt no fear. When he turned to face the onrushing beast he was smiling like a wolf.

Malus stepped into the shaggoth's charge, swinging the warpsword in a clean, perfect arc that was the virtual twin of the blow he'd struck before. The bright edges of the blade left an arc of ghostly light in the darkness as it sliced through the dragon ogre's midsection. The beast screamed, hurled backwards by the force of the blow. It landed in a broken heap close to the mouth of the cave, its armour half melted and smoke rising from the fearsome wound in its abdomen. The beast was dead, almost as if the blade had reached into its huge body and snuffed out its life like a candle.

The highborn stared at the sword in wonder. Its warmth coursed through him, banishing Tz'arkan's black ice. His heart hammered in his chest, and his mind was suffused with an emotion he hadn't felt in many months: hope.

'Good sword,' Malus said in an awed whisper. 'No wonder you wanted it for your collection.'

The daemon seemed to shrink inside Malus, dwindling in presence until it coiled like a serpent around the highborn's black heart. 'I despair of you Malus,' Tz'arkan said hatefully. 'When the final task is done there will be *such* a reckoning.'

Malus stared into the depths of the blade. A faint smile tugged at his lean face. 'I'm counting on it,' he said.

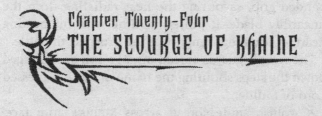

Chapter Twenty-Four
THE SCOURGE OF KHAINE

MALUS DARKBLADE RODE into the city of the Ageless Kings with a gleaming sword in his hand and a Chaos storm raging at his back.

Lightning roiled the crimson skies, etching the broken walls and crumbled towers in stark relief. Thunder rolled, matched by the terrible growl of the nauglir as it stalked down the debris-choked lanes. Tribesmen rose from the furs they had been sleeping on, clutching axes or swords, and peered into the night, sensing something terrible was at hand.

Malus rode through the plaza of impaled men, passing the crossed timbers where he himself had hung mere hours before. The dark bulk of the temple reared before him, its skull adorned flanks silhouetted in flickering displays of brazen lightning. He reined in his cold one at the base of the towering steps and regarded the sealed doors coldly. Spite reared his head at the ancient building and roared, a raw sound of fury that echoed roughly from the temple's thick walls.

The double doors swung open within moments and a troop of temple guards swarmed out, brandishing long, heavy pole arms and axes. Malus slid from the saddle and took the warpsword in a two-handed grip, savouring the heat radiating from the unearthly blade. It pulsed in time with his beating heart, quickening hungrily at the prospect of battle.

The temple guards spread out at a run and charged down the steps shouting the name of Khaine, blessed Lord of Murder.

A wolfish smile spread across Malus's grim face. 'Blood and souls,' he whispered, and ran to meet them.

He saw the battle unfold with dreadful, icy clarity, as if it was a ritual dance unfolding in slow motion. A guard rushed in from the highborn's left, stabbing with his pole arm. Malus hacked off the spearhead with a desultory sweep of his blade and cut the man in half with a backhanded stroke. Without pause, Malus swept his sword to the right to block the sweep of another guardsman's axe, before reversing the blade and cutting off both of the warrior's legs just above the knee. Armour parted like rotted paper; flesh blackened and bone splintered at the sword's ravening touch. Men's screams wove a brutal threnody around Malus as he wove among his foes, scattering arcs of hot blood that sizzled and steamed in the air.

One guardsman swept low with his pole arm, aiming to knock Malus from his feet. Before the blow could land the highborn reached out and sank the point of the warpsword into the onrushing guard's neck, and then spun on his heel and severed both arms and the helmeted head of the guard charging at Malus from behind. The highborn laughed like a drunkard, spinning and cutting with the seething blade and climbing ever higher towards the temple doors.

A guard screamed in fury and leapt for him, heedless of the long fall to the plaza below. The move caught Malus off-guard for a fraction of a second, but with the battle fever on him his foe seemed to hang languorously in the air, his muscular arms outstretched like a child's. Fluid as a blade dancer, Malus half-spun and dropped to one knee, bringing the sword up in a glittering stroke that sliced the man open from groin to chin and propelled him in a bloody arc to the grey stones at the nauglir's feet.

There was a droning sound humming lazily towards Malus. He turned and swatted the thrown axe aside, and then dashed up the last few steps to the sole remaining guard. The warrior had barely enough time to unsheath his dagger before Malus reached him.

Both men regarded one another. The armoured giant towered over the lithe highborn, his masked face looking down at the druchii as if in startled bemusement. Then the guard let out a bubbling sigh and bright blood erupted from the air holes in his visor as the highborn pulled the warpsword free from the man's breastplate. Malus stepped gracefully to the side as the giant's body crashed face first onto the stone steps and slid towards the bottom on a dark trail of gore.

A pale figure regarded the highborn from just outside the temple doorway. The blood-witch sank slowly to her knees, her marble-like eyes glittering fearfully as Malus approached her. Thin, wrinkled lips pulled back from yellowed fangs in a frightful grimace of dread.

'I knew you would return,' she groaned. 'I tried to tell the others, but they would not believe what I had seen.' The ancient blood-witch spread her hands. 'You are death and ruin given form, oh son of the house of chains, and the blessings of the Dark Gods go with you. Our time is finished. Let the Time of Blood begin.'

She raised her chin, and the warpsword seemed to leap in Malus's hands. The black blade flickered through the air and the blood-witch stiffened in the wind of the sword's passing.

Malus studied the witch coldly for a moment. A trickle of dark blood welled in a thin line across her narrow throat. The highborn stepped up to her and reached out, taking a handful of her white hair in his fist and lifting her severed head from her neck.

The highborn hung the witch's head from his belt and stalked past her still upright body, heading into the darkness of the temple beyond.

WHEN MALUS EMERGED from the temple a short while later the tribe of the red sword was awaiting him.

They filled the plaza at the foot of the temple, standing like wraiths amid the forest of impaled men.

Lightning picked out steel helms and glittering mail, sharpened swords and bared fangs. Warped faces turned upwards as the highborn's armoured figure strode to the top of the stairs, and every eye beheld the steaming sword and the trio of severed heads gripped in Malus's hands.

Shebbolai stood at the head of his tribe, waiting at the foot of the broad stairs with a look of grim joy on his face. Malus regarded him balefully, and then his gaze swept across the gathered warriors. Thunder rumbled from the north.

'The rule of the Ageless Kings is no more,' Malus said, his sharp voice ringing out across the plaza. 'They forgot their duty to the Lord of Murder, and Khaine has meted out his wrath, but their taint has spread to you, warriors of the red sword. The sons of Khaine do not hide in cities of stone and turn their faces from the battlefield! The glory of the Bloody-handed God lies in death, not in slaves, nor gold, nor stone walls. The Ageless Kings chose to cling to life, and you joined in their depravity.'

A groan rose from the assembled warriors at the highborn's harsh words. Malus cut them off with a shout.

'When Khaine sent his chosen Scourge to claim his birthright from the kings, they were sunk so far in their iniquity that they did not know him.' Malus raised the terrible blade. 'Look upon the Warpsword of Khaine and know that his Scourge has arisen!'

The warriors replied with shouts of anger and despair. Men slashed their cheeks and their chests, offering up their bloodstained blades to the highborn.

Warriors turned on the weaker men of the tribe and hacked their bodies apart, throwing glistening bits of flesh and bone upon the steps of the temple.

'We live to serve!' Shebbolai cried out, his face a mask of shame and despair. 'Forgive us, dreadful Scourge!'

'There is no forgiveness in the eyes of Khaine,' Malus snarled, 'only death. Blood alone can wash away your sins.'

'Then blood it will be!' Shebbolai roared. 'Show us the way, holy one. We live and die at your command!'

The highborn looked down upon the chieftain and smiled an executioner's smile. 'Follow me, sons of the red sword. Death and glory await.'

MALUS LED THE tribe out into the wasteland, returning to the place where the Vermillion Gate had left him. He had no idea if it would make any difference, but it gave him some time to think and take stock of the forces at his command.

The Chaos warriors did not march as an army of Naggaroth, in ordered lines and divisions. They swept over the plain in a ragged mob, perhaps two hundred strong, riding swift, lean horses that moved as if they shared a single mind with their masters. Hoarse shouts and lusty war cries echoed in the darkness as the warriors followed the Scourge from the city. The prospect of battle had quickened their blood, banishing doubt and fear.

The same could not be said for Malus. He rode ahead of the unruly mob with the warpsword riding in its scabbard against his hip. With the weapon sheathed he felt cold again, the heat of Khaine's hunger leaching slowly from his muscles and leaving him wretched and weak. Every few moments his hand would stray to the weapon's hilt, as if he was warming himself by the side of a small fire.

Tz'arkan stirred within Malus. Where before the daemon's presence seemed to swell within the highborn's chest, now it caused his whole body to tremble. 'You grow overbold, little druchii,' the daemon sneered. 'You trifle with forces beyond your understanding, and you think to lead this pitiful mob to war with your brother?'

Malus looked back at Shebbolai, riding just a few yards behind the highborn, and beyond to the shifting crowd of riders spread out across the plain. 'I don't expect them to triumph,' he said coldly. 'I expect them to die, in as dramatic a fashion as possible. I will need a grand diversion if I'm to reach the Sanctum of the Sword and deal with Urial.'

It was a gamble, to be sure, and a desperate one. As fearsome as the warpsword was, Malus didn't care to pit himself against Tyran and his entire band of zealots. If he could distract them with a sudden attack inside the walls of the fortress, it might buy him enough time to reach the temple and confront Urial directly. He hoped that with his half-brother dead the zealots would accept him as the new Scourge or else lose heart and scatter into the night. Then he could deal with Rhulan or whoever was commanding the forces of the temple.

'You think that you can defeat Urial by yourself?' the daemon sneered.

Malus's hand strayed towards the hilt of the warpsword. 'With this I can.'

'You are a fool, Darkblade!'

'No, daemon. You put this sword into my hands. If you didn't think I'd take it up and use it to slay my enemies then you are the fool, not I.'

As he spoke, Malus caught sight of a trio of ragged shapes lying upon the lifeless ground and realised they'd reached the site of his battle with Shebbolai's champions. He prodded Spite into a canter and rode halfway up the shallow rise so he that could turn and regard the tribesmen. As the nauglir heeled about the riders brought their mounts to a halt and waited expectantly.

Malus drew the warpsword, shuddering slightly as the rush of heat flooded his body. 'Warriors of the red sword,' he cried, 'the hour of your redemption is at hand! Follow me and cleanse your souls in the blood of the foe! Kill every man who stands in your way!'

Shebbolai drew a fearsome, curved sword and waved it in the air. 'Blood for the Blood God!'

The night air erupted in a cacophony of bestial shouts to Khaine. Malus smiled, and focused his will upon the sword. *Open the gate,* he commanded. *Return us to the temple, you damned Lord of Murder, and we'll reap a red harvest in your name.*

An angry rumble shook the air. Whether it was thunder or the growl of a bloodthirsty god Malus could not say, for at that moment the warriors of the tribe cried out in terror and the world turned inside out.

* * *

THEY APPEARED UNDER clear skies, with a bright pair of moons overhead. The transition was so jarring that for a moment Malus was completely disorientated.

Horses screamed and men shouted in wonder and fear. The night shook with the stern cry of trumpets and Malus heard shouts of alarm echoing down the lanes of the temple fortress. Then the world snapped back into focus.

Malus and the warriors found themselves in the broad avenue between the Citadel of Bone and the dwarf-built temple. White-robed zealots were charging from every building and pathway, and the alarm trumpets continued to sound. It was as if their arrival had been expected somehow, the highborn thought. If so, his gambit had already failed.

The sounds of battle revivified the Chaos warriors, however, and already screams and clashes of steel echoed across the avenue. Malus stood in his saddle. 'Warriors of Khaine, redeem yourselves in the blood of your foes!'

With a bloodthirsty roar the marauders spurred their horses and threw themselves headlong at the zealots, and in moments a fierce, swirling melee raged along the length of the avenue. More zealots were streaming in from every direction, but for the moment the horsemen had an edge in both numbers and mobility. The highborn knew the tide would turn soon enough.

Malus put his heels to Spite's flanks and dashed for the temple.

White-robed warriors raced across his path from left and right, trying to cut him off. The highborn pulled on his reins and headed directly at the zealot on his right. To his credit, the zealot held his ground, readying his weapon to strike at Spite's head, but at the last moment Malus changed direction again, veering left and swiping his sword at the warrior as he went past. The zealot's draich bit into Spite's shoulder just as Malus took off the top of the warrior's skull.

Steel rang on Malus's left side. He glanced over his shoulder in time to see the second zealot's headless body collapsing to the ground. Shebbolai and half a dozen marauders had fallen in behind Malus, using spears and swords to kill anyone who came too close. The marauder chieftain raised his sword to the heavens, laughing like a fiend. Malus grinned cruelly and put his boots to Spite's flanks.

The doors to the temple were open as Malus reined in before the building's broad steps. Fearing an ambush, he dismounted quickly and let Shebbolai and the marauders take the lead. The Chaos warriors raced across the threshold, and almost immediately Malus heard screams and the sounds of battle. As he charged through the doorway, he found the marauders slaughtering a group of temple servants who had been stacking a new set of trophies near the doors.

'This way!' Malus shouted as he dashed across the large chamber. Shebbolai and the men followed the highborn as he raced up the stairs to the chapel. He burst into the chamber expecting at least a handful of zealot guards, but the smaller chamber was empty.

Something's wrong, Malus thought, feeling the first twinges of dread tickle at his heart. The Cauldron of Khaine seethed and bubbled on the ceremonial dais with no one to attend it. It felt like an ambush, but how could Urial have possibly expected this?

Gritting his teeth, Malus decided that it didn't matter. He was committed, one way or the other, and would have to see things through to the bitter end. Taking a deep breath, he made his way to the sanctum stairs.

Shebbolai and the marauders gasped at the towering statue of Khaine as they worked their way around the dais and climbed to the red-lit doorway. Malus gripped the warpsword tightly, drawing strength from its heat as he approached the door. He remembered all too well what had happened the last time he'd stood at that narrow threshold.

Raw power seethed from the doorway, washing over Malus's skin and making the warpsword vibrate in his hands. 'Be ready for anything,' the highborn warned the marauders, and stepped inside.

Malus was not prepared for what he found.

THE VERY AIR howled and shimmered with pain.

Malus stood at the foot of a broad bridge fashioned from skulls that crossed a sea of seething red. Heat and light rose from its surface like the glow of a furnace, searing his skin and filling his ears with the cries of the damned.

At the far end of the bridge stood another doorway leading into the sanctum, and at the bridge's midpoint, naked and gleaming in the ruddy light, stood Yasmir.

Malus looked upon her and felt smaller and weaker than he'd ever known before. She was unearthly, radiant in her lethal beauty. Her dark eyes met his and she smiled, revealing her leonine fangs. Behind Malus, one of the marauders moaned like a frightened child.

'Who is she?' asked Shebbolai, his voice full of dread.

Malus didn't know what to say. Finally he shrugged. 'She is my bride,' he said grimly, and went to meet her.

She waited for his approach, spreading her arms slightly. Had it not been for the slim, needle-like knives in her hands she might have been offering herself to her lover.

The highborn clenched the warpsword tightly. One did not fight Yasmir; one offered oneself up to die. For an instant he thought of the daemon, but he pushed the idea away. The warpsword would have to be enough.

Her gaze was inscrutable. It was as if she stared through him, seeing some vista beyond the ken of mortals. When she was within reach of his longer sword he came to a halt. His fingers flexed on the sword's leather wrapped hilt.

Yasmir made no move. She continued to stare through him as if he wasn't even there. Malus frowned. 'Hello, sister,' he said.

At the sound of his voice her expression changed. Her eyes shifted slightly, as if she was seeing him for the first time, and then she was flying at him, her daggers reaching for his throat.

Malus brought the warpsword up in the nick of time, barely deflecting the lethal strikes, but there was no time to recover, as the living saint switched targets and began a series of deadly thrusts at his face, chest and groin. She never stopped moving, flowing towards him like a dancer and making a lethal move with each and every step.

He had no time to be afraid. The warpsword seemed to move of its own accord, matching Yasmir blow for blow. Once again, he saw the fight unfold with a detached clarity, as if he was a spectator rather than a combatant. Her speed and grace were devastating. Even though he could read Yasmir's next attack his body was hard-pressed to counter it.

She drove him back steadily, keeping him constantly on the defensive. A dagger thrust sank a quarter of an inch into his throat, but he scarcely felt it. Another blow stung him like an adder just below his eye.

The next one was going to hit his hip, right where the breastplate met his fauld. Malus waited until the last possible moment, and then pivoted on his left foot and let her thrust slide past. He continued the spin, turning it into a lightning quick backhanded cut aimed for her neck. The warpsword hissed through the air, but Yasmir was already gone, rolling forwards out of the sword's path.

Malus rushed at her, but Yasmir recovered from the roll at once and whirled, knocking aside his stop thrust, and making a blurring stab for his neck. The highborn sensed the strike and faded back, deflecting the thrust with the flat of his blade.

Two marauders charged at Yasmir, their weapons aiming for her slender back. She reversed her daggers with a flourish and stabbed both warriors through the heart, before pushing their corpses off and tucking into a tight roll towards the highborn. When she came up out of the roll her blades were reaching for his throat and a terrible smile of joy lit her unearthly face.

Malus had anticipated her attack and ducked beneath the thrust. His sword swept up at her torso and her knives fell into a cross block, trapping his sword. Malus yanked his sword clear, feinted low and then thrust at her neck, just as she twisted her body, deflecting the attack with her right hand dagger and stabbing at Malus with her left.

The point of her dagger scratched the hollow of his throat and stopped. She could reach no further with her right hand blocking Malus's sword. They were at a deadlock.

Yasmir looked into Malus's eyes. She seemed to truly recognise him for the first time. 'I cannot kill him,' she said breathily.

Malus gave her a bemused frown, and then realised that she wasn't speaking to him.

From behind the highborn, back towards the doorway at the far end of the bridge, he heard Urial's angry voice. 'What is this foolishness?'

Malus thought quickly. 'She cannot kill me because we are too evenly matched,' he said. Slowly, carefully, he stepped away from Yasmir and lowered his sword. She mirrored his moves exactly. 'As befits a bride and a groom, don't you think?'

Angry shouts from the other end of the bridge caught his attention. The marauders were retreating from a group of bloodstained zealots, and two fearsome grey figures that crawled like spiders down the stone walls above the doorway to the chapel. The

Chaos beasts lashed their tentacles hungrily as they sank closer to their prey.

There was a meaty *thump* near Malus's feet and something bounced heavily off his calf. He looked down and saw Arleth Vann's bloodstained head roll to a stop at his feet.

'He told me everything,' Urial hissed. 'An assassin's body can resist torture, but his spirits are powerless to one such as I.'

Malus turned to face his half-brother, pure murder dancing in his eyes. 'If he told you where I went,' he said raising the warpsword, 'then you know what *this* is.'

Urial stood at the far end of the bridge, the copy of the warpsword clutched in his left hand. His face twisted with rage. 'It is not yours, you misbegotten cur! It is meant for *me*! I was reborn in the cauldron while you were whelped by that Naggorite whore. If you are here it is because Khaine willed it so. You are here so that I may take the sword from your broken and bleeding body.'

Malus smiled. 'Do you want it, brother? Come then, and take it.'

Urial screamed like one of the damned and charged at Malus, his sword held ready. Behind the highborn Shebbolai roared a challenge at the zealots, and suddenly the air rang with the clash of steel and the screams of the dying.

Malus charged at his half-brother, a war scream bursting from his throat. He read Urial's every move, knowing his blade would come slashing down for his shoulder half a second before the blow fell. The warpsword swept up, knocking the blow aside. Then Malus reversed the stroke and sliced at Urial's chest. Before the blow could connect, however, Urial's form blurred, and the sword passed through the space where he had been.

Damned sorcery! Malus whirled just as Urial's blade whipped at his face from an unexpected angle. Caught by surprise, the sword sliced neatly across his cheek. Hot blood poured down his face, and Urial laughed.

Malus stabbed at his half-brother, but again, the sorcerer's form blurred and seemed to coalesce three feet to the left. Urial's sword stabbed out, glancing from Malus's armour, and the highborn spun and slashed down at the extended arm, but once again, it was like cutting at air. Urial blurred and then reformed again to Malus's right. This time the highborn was expecting an attack and was ready when Urial lashed out at his neck. Malus parried the blow and stepped in for a thrust, but again, his half-brother turned to smoke and reappeared three feet to the highborn's right. His half-brother's sword flashed, and Malus felt a spike of pain lance through his right thigh.

The highborn roared in anger, and rushed at his half-brother just as a heavy weight landed on the bridge behind him. He heard the tentacles hissing through the air a fraction too late as the Chaos beast entwined his sword arm and waist and lifted him into the air.

Hissing, gobbling howls rang in Malus's ears as the beast reared onto its hind legs and lashed at Malus with the rest of its tentacles. Barbed hooks grated across Malus's armour as he was spun through the air.

He could hear Urial cursing the beast, but the hunter paid the sorcerer no mind, intent on drawing Malus towards its clashing beak.

Snarling, Malus shifted the warpsword to his free hand and slashed at the tentacles holding him. The warpsword parted the flesh whips in a spray of steaming ichor and he plunged face first to the bridge. He hit hard on his left shoulder and rolled away down the beast's right flank. Malus rolled to his feet as the Chaos beast rounded on him, and he buried his sword in the creature's neck just as two of its tentacles smashed against the side of his head. The blows knocked the highborn to the ground and he rolled clear, dragging his sword with him.

When his vision cleared Malus found himself facing back towards the chapel end of the bridge. The second Chaos beast had leapt from the wall and clung to the side of the stone span, snatching men in the midst of the melee and lifting them clear. As Malus watched, the hunter snatched one of the marauders from the battle and lifted the wriggling body high overhead, whereupon it began to pull the man limb from limb.

Tyran and Shebbolai faced one another, trading blows with their curved swords in a blur of razor edged motion. All around them zealots and marauders tore at one another with single-minded ferocity, although it was clear that with the Chaos beast on their side the zealots would soon gain the upper hand. Yasmir stood apart from the battle, watching the slaughter with dispassionate interest.

A shadow loomed over Malus. Urial's sword whirred through the air and struck the bridge where the highborn had been, but Malus had rolled away and was clambering unsteadily to his feet.

Roaring with hate, Urial charged at his half-brother, launching a series of powerful blows that Malus blocked with steady, deft strokes. Malus didn't attempt to strike back, knowing that it would only give Urial a chance to discorporate and strike him from an unexpected angle. Instead he gave ground, defending himself easily and trying to think of a way to turn the tables.

With every step Malus drew closer to the melee at the end of the bridge. On impulse he blocked Urial's next attack, and turned and ran towards the battle. Behind him, Urial laughed in disdain and lurched after him, dragging his twisted foot across the smooth stone.

A zealot struck down one of the Chaos warriors and stepped in Malus's path. The highborn cut the man in half and dashed past before the bloody halves hit the ground. He raced right for the last Chaos beast, which saw him coming and reached for him with eight thrashing tentacles. He seemed to race directly into the creature's embrace, but at the last moment he threw himself to the ground and rolled beneath the creature's head.

As he'd hoped, Urial ran headlong into the monster's clutches. The Chaos beast, not able to tell the difference between friend and foe, reached for Urial as eagerly as it had tried to grab Malus, but again the sorcerer's form blurred and he appeared three feet to the left of where he'd stood. Half mad with fury, Urial stabbed the beast in the eye, and it plunged from the edge of the bridge with a shriek. One of the last marauders leapt at Urial from behind, but the usurper twisted at the waist and sliced the man in half with a savage swipe of his blade.

There was a scream to Malus's left as the last zealot leapt at the two remaining marauders. Both Chaos warriors buried their blades in the druchii's chest, but the zealot crashed heavily into the two men, bearing all three over the edge of the bridge and into the red sea beneath. Their screams ended as they sank beneath the heaving liquid and did not rise again.

Only Tyran and Shebbolai were left. Both men circled one another warily, bleeding from scores of deep wounds on their chests and arms. Shebbolai raised his sword and charged Tyran with a fierce roar, as Malus looked on. The zealot leader watched the man come and ducked the chieftain's swing at the last second, thrusting with his draich and taking Shebbolai squarely in the chest. The onrushing warrior impaled himself on Tyran's blade, the draich bursting from Shebbolai's back. Before Tyran could pull his blade free, the chieftain grabbed the zealot leader's wrist. Smiling madly, the chieftain pulled Tyran towards him, driving the man's sword deeper into his chest. Tyran tried to pull away, but the Chaos warrior's grip was like iron. Shebbolai's sword flashed, and Tyran's sword arm was hacked away at the shoulder. The zealot staggered back with a hideous scream and fell backwards off the bridge. Still smiling, Shebbolai sank to the ground and toppled over dead.

Urial charged Malus with a roar, thrusting at the highborn's neck. Malus blocked the thrust and swung at Urial's head, but again the sorcerer's body blurred and reappeared three feet away. The usurper's sudden counterattack nearly took Malus's head off, but he saw the blow just in time and ducked out of the way.

Malus's half-brother laughed. 'You're done for, Darkblade,' he taunted. 'I can do this all night long if I must.'

'I know,' Malus snapped, swinging at Urial's chest. The sorcerer's form blurred – but the highborn continued the swing, aiming for a point three feet to the left.

Urial screamed, staring down at the black sword jutting from between his ribs. Blood poured down the length of the warpsword, turning to steam against its hot edge.

'It makes you predictable,' Malus said, and pulled his sword free.

Urial staggered backwards, his sword falling from his hands. Blood poured in a rush down the front of his armour. He fell back, and found himself enfolded in Yasmir's slender arms.

She laid him gently on the ground, cradling his head in her hands. Urial stared up at her, a look of longing in his eyes. His mouth worked breathlessly.

Yasmir rose and walked around him, kneeling at his side. Smiling lovingly, she placed her hands at the join of his breastplate and pulled. Rivets popped and straps broke as she tore the armour away, revealing Urial's misshapen chest. Then the living saint ran a delicate finger down the usurper's uneven sternum until she found the spot she wanted, and dug in with both hands. Cartilage popped wetly as Yasmir ripped her brother's chest open.

The last thing Urial saw was his beloved sister feeding on his still beating heart.

As IT HAPPENED, the warriors of the red sword acquitted themselves far better than Malus had ever expected. After slaying all the zealots and temple servants they could find, they opened the gates of the fortress and rampaged out into the ravaged city. Several of their bodies were found as far away as the warehouse district when the warriors of the temple made their way back into Har Ganeth.

Malus sat back in the throne of the Grand Carnifex as Arch-Hierophant Rhulan entered the council arena, attended by a handful of priests and priestesses. When the elder saw Malus, his relieved expression turned to a look of abject horror.

'You!' he exclaimed. 'What happened? Where's Urial?'

The highborn eyed the elder contemptuously. 'Why, Arch-Hierophant, don't you remember the plan? I said I would find a way to strike at the usurper directly, and so I did. He will trouble the temple no more.' He leaned back in the throne, his right hand resting on the pommel of the unsheathed warpsword. 'I would have resolved this more quickly, but the diversion I'd been led to expect never materialised.'

Rhulan gaped at Malus, his eyes widening in fear. 'It... that is, we tried, but the citizens had gone mad. We couldn't reach the temple–'

'Where is that other elder?' Malus interjected, 'the striking one with the tattoos?'

'Mereia?' Rhulan stammered. 'She… she died trying to reach one of the more isolated warbands.'

'Meaning she tried to fulfil your part of the plan and died fighting while you cowered in a basement somewhere,' Malus snarled.

'Do not presume to judge me,' Rhulan cried. 'I did what I thought best.' He looked back at his attendants, and then fixed Malus with a conspiratorial stare. 'You couldn't have beaten Urial. He had the warpsword. He couldn't be defeated in battle.'

Malus smiled coldly. 'Ah, yes, the scriptures, so, let me understand this correctly: in the interests of doctrinal veracity, you betrayed me and left me to die. Is that right?'

Rhulan began to tremble. 'No, no, it wasn't like that. We had to wait for Malekith to arrive. He could have found a way to stop the usurper.'

'Fortunately for our people, he won't have to.' Malus rose from the throne, holding the fake warpsword in his left hand. Stepping to the edge of the railing, he jumped off and landed on the arena floor. A flare of pain in his wounded leg made him wince, but he pushed the feeling aside. Actually, the discomfort was a good sign. It meant that the daemon's power wasn't healing him as well as it had been. The power of the sword was somehow counterbalancing it. He didn't know how, but he wasn't going to question it for the time being.

Malus straightened and stalked over to Rhulan. 'This, I believe, belongs to the temple,' he said, dropping the fake blade with a clang at the Arch-Hierophant's feet. 'The Grand Carnifex can return it to the sanctum, and as far as the rest of Naggaroth is concerned, it never left its home.'

Rhulan frowned. 'I don't understand–'

'I know,' Malus said, and beheaded Rhulan with the warpsword.

Men and women screamed in horror as the Arch-Hierophant's body collapsed to the floor. Malus silenced them with a cold glare. Then he levelled his sword at one of the priestesses. 'You, come here.'

Niryal stepped from the crowd. She'd put aside her axe at some point, and changed into better clothes. Unlike Rhulan, she mastered her fear, keeping her chin up as she stepped closer to the bloodstained sword.

Malus gave the priestess a murderous look. 'You weren't taken by assassins. You slew the other sentry and then betrayed us to Urial.'

The priestess never flinched. 'I was certain you were deceiving us, and, as it happened, you were.'

'Then, as soon as Urial was dead you switched sides again.'

'I serve the temple,' Niryal said.

Malus smiled. 'I thought you would say as much. That's why I'm making you the new Grand Carnifex. Of all the people in this damned fortress you're the only one whose motives I can understand.'

The other attendants gasped. Even Niryal was stunned. 'You can't do that,' she said.

Malus raised the warpsword. 'I am Khaine's chosen, Niryal, I most certainly can.' He surveyed the other loyalists. 'And they shall be your new Haru'ann. They seem a dim sort, but since they know the truth about the sword, we can either kill them or make use of them.'

Niryal struggled with her sudden change in fortunes for a moment more, and then managed to recover her composure. 'What would you have us do, holy one?' she asked.

The highborn smiled. 'That's better. You will return the counterfeit sword to the sanctum. At this point, no one who saw Urial with the blade is still alive except for us.'

'What about the Witch King? He is probably marching up the Slavers' Road even now.'

'When he arrives you'll receive him with luxurious hospitality and inform him of Urial's usurpation,' Malus said. 'Tell him that Urial and a cabal of zealots used Chaos magic to sow discord among the citizens and slay the temple elders. There was fighting in the streets for almost a week, but in the end you sent a group of volunteers through the tunnels and they managed to assassinate the usurper and the ringleaders. The Witch King will probably want to publicly execute some citizens to vent his pique, but other than that he should be satisfied with the outcome.' He raised the sword in warning. 'You will not tell him anything about me, or Yasmir. She is to remain in the sanctum until such time as the Witch King departs. After that, she may do as she will.'

Niryal thought everything over and finally nodded in satisfaction. 'It shall be as you say, holy one, but what about you?'

'I am leaving,' Malus said. 'Summer is almost done, and I have pressing business elsewhere.'

Malus reluctantly slid the warpsword into its scabbard. Spite waited in the fortress's beast pen, packed and ready to ride. Somewhere out there was the Amulet of Vaurog, the final relic the daemon required. Time was growing short.

He pushed his way through the crowd of stunned attendants, walking briskly to the door, when Niryal called out. 'I don't understand. You're the Scourge. The Warpsword of Khaine is yours. What about the Time of Blood? Are you not here to lead us into an age of death and fire?'

Malus paused. He looked back through the crowd at Niryal, his hand straying to the hilt of the burning blade.

'Perhaps,' he said with a ghostly smile, 'but not today. The apocalypse will have to wait.'

ABOUT THE AUTHORS

Dan Abnett lives and works in Maidstone, Kent, in England. Well known for his comic work, he has written everything from the *Mr Men* to the *X-Men*. His work for the Black Library includes the popular strips *Lone Wolves*, *Titan* and *Darkblade*, the best-selling Gaunt's Ghosts novels, and the acclaimed Inquisitor Eisenhorn trilogy.

Mike Lee was the principal creator and developer for White Wolf Game Studio's *Demon: The Fallen*. Over the last eight years he has contributed to almost two dozen role-playing games and supplements. An avid wargamer and devoted fan of pulp adventure, Mike lives in the United States.

Glossary

Ancri Dam

Literally 'Heart of the Stag', an arcane talisman worn as a symbol of rule by one of the larger Autarii clans. Thought to possess potent magical powers.

Anwyr na Khaine

Translated as either 'The Blessings of Khaine' or 'The Brides of Khaine', these women are the warrior-priestesses of the God of Murder.

Autarii

Translated as either 'Shades' or 'Spectres', it is the name adopted by the druchii mountain clans north of Hag Graef. Superlative woodsmen and hunters, the Autarii are considered cruel and pitiless even by druchii standards.

Caedlin

A mask, usually of silver or gold, worn by highborn citizens of Hag Graef to protect their faces from the fog that sweeps over the city each night. Sometimes called a nightmask.

Courva

Root extract from a plant found in the jungles of Lustria. When chewed, it acts as a stimulant, sharpening the senses, and is believed to increase reflexes. Favoured by duellists and assassins. Mildly addictive.

Drachau

Literally 'Fist of Night', the title held by the six rulers of the great druchii cities as appointed by the Witch King Malekith. The Drachau serve as the Witch King's lieutenants and his inner council, each fulfilling a specific function in that capacity. Traditionally the Drachau of Hag Graef serves as the general of the Witch King's armies in times of war.

Draich

A powerful two-handed sword with a single edged, curved blade. The favoured weapon of Khaine's executioners, these weapons are swift and deadly in the hands of a skilled user, but require extensive training to use effectively.

Draichnyr na Khaine

Loosely translated as 'The Blessed Swords of Khaine', these warriors of the temple are also known as Khaine's executioners.

Druchast

The written language of the druchii.

Druhir

The spoken language of the druchii.

Hadrilkar

Literally 'collar of service'. A torc worn by members of a highborn's retinue or followers of certain religious cults or professional guilds. The torc is typically made of gold or silver, and etched with the highborn's family sigil.

Hakseer

The 'proving cruise' made by every druchii highborn upon reaching adulthood. Every highborn is expected to lead a yearlong raiding cruise to demonstrate his skill and ruthlessness and establish his reputation in highborn society. Oftentimes, success on the cruise depends on how much the family spends to outfit it. It's not uncommon for a Drachau's son to take to the sea with a small fleet of ships at his command, for example. The commander of the cruise keeps the lion's share of the plunder, as is customary on all raiding cruises.

Hanil Khar

The 'Bearing of Chains', an annual ceremony held in all six of the great druchii cities, where highborn families restate their oaths of allegiance to their Drachau and present some form of tribute as a symbol of their fear and respect for him. The Hanil Khar marks the end of the raiding season and the beginning of the long winter of Naggaroth.

Hanumaika

The 'flesh-price' – tribute paid to druchii corsairs by some human towns to avoid being attacked. Frequently paid in a combination of coin, goods and flesh – usually town criminals or unfortunate travellers caught in the wrong place at the wrong time.

Hassariya

The game of 'Dragon's Teeth', a game of chance played with shark or eel's teeth that is a favourite pastime among druchii sailors. Also used as a fortune-telling tool in coastal cities such as Clar Karond and Karond Kar.

Heshyr na Tuan

The 'Keepers of the Dead', an archaic term for the blood witches of the Temple of Khaine.

Hithuan

The druchii, with their passionate and murderous nature, have evolved a rigid etiquette of social space that allows the highborn to function socially without the near constant risk of bloodshed. Distance is measured in sword lengths; lowborn may not approach closer than three sword lengths (approximately twelve feet) without being summoned, while retainers may stand as close as two sword lengths from their master. Valued retainers, lieutenants, and lower-ranking highborn stand just out of sword reach. The closest, most intimate space is reserved for lovers, playthings and mortal foes. Hithuan does not apply to slaves, as they are expected to shed their blood at a druchii's whim.

Hushalta

A thick, acrid liquid also called 'Mother's Milk', made from plant extracts taken from Tilea and alkaloid substances found in the mountains of Naggoroth. The drink induces a deep sleep, characterized by vivid nightmares and lingering hallucinations after waking, though it also speeds the healing process for the druchii. High doses can result in memory loss and even dementia over a prolonged period of use.

Jhindara

The feared sea witch of druchii legend – supposedly spirits of drowned women slain in the sinking of Nagarythe who haunt ships at sea. They are said to be jealous and cruel, seducing corsairs and dragging them off to cold beds beneath the waves.

Kheitan

A thick gambeson of leather and cloth worn over a dark elf's layered robes, covering his upper and lower torso. Typically worn beneath a coat of fine mail (in social situations), or an articulated breastplate (in wartime), the kheitan provides both added protection and insulation from the elements.

Maelith

Malevolent spirits, supposedly the ghosts of druchii who offended the Dark Mother and were consigned to haunt the earth until the end of days. They feed on the blood of the living, and cannot be harmed save by the touch of cold iron. Occasionally used by powerful sorcerers as familiars and guardians.

Nauglir

Literally 'cold one', the druchii name for the huge, lizard-like predators found in the caverns beneath Hag Graef. Mistaken as large reptiles by humans, the nauglir are in fact a distant relative of the dragon, and are used by the highborn as cavalry and hunting mounts.

Raksha

One of the autarii's many names for the restless dead. In this case, the name specifically refers to a vengeful ghost that preys upon the living.

Sa'an'ishar

A shorthand of the command 'Shields and spears!' – the standard druchii order for a formation to ready themselves for action. Druchii lords often use the phrase as a general command for attention.

Shakhtila

A mounted game of mock warfare where riders attempt to ride down armed slaves and gather more severed heads than their opponents within a set period of time. Though the slaves have little hope of injuring the heavily-armed riders, fights between opposing teams often cause the deaths of numerous players each year. A popular sport among young druchii of both sexes.

Slachyr

Literally 'Render', an ancient magical weapon forged in lost Nagarythe and carried into battle by the Vaulkhar of Hag Graef.

Urhan

Literally 'High One', the title of an *Autarii* clan-leader.

Vaulkhar

Literally 'Maker of Chains', a title held by the warlord of a Drachau's army. The title comes from the warlord's right of indenture – rather than kill or ransom prisoners of war, he can enslave them if he so desires.

Vauvalka

Literally 'Shadow-casters', illegal users of the dark arts who can raise angry spirits and inflict them on a druchii's rivals — for a price.

Vrahsha

A thick liquid made from nauglir slime that cold one knights must periodically apply to their skin in order to convince the cold ones to accept them as 'pack mates'. Without the vrahsha, the cold ones would turn on their own masters. The liquid is quite toxic, and causes damage to the knight's nerve endings over time, requiring expensive remedies to correct.

Vraith

The paired blades of a highborn, worn both as a symbol of their rank and as deadly battlefield weapons. Each sword is a single-edged, slightly curved blade with a hilt long enough to accommodate two hands. Few highborn actually wield both swords simultaneously, but schools of vraith fighting do exist.

Yrila

Loosely translated as 'crone' by humans, a Yrila is a seer, a sorceress who has mastered the art of divining the future. The art is both feared and highly prized by the highborn of Naggoroth, and not every druchii city can boast of possessing one. Eldire, consort to Lurhan of Hag Graef, is considered the strongest seer of her time next to Morathi herself.

Ythrum

A bitter, acidic drink made from boiled courva root and favoured by the nobles of the black ark.